Praise for *I'm Losi*

"Ruthlessly hip and very funny."

—*Wired*

"Edgy, sublime."

—*New York Newsday*

"Wagner's verbal animation rarely flags. . . . His prose writhes and coruscates."

—John Updike, *The New Yorker*

"The author's images, tones and language give *I'm Losing You* a hard beauty that glints like a black crystal."

—*Time*

"Wagner's latest novel makes all other Hollywood satires Capraesque in their innocence."

—Will Self

"One of the year's most notorious books . . . a living satire of a dying Hollywood . . . a must read."

—*Entertainment Weekly*

"A black farce played with brute force. . . . Wagner improves upon the Hollywood-equals-hell novel . . . with an intricately woven jump-cut montage of deeply twisted parents, children, doctors, filmmakers, agents, writers, and actors who lay waste to each other's lives and score movie deals from the carnage."

—*Details*

"Mr. Wagner . . . treats us to many glorious phrases and whole passages that have the self-propelled rhythm of great prose."

—Adam Begley, *New York Observer*

"Makes the nonfictional *You'll Never Eat Lunch in This Town Again* look like a Hollywood valentine."

—*Glamour*

"A deliciously guilty pleasure . . . perfect beach reading for the millennium."

—*Newsday*

"The most distinctive Jewish novel since *Portnoy's Complaint.*"

—*Jewish Journal*

"A meditation on moral corruption and loss which is at turns hilarious, tragic, and at times as caustic as a shot of kerosene."

—*Detour*

"Compared to this novel, the Hollywood disenchantments of Nathanael West and F. Scott Fitzgerald seem gently nostalgic."

—*Books of the Southwest*

"An ambitious and complex literary novel . . . one of the best serious books published this year."

—*Sun-Sentinel*

"A dazzling prose stylist."

—*Hartford Courant*

I'M
LOSING
YOU

Also by Bruce Wagner

Force Majeure
Wild Palms (graphic novel)
I'll Let You Go
Still Holding
The Chrysanthemum Palace
Memorial
Dead Stars
The Empty Chair: Two Novellas
I Met Someone
A Guide For Murdered Children
(writing as Sarah Sparrow)
The Marvel Universe: Origin Stories
*ROAR: American Master, The Oral Biography
of Roger Orr*
The Met Gala & Tales of Saints and Seekers

I'M LOSING YOU

BRUCE WAGNER

Arcade Publishing • New York

Copyright © 1996 by Bruce Wagner
Arcade Publishing paperback edition © 2024

Arcade Publishing books may be purchased in bulk at special
discounts for sales promotion, corporate gifts, fund-raising, or
educational purposes. Special editions can also be created to
specifications. For details, contact the Special Sales Department,
Arcade Publishing, 307 West 36th Street, 11th Floor, New York,
NY 10018 or arcade@skyhorsepublishing.com.

Arcade Publishing® is a registered trademark of Skyhorse
Publishing, Inc.®, a Delaware corporation.

Visit our website at www.arcadepub.com.
Please follow our publisher Tony Lyons on Instagram
@tonylyonsisuncertain

10 9 8 7 6 5 4 3 2 1

Library of Congress Cataloging-in-Publication Data
is available on file.

Cover design by David Ter-Avanesyan
Cover painting is *Ophelia* by John Everett Millais

Print ISBN: 978-1-64821-049-5
Ebook ISBN: 978-1-64821-050-1

Printed in the United States of America

AUTHOR'S NOTE

I'm Losing You is a work of fiction. The characters, conversations, and events in the novel are the products of my imagination, and no resemblance to the actual conduct of real-life persons, or to actual events, is intended. Although, for the sake of verisimilitude, certain public figures do make incidental appearances or are briefly referred to in the novel, I have included them here without their knowledge or cooperation; their interactions with the characters I have invented are wholly my creation and not intended to be understood as descriptions of real events or to reflect negatively upon any of these public figures; nor to suggest that they ever sought or participated in any psychiatric or psychological treatment.

Ognuno sta solo sul cuor della terra trafitto
da un raggio di sole: ed è subito sera
—Salvatore Quasimodo

(Each alone on the heart of the earth, impaled
upon a ray of sun: and suddenly it's evening.)

CONTENTS

Book 1

IMPALA

It seemed only yesterday that Serena Ribkin was a vibrant, no-regrets member of the Lie—that seventy was "young"— but now she lay bedridden in her frazzled palace with a bad case of colon cancer. Ten months ago, her party, so to speak, had been crashed by a painfreak hooligan; she duly protested, thinking the intruder could be sassed or paid off, cajoled to leave. Unflappably, she submitted herself to resection and the roughing-up of a good chemo. But when they indecorously cut away thirty-six inches of bowel (not to would be suicide, Donny said), everything changed: the skinhead sodomized her in front of the guests and she had no choice but to give him run of the house. She knew all would be smashed now, every secret recessed thing. At least, while revelers were slaughtered below, the invader allowed her lucidity and television privileges— that was something, anyway. Now Serena lay stuporous in her cloacal chambers, on the protective-plastic-covered California King. Far from the madding crowd, as they used to say.

She doped herself and dreamed a parade of Judith Leiber handbags all in a row, marching up and down Rodeo Drive, escorted by fife-and-drum Barneys New York blackamoors. The purses' famed claw clasps detached, nostalgically carrying her from the house on Carcassonne Way, above the town of Beverly Hills. On a carpet of Demerol she floated over certain personal monuments, joined by a dutiful panoply of royalist flak—a clique of Chanel ensembles that had served her well hovered now like woolly choppers—while she gazed downward, striving to recapitulate what had happened to her life.

Serena had become nocturnal, the four-thirtyish earthquake hour her comforting noon. She flipped through the expensive photo album she had filled with images from *National Geographic,* a legless beggar-boy flogged by his "manager" on the streets of Cairo, a Vietnamese girl feeding mush to catfishes through a trapdoor in the living room of her floating house, the X ray of a pelican that had eaten a gopher—the gopher having burrowed out through the larynx in its death throes. In her mind, she called these images *curiosities* but wasn't at all sure how she'd become their curator.

She told Farfina (a night nurse, Donny insisted, was a "given") not to disturb her, then slid open the heavy glass door and lit a cigarette. Serena held a slice of angel food cake in her palm and it shivered there while she watched for the floating snakebite eyes of the raccoons. They were late tonight. The old woman stared at the dark hill abutting the backyard like the hump of a beast she'd soon ride off on. Where would it take her? To the lush coast of Raccoon Cove, where hedgehog traffic cops with Gucci scarves stood under sugar-teat streetlamps. She brought the chair closer to the darkness.

At her fiftieth high school reunion, there were three people she wanted to see—two old flames and the girl who stole them away. She called the alumni association and found out the trio was planning to attend. Serena knew how good she looked and wanted to rub their noses in it; haul them down by their scalps to lick the salt off her cunt, if she could. She hadn't seen them since the Big Twenty-fifth, but the dull, chatty alumni newsletter kept everyone au courant. Victor ran a bank and had a successful bypass. Glynis was a widow, remarried (nineteen eighty-eight) to a manufacturer. Ted had fourteen grandkids and started a trust with the eleven-million-dollar lottery he'd won in their names. And what of Serena? Divorced from a Hollywood producer, her son a powerful agent, a Senior Veepee at ICM. AlumNotes ran a pre-cancerous photo Serena had sent, she of the twinkling eyes and the Scaasi chiffon, she of the I-shit-on-you mouth—like some centimillionairess out of *W*.

The reunion looked like a collection of fat old talking candles. The banquet ended just after ten. As the pallbearers of the student body returned to their rooms, Serena heard music blaring from a sidebar ballroom. She wanted to investigate. Victor and his wife went up to bed, beat. Serena had to pull Ted by the elbow; Glynn and hubby indulgently followed. Sad to say, but wandering like that with Ted on her arm was the most fun yet. The music grew louder and the air seemed to change, supercharged by the molecules of the young. A prom. Serena wanted to crash, but the others backed off, laughing gray-skinned dumb-asses. Serena made Ted buy her a drink in the bar while they cut up old times. After Ted walked her to the room and kissed her with his dead fish mouth, she went back down and tipsily danced with the kids. They didn't know what to make of it but liked her energy. She grew light-headed and a leg felt numb; Serena thought she was having a stroke, but it was only the carousing and champagne. She sat at a table, pale, dizzy, staring at souvenirs not of her time—then cried all the way to the

elevator, like hosing vomit off a sidewalk. By the time the
doors sealed her in and the car began its skyward rush, she
knew her life had ended.

*

On Saturday, Donny Ribkin rose early. He exercised, spoke to
his mother's night nurse and speed-read three scripts before a
solitary hotel breakfast. Saturdays were the best; Sundays were
too close to Monday to be anything more than exemplary. In
the afternoon, he drove to the beach. He toyed with taking
the Impala—the car his father bought him when Donny was
sixteen—but settled on the Land Cruiser because of its height.
In the Toyota, he could watch the naked, hair-strewn legs of
the women and children, worn out from the water.

He was thinking about Leslie Trott, fag dermatologist and
celebrity adept. As an agent, Donny was immune to anything
more aberrant than a fleeting client crush—excluding directors (at least, good ones), he felt superior to those in his charge.
He'd met all kinds of Big Star-fuckers but never anyone so
consumed, attuned and addicted as Dr. Trott. Les had a large
staff of young borderline-attractive nurses, also enslaved; the
one-two punch of awe and resentment delivered by the stellar
clientele had pushed his retinue to the reedy marshes of phar-
maceutical abuse. How surreal and achingly unfair to be on
such casual, familial terms with world-class icons—sneaking
them through the Private Door, trading high-end gossip of
love trouble and HIV death, apportioning devoted guffaws and
unsolicited Percocets, being kissed, teased, quasi-missed and
token-gifted by the most famous men and (mostly) women on
Earth. A television comedienne handed out thousand-dollar

Bulgari pens like they were Snapples—general thank-yous for being such staunch, discreet Big Star Acolytes in Les Trott's fucked-up swanky codependent parish. Hired more for a talent to soothe and schmooze, Mother's little helpers were duly outfitted in sanitorium whites and signature Mephisto tennies, their minimal skills enhanced by crash-course on-the-job training. They became cyst-popping confidantes, handmaidens to media immortals: after all the in jokes and injections and periorbital peelings—while dope-nodding Big Star snaked and lurched on the table, squeezing Acolytes' hands like a pioneer sister having an arrow-wound cauterized—after all the shushing, sloughing, scraping, flaking, flecking and sucking up, after the poke, prod, swab and salve, the plucky divinity would evanesce (Private Door) to the limo for a stoned shopping spree while hydra-headed Cinderella mopped the pus and dermal dandruff in its wake.

Les treated most of Donny's clients, appearing at screenings and charity balls, art openings, award shows, tapings, shootings, bar mitzvahs, weddings and funerals. The reason the sultan made time for the agent's occasional eruptions (when Donny got a pimple on his nose, he liked it injected ASAP) rather than shuffling him off to, say, a partner with offices in the megasuite's Siberia, was owing to Donny's official role as wrangler to three of the doctor's seven key Big Star fetishes. In fact, Les Trott had only three observable modes of discourse: (one) *that while with an unempowered, non-celebrity stranger* (this sometimes occurred inadvertently. He remained coolly cordial and glassy-eyed while plotting his trajectory from sandtrap to nearest Big Starlit oasis. It was during such encounters Les convinced himself he was a normal person, capable of self-effacing civilian banter); (two) *that while with a powerful yet non-celebrity acquaintance* (in such an instance, he might affably field medical queries, overwhelming one with minutiae. He assiduously kept current on the journals and enjoyed regurgitating their contents to laymen, a kind of parlor trick with the dual function of helping him retain what he'd read.); lastly, (three) *that while interacting with a Big Star.* Donny Ribkin, whose whimsical scrutiny of Trott was an extension of his student anthropology days at UCLA, breezily noted gradations therein: a breath of alacrity, almost subjective, an *iridescence* discerned in the jump from Victoria Principal to, say, Jane Seymour. Then one watched a Seymour fall to an Ali MacGraw, who then fell to a Helen Hunt; a Hunt to a Bergen, a Bergen to a Bening (more so, of course, if Bening spouse was present), a Bening to a Midler, a Midler to a Whoopi, and so on, until all fell to Streisand or Taylor or Streep. It was banally, bizarrely riveting.

A few weeks ago, Donny brought his mom to the Cedars-Sinai office so Les could look at her moles and tags. Donny knew they were harmless, but Serena was vain. Since the surgery, she'd spent countless hours poring over the map of her skin—though the cancer inhabited her desert's dark hole, not the negligible cacti growing on chaparral of tummy, pelvis and neck.

Serena always liked Les, having visited through the years for age spots, spider veins and cortisone. He seemed genuinely to enjoy her company. Dr. Trott knew she was dying and, after all, such imminence conferred a kind of celebrity too, linking her to the power-sodden, ticking-clock clan of his H.I.V.I.P. friends. Thus, Les was able to enter a makeshift fourth mode of tender ministrations: the incongruous one of healer. The wry, happy-face Acolytes, never more than an hour or so away from the next Big Star fix, garlanded the agent's mother with queen-for-a-day benedictions and real sugarless-candy give-aways—actual lollipops of affection—just as they had Bette Davis in *her* pre-mortem dermo once-over. Outside the windows, birds chirped a Technicolor musicale and even the nurses seemed less stoned; angelic, whitewashed sisters of charity, loving the agent for bringing his mum, lifting her spirits like that at death's elaborate, unfunny door.

Serena loved them back (but brought no Bulgari nibs). Here was a doctor who wouldn't snip away at her guts! Here was the clinic as vanity fair, a fluorescent cotillion with a smooth maestro of emollients—here was a doctor with his gorgeous gals to coo over her Sandrine Leonard handbag and antiquarian brooch; to overlook her shrunken, balding frame; to studiously ignore the fecal odor following after like the devil's courtship cologne.

Donny went down to the street to smoke and that's when he saw Katherine Grosseck, love of his life. He wanted to run but managed a sickly smile as they collided. She was sleeveless and her chic workout arms carried bags from agnès b. "My mother's seeing Les."

"I heard she wasn't well. I'm sorry." Serena and Katherine had always gotten along. "I have to go now," she said, then winced as if she were passing a stone. Donny got that hit-and-run feeling.

It was two years since the breakup, but their life together—for him—continued on a parallel, spectral track. He watched it unfold from a shadowy place he called the Imaginarium (after the toy store in Century City), watched as shadow-Donny and shadow-Katherine went about their daily couple-life: saw them vacation and marry, go to movies, buy a house. Saw belly swollen—saw child come. Watched them banter through the day the way they always did, like no two people in the world in the history of time. For the last two years, whenever idiot things happened (in the office, on the street, something glimpsed or overheard), he saw Katherine look at him the way she used to, the way no one ever had, no person in the world or in time, sly and throaty, sexy, knowing—watched them laugh away the nights and days the way they did—his shadow self staring into the sturdy well of her chocolate eyes with the kind of hyper-realism he imagined preceded psychosis.

Their love continued to grow the way nails were said to grow on a corpse.

*

"I'm the Dead Animal Guy."

The family in the house at the end of the Downey cul-de-sac had been waiting a day and a half. When the handsome man with tight gray curls opened the screen door, Simon Krohn was already kneeling at the foundation to sniff a mesh-covered vent. Inside, the disdainful Latina was sorting her husband's freshly laundered Water and Power shirts. She hated Simon on sight; his quirky metabolism put her right off. He was so white his skin glowed. "Make sure you show him the den," she said. The smell was here, there, everywhere. She couldn't be sure anymore—it was stuck to her nosehairs. After holding forth on the importance of durable screen installation, Simon was led to the bathroom. She didn't want to get too close to this coveralled emissary of Creep. Like having a gravedigger in the house.

The door to the bathroom was shut, as if to trap a poltergeist. Simon the Discursive squatted at the bath.

"As I explained over the phone, if our friend has found himself a little home between the walls, that's a problemo. There's not much I can do short of busting in there, which doesn't thrill me and I'm *sure* won't thrill *you*. To summarize, if that's the case, there's not much to do but wait for our fine furry friend to burn itself out—you're looking at anywhere from three to seven days. Sometimes," he said, tap tap tapping, "they die just on the other side of the tub. And—as I said over the phone—that can also be a very large problemo."

The eavesdropping wife flinched from her post by the Naugahyde E-Z chair. This asshole was saying the only thing that separated them from the infested, debris-strewn Valley of Mexico was a thickened toenail of bathtub porcelain. She wished they had called a professional, a proper man in proper uniform; she'd pinched pennies, and here they were at the mercy of an inept, cut-rate reaper. The husband, a city worker with a broader band of experience, was more tolerant.

Simon stood. "I made a kind of covenant with God when I started this business—not that I'm a fervent believer, but I'm probably the most religious in my family. That's an understatement. My mother's an atheist and my sister's a total agnostic. My little family joke is that we're really pagan Jews. Anyway, I have two cardinal rules: never endanger public health, and never gouge the customer. Even though I charge one hell of a lot less than an exterminating company, before I actually come out I want people to know I can't always save the day. In a situation where little Fluffy is trapped in a wall space, for example, I always try to make it *very* clear that coming to a site will cost you. I mean, it's sixty-five dollars just to say hello. Depending on the amount of time I spend under the house, the supplies used, that can go high as a hundred and thirty-five. In your case, if everything's cut-and-dried, I imagine the charge could be one-oh-five or one-oh-seven. That's why I wanted to make it *very* clear as I said in our phone call this morning that if I go under the house and can't *find* our friend Fluffy, I can only assume that, unhappily, Fluffy is between walls. And that is una problemo grande because equipment would be required to actually go through that wall and said equipment won't make either of us very happy. Besides, I don't do that. I work strictly under the house, as I said on the—"

Simon retrieved a stained sack from the Datsun. It held flashlights, Hefty bags, Lysol, gloves, surgical masks and a deodorizer called Zap. He slipped on the mask and went to the side of the house to another mesh-covered vent. Fur was stuck to its torn edge. He saw the cadaver right away and Lysoled the maggots. They sizzled—like the Top Ramen commercial, he noted aloud. Simon's anarchic humor was his strong suit. He thought of himself as a *Wired* generation hepster, a kind of homegrown traveling cyberfolk Dadaist. He wouldn't be crawling under houses forever; one day he'd write paperbacks or screenplays. These were preliminaries. Like Burroughs and Fante before him, the oeuvre would be drawn from *this,* from now. That he was thirty-five didn't matter. At thirty-five, Van Gogh was barely painting with oils; Leary hadn't even tripped, heh heh. As Lysol fumes hammered through the mask, he thought of Burroughs's *Cities of the Red Night.* "You must touch Death, you must get close to Death." Fuck that, he said loudly, and laughed. The haughty Latina was probably upstairs listening, ear to vent. She was the kind that would try to make him feel guilty when he asked for the money, even though it was half what anyone else would have charged. Simon put the saprogenic mophead of possum in the bag, Zapped the area and collected his due. His pager beeped but the third-world prig wouldn't let him in the house to use the phone.

He drove straight to the pound (tossing the thing in a Dumpster would have been an outright violation of the covenant). He circumvented a long line of people adopting pets until he reached the hosed-down concrete outback, where an albino girl sobbed over a euthenized cat. *Turn, turn, turn.* A worker took Simon's thoughtfully double-bagged quarry for incineration. The Dead Animal Guy was a familiar face, so they let him use the phone.

"Did someone page me? I'm the Dead Animal Guy."

"Hello?" said a raspy voice.

"Did you page me?"

"Yes." It was a woman. "Can you come?"

"What seems to be the problemo?"

"I think something died in the basement."

"Are you on a slab?"

"I beg your pardon?"

"The house—what kind of foundation do you have?"

"I don't understand what you mean."

"Tell you what. I can come out and have a look, but I can't guarantee anything. If it's a situation where our friend Fluffy decided to take his permanent vacation inside a *wall*, there's not too much I can do but tear the wall open, which I'm not actually equipped to do and which I don't think would please either one of us—"

"Who is Fluffy?"

"Whatever's down there, I call Fluffy. What I'm trying to say is, there are various situations where I can't really be of great help, other than to make certain recommendations I could do just as well over the phone."

"I would like you to come."

"That's fine, happy to, we all like to make money. At the same time, to summarize, I want you to know that I will have to charge you sixty-five dollars just to say hello. If I do find our furry friend, depending on the size of el problemo and the amount of time I spend, I could wind up charging you anywhere up to a hundred and thirty-five."

"Well . . ." Simon thought he had talked himself out of a job. That's what happened when you tried to do the right thing. "I don't care what it costs. How quickly can you come?"

The address was on Carcassonne Way, not far from where he grew up. His mother, the well-known psychiatrist Calliope Krohn-Markowitz, still lived in the old Brentwood family digs. Her second husband was an analyst, and the couple worked at home, seeing patients from opposite sides of a quaint guest cottage. Simon resolved to drop over when he finished with the new client.

*

In five months of therapy, Donny hadn't revealed much. He'd seen shrinks on and off for twenty years; it wasn't like he didn't know the game. Then why was he being such a tightass? He hadn't even mentioned his obsessive fantasy life with Katherine. He sat in Calliope's office week after week, bullshitting—agenting. And he knew she knew it. Donny was starting to feel the pressure to unkink. Sometimes he thought he would have been better off with some out-of-the-way therapist, say in Sherman Oaks, one who wasn't so hardwired to the business.

There was no denying Calliope Krohn-Markowitz's charisma. In her mid-sixties, she looked like a collagened Georgia O'Keeffe. She was fit and authoritative, with twinkly eyes and actor-perfect teeth. Like Dr. Trott's, her clientele was almost strictly the scarily famous. Calliope didn't believe in lengthy analysis, preferring short-term crisis intervention, usually seeing patients in three-, six- and twelve-month modules. On cynical days, Donny saw true brilliance in the high-octane turnover of this imperative; no one was immune to the seductions of the Big Star—fuck, let alone the renowned shrink who had given herself the celeb gangbanger's supreme gift of a gossipy gigawatt carriage trade. As Donny waited outside in a green Adirondack, he turned on the spigot and let the petty resentments flow.

Celebrity psychiatrics was a specialty as bona fide as diseases of the retina or surgery of the hand. It seemed to Donny that famous people were probably less interesting on the couch than those who'd never known the effluent murmur of publicist and toady—by the time Big Stars found their way to the now-itself-famous cottage, they cathected with all the drollness and showy urgency of a talk show appearance (at Calliope's, clients flogged themselves instead of a film). Simply letting others know one was "seeing Calliope" was enough to set peculiar alchemical forces into play. One instantly garnered a quiet, casual dignity that was almost spiritual; an admittedly lower rung from, say, the level of dignity conferred by the purchase of a Vajrakilaya Center for one's pet Tibetan master—but a rung nonetheless. Donny noted a distinct symbiosis in transaction of analyst and analysand: Calliope blushed and swelled with the borrowed energy of her temporary acquisitions. The interesting thing was that during visits he never saw Big Stars come or go. This, he surmised, was because Thursday morning—his time—was probably C-list material: potluck, charity, favors, dross. Most of his visits were bracketed by a Castle Rock business-affairs gal and Hiram Joggs, Oscar-winning cinematographer. Donny wondered what they had on the shrink—they seemed more like material for husband Mitch.

Donny was thinking he should probably start telling her things, otherwise she might fire him. Shrinks did that these days, especially one who was turnover-crazy. Make way for that Big Star coming 'round the bend. He was at a temporary loss. His tried-and-true litany of early sorrows (recited to shrinks throughout the years) was exhausted—not an abreaction in the lot.

"I ran into Katherine the other day."

"Where?"

"On Bedford. I took Serena to the doctor. Did I tell you she was with a woman?" Calliope looked like a tourist who'd asked directions but got gibberish instead. "Yeah. Katherine's supposedly been having this hot woman thing for months now."

Her dim, abstractly sympathetic smile reminded him of the mother on *Little House*—all "rerun." The expression shifted to that of tender inquisitiveness; the paranoid agent took it as the veneer of a shrieking tabloid curiosity.

"Do you know this person?" she asked.

Donny shook his head. "A novelist, with a Kathy Acker haircut."

"How do you feel about that? Are you angry with Katherine?"

"I don't know. If I wasn't on Zoloft, I'd probably be depressed." He paused. "I still think about her—actively. Sexually."

Calliope had the Give Me More look and Donny told her about the games. How Katherine would lie in back of the Land Cruiser like she was unconscious, panties off. They'd pull up to someone, anyone—a mechanic or a Mexican selling maps to stars' homes—and the agent would ask if he knew where the hospital was because his girlfriend was sick. Shifting and showing herself while Donny got directions. On the freeway, too: Katherine in back like she was asleep. The truckers went insane.

In the last few months, they picked up people in bars. He remembered the first time they did that. The fantasy was that the guy would give her head, nothing more. Safe. They had to be in agreement on the candidate. No women—boring, that. Passé. Someone who they thought could be trusted was usually to be found, but the danger was still there. They liked the danger. When they found their mark (or Joe or Jim), they took him home and had a few drinks. Smoked some pot, Katherine fumbling at cold Thai, self-conscious laughs. This guy was cute and tried to kiss her in the kitchen but Katherine said Hey! the deal was head only. More laughs. She kissed him anyway. They "adjourned" to the bedroom and she tried chickening out, but Donny could see the chickening was only pretend and that made it hotter. Donny tied a kerchief around her eyes and the guy started licking her and she groaned "Oh God" as Donny left the room. Where are you going! she shouted, splayed like an animal on their bed, saliva-stained thighs gripped and spread by the hands of a stranger. Her neck crooked, the blindfolded eyes: Donny? I'm just getting a drink, he said. Katherine said she didn't want him to go—already overcome. The whole time never taking the scarf off. Donny, love of her life, taking that as a sure sign of abasement and delirium. He left them there and

had the drink, pulling at himself as he listened to the moans
of his wife, the woman he loved to annihilation, saw them
moving in the distance in the dim bedroom light. It excited
him beyond belief. Donny? she called again and he thought
he'd pass out he was so aroused. *Donny*—token bleats now, the
name meant nothing in her mouth, something he'd read in a
book flitted through his head, how a girl had been raped and
the men let her use the bathroom before they poured Drano
down her throat and how she'd padded back after doing her
business, terrified, nude except for smelly socks and said,
Guess I really had to go, huh? The agent circled around the house
and watched from the terrace. He deliberately left the sliding
glass door open when they first arrived and now the stranger's
pants were down around his ankles and Katherine no longer
called for her love. The guy put her hand on his cock and the
mask rode up on the ridge of her nose enough for her to see
the show, to watch with a horse's crazy eye as he sank it in,
grinding, and after a minute she bellowed as the scarf came all
the way undone. . . .

It was impossible to gauge Calliope's reaction; she was a
pro. Her expression might have been the same had he spent
the hour bitching about office politics. On the way out, in
place of the Oscar-winning D.P., sat Phylliss Wolfe. Donny
had promised to help with casting on her go-nowhere indie
remake of Pasolini's *Teorema*. They laughed when they saw
each other.

"Ho ho. Ships in the night," said Phylliss.

"It's like a *New Yorker* cartoon," he said.

"Only better drawn."

*

The diminutive man in coveralls squinted as the day nurse led him to the living room. In the center of the space was a round marble table with a gigantic flower arrangement befitting the lobby of a small hotel. Modern paintings—little Dines and Twomblys—mixed with sculptures of antiquity and a piano so grand it seemed a parody; upon it, a thicket of family photos in the small, elaborate, variegated frames favored by the rich. Serena Ribkin sat on a Donghia sofa, on a slice of bedsore-repelling sheepskin. Simon realized what he'd smelled at the door was emanating from the frail, elegant woman with black bangles and grayish skin.

"What seems to be the problem?"

"There is a family of raccoons on the hillside," she began, most grandiloquent, "and I am worried one of them has died in the house."

"Okay. Yes. That could be una problemo."

"It's particularly strong in the guest room and den."

"Okay. Right. How long have you been aware of the smell?"

"Juana?" Simon thought it an odd name for the nurse, who looked Danish. "Juana, how long have we had that smell?"

"A few days." With this, the saturnine aide took her leave.

"What makes you think it's a raccoon?"

"I feed them at night. They come right down the hill, a mama and her two babies. But now they don't come."

"Right. Okay. And you think one of our friends died under the house."

The woman looked stricken. "I hope not! If it was one of the babies, do you think the mother would—what would she do? Keep vigil by the body?"

"Right. Uh huh. Okay."

"Would she try to *bury* it?"

"That's one for Marlin Perkins. Can I go to the—den, did you say it was?"

"Please. What is your name?"

"Simon. But people know me as the Dead Animal Guy."

"I am Serena Ribkin."

"Beautiful home. Used to live a hop, skip and a jump from here, on Saltair. My mom still does."

"The smell is so awful."

"It tends to be—always part of the problemo. If our critter's found a nice little niche to make his quantum leap to the Great Unknown, there's not a whole heck of a lot I can do short of taking a few bites out of your wall—which I don't think would thrill either one of us. To summarize, I'm not actually equipped to do that. I pretty much go under houses, and that's all she wrote. To summarize, the last time I looked, I didn't have the Jaws of Life handy. If that *is* the case and Fluffy has gone and wedged himself in a remote area, these things usually burn themselves out in three to seven days. I'll still have to charge you sixty-five dollars just for saying hello. Now, if we *find* our Roger Raccoon or Peter Possum or what have you and it's purely a matter of crashing a maggot party, we have no problemos. While I'm here, I'll take a nice look at your screens. I have to tell you that I am against hiring someone to do a patch job; it's almost part of my covenant. They will rob you blind. If you're not all that worried about aesthetics—judging by this place, you are!—but if you're *not* all that worried, you can spend a fraction of what a professional would charge, by doing it yourself. But I'll take a nice long look. Part of the package."

Knowing that this American Gothic, this spindly hired hand, was rooting around below was a source of immense comfort to the old woman, who closed her eyes and listened for subterranean maunderings. She hoped he would find no coons yet the satisfaction derived from knowing the thing was being faced head-on gave her a moment of peace that felt innovative, potentiating the effects of the Demerol. All her life she had taken solace from the good offices of those involved in service—the handymen of Rockwell's America, armies of commonsense illuminati with natural born dexterous gifts, men who dismantled and trimmed, gutted and washed away, improvised and cobbled, unstopped, unplugged and unstuck; men who removed unwanted things, useless or dead. She wanted him down there forever, guard of the underworld; now and then, he could surface for a meal, sitting with her at the captain's table of the kitchen banquette as she sipped her painkiller, telling all the Huck Finn things he'd seen from the mystic engine room as they trawled their way to the far sodalities of Raccoon Cove.

It was cool and vast beneath the house. The place was like a showroom, tightly packed dirt so clean it might have been the floor of a natural history exhibit featuring basements of rich suburban hillside dwellers of the late twentieth century. The Dead Animal Guy liked this woman and was faintly embarrassed for her. He knew he would find nothing.

Suddenly tired, Simon sat cross-legged, lighting a cigarette. Maybe he should call Calliope before dropping in—sometimes she went nutzoid if he didn't. Oh the hell with it. He was so close, he'd stop and have a sandwich on the way back to Huntington Beach. What was the problemo? Visiting the old homestead was a bit of a dysfunctional detour. He should really go straight home to work. Eight months ago, he'd bought half a dozen *Blue Matrix* episodes at Script City in Hollywood. They'd been gathering dust on the floor beside his bed; it was high time to enter ye olde Writing Phase. Back at Three Strikes Exterminators, before he was an independent contractor, he'd met one of the *Blue Matrix* producers on a job, removing what looked to be a mephitic, larva-shimmering leather shoe from the crawlspace beneath a Studio City home—*ur*-Fluffy, in fact. Simon had a *Matrix* premise concerning a dying Vorbalidian emperor, and the producer, Scott Sagabond, had been encouraging. The veterinary mortician still carried the man's scuffed-up card in his wallet.

"Mother?"

The voice resonated with eerie clarity, and Simon scurried to a vent. Pairs of feet shuffled above.

"Is that you, Donny?" Serena asked.

"Juana called me in the car."

"Why did she do that?"

"Actually, I called *her.* I had a meeting nearby and wanted to pop in."

The old woman coughed with displeasure. "I don't know why you called him, Juana."

"I didn't, Mrs. Ribkin."

"I don't like being spied on."

"Mother, you're being silly."

"No one's spying, Mrs. Ribkin."

"Don't you patronize!" A pause. "Are you hungry?"

"I'm fine."

"Juana, will you tell Veronica to make a tuna salad?"

"Is someone here?" Donny asked.

"What do you mean?"

"Juana said someone was here."

Simon stubbed out his cigarette and emerged from under the house. He knocked on the door and the man answered. He was around forty, pudgy, with thinning orange hair. He wore a deep blue suit and glary, tieless white shirt fastened to the top, each button a different size and shape, ranging from chunks of ivory to tiny animal horns. As Simon began his spiel, Donny Ribkin was already digging in his pocket for cash: He sent the Dead Animal Guy packing without benefit of a migratory discourse on vent-cover aesthetics.

As he left, Simon heard the old woman call to her son, the nurse and whoever else might listen: "I tell you there is something dead in this house."

*

"Oh hi, Mitch."

Simon poked his way through the Traulsen fridge. The view of the yard—his erstwhile domain—was panoramic. Gardeners moved like beadles through hedges; swimming pool generator hummed. The guest house presented its anodynous, photogenic façade.

"Didn't see you come in." His stepfather's bogus, in-patient smile lit up the room like a hospital cafeteria.

"I had a job over in Bel Air."

"We haven't seen you in a while."

"I've been a wee bit frantic—no estoy el problema."

"Does your mother know you're here?"

"That's a negative."

"There's some wonderful cheese in there." Mitch took over the Traulsen, reestablishing supremacy. He grinned, scanning Simon's coveralls. "I hope you're pretty well dusted off." He went to the cabinet and got a plate. "How's business?"

"Things were dead but now they're picking up." Simon heh-heh'ed and gulped a Diet Sprite. "Mom with a patient?"

"You mean *client*." Mitch smiled correctively at Simple Simon. "*Patience* is something we *lose*. We don't lose *clients*—not hopefully, anyway." Through the window, an Asian girl lingered by a table in front of Mitch's side of the cottage. The stepfather took note then said, "And yes, she's with a client."

"I probably won't see her then. Need to get home to write."

"I'll tell Calliope you said hello."

"You know, I usually charge sixty-five for that—to say hello," he said, nonsensically. Simon took a parting smear of Brie. "She's getting a real deal. Tell her the Dead Animal Guy stopped by, she *hates* that. No! Tell her Ace Ventura, Dead Pet Detective, was here."

"I think I'll just say, 'Your son came by to see you.' So long, Simon. And clean up after yourself, okay?"

Simon watched through the window as Mitch made a hammily breathless entrance, greeting the Client as if graciously squeezing her between photo shoots and tribute dinners—all he ever wanted, Simon thought, was to be famous like his wife. By the way the Asian looked at him, she was clearly in the honeymoon of transference. Probably some TV exec, but to Simon, she was a dead ringer for the sniper in *Full Metal Jacket.* "Me so haw-nee. Me analyze you long time." Simon laughed, warm Sprite fizzing from a nostril. Mitch unlocked the door of his office, each movement performed with craftsmanlike felicity, a kind of in-the-now small-town ardor, a joyous, fraudulent humility that insidiously celebrated *himself* while reasserting the Client's pathetic station. Yes: if Dr. Markowitz was on a steady jog through leafy Brentwood

byways, then his troubled flock was on a nude, witless jag
through Bosnian streets.

Moments after Mitch and the whore from Saigon vanished,
a large, elegantly dressed black plunked himself down in one
of the Adirondack thrones. Simon did a double take: it was
Hassan DeVore—aka Fista, the Vorbalidian antihero of *Blue
Matrix*. The Dead Animal Guy fairly yawped. His very own
mother just happened to be therapist to the Chief Navigator
of the Starship *Demeter!* Simon glanced at the clock; twelve of.
He swiped his lips and raced outside.

"Uh, excuse me . . ."

DeVore gaped at him, thinking he was an intruder.

"I'm Calliope's son."

He broke into a smile as wide as a starship bridge. "Nice
to meet you!" The actor was known for his basso profundo, as
for his courtly, theatrical manner.

"She'll kill me for talking to you—"

"No," he said stalwartly. "I won't let her. *And* it would be
bad for her practice."

"I just had to tell you how big a fan I am."

"Why, thank you very much!"

"I'm Simon—Krohn."

"Pleased to meet you, Simon. I'm Hassan."

He warmly shook Simon's hand before settling back onto
the chair.

"I went to the last *Matrix* convention. I didn't feel great
about spending forty dollars to get in—"

"It's terrible," he said, with real sympathy. "It's a lot of
money, I know."

"Some friends and I wound up counterfeiting passes."

"Counterfeit passes! That's *marvellous*."

"We have a kind of street-gang thing going. You know—hip-hop crypto-terrorists." DeVore was baffled but charmed. "A little postmodern Yippiedom. It's retro, but it keeps Big Brother away."

"How old are you, Simon?"

"Thirty-five going on sixty-four going on twelve."

As DeVore burst into laughter, the cottage door opened, disgorging Laura Dern. Calliope loomed behind her. When she saw him there, the psychiatrist's features hardened like ice around the fishing hole of her mouth.

"Laura, this is Simon, my son."

"You were so great in *Jurassic Park*," said Simon.

She thanked him, before exchanging exuberant, fraternal hellos with the waiting Vorbalid.

"The Jeff Goldblum character was my favorite," simple Simon said. "The whole 'chaos' thing. But what I really want to ask about is *Rambling Rose*—"

"If you'd like an interview, you'll have to call her publicist," said his mother, moving between them like Secret Service ready to take a Big Star bullet. Laura made a quick and gracious goodbye. Hassan went into the office.

"I am *furious!*" she shouted, steering Simon through the halls to the front door. "You are *never* to approach clients, you *know* better. This is a safe haven, not the tour at Universal! They come here to get *away* from that, do you understand?"

"I'm sorry—"

"*Not good enough*. Jesus, look at you! You embarrassed me!"

"Yeah, I forgot my Armani."

"You are *always* to call, I thought that was our *agreement*." They paused at the chandeliered entrance while Calliope caught her breath. "You came from a job, didn't you?"

"That's me, Mom—Ace Ventura, Dead Pet Detective."

"Why do you do this to me?"

"Show business is my life."

"What is your delight, Simon? *Why?*"

"I'm sorry, I'm sorry. Look, I'll prostrate myself." He kneeled before her, hoping to make her laugh, but she just glowered. "I'll even *prostate* myself—only with a urologist present, of course."

She yanked him by the elbow like she did when he was a kid. "Get up!"

"Oh come on! What do you want me to do? Not be your son?"

"Right now," she said, "I want you to leave."

"Is that what you want me to do? Not be your son? Because that can be arranged!"

She opened the door and pushed him out.

The ignobled psychiatrist composed a mental sentence or two explaining to Mr. DeVore her son's "history of problems," but when she reached the cottage, she decided to let it be.

*

That afternoon, Les Trott was accused of over-prescribing painkillers to Oberon Mall, the famous singer and actress. A bitch from the DEA dared visit while he was needling cow protein into Phylliss Wolfe's nasolabial furrows. He made the woman wait in his office so she could stare awhile at the photos of bagged and framed Big (Star) Game: Les with international icons, royalty, H.I.V.I.P.s. When he came in, she got right to it, said a whole ring of abusing medicos were implicated. He didn't believe her, but the piece of shit named names,

and except for one, all of them were colleagues. The woman
wanted to know why Oberon had a note in her purse written
on one of Les's prescription pads alerting ERs to her chronic
migraine condition—a kind of backstage pass to the concert
of anesthesia. Les smiled and sweated while an Acolyte futilely
tried his lawyer on the phone. Was he under arrest? He wasn't,
said the harridan. He had watched enough television to know
it was time to ask her to leave.

He sat there shaking. His support team—soft-treading
Mephisto-hoofed angels—fed him Xanax and evinced
outrage. Les called a few of the men she'd named. He got
through to the one he knew least, an ENT guy who shrugged
it off. "They came after me before, the dicks. Listen, they
got nothing else to do. I tell 'em to get a life." Les canceled
his appointments and holed up in the Game room, waiting
for Obie and Calliope to return his calls. When Les hurt,
the Acolytes hurt; they bused in fried chicken from the Ivy,
but he wouldn't eat. Calliope was finally on the line. She
heard the familiar panic in his voice and told him "not to
go there." The shrink said it was probably some sort of scare
tactic, not that she knew so much about this sort of thing.
She asked him point-blank if he *had* over-prescribed. He said
it was all insane. Four thousand Percocets and Vicodins, the
woman said, over fourteen months! How was that possible?
Obie was his closest friend. He lived in her house for five
months after the earthquake while his place was redone.
He'd been through the wars with this girl: surgeries, depres-
sions, divorce. He had been there for her, and she for him—
when boyfriends stomped his heart. Obie was childless. In
sweetly hushed, narcotic late night phone calls, from one
wing of the house to the other, she told him to give a gob

of sperm so they could make a baby; she was burned out on relationships, she said, but wanted a kid. Les never took her seriously (such a terrifying merge was beyond his wildest fantasies of celebrity bonding) but was flattered and moved nonetheless. He made her repeat the proposition at parties, so everyone could hear.

"Four thousand pills is a lot," said Calliope.

"It's *not* four thousand, it *couldn't* be. Are you turning against me?"

She changed tack. "Les, I don't want you getting paranoid."

A little after six, he left through the Private Door. His advocate got through to the Lotus (with the LESISMOR plate) and told him not to worry—"there's no case." There was something troubling and possibly illegal, he said, something *political,* about the entire visit. He'd make a few calls; he had DEA friends who would give him the skinny. Not to worry. Les felt better, having mustered the troops.

He couldn't sleep. He talked to Obie and she was loaded. She said it was all a "bad joke" and was going to break the next day in the *Times.* They talked about a name on the DEA list, a man Les knew only in passing. He'd seen him at Obie's and other Big Star homes. For six hundred dollars, Stuart Stanken made housecalls at any hour of the day and night (he had an answering machine instead of an office). If Big Star had root canal or migraine or hint of kidney stone—or if Big Star was depressed over AIDS death or bad breakup, hair loss or loss of movie role—Stu Stanken was there. He'd shoot them with morphine and stay awhile as they nodded, chit-chatting, admiring the decor and general Big Starness as the systemic valentine was delivered. An hour later he'd dispense an intramuscular booster, just to be safe. I don't want your pain coming back when I'm fifteen minutes out the door. *You need never suffer from pain again,* he intoned, *not so long as I am here to help.* Les used to bridle on running into him at Obie's parties, and he told her so. Being with Stanken was like having a dipso chiropractor in your midst—or an abortionist out of Faulkner. Now, it looked as if they'd be sharing a line-up.

Three in the morning. Propelled from bed by a nightmare, he stood in his Charvet robe before the bathroom mirror of his eighty-five-hundred-square-foot Santa Monica Canyon house, staring at a pimple. All day long he'd felt its achy inchoation. In adolescence, he suffered from acne vulgaris and bore the scars to this day, minimized by dermabrasion. His years of papular plague had been something out of the Middle Ages—weeping pistachios on forehead and cheek, walnuts on shoulder, pecans on back and buttocks, groin and nasal fold. Sometimes, at the whim of jaded acne gods (having feasted on his worried flesh, they sat at table, sated and snoring, turkey drumsticks still in hand), a lone pimple was sent like a scout to unlikely, mind-bending territories: back of the hand, kneecap crown, achilles heel. The men didn't seem to care— the men in movie theaters and coffee-shop bathrooms, some sandy-haired, muscular and trouble-free, others with afflictions of their own. The men who picked him up in cars on the boulevard desired him, with or without his mother's concealing makeup (he could still summon Max Factor's somewhat acrid, hopeful smell). The piratical flesh of Leslie Trott became his enemy. He resolved to have dominion over the landscape that had ostracized him with such methodical, unforgiving cruelty. In medical school, he envied the Jews their baby faces and wispy beards, their unblemished certitude. They were funny and kind. He was their mascot, the over-achiever with bad-news oil glands, a living laboratory of follicular mayhem. He would show them all.

He took a syringe from the drawer and injected the thing with cortisone. Les still ruled over the dermis—he would save his own skin, at all costs. He padded to the kitchen and sat under the bright lights. The hum of silver appliances and halogen allowed him to ponder what he had dreamed. He had been walking, or gliding, down the middle of Sunset Boulevard. No cars. Something lay in the road ahead. A body. His mother hovered over it—not his mother, but rather a succubus: the DEA inquisitor. When the demon said the body needed to be buried, Les laughed and fled. Next thing he knew the demon was upon him, hurling him face-down. Les's teeth shattered on the asphalt. That was when the dermatologist felt the weight of the cadaver, its hands clinging to his neck. The demon forced him to stand with his burden, having strapped the body to Les's back like a nidorous papoose. He was warned that this latest development was born of his attempting to run; if he didn't obey, the consequences would be unimaginably worse. Les asked the demon its bidding. The demon said the body must be buried before dawn in the yard of a distant house. When he began to walk, the weight was almost insupportable, like trudging up a muddy hill carrying a two-hundred-pound man. He tried desperately to awaken. Then he found himself at the gates of a house. The succubus waited there with pick and shovel in hand. The gates opened slowly, as in a cheap horror film but with chilling effect: the house was his own.

*

Donny Ribkin sat at a table with Oberon Mall and the producer Phylliss Wolfe. They were lunching at Sweets, an ICM haunt on Beverly and Sweetzer. Phylliss really owed him for this. She'd been trying to put together an indie remake of Pasolini's *Teorema* for years now, with an interesting spin: the Terence Stamp role of the libertine stranger would be played by a woman.

Phylliss Wolfe was lanky and elegant, with buttery hazel skin. She apotheosized all the New Yorkers Donny'd ever known—brusque and intimate all at once, quick to laugh and trigger-haired when it came to perceived affronts. Although she'd been a fixture on the independent scene for more than a decade, the last few years had been colorless; Phylliss hoped *Teorema* would change all that. She knew how difficult it must have been for the agent to have gotten Obie's attention, let alone nailed down a lunch. The fact that Katherine Grosseck, his beloved ex, happened to be the writer on the project further martyred him.

"Did you go to the screening at Zev's last night?" asked Donny.

Obie nodded, attacking the chef's salad. "I have *never* laughed so hard in my *life*. I was *hemorrhaging*."

"What movie?" Phylliss had a mouth full of onion rings.

"The new Batman. It was horrible."

"Let's cut to the chase," Donny said. "Did you play Rim the Host?"

"He had the runs—how could we resist?" Phylliss laughed, and Obie lit up. "Can you smoke in here?"

"Can *I*? No. Can *you*? Probably."

Just then, a waitress approached and said she'd have to put out her cigarette. Obie scowled at Donny while she stubbed it in a butter dish.

"Told you," he said.

"Anyway, Moe—Trusskopf—started coming up with titles for porn movies. Mostly gay, of course."

"This is so much more wholesome than I imagined."

"There were all these categories and sub-genres . . ."

"She used the *S* word!" interjected Phylliss.

"The *S-G* word," Donny added.

"We did movies: *Sleepless in the Saddle* . . ."

Phylliss submitted *Forrest Rump.* Obie practically spit onto her plate, gratifying the producer.

"We went on for *hours*," Obie said. "I *wish* I could remember—why didn't I write them down? I am such a pig. We did this whole *music* thing. Mamas and Papas . . . 'California Reamin'—' "

"Now we know why all the leaves are brown," volunteered the agent.

Obie guffawed and Phylliss took another shot: " 'Long Time Coming'?"

"That's good," said Obie, cordial and imperious, "but it's the wrong group. You have to stay with the *group*." The producer deflated.

"I have the *best*," Donny said, pausing dramatically. *"Thirty Days in the Hole."*

Cachinations all around.

"I *love* that. Then we got *literary*."

"A Hard Man Is Good to Find," offered the producer. She knew she had a winner.

"Oh my God!" said Big Star. "That is *so fantastic*."

"Wait a minute," said the agent, clinking a glass with his fork. "I have it. I have the *ultimate*."

"Tell us."

"Are you ready?"

"We're ready! Tell us!"

"The Catcher in the Y."

No one would top it. Obie exploded with glee.

"I don't get it," said Phylliss.

"You're so unhip," said Donny, disgruntled.

A handsome young man with five or six tiny hoops in each ear was led to their table—Phylliss's assistant. He handed his boss a packet.

"Eric, you know Donny. Oberon, this is Eric, my guy Friday."

Obie gave him the lech. "We should put him in *Catcher in the Y.*"

"Been there, done that," said Phylliss. "Right, Eric?"

"If you say so." He smiled.

She turned to Obie. "You're an icon to him."

"It's a dirty job," said Big Star, "but someone has to do it."

Phylliss raised an eyebrow at the loitering Eric, then sarcastically gave him his walking papers. "Well . . . we'd *love* it if you could stay but—"

Eric adored Phylliss, and was used to her public paddlings. He smiled shyly, bowed his head then left.

"Thank you, Eric!" Phylliss called out musically.

"Cute," said Obie.

"Here's the cassette," said Phylliss, setting *Teorema* by Obie's purse. "Latest draft's in there too—the Grosseck draft."

"Efficient little fuck," said Obie, looking Donny's way.

"I wouldn't know," he said. "But she *is* full-service."

They gossiped about people who were dying. Phylliss mentioned a friend, a screenwriter with AIDS who recently took a turn for the worse. Suddenly, he was getting ghoulish e-mail: prayers and solicitations from a network of God freaks he called the Internuts.

Donny, the good agent, dutifully brought them back to Phylliss's project. Obie said she'd recently screened *Salò,* and Phylliss was surprised to hear the filmmaker fascinated her enough that she'd once considered optioning a biography, *Pasolini Requiem,* with the intent to produce. Naturally, the idea of playing a young woman who becomes the sexual obsession of a suburban family appealed to her immensely; Obie's instincts were always to shock. Though Phylliss knew Big Star was bold (most often for the wrong reasons), she cagily emphasized the commercial elements along with the avant-garde.

"It's like a darker version of *Boudu Sauvé des Eaux*—the Renoir film."

"*Down and Out in Beverly Hills.*"

"Yes!"

"Then it's a comedy?"

Phylliss scrunched her mouth up, a translator pondering nuances of an ideogram. "It *is* funny—*unbelievably* so. But I don't think I'd call it a comedy."

Donny laughed. "It's *definitely* not a comedy."

"Do you have a director?"

"We're close."

"Jane Campion would be so great."

"I love Jane," Phylliss said, "but I don't think she's available."

"Well, I love what this is about. And your stuff is always so great—*I love your shit.* And I'm *so* fucking sick of the studios. I need to *do* this."

"It's not a very long shoot," said Phylliss. "And it's all in L.A."

"I wish it was in Miami—or New Orleans."

"If that's really an issue—"

"Naw. I don't wanna fuck you up."

"She just bought an amazing house in Palm Beach," offered the agent.

"The two cities are so similar," said Phylliss.

"Fuck it, I'll do it in L.A. I'll be cool."

They toasted each other. They were having their *Get Shorty* "done-deal" moment—a sort of druggy group hysteria that Phylliss knew usually led nowhere. No matter. Strokes from Oberon Mall were better than a pass from Sandra Bullock. More fun, anyway.

"By the way, we *are* changing the title."

"*Teorema* would be kind of a tough sell."

"Too artsy."

"*Thirty Days in the Hole?*" Donny shouted.

"*The Man Who Came at Dinner.*" Phyllis was choking.

"No! No! *The Man Who Came on Dinner.*"

*

Airborne again with her flotilla of Chanels, up, up and away, sucked from Bel Air over park and Palisades, Topanga and Pepperdine and Point Dume, ocean and asphalt and greensward, then the buses of Hearst Castle, faraway confetti of tourists filling Serena with the kind of mournful nostalgia roused by the drone of prop planes or secret garden wishing wells. She felt a fathomless burning. She sat atop a maypole, like the novelty eraser on a child's pencil, remembering the Great Intruder. That's what she was on, then—a metastatic tour of the Americas, a Cook's cancer carousel of the Western world. Impaled thus, riven by pain and douched by morphine, she kept her stabbing vigil on the highest sail, nightwatch on the old crone's nest. She'd be first to sight Raccoon Cove, the gelatinous waves of its mossy harbor flecked with sodden offerings: crumbcakes, sheepskin shag and tiny buoys of meperidine ampullae.

There was Sy, waving from the dock. They first met at Beth-El, the Wilshire Boulevard temple where Donny went to Sunday School. Her marriage was on the rocks. Sitting at those services, Donny's little hand in hers, she fixated on the tall gray cantor while Bernie fidgeted, dreaming of Vegas or studios or whatever it was Bernie Ribkin dreamed, sitting with sore and stinky cock, unwashed from last night's whore-fuck. To Serena, the burnished wood of the pews always smelled like coconuts and musk—as she imagined the skin of the cantor—and for her, this odorously illicit concatenation made her pulse pound. Rejoice: she watched the deadpan cantor silently clear his throat, neck shifting mysteriously, Sy Krohn, the inscrutable religious pro, and the Ribkin family stood along with all the others when his songs began, prayerbooks open for talmudic anthem, this soignée, beaten-down housewife who could actually smell the cantor's balmy breath, redolent of Listerine and borscht, matzo brei and brisket, beer and kugel; she built an aromatic bridge to him, tendons of ambrosia, sandalwood and heliotrope, jasmine and rose—high altar of attar. He lifted the span with the tension of his voice and held her aloft while Bernie vanished to the men's room or sidewalk with a sixty-dollar cigar. They journeyed together, cantor and mistress, a powdery pilgrimage to Mecca and Medina, Gaza and Alexandria, Palmyra and Damascus. Skirting the Empty Quarter—Rub al

Khali. To Athens they went—along the way, eloping from the caravansary and camping in a grove of tamarisks, near a spring-fed pool. Sy roasted a young goat over thuriferous firewood and served tea thick as molasses. He tore into her Arabic tail, slicing it open, licking her spit. Come morning, she awakened in his arms beneath a cloudy anvil of monsoon.

The congregation sat again, jarring her reverie. As the rabbi spoke, Sy faded to the wings to begin his trademark mucosal rumblings. Once she was his, Serena resolved to do a makeover. A few adjustments, that's all. Get him to stop putting grease in his hair, that's why he had the dandruff. Then, in the middle of these absurdities, Donny looked into her eyes, freed by the absence of his father, a strange beseeching look, the abstract, abject entreaties of a small boy's nameless misery. The seven-year-old could not give his heartbreak a voice—the cantor would have to speak for them all. The congregation would rise again as Serena fell back on her fantasia: East of Aden, there they were amid merchants and drovers, wending through souks with the imperturbable charm of post-coital complicity: stalls of cinnamon, cardamom, turmeric and thyme, ivory, indigo, coffee and galls. He gave her myrrh for menstrual cramps, and ground red coral for the abrasions from their lovemaking, resin from the dragon's blood tree. The cantor wore blue loincloth, scabbard and *jambiyya*. Gone were the grease and the talis, the flaky skin. Under hallucinatory skies of eagles and crested hoopoes, through fields of wheat and fire-red aloes, rock-laden baboon-screeched wastelands and stands of lemon trees they went, Sy and Serena, until reaching the vulcanean cliffs of Hisn al Ghurab.

Bernie rejoined them, sliding onto the bench (that reeked of the mucus of her love), soft and honey-smooth as a bowling lane. It had been hell for almost four years; he hadn't touched her in three—why didn't he leave? Because of the child, he said. *But we're killing the child!* Their rancor was sloppy and public. Why hadn't she forced him out? Because of the child . . .

Soon she would go to the cantor, to save her soul. She didn't care what it took. She would corner him, talk to him, make him touch her. He had a wife but that meant nothing. She would ask him to sing—to her alone. She would tell him that spices rode on his voice and that he should stop putting grease in his hair. She would say she was lost in the Rub al Khali and would he please take her arm lest she be swallowed by the dunes.

*

Simon decided to wait a few weeks before calling Calliope to apologize. They'd been through this type of blow-up before. The bad part was, this time he needed rent money.

He came up with a great idea for a *Blue Matrix* episode. Simon would call it "Heart of Arknes," Arknes being the name of the Vorbalidian navigator's long-lost mother, a fierce warrioress who died in a tribal feud when Fista—Hassan DeVore—was a boy. His idea was to bring her back as a hologram, the computer-simulated virtual images of dead loved ones made available to lonesome crew members on request. Fista "checks her out" at the library but begins having doubts; the ectype seems too *real*. What if it's *more* than just a hologram? Fista starts seeing Mom everywhere—on the bridge, the engine room, infirmary—this time wearing nurse's whites; that time, ensign's blues. Fista fears for his sanity. After a violent outburst, the Captain throws him in the brig to cool off. Only one person believes him: Statler, the Malclovian hermaphrodite and ship's cook.

He fantasized about success. After all, his story idea was sound and there was personal entrée—not only was a *Matrix* producer a former client, but the series' star was emotionally dependent on his mother. Simon surmised that psychologically, on all kinds of weird Freudian levels, Hassan DeVore would be dying to please Calliope by doing her son this favor, even if the whole business might appall her. He would have to keep his mother from finding out until after the fact, until the thing was on the air, if that was possible. He'd make sure to inform Hassan that secrecy must be maintained, this was an adventure, a "gift" to her from the two of them. Simon ached to be another Harlan Ellison—or Dean Koontz. He read in *People* that Koontz had a full-time staff whose sole function was to keep track of worldwide royalties. Things would be different once Calliope saw the *In Style* photo spread of Simon at his Santa Ynez ranch, romping with Arknes 1 and Arknes 2, his purebred Rhodesian ridgebacks. He'd make sure the guards turned her away at the gate if she didn't call first. Mitch the fame-slave would kiss Simon's ass so deep they'd need the Jaws of Life to pry him out. No estoy problemo! Simon would still go on dead animal treasure hunts, for the sake of photo op and keeping his hand in. It'd be good press to show the Emmy-winning oddball under a house, doin' what came naturally. Harlan typed short stories in bookstore windows; Andy Kaufman bused tables; Larry Hagman wore chicken suits to his own black-tie galas. Why shouldn't Simon Krohn man the maggot brigade? The Pet Sematary pinup would even keep the scurvy Datsun pickup—that's right, leave it right there in the garage between the Corniche and the Cobra. He might eventually buy an exterminating business, that would be the coup d'éclat. A profitable one, at that.

The phone rang. Serena wanted him to come to the house again. He reflexively began the sixty-five-dollars-just-to-say-hello spiel but stopped himself. She had pots of money; that made it easier. She was lonely, that's all. He'd make a token inspection, then sit awhile, like a volunteer at a hospice.

When he got there, it was late afternoon. Simon hung back in the entryway. The regressed old woman sat on the living room couch while a doctor gathered up his medical bag. "If the spasms return, I want you to call." Serena nodded meekly. The nurse stood by the piano watching, vaguely aroused, vaguely punitive. "You'll promise to call then, Serena?"

She bowed her head contritely. "Thank you, Dr. Stanken."

"You know, this business of being brave is for the birds. And I know Donny has encouraged you to use the phone. Serena?" He squatted before her, staring into her drifting, blepharotic eyes. "You need never suffer from pain again—not so long as I am here to help. Do you understand?"

"Thank you," she mumbled, mouth pursing involuntarily in the wake of the gentle scolding. Stuart Stanken took his bag and said goodbye. They were suddenly face to face in the front hall.

"I—I'm the Dead Animal Guy," he whispered. Nothing else came to mind.

"I'm the pain guy. Nice to meet you." The doctor smiled, sailing out.

The nurse swooped on Simon officiously. "You'll have to go—Mrs. Ribkin isn't feeling well."

"Sorry to hear it."

"I don't think she really needed you."

"I'll just take a quick look under the house and be on my way."

"This *nonsense*—if I had known she called—"

"Juana? Is that the young man?" Simon muttered "Baby Jane" under his breath as the nurse turned back to the living room, steeling herself. He followed her in. "Why didn't you tell me he was here?"

"You should be going to bed now. You'll be passing out from what Doctor gave you."

"I want to sit on the terrace."

"You should be lying down."

"*I want to sit on the terrace, goddammit!*"

Outside, they propped her on a chaise, and Simon tucked a Ralph Lauren throw around. His knees acted as a hedge to keep her from falling.

"Can you smell it?"

"I smell skunk, but it's far away."

"Poor raccoons—it's their mama, I *know* it. How awful!"

"How long have you been sick?"

"Awhile. But I'm just about done."

Something stirred on the hill.

"I could take another look. I mean, under the house."

Serena coughed, and he asked if she needed water. She waved him away. "I heard a marvelous joke. Farfina told me, she's the night nurse. Stupendous gal." She pointed toward the house with a hitch-hiker's thumb and coughed some more. "*This* one—Juana—is a Nazi."

"I'm not excessively fond of the ladies in white myself. They're all Nurse Ratcheds."

The old woman was fading. He morphed her face into younger versions of itself, to pass the time. Serena coughed, bad one this time, eyes opening wide in an alarm of pain. She fidgeted and the blanket fell. Simon helped her cover up.

"There's a man, he's dying. His wife and him don't get along too well, physically—haven't done anything for years. He knows he's not going to make it through the night. He tells her that, and asks for sex. She turns him down. He says, 'How can you do this to me' The wife says, 'I'm tired, I'm exhausted, I worked all day.' He's shocked, of course—like they all are. And he says, 'But I'm dying! How could you be so tired that you couldn't give me sex on my last night on earth?' She looks at him and says, 'That's easy for you to say. You don't have to get up in the morning'!"

She laughed and coughed and Juana gathered her away.

*

He was in his office at ICM, thinking about Katherine and her lover. Phylliss Wolfe had told him about as much as he could stomach. Well, his ex could have done far worse than Stocker Vidra, tribadic film critic, book editor and part-time novella-ist: Katherine might just as easily have wound up in the arms of some agent-turned-successful-producer. This way, there was less exposure. Less embarrassment for him. Better a récherchée *clitterateur* than some art-house director in the thralldom of a freak crossover hit. Better some dyke of Academe than a lawyer-turned-screenwriter. Lawyers-turned-writers were the worst.

He sat there, Dirk Bikkembergs pants at mid-thigh, hand around dick, wondering what they were up to. Probably in Joshua Tree, fisting each other between hits of ecstasy, laughing over his stubby, herpes-ridden shlong.

Taj let him know Phylliss Wolfe was on the phone.

"Hi, Donny. It's Eric."

"Hi, Eric."

"I met you at Sweets. I brought Phylliss the script."

"I know that, Eric. You're very memorable."

"She's just getting off this other call. I thought I had her but—"

"Old gal's slippery."

"Would you like me to call you back? Or would you mind holding a second longer?"

"I don't mind holding." Donny looked down at his lap. "Do you?"

"Do I—?"

"Do you *mind*."

"Holding?"

He was actually flirting with Phylliss's assistant. She jumped on, interrupting the volley.

"Donny *dearest,* is that you?"

"Yes, Mother."

"I want to thank you again for the lunch. I thought it went *very* well."

"It was a stone groove, Mother."

"Have you heard from her?"

"Don't be desperate, Phyll."

"Does she hate me?"

"She thinks you're the best."

"Well, I think she's *wonderful.* So we'll see. And if she doesn't do it, she doesn't do it. Fuck her and fuck you."

"That's my girl." A message flashed on the Amtel: YOUR FATHER ON 4. Donny hiked up his trousers. "Phyll, I gotta jump."

Twenty-five years ago, Bernie Ribkin produced a string of low-budget horror films that made a fortune. An over-tan Mike Todd wannabe, he disappeared in the mid-seventies, after the divorce. The story was he'd been living in Europe, producing films, but Donny didn't buy it. He resurfaced a few years ago and was living in a stuccoplex on Burton Way. On occasion, the agent ran into associates after Bernie introduced himself at Eclipse or Drai's the night before ("I didn't know you had a father!"). The Veepee always cringed. He called him "my crazy stepdad."

They exchanged guarded hellos. Donny promised himself he wouldn't blow up. That would be his meditation exercise.

"How's your mother?"

"Why don't you ask her?"

"I'd like to be able to. I put *several* calls in but she won't answer."

"Serena's not doing too well."

"Somehow I don't think she's too eager to see me."

"Guess you'll never know."

"She wasn't all that eager to see me when she was tip-top!"

The agent could smell the cigar and the lox, eggs and onions. "Listen—Dad." He hated himself for calling him that. Mistake, mistake. "I got five people waiting for me on a conference."

"I'll let you go. Do you think we could have lunch?"

"Talk to Taj."

"What's his last name, Mahal?" laughed the old man. "Looks like I've finally got my fucking sequel in place."

"Great."

"Can you believe it took me thirty years?"

"That's Hollywood. Gotta jump."

"I could use some of your casting ideas."

"Talk to Taj and he'll make a time."

*

He found himself on the freeway, heading downtown. He got off on San Pedro and there was a woman with a sign: **GOd BLeSS.** She had a little girl with her. Donny pulled over and gave her a twenty. The woman was pretty and had all her teeth. He asked what had happened and she said she was working for an insurance company. Her employers were hit hard by the quake and had to let her go; people were still dining out on the fucking earthquake. Donny wondered what the real story was, as if a simpler truth lay hidden behind the insipid lie—as if being jobless and alone with a kid wasn't enough to make you destitute.

Her name was Ursula, and Tiffany was her daughter. He asked if they wanted to get something to eat. She thanked him but declined. He could probably get her to say yes, but what was the get-off? What would he do with them? They probably had the virus—she'd cozily left that one off the verbal résumé. So big deal. Donny figured he wouldn't have to touch her. For thirty dollars cash money she'd suck him off with the kid watching, gratis. Or do the God thing. That could be fun—rent her a place in Toluca Lake right *now,* stock it with cutlery, soaps, mops, candles, all that Smart & Final Iris crap, Trader Joe's cheese, thrift-store bean bags, fifties dinette set, water bed, aquarium for the kid, wardrobe and lingerie, give her the old Bernie-bought Impala, the whole *schmear.* Do the impossible in just a few hours. Ensconce them in a super-clean utility apartment on Barrington somewhere and pay the rent a fucking year in advance. How much for the whole package? Ten grand? Twelve? That was shit. When it's done, lay five K on her and disappear, like some saint. Let six months go by, then drop in to see what's what. What else could he do with her? More immediate. Clean her up. Get her to the doc for a little Private Door dusting, douching and delousing. Have her tested. If she's negative, go the whole Pygmalion hog: Dr. Les's magical mystery collagen tonic, creams and unguents and Retin A, plucking and waxing—shave the pussy and storm the blackheads. Shopping at Trashy Lingerie, gallery-hopping at Bergamot Station, Planet Hollywood with the kid. Get Tiffany into a private school. A fourth grader's tuition at Crossroads was only eleven thou. Be fun having a kid out there in the world, one you never needed to see, who worshiped and was terrified of you, like some miniature Manchurian Candidate.

Donny passed her a business card. He said he could find her work cleaning houses. She plucked a book from her knapsack, a two-thousand-page tome called *The Book of Urantia,* "Urantia means Earth," she said. "Our planet's only one among many, you know." Donny said he would hereby call her Ursula Major. She smiled and gave him the book, as a gift. He took it, forcing on her a hundred-dollar bill. The homeless woman got weepy and kissed his cheek. Tonight, they'd stay in a Best Western instead of God knew where.

He read Katherine's draft of *Teorema* in bed then scanned *The Book of Urantia.* He flipped through its elegant, tissue-thin pages until he found a passage to read aloud:

> *For almost one hundred and fifty million years after the Melchizedek bestowal of Michael, all went well in the universe of Nebadon, when trouble began to brew in system II of constellation 37. This trouble involved a misunderstanding by a Lanonandek Son, a System Sovereign, which had been adjudicated by the Constellation Fathers and approved by the Faithful of Days, the Paradise counselor to that constellation, but the protesting System Sovereign was not fully reconciled to the verdict. . . .*

The agent drifted off, rising like a kite toward interplanetary zones.

*

It was easy getting onto the Sony lot. At the Thalberg Building gate, security was focused on cars, not pedestrians. There was only one guard on duty. Just to be safe, the Dead Animal Guy waited for him to become embroiled in the usual drive-on snafu, then strode right in. Wasn't this the same studio someone drove a flaming truck into a few years back? Simon remembered that in the news; happened around the same time those guards were shot over at Universal. Bad week for showbiz. But maybe trespassing *wasn't* so easy—maybe his furry netherworld shenanigans, veteran wayfarer that he was, had imbued him with a debonair invisibility. He imagined himself in a tux, the Dead Pet Society's mystic Double-Oh Seven.

Simon thought of looking up his sister, Rachel. According to Calliope, big sissy now worked for Perry Needham Howe, the guy raking millions off that syndicated cop show. Howe had offices somewhere on the lot—probably even knew the *Blue Matrix* boys. At a certain level of moneymaking, everyone knew everyone.

He decided to head for safe ground: the company store. He bought a *Blue Matrix* sweatshirt and the cashier told him which stage to go to—asking a guard could have invited trouble. The sparkling backlot had a ritzy Deco theme. He passed a whole block of buildings with wharf-related façades, imaginary fish importers and the like. Rolls-Royces, Hum-Vees and Range Rovers threaded the posh alley-like streets. People drove around in golf carts, as in studio days of yore.

A red ambulance light flashing at the Stage Six door meant they were shooting inside. Simon waited with a small group. When the light went off, they entered the cavernous darkness through gunmetal doors. A girl with a walkie intercepted him.

"May I help you?"

"I'm here to see Hassan."

The girl was listening to voices in her headphones. She said a few words to the walkie that referred to some humdrum crisis.

"You are—"

"Simon Krohn. Hassan's a family friend."

She held the walkie to her mouth, waiting for an audio runway to clear. Finally, she abandoned her efforts and waved him in.

The bridge of the U.S.S. *Demeter* rose before him like the flagship of an exterminating angel. The legendary players were frozen in grandeur between takes, a tableau vivant for Simon's delectation. There was Captain Trent Wildwood, with his shock of blond hair and vermilion tunic; the tapir-like Commander Stroth, clacking fingertips poised at ellipsoid console; Lt. Livingston T. Cloud, witty diplomat in residence, a hundred-year-old being encased within the body of a pre-adolescent boy. Someone yelled *Take five!* and the crew scurried while the actors exhaled, awakening somnambulists.

Simon rounded the set. Before him stretched an aboriginal landscape of lava rock and sand that he recognized as the Fellcrum Outback, sacred burial- and battleground of Vorbalidian gladiators. Grips raised giant blue screens on its periphery. The budding teleplaywright was about to ask

directions to Hassan's dressing room when he saw the impos-
ing figure of the Chief Navigator heading toward him. His face
wore the characteristic calcium plating of the Vorbalid race, a
dignified mosaic of features that made him resemble a cubist
prelate. Mr. DeVore smoked a long thin cigarette and seemed
oblivious; he had the judicious, wistful mien of an actor making serious money, at last.

"Hassan?" The shaled head swiveled. "It's Simon—Krohn."

The Vorbalid brooded and blinked, cracking a smile.
"Well, hello!"

"I hope you don't mind my dropping by."

"Well—I'm not sure!"

The smile became a froggy grimace. The actor began to
loudly hum, as if preparing for song.

"Scott Sagabond is a friend."

"Who?"

"Scott Sagabond, one of the producers."

"He's not with the show. Left last year."

"Okay, no estoy es problemo. He was a friend—of my
mother's too. I had an idea for a script, a long time ago, and
when I met you the other day, things fell quickly into place."

"Yes, they did, didn't they! I can see that."

"Since my story mostly revolves around you, I wanted to
get your input."

"Revolves around me?"

The girl with the walkie came and stood a few feet away,
listening to her headphones. She was waiting for a cue to usher
in Mr. DeVore; head slightly atilt, her eyes had the dull, frank
look of someone making potty.

"Perhaps," said the thespian navigator, "we can talk about
this some other time."

"Oh sure! I can come to the house. I saw it in *In Style*, by the way—your place in Encino? I *love* the grotto your wife designed. She's a very talented lady!"

The girl stepped forward. "Hassan, they're ready for you."

"Karen, this is Simon Krohn. *Actually*, he's my psychiatrist's son." The actor sneezed violently but Simon realized it wasn't a sneeze at all, but a strangled guffaw. Karen grinned, absorbed in finding a free channel.

"Why don't you send the précis to my agent?"

"But I have a copy with me."

"Better to send it—Donny Ribkin at ICM." The Vorbalid was ditching him before Simon could lock on to his coordinates. "But thank you much. Kind of you to drop by."

"My mother thought it would be a good idea to cut through the normal channels—you know, eliminate the middleman."

DeVore stopped in his tracks. "Calliope said you should come here?"

Neither of them looked as if they believed it.

"Well, actually, she suggested I drop it off at the guest house for when you come on Wednesday—at five o'clock. Five's your time, isn't it?"

"I see. Then let me have it."

"I can still send it to your agent."

"Hand it over and I'll look at it tonight."

Hassan made his exit, "Heart of Arknes" in hand. Simon crouched at the edge of the Fellcrum Outback, collecting thoughts and breath, amazed at the adrenaline the afternoon had required. On the other side, they readied for camera. The Dead Animal Guy sat cross-legged amidst the rocky purplish wilderness, contented, a solitary celestial soldier. Only the presence of a lone grip, Styrofoam cup in hand, surveying a table of pastries, fruit and trailmix, invaded his fantasy, rooting it in the workaday.

*

Gliding down Sunset Boulevard. Something in the road. Harpy upon him, hurls him to the ground, scattering teeth to curb like a bloody herd of mah-jongg chips. The dreaming physician ran eastward with the piggybacked cargo, necrotic hands clapped around his neck—trying not to glance down at the wormy holes in the cuticles—apocryphal howling wind chilling him to the bone. Rounding the recurring corner and standing at recurring gate . . .

On the way to Malibu, Dr. Trott turned over last night's images; they still had punch. Same dream, of varying degree, for weeks. Tranquilizers didn't help. He wondered if soon he would be in the grip of agrypnia, the insomniac's insomnia: total inability to sleep. *This disorder,* said the literature, *fatal if it lasts much longer than a week, is also seen in diseases and intoxications—especially* encephalitis lethargica *and ergot-poisoning.* He felt foolish and anachronistic, the "recurring nightmare" concept itself a throwback to the fifties, to the time of shelters and tailfins and Miltown. *The Three Faces of Les.*

It was a big blue Sunday and Obie invited him to the beach house for a screening of *Teorema*. The old friends had had a few whispery, dishy early morning phone chats (Obie saying everyone was full of shit and no one would be able to prosecute, Les trying to believe, scared, needy, unconvincingly cavalier, hanging on Big Star skirts through the

incessant hiccups of her call-waiting; just when the paranoia
started to recede, Obie would click back on and ask if he'
had any Percocets. Les would panic, wondering if the feds
had tapped the line, and ask, stilted and absurd, if she was
kidding. "You know, you should really try to stop being such
a fag," she'd say—so cutting and unnecessary—then take
another call and leave him dangling, marooned and pun-
ished) but this would be the first they'd seen of each other
since the "controversy."

Moe Trusskopf, Obie's personal manager, lay sunning on
the deck with a new boyfriend, a sweet-faced gay mafia moll
who'd been on the circuit awhile and was looking to settle
down. Les remembered him from the office. About a year ago,
he came in with a boil on his ass; he lanced it, then jacked him
off. (Moe knew the story, and introduced the boy as Lancelot.)
He'd met Cat Basquiat before too, but not in the comfort of
his professional offices. At twenty-three—ten years younger
than the hostess—his fee was in the mid-sevens and rising.
His mother had recently died, rendering the tiny MOM tattoo
on his hairless chest mildly poignant. He had a manta ray–
shaped birthmark on the upper left quad and pierced nipple as
lagniappe. Les scanned greedily. The whole package gave the
potential indictee a stony hard-on.

The viewing room had a clarinet-sized Giacometti, a
Noguchi landscape table, a Kitaj pastel and a Baselitz "inver-
sion." The projection screen dropped down over one of those
big Ed Ruscha movie paintings that spelled The End. Baccarat
bowls brimmed with blue M&Ms and rock candy. The doctor liked Pasolini well enough but wasn't up for it. He let
his thoughts drift back to a year ago, Lancelot face-down on
the table, Les numbing and pressing and draining. Time for

some dilatation and curettage . . . When his rubbery attention snapped back to the screen, the father was about to discover Terence Stamp in bed with his sleeping son.

"Like to have been a fly on *that* wall," said Moe.

"How 'bout a fly on those jeans?" said Obie, and everyone laughed.

Les wandered again, rudderless, this time to a recent meeting with the lawyer. While the attorney general's formal accusations were imminent, counsel was confident the matter would end in a letter of reprimand from the Medical Board—a slap on the wrist. If that wasn't forthcoming, an alternative might be probation and community service; at worst, a DEA administrative hearing aimed to revoke or curtail the dermatologist's prescriptive powers. Les sucked on a saccharine crystal. The baronial law office yanked inside-out like a sock, reborn as a dungeon with a Philippe Starck sink—the freefloating physician now in protective custody at the downtown jail in all its slabby *City of Quartz* splendor, co-starring with Terence Stamp in *Kiss of the Spider Woman*. Stamp sure was gorgeous. Could've used a nipple ring, though.

Cat Basquiat had his tongue in Obie's mouth. When Les reached for the M&Ms, Moe said, "What are those, Percocets? I got a headache Les. Gimme." Lancelot laughed. Obie said, "Don't tease, Moe, you know how delicate he is." Les managed a smile as he faced the screen again, then *whoosh* back to the clink for some requisite cyst-popping and rimming of trusties *whoosh* to a DEA meeting, where he stroked out in mid-testimony, crapping his Tommy Nutter trousers as he fell from the witness stand. The rest of his days would be spent in a gold-plated wheelchair, feet drooping down like an unemployed marionette.

Les shuddered, shrugging off this specialized humor-esque, knocking a loafer askew and propping a foot up. He reached into the bowl and licked another sugarcane pebble, dreaming of Rock Candy Mountain mistily shrouded by this boy Basquiat's anal fumes, all vinegar and tuberoses.

How thrilling the proximity, and how improbable to share the citadel! He would have accepted the lowliest position—polishing marble there, or candlesticks. For Big Stars were different than you and me, this he knew from an early age. The boy who watched reruns (*The Rifleman, The Adventures of Ozzie and Harriet, Father Knows Best*), too ashamed of his looks to go to school, knew. The boy who locked himself in the bathroom, tetracycline vials around the sink like votive candles, his face an angry mask of suppurating knots, knew—fussing with them till they wept clear fluid, as if drawn from spinal waters. All he wanted was to be Kurt Russell. Won't someone make it so? Jan-Michael Vincent . . . any old sunbaked smooth-faced boy in hip-hugger jeans would do. He longed for fields of undamaged skin, craving Sal Mineo's buttery cheeks—when they finally came (still sitting on bathroom floor, eyes clenched shut, mirror forgotten for now), he rode to the dusty ranch and necked with Johnny Crawford while his father was at the General Store. The things they did in that barn . . . he would have "Lucas" next.

Les planned to become a psychiatrist—he would listen to Big Star woes, a shoulder for Big Star tears—but changed course in midresidency. He was moonlighting at a Malibu emergency room when Streisand came in with an allergic reaction to fish. She was hyperventilating and badly mottled. He shot her up with Benadryl and right away she could breathe again. Any intern could have done it, but Streisand thought he was God. She invited him to her home for a troubled-youth charity hoedown. Les didn't know a soul yet there he was, bonding with Larry Hagman and Ray Stark, Ann-Margret and Shirley MacLaine. *That's* when he had the vision, more like a religious exfoliation: skin as the Comer, hotter than plastic surgery. O Pioneers! Now, after all these years, they wanted to drag him from penthouse to pillory and march him down Wilshire to the hillock of Via Rodeo, for all the Big and Little Stars—and the nothings—to see.

*

"How are you?"

Obie tucked herself into the chair, hunched in a fetal position. "It's been a real shitty week."

"What happened?"

"Stuff with Cat. Career shit. *Bull*shit."

She was going to cancel, but had canceled the last three sessions already. She blew her nose and Calliope pushed some Kleenex.

"Are you sick? You don't look like you're feeling well."

"I think I have a—this sinus infection. And there's . . . this drug thing, so *stupid*. With Les. It's more a pain in the ass than anything else. Have you read about it?"

"I saw something in the paper."

"It's like, *enough*. It's so *ridiculous*. Poor Les—he's *really* upset, he's like, *shaken*. You know, he's concerned about his career."

"As he should be."

"Has he talked to you about it?"

"You know I wouldn't share something like that."

"Nothing's going to happen."

"There are no guarantees. And it can't be much fun."

"I know—I'm not in denial, I'm not saying it's *nothing*. It's just, I'm so used to—*he's* not. He's never been in the *glare* of the whole whatever. But there's no *way*, that would be *insane*. I mean, for them to—*I'm* the one, if anyone. And it's such a *victimless* crime, if a crime at all. I mean, don't these people have better things to do? I want to talk about something else."

"Did you take anything today, Oberon?"

"What?"

"Did you take anything today?"

"No! Why?"

"You're slurring some of your words."

"I *am*?"

"Yes."

"It's the Zoloft."

"Zoloft doesn't make you slur."

Obie blew her nose again, then closed her eyes. "There's something I really need to talk about."

"In a moment," she said, sternly. "I don't want to see you in here under the influence."

"I'm *not*—"

"That's a rule, Oberon."

"I haven't slept in two days and I have this sinus thing that I took some—what's it called, Atarax?—it's like *unbelievable*, they're like *reds*. I haven't felt this good since high school. I'm kidding. I mean, I could barely drive over here."

"Just so we're clear on the rule."

"We're clear on the rule."

"If you can't drive, we'll call your assistant to pick you up."

"There's an idea. It's just I've been sneezing for, like, *forty-eight hours* and this is the first time I've stopped. I was freaking out 'cause I read somewhere about someone who had to be hospitalized because he couldn't stop sneezing and then he *died*."

"What did you want to talk about?"

"I've been offered this really interesting role. A remake, for no money. Italian film. Pasolini. But *really* interesting. And I did something—I think—I *know* it was connected to the part and some of it was the *drugs,* which I've now stopped. But I feel weird about it and wanted to talk."

"Something with Cat?"

"God, I *wish*. Someone I know befriended a homeless woman. I don't want to say who it is. He picked her up on the street and gave her money. Put her up at the St. James—or the place that used to be the St. James. She has a little girl. Anyway, they came to the house and she blew lunch over the whole celebrity thing. Meeting me. I mean, this is a woman who has been living in *weeds* off of *freeways.* We all got loaded and fooled around—I mean, she's clean, *not* your standard homeless person, I know that sounds terrible. But *very* pretty, kind of like Annette Bening. My friend wound up taking her to another room. You could hear them . . . *fucking* so I took the girl to the other side of the house."

"How old is she?"

"Around seven. Calliope, it's really awful!"

"Why are you so upset?"

"I just feel so *weird* about this but I *know* why I did it. *God,* sometimes I wish I wasn't an actress—the fucking *burden*. See, in *Teorema*—that's the project I'm going to do for, like *no* money because it's so great—this character I'm supposed to play is totally free, totally uninhibited. She has no . . . sexual morality. That's what attracted me to the part. She's a *seducer*. She sleeps with a whole *family:* husband, wife, daughter, son, the whole deal."

"You're saying there are no boundaries."

Obie closed her eyes and nodded. "We played this game where I made her reach inside me."

"You what?"

"I'm *not* a monster and I *know* she wasn't . . . aware— what was happening. She was already sleepy because I think her mother gave her part of a pill, a Valium or something. So she was groggy, whatever, to begin with. My friend said that's what she did, and I remember thinking how weird it was to give your kid a pill. But my mother did that too. So—she was half awake and I—took her to the guest room."

"And what did you do?"

"I was going to put her to bed—should I . . . can I *tell* you this?"

"Yes."

"You won't judge me?"

"I won't judge you."

"This is *exactly* what the *woman* would have done—"

"What woman?"

"The *character.* From *Teorema.* I was *totally* covered by a blanket and she was *more* than half asleep, Calliope, I *know* I was *completely* covered the whole time. I feel weird but I'm not even sure it's wrong—there's *no way* she had any idea. 'If an arm falls in the forest'—"

"She put her arm inside you? *How?*"

"I said I lost a diamond and if she found it, she could have it. I pushed it in . . . I mean, there was no way—it was only like ten seconds and that was *all*. She went to bed *immediately*. I mean, she was half-asleep *during*."

*

"Simon? It's Mitch."

"Oh hi, Mitch."

"Your mother's very upset. She's so upset that she asked me to call."

"What's up?"

"You know what's up."

" 'Fraid I don't, Mitch."

"Did you pay a visit to Hassan DeVore?"

"Pay a visit is a bit much, Mitch. I *saw* him, at the *studio.* Did he tell her that?"

"How else would she have found out, Simon?"

"What's the problemo?"

"I think you *know* what the problem is."

"Frankly, I don't, Mitch. To summarize, why don't you tell me."

"Come on, Simon. You have a head on your shoulders, though you don't always use it. That man is a *client* of your mother's. Going to see him like that is not only a gross invasion of his privacy, but an act of aggression toward Calliope. I can't believe you would have exploited her in that way. *Or* him."

"I went to see Mr. DeVore as a *courtesy,* Mitch. I'm a writer! I'm not playing games! I know a *producer* on that show—"

"I can't believe you'd even *defend*—"

"It's *moot* that Sagabond's no longer there, Mitch! The man extended me an *open invitation*—"

"Simon, I *don't care!* Do you understand? Can you imagine her embarrassment? A client confronting her like that? With stories that her son's *soliciting work*—"

"*Confronting* her? What does *that* mean, Mitch? Did *Mister Vorbalid* say he was unhappy I stopped by?"

"Mr. What?"

"He's a fucking *Vorbalid,* Mitch—we're not talking Anthony Hopkins here! We're not even talking Michael Douglas!"

"This is pointless. I'm just calling to convey a message from your mother, okay, Simon?"

"But this is *important,* Mitch, this is *subjective.* Did my mother say DeVore was unhappy about my visit or *didn't* she? Did she actually *hear* DeVore say—"

"This isn't *Court TV,* okay, Simon? What you did was wrong and you know it! Calliope doesn't want you to call, she doesn't even want you at the house."

"Oh, *really.* And what does *that* mean?"

"It means what it means. She doesn't feel safe."

"She doesn't feel *safe,* Mitch?"

"That's right and I can't blame her. You crossed a line, Simon."

"And now I'm the Unabomber."

"I didn't say that."

"Now I'm stalking my own mom, a *moser!* Pursuer of Jews!"

"You're not to come by the house."

"The house I grew up in. Oh. I see. Great. Wonderful, Mitch. I'm not to come by the house that I grew up in and the house *you've* inhabited for a relatively short while."

"Don't drag me into this."

"You've done a pretty good job already."

"This has nothing to do with me, Simon."

"Oh. And what *does* it have to do with?"

"Your inappropriate behavior."

"Oh. Right. To summarize. I see."

"Let's not belabor this."

"I know you're pissed off because she's famous and you're not."

"I won't even dignify that asininity with a comment."

"You never *will* be, Mitch. I know that must hurt."

"Goodbye, Simon."

"Just one more thing. I was just wondering."

"This conversation is over. *Just stay away.*"

"I only want to know one thing, it's important."

"What is it?"

"I was just wondering what your clients say when you show them your weasely non-famous little dick."

*

When Simon got to Bel Air, Serena wanted to take a drive. The new day nurse was refreshingly indifferent to the announced itinerary. They brought the sheepskin from the couch and laid it on the cracked leather of the old Jag.

"This is a bit unusual for me," he said as they got under way.

"Being abducted by a sick old woman?"

"But I have to say I like the anarchy quotient."

"You're a funny young man." Serena coughed, readjusting herself beneath the strap of the seat belt. "I'm going to take this damn thing off," she said, trying to undo it. Simon reached over and freed her. "Thank you. Silly for me to wear it. For you, no. But for me . . ."

When they got down the hill, she said she wanted to go see raccoons at the zoo.

"I'm not sure they're part of the repertoire."

"Well, *of course* they have raccoons, it's a *zoo*."

"Could be, could be. Maybe so."

"You *are* funny."

"*Rocky Raccoon*," he sang, "*went into his room . . .*"

A tear spilled to her cheek and she wiped it away with the quavering back of a hand. "I'm so worried, Simon." It was the first time she had called him by name, and he felt a deep tug within. "I can smell the mother—I *know* she's unwell. What will happen to the babies, with the mother gone?"

They stopped at the park across from the pink hotel, to sit awhile. Serena didn't look well, and Simon was afraid she would die on him. She thought about Sy Krohn with a drowsy, bluesy yearning; every once in a while his voice keened on the radio of a passing car. She got loopy and asked Simon if "the old Jurgenson's still sold fumigants"—frankincense and myrrh—"anything to blot the smell." Serena wanted to know if he'd ever been in love and Simon said he didn't know. Of course that meant he hadn't, she said. Simon felt an unbearable melancholy, like a weed killing his meager gardens. He remembered a boy in grammar school he thought he loved, and a girl too. The boy smelled like Zest soap and the girl, Jungle Gardenia—now, they were barely memories. Serena asked about his family and Simon said his father died long ago, a mythic figure distant as a king on the cover of a vintage comic. He thought of telling her more, but Serena was in pain and asked that he drive her home.

If they had stayed a while longer, Simon might have spoken of his father as a murdered man, a cantor. "His name
was Sy Krohn," he might have said. It can only be wondered
whether Serena, already hemorrhaging, would have felt the
impact of this rogue revelation and held it long enough to bony
breast to declare the fallen idol as the very one she'd loved to
near madness; how she had been with him when he died and
for years after wished to die herself. For better or worse, those
details would remain under shifting sands, consigned to the
Rub al Khali of memory for all time.

*

After a few sleepless nights, she called an old therapist friend.
They met at a coffee shop, Calliope in her big dark glasses. Of
course, she didn't name names. Her colleague said, "You must
report this." You are not an attorney, he said. Hence, certain
things your client tells you are not privileged under California
law. But if the child is indigent? Calliope heard herself asking,
knowing it came out wrong. She meant it in a habeas corpus,
not a class sense—the child would have to be submitted, no?
But you told me they're with this person's friend, said the colleague. So they are not indigent. Aside from the actions of your
client, which are criminal, this little girl is being put in harm's
way by her mother—your client said the mother is feeding her
pills. Not only is she negligent but her judgment is impaired.
You'd better do some serious thinking, said the colleague.
Because you have a serious problem on your hands.

Calliope went to bed, where she remained for three
days. How could this have happened? If the esteemed psychiatrist acted according to law and contacted authorities,

her assiduously cultivated practice might easily topple; the legal nuances of confidentiality were not an issue her paranoid, illustrious clientele cared to grapple with. Anyhow, it was Oberon's word against hers. The claims might be thrown from court, and Calliope left with libelous egg on her face—Obie could even countersue. The psychiatrist would become tabloid-fodder.

She lay there sweating and channel-surfing. One moment, she was reaching for the phone to make the Call; the next, freeloading on Big Star's twisted reasoning, wondering if, in fact, there really was a crime . . . if the girl truly had no knowledge of what transpired—she groaned, seized by a wave of self-revulsion. What is *wrong* with me? Yet what was the alternative? She'd talk to Oberon and share her dilemma, that might help her decide. Describe the hard-and-fast legal obligations of a California therapist—frighten Obie to death. *I want you to think carefully about what I've told you, Oberon. And I want you to tell me . . . whether what you said happened with that child was the fantasy of an actress preparing a role—or was it* real? Pause, while the actress took in the full import; answers it was "fantasy." *Good. That's what I thought. I'd like to know: did the drugs have anything to do with this active* fantasizing? Pause. Says yes, "Yes, they did." Drugs. *Good. Very good. It's good to be honest. Now, I want you to enter a drug treatment program—today. Do you understand, Oberon?* Somber nodding of the head, along with expiatory tears. Calliope would make it clear that when she got out of detox, they'd get to the bottom of this perverse, *imagined* act—the tough-love therapist wasn't about to let her off the hook. They would face Big Star demons together. She would *help* Obie because that's what Calliope *did,* that's how she'd built her practice—helping and healing, not destroying clients' lives. Or wreaking havoc on her own. If the Obie thing broke, the famed cottage (therapeutic oratory, refuge and sacrarium, Brentwood's own confessional Taliesin of above-the-line tears, fears and renewal) would be the sudden locus of *Hard Copy* helicopters, *Vanity Fair* layouts and O.J.ish lookie-loos. No one should be subjected to that.

Calliope reached for the phone, wondering why she'd ever faltered. She left a message for Obie that it was imperative she didn't miss her next appointment.

*

The carnival-themed Children with AIDS benefit was on the Twentieth Century-Fox backlot. Everyone wore baseball caps that said HERO—even the agents. Dustin and Goldie and Meryl manned the booths. Tom Hanks got dunked by Bob Zemeckis, Roseanne worked a Hula Hoop and Oliver Stone demonstrated a ring toss. There were lots of children and rich wives, paparazzi and studio heads and an army of people with the lean, mean walking-stick look of waning T cells. As Mitch and Calliope snaked through the crowd, the therapist rehearsed her attitude should she bump into Hassan. They'd only had one session since the Sony incident; he had been understanding, but she couldn't control who the television star would tell. Somewhere down the line, more scandal awaited.

They found themselves on line for a hot dog behind Oberon and Dr. Trott. A little girl stood on his shoes. He introduced her as Tiffany, and the child extended a hand for Calliope to shake. Calliope asked Obie if she'd gotten her message. Obie said she hadn't. They were joined by Donny Ribkin and Ursula, Tiffany's mother. Les made a joke about therapist gridlock, then Donny said seeing Mitch and Calliope in public was like walking in on your parents while they were doing it. Phylliss Wolfe came over and said they almost had enough for a minyan. Ursula asked what a minyan was and Phylliss said it was "Yiddish for encounter group."

Only on the ride home did Calliope realize the mother and child she met were the players in Obie's hellish home-movie, with Donny Ribkin as co-star. She shivered, recalling the hairless white arm and the girl's tender grip, limp as a rag doll's.

*

The Dead Pet Detective had a job in Laurel Canyon; Fluffy was in the cellar, party-heartying with the larvae. It was strictly a BYOL scene—bring your own Lysol—and before you could say *yech,* the little wrigglers were doing the Top Ramen tango. After, he stopped at the Canyon Mart and impulsively bought flowers and sandalwood incense for Serena.

There were police cars in the driveway. The front door was open and Simon stepped inside. Men in suits were questioning the new nurse, who was near hysteria. Seconds later, Donny Ribkin barreled from the kitchen.

"This is *insanity*! How could this fucking *happen?*" He locked eyes with Simon. "What are *you* doing here?"

"I just stopped to give these to Serena."

"Thank you, but you're going to have to leave. I'm sorry."

"Is she okay?"

"Look, you have to leave, okay? Thank you very much."

He jostled Simon out without even taking the flowers. Had Serena died? She'd been sick enough that her death shouldn't have aroused such mayhem. What did Donny's words in the hall mean? The mood of the house seemed more interrogatory than postmortem. Might she have been killed by a burglar? That was too farfetched . . . maybe the old woman took an overdose and that's why the nurse was being grilled. Yes—that made most sense. Or maybe she wasn't dead at all. But if that were true, where was the ambulance? And if she was already at the hospital, what was the son doing here? If she *was* dead, who were these people? Where was the coroner? It felt like something had just happened: they never rushed a body out of a house like that.

His car was parked curbside. Simon tossed flowers and incense onto the front seat through the open window. A policeman left the front porch of the home across the way. A woman in a bathrobe covered her mouth with a hand, stricken.

"Do you think she's wandering the streets somewhere?"

"If she is, I would hope someone will take her in and give us a call."

"Poor darling! She's been *so* ill."

Simon ran to the side of the house.

He could smell her as he shimmied through the access. She was ten yards in, sitting against a post. He whispered "Serena" and hunchbacked toward her. The eyes were open. A horde of disorganized ants in the superheated throes of discovery laid claim to the darkening ground beneath the bloody, blown-out engine room of her bowel. They would say it was delirium, but Simon knew why she had come. He choked back tears, wondering what to do next. She looked so perfect there, timeless and untroubled—Serena. He would keep her from the maggots.

Above came the querulous footsteps of the son and the men, and Simon wished this house could lift off, basement jettisoned, to find its lonesome orbit somewhere near the Fellcrum Outback. The Dead Animal Guy in Space would petition the Vorbalidian Elders for mercy and they would grudgingly comply, resuscitating her with the proviso she could never return to Earth. Together, they'd cross the firmament of the cellars of eternity, performing obsequies over the dead.

*

On the eve of burying Serena, the agent had a massage. He got a name from Laura Dern's chore whore. The masseuse spent a lot of time moving her hands over his body without touching—"dispelling dark energy," she said. Someone must have blabbed about his mom dying. It was lovely being rubbed out there on the patio. He got sleepy. The fountain tinkled and the hill rustled with scavengers. The girl said she saw a big raccoon.

All day long, he'd been airing the place out. Donny loved this house; maybe he'd move in for a while. Strange, but he'd never bought, always rented—he thought he must have got that from his father. Bernie was always bouncing from duplex to hotel. Serena had kept things up pretty well, though the lot was probably worth more than the house itself. Whole thing might bring two-point-seven—with the market the way it was, who knew. Maybe two-three, two-one. He'd find some Persian schmuck-Jew or Big Star wannabe, sell it for cash, then buy a place in Mandeville or Rustic Canyon. Three acres felt about right. He could actually afford to spend five mill, if he had to. Five mill on a house. You could get something really decent for that. Lying there, getting his bad energy laundered, Donny performed a sprightly minuet of acquisition: he could retire in Fiji or the Côte d'Azur if he chose, or spend a million on a Pissarro. Lasso koi from the Sargasso or bid on a boulle Louis XIV *bureau plat* at Sotheby's, three million for a piece of fucking furniture, thank you very much. Something to set the teeth of his colleagues on edge—they were always jockeying for rarefied outside investment interests that made them more than "just agents." How about the Donny and Serena Ribkin Foundation? Generous and unconditional stipends to radical artists. Whatever he came up with, the grieving son promised himself Jessye Norman would sing at his next birthday.

The service at Hillside would be small. He hadn't yet called his father. The old man was probably gambling at some West Hollywood card club or standing at the Peninsula bar, informing a hooker his son was king of ICM. He could see it: Bernie at the cemetery, sussing out the gallery, slithering up to a mark, one of the agency crew, pitching his loser sequel there at the open pit as the casket ratcheted down. Well, fuck *him*. He'd have to read about the death of Donny Ribkin's mother in the trades. Then he could make his phony graveside communion—*oh, the way we were!*—hike up the hill for the big false moment, standing on the grassy doormat of her remains with supermarket flowers and crocodile tears. What a ham. His drinking buddies from the Golden Years were buried there, Dick Shawn and Vic Morrow. On the way back to his bunged-up Range Rover, the old bag of semen might even take a walking tour, stop and say hello. All that gloom sure made a fellow want to play an exacta or two—from the memorial park's gentle slopes, you could practically see the track. . . .

Donny was hard for half the massage, cock straining against the sheet like a dumb, friendly ghost. He didn't feel remotely erotic, but that was of no consquence; day after night after day, the absurd beggar made its demands. Energy Girl worked around it, never making a move. Wouldn't toss it a nickel.

The agent got restless and went to see Ursula. On the way, the radio said Oberon Mall had overdosed. He doubled back to Cedars. When he got to the hospital, the media circus had already staked its tents. Donny parked across and sat in the darkness, immobilized. He didn't have it in him tonight, not just because of his mother's death, though that was handy. No one would exactly expect him to show up at the ER with the lawyers and publicists. He was thinking more along the lines that it was time to change his life, disappear somewhere in a three-hundred-thousand-dollar motor home; cliché agent burnout thoughts, life as Lynchian road show. Nic Cage could play him in the movie of his life. Donny began to laugh, then saw his mother drifting before him in a Valentino; she hovered outside the windshield, an ancient dulcinea on the hood, trying so hard to charm the Acolytes at Les's, so valiant, smiling through a veil of eviscerating pain. The agent wept convulsively until the windows fogged, shielding him from the prying searchlight eyes of *Entertainment Tonight.*

*

A tube snaked down the hole in Obie's throat. Les was the only one she "talked" to—grunts, clicks and tortured exhalations amid farts and yowling tears. He sat with her every day after work and on weekends. One blink for yes and two for no assured she was compos mentis. He wished, mercifully, that she weren't.

It wasn't an overdose at all. Oberon Mall went in for a root canal and bacteria got in the blood, attacking a congenitally weakened valve in her heart. It festered there before unleashing a shower of emboli to effervesce the brainstem, blocking supply of blood to the pons—the area commanding movement. When the tide rolled out, death of tissue left her marooned—"locked-in," went the jargon—a Big Star cognitively undamaged, sensoria intact, dungeoned in a useless body, a catheterized sandcastle princess on a wide dead sea.

He left her to the caretakers when it became too much, Obie with her ungodly wail, blind but sensing his departure, the distraught dermatologist rushing for the elevator while nurses unstuck watery carbuncle of bedpan, rotating her so she wouldn't grow decubiti. A few days in, two attendants were caught photographing her nude, their hands on her.

*

Les wondered how much she could see. Once in a while, when he held her, an eye rolled up and looked into his like something from Sea World. Her doctors, most of them friends from medical school, said Obie would never recover movement or speech. Les couldn't imagine that. Perhaps he'd assume care once she was discharged. When she got over her depression (if that were possible), she would require a van, with driver and attendant, like the Getty boy. He would have to get with her accountants. She was completely vulnerable now. The court would need to appoint an executor. The only relative he knew of was the mother, and Edith wasn't able. It would be easy for him to step in. They shared the same attorneys, and he knew Obie would agree to such an arrangement. But could he afford it, emotionally? Professionally? There was still the matter of the Medical Board investigation. If Obie fell to his care, he would hire a publicist for a few months, a friend at PMK. He'd been thinking of doing that anyway. He was already being slandered—there were whispers of the root canal story being a cover, that Les had furnished the drugs that destroyed her. People would say he was just doing penance with his attentions, Big Star–martyred, reading aloud to her for hours, Tolstoy and George Eliot, arranging on-line chats with Chris Reeve, visits from Deepak Chopra, injecting collagen here and there for old times' sake. Hosting morbid dinner parties . . . Who cared what they said? He loved her and would do the right thing. Yet he knew what happened to "love"—he'd been through that with his mother during her slow decline. How many times he had wished her dead, wanting to piss into that hairy, sleeping scowl of a mouth.

He would accommodate. Les's spirits rose as he saw himself arriving at a benefit with Oberon and her pharaonic attendants—a famous pair the Doctor and Big Star would make, odd and legendary, real *New Yorker* material, Avedon'd and Yohji'd in summer whites, Obie tied by Hermès scarves to a high-tech wheelchair, atrophic and glorious in her Anna Sui, gums overgrown from anti-seizure meds.

*

Once Obie's mom was coaxed into coming, she didn't want to leave. The ICU nurses bent the rules and let her sleep in a cot in the room. Les took her to Mortons while the medics fiddled with the Big Star gastrostomy tube.

Edith had gained about a hundred pounds since he'd seen her last. She was remembered as a tall, lanky woman, a big-boned American classic—pasty and menstrual-smelling now, cheeks like slabs of halvah, wet with tears. A borderline schizophrenic, she lived alone in a building Obie had bought and christened the Edith-Esther. Her mother was holy to her. Big Star had managed to keep her existence from the world and that was good, because Edith-Esther Gershon was not built for scrutiny; she was gentle and alien and rarely left her rooms. Les remembered stopping over one night after a premiere. Edith giddily showed them the bawdy printouts of her dialogue with AOL lotharios. One of them, a Turk, owned a strip club in Akron. He wanted to know how "tall" Edith's breasts were and Obie laughed until she cried.

*

Calliope told Les he didn't look well. She said he needed time off and gave him "permission" to recharge in Rancho Mirage.

Les left Thursday and drove back Sunday night, top down all the way. He hadn't done that since college. The freeways were clear, the night a velour, spangled dome. He thought about Obie, turning the pages of the memory album while "Streets of Philadelphia" repeated itself on CD. They had some hilarious times. As the air knifed around him, the physician felt grateful and alive. *I'm not paralyzed,* he thought, then said it aloud. And said it again, louder this time, as if courting danger, shouting his Schadenfreude to the stars. The words soured in his mouth and he felt naked and foolish, unclean, ashamed. He recoiled as he heard the voice: *You should really try to stop being such a fag. . . .*

Les drove to the hospital.

The cot was empty and a curtain was drawn around Obie's bed. A small light shone within.

He hesitated to enter, thinking her in the midst of some intimate minor procedure. He tried to discern silhouettes, then went in. The two laid atop the sheets, Oberon in her mother's puissant arms, mouth fastened to nipple. Edith's tear-streaked face looked up and smiled, lips trembling like an ecstatic clown. Les's mouth was open too and he covered it with one hand while the other felt for a chair. Eyes riveted, he backed up, noiselessly lowering himself as if onto a pew.

*

"Hey, there."

Eric was at the Sweets bar when Donny walked in.

"There he is," said the agent.

"Here for dinner?"

"No—I was at Muse."

"Can I buy you a drink?"

"Absolutely. Absolut."

It was a Monday crowd—the place had become so hot that Monday was the only hip night left.

"Have you been to see her?"

"Yeah," Donny lied. He hadn't visited once.

"Pretty horrible, huh."

"Pretty horrible."

"Do you believe—is it true about the root canal stuff?"

"Yeah, it's true."

"Jesus. Phylliss was really freaked out."

"A lot of people were."

"She went over to see her."

"To the hospital? You're kidding."

"It *really* freaked her out."

"What did she say? That she was rewriting the part for a quadriplegic?"

"Yeah, right!"

They laughed darkly and sipped their drinks.

"I heard your mother died," Eric said. "I guess this hasn't been a great couple of weeks for a lot of people."

Donny impulsively asked if he wanted to go somewhere else. The assistant was flattered and surprised. He ducked into the men's room while the agent waited for the valet. A few boisterous associates came and went, and Donny was grateful to have been standing there alone. Eric said he was parked on the street. They left his car and wound up at a club in Silverlake.

"I thought you were straight," said Eric as they got out of the car.

"As an arrow."

They drank and watched men dance. They were joined by a friend of Eric's named Quinn. Quinn had some coke, and ten minutes later, Donny actually found himself on the dance floor, two-stepping with the boys. They had more drinks and more coke and he invited them back to Carcassonne Way. Quinn followed on his blue-and-white Harley.

Donny showed them around the house. When they got to the patio, Eric stripped off his things and jumped into the pool with a whoop. Donny asked Quinn if he was into cars, and they went to the garage.

The day Serena died, he brought the old Impala over and left it there, as if for a period of mourning—wild car of his youth back in the coop to pay its respects. Quinn ran a finger over the hood. Donny opened the door and climbed in. Quinn slid behind the wheel, shirtless. He asked if they could hear music and Donny handed him the key. Quinn turned the radio on then leaned over and kissed the agent on the mouth. His hand snaked into Donny's pants.

"You don't remember me, do you?"

"You're Quinn," Donny said, blankly.

"You're married, right?"

"Uh, was."

"Your wife has an angel tattooed on her butt, right?"

"Last time I looked." The agent was curious now.

"I went home with you. You live in Laurel Canyon, right?"

"Jesus."

"With the scarf, remember? That was pretty hot."

"All in the family," the agent said, unbuckling his pants. The old acquaintance got out a tiny tube of K-Y. Donny took it and greased Quinn's cock. Donny asked if he'd tested and Quinn said, Every three months. Donny just wanted it inside him. They did some coke and the agent leaned back against the door, legs up in the air. The windows fogged and the Senior Veepee winced. Is this what his mother felt? This kind of cancer . . . A shape appeared through the misty glass. Bracing with his body, wet from the pool, Eric carefully opened the door, so the agent wouldn't fall out. Donny arched, groaning as he rode up on Quinn. Eric braced Donny's back and neck while Quinn scooted back like an insect, taking the stuck agent with him. Eric put his knees against the seat and his balls in Donny's mouth. Donny twisted his head so that in his agony he could get at Eric's prick. The agent was stoned enough that the twisting nearly made him black out.

When his father first bought him the car, Donny took
Serena for a ride. She sat in the back and he chauffeured her
to Linney's, the deli on south Beverly Drive. When they got
back home, she sat and wept. "You're all I have now, Donny."
It would be years before he learned what she meant.

Eric watched like a naturalist as Quinn began fucking
faster. The agent conjured his mother, sitting in back, staring past them; a coliseum-sized roar as Serena was torn from
the prow, a whirligig Ursula taking her place, with Tiffany in
tow—mascara of dirt and tears, firecracker eyes. Donny jacked
himself, hand crushed by Quinn's hard belly, Eric slowly pulling his own gummy head at the agent's crown like a deep sea
geiger; Bernie and Calliope before him, agent close to puking
now, two-step funhouse vertigo, father's B horror trailers—
entrailers—blood hammering, hilarious vaudeville pneumatic
sucking of Donny's asshole; Katherine, love of his life. Donny
beside her on the Laurel Canyon bed, Quinn fucking both
like a piston, cold Thai on the counter, forgiving her beloved,
forgiving him everything, never a bigger love, never bigger
than theirs, never could be, staring at each other, Bonnie and
Clyde just before the bullets but senses dead, no Pop poet-
ics, Donny holding back the tears, awareness searching like
a snail's antennae for something to hold on to, something to
hold him down, to ground him, he found it, the crazed wet
smacking of the vinyl seat and the painful button at the small
of his back kept him conscious. Then the beauty of the hood
ornament glimpsed through mouth fog carried him over. . . .

As soon as it was done, he could join his mother—wasn't
he all that she had?—under the house.

*

On weekends, Les put in time at the Venice free clinic. The Medical Board asked for two hundred hours; the six months he spent there revitalized him. He felt like a real doctor again.

Obie remained paralyzed and there was no improvement in her speech. Still, he understood her better than anyone. He painstakingly assembled something of a secret language, until one day he gained fluent trespass to the sandcastle's sodden, crumbly rooms. Visitors and nurses alike marveled, though sometimes Obie's requests, as channeled through Dr. Trott, were filigreed enough to elicit unspoken derision. The day she asked him to kill her, he immediately called Calliope. The psychiatrist warned of the consequences, legal and moral. Until he was able to separate Oberon from his mother, she said, his motives would be tainted. Luckily, Big Star pulled out of her depression—or seemed to, anyway. She stopped bringing it up.

He had a week of vivid dreams.

Most began at the Children with AIDS benefit but ended with the doctor on Sunset, standing over the familiar corpse. (The impingement of the carnival seemed to signal an end to the haunting of Les Trott.) At the pre-succubus open-air gala, the Duke of Dermis wandered through Big Star–manned booths, searching for Obie. The strange thing was, only civilians used a language Les could understand. Television actors spoke pidgin English unless they were cultural icons, which rendered them practically incomprehensible. Big Stars spoke "Catalan," or its dream version—beyond translation. It was actually with relief that Les would find himself erased from that scene and propped in the middle of Sunset near the pink hotel, its refurbished, too-perfect grandeur and Disney World pastels suitable dressing for all manner of night terrors. As usual, the body lay ahead and relief turned to apprehension.

Teeth shattered against curb and the demon seized upon him like always, fastening the cadaver to his back. Again, the instructions he'd heard time and again: burial before dawn in the yard of a house which of course, turned out to be his own. Les broke ground with the shovel, but this time was allowed to complete his chores before awakening. The body slid off him like a bangle into the grave.

It was Obie.

He floated up through inky waters, startled by his own sobs, his bed a set of dice, and then a lily pad. He was ravenous. He wolfed steak and eggs and began planning a cruise through the Suez to Safaga, on to Bombay and Colombo, Phuket and Penang, Kuala Lumpur. The Seychelles—the lagoons and atolls of the Indian Ocean, trade winds of an equatorial sky: Aldabra, Cosmoledo, Astove, Assumption. He'd invite a young man he met at the clinic. Thirty thousand apiece for Cunard's "Owner's Suite," but Les could afford it. Calliope would think it a smashing idea.

Friday, the doctor was over-booked. He shot a lot of collagen and pimples, soothed a lot of Big Star egos. He worked late and went to a premiere. He came home around eleven, showered and threw himself into bed. It was only minutes before sleep that Les realized he hadn't thought of her the entire day—not once. The feeling of the nightmare came back, but instead of fear he was suffused by a corny, esoteric nostalgia. He knew he'd never have that dream again.

All at once, it came to him. He would buy something for Obie before he left, something expensive, a brooch or diamond anklet. She'd love that. He smiled excitedly at the prospect. How fortunate he was, he thought, to be able to make such a kindness. He hugged a downy king-sized pillow and thought about where to shop. He was supposed to be in Santa Barbara tomorrow for a party at the Zemeckises'; the gift could wait till next week. He didn't want to be compulsive about it—that was the old Les, the Les that needed to be loved, right now, right away, at any cost. Something silky, maybe, or something soft, like those eight-thousand-dollar shahtoosh scarves in vogue with Big Stars these days. Well, he'd think about it; had to be right. Besides, he could always get something on the cruise—*that's* what he'd do. She'd miss him so while he was away. Les would have to break it gently, tell her the day before he put to sea. He'd give Edith-Esther exotic postcards with funny little messages from whimsical, imaginary ports of call, to read to her out loud. He'd buy Obie pearls—strands of duty-free black pearls. Docking in Long Beach at trip's end, he'd limo straight to the hospital. He'd kiss her cheek and say he had a surprise, putting the necklace in her hand, wrapping it around the wrist like a rosary. Edith-Esther would tell everyone "Dr. Les got her those" and no one would doubt his love.

Book 2

WOMEN IN FILM

You'll Never Eat Me During Lunch in This Town Again
by Phylliss Wolfe

Strange-ass developments at hand! Wound up on the red eye to New York with Katherine Grosseck's inamorata. (You haven't met her yet, have you Eric? *Very* talented writer along the Kathy Acker line. It's a dirty job but someone has to do it— Obie Mall used to say that about *everything.* Poor Obie.) The plane was totally, scarily empty. I drifted to coach at around thirty-two-thousand feet and we worked our way back to Business, tiny bottle by tiny bottle: high-larious! I did my whole "Let Me Entertain You" number and Vidra was laughing non-stop (she's really "Stocker Vidra" but everyone calls her Veed; can't quite bring myself to yet). I think I was a little nervous that maybe she was going to slip a finger in my twat so I kept the patter going. Just kidding—we had a great time. Turns out that not only does she write award-winning experimental "fictions" . . . *is* there such a thing anymore? I think prose is so endangered, any kind of fiction writing should *automatically* be called an experiment! Not only does she write but she's doing a three-month teaching stint in Ohio *and* she's a consulting editor at Grove. How she manages to eat pussy with a schedule like that::::::::::where was I? I have the bladder from hell. Bladder transplants are gonna be the new hip thing, just wait. Leaking to the press, ha ha. The long and short of it

is, Vidra says I should keep a journal or a whatever—wants to
peddle my memoirs! I mean, she's *serious,* says Grove would
buy it in a heartbeat. We futzed around with titles. I liked *Cry
Wolfe!*—*Slouching Toward Sundance* but I'm a silly cunt, aren't I?
You *know* you've got the fucking best job in the whole world,
Eric. And if you show this to *anyone,* I'll hang you by your
pierced tits (probably like that, huh). But I really do love you,
E. You and the eighty-one T cells you rode in on. (Buh *dum*
bum.) But I wanna tell ya . . .

Then Vidra came up with the Julia Phillips variation and
we *died.* I mean, I *have* to do it now, just so I can use the title.
(Though maybe the whole reference is already passé?) I'm
still not quite sure what Vidra wants from me. She said, "Just
start," so here I am. Guess it's my own insecurities . . . am I
supposed to be Jackie Mason or Oscar Wilde? Carrie Fisher?
(She's kinda both):::::::::::I talk into a long silvery Sony micro-
cassette recorder with a brown suede sack—very *President's
Analyst,* very Jay Sebring. Starting from about fifth grade,
I promised myself I'd keep a diary, but never did (call me
Anaïs the Ninny)—guess I needed Vidra for a jump-start.
Went to Book Soup to get Keats's letters (on Katherine G's
recommend) but wound up flipping through Dawn Steel's
book instead (for research, okay?)—*They Can Kill You . . . But
They Can't Eat You.* It's like she won the Worst Title lotto.
(Maybe I should call my book *They Can Kill You . . . But
They'll Never Eat Me During Lunch*—!) There's a bizarre chap-
ter where Dawn befuddledly wonders why various famous,
powerful men would want to befriend her—deeply absurd
low-self-esteem weirdness. Like looking at a stiff cock and
saying, "I couldn't figure out for the life of me how shit got
on there." She *does* answer her own perturbation in the next

paragraph, with a power-Zen retort: "By the time I knew, I
didn't care. I already had moved on to Touchstone."

Oh, E, am I trying too hard? Maybe I shouldn't even be
doing this:::::::::*Hate* the sound of my voice, I sound like a
man—worse! An *angry* man:::::::::Calliope thinks it's a good
way to examine my so-called life. Still can't believe I see a
shrink named Calliope . . . wasn't there, like, at least *one* friend
everyone had when they were growing up who had an out-
of-control alcoholic mom named Calliope? Reminds me of a
toga'd Carol Lynley–haired bimbo from one of those ancient
Star Treks—no! Yvette Mimieux in *The Time Machine*—no!
Anne Francis in *Forbidden Planet.* Lyre-toters! Deep-space air-
heads! You know, where the action always takes place on some
drugged-out, asexual trans-stellar Pompeii. Uh . . . was I trash-
ing my shrink? A sure sign I've run out of things to say. (Stop
me before I shrill again—ugh. Call the pun police.) Calliope's
husband's a shrink too, you knew that, didn't you, E? Only he
doesn't have a funny name. They work out of this perfect little
Laura Ashley Cape Cod guest house in Brentwood. It's like that
old movie with Robert Young, *Enchanted Cottage* . . . or maybe
it isn't but who gives a fuck. Gotta get those film references
in there, sez Vidra. I'm always afraid Calliope's gonna dump
me on the husband—Mitch's psychiatric specialty being the
"below-the-line" personality. Am I not heartless? Funny if I
met a guy that way (if I met a guy *any* way)—I mean, while we
were waiting to see our shrinks. Good premise for a bad one-
act:::::::::Tell you one thing: Dawn Steel would *not* do a remake
of Pasolini's *Teorema.* She's too smart for that . . . . But fuck all
if it doesn't seem my ten-year dream is *finally* on a fast track in
this grand New Year. Would still kill for Jane Campion (I BRAKE
FOR BERTOLUCCI), but Saul says she's booked for like six years.

(He actually suggested Amy Heckerling.) I remain *adamantine* about having a woman at the helm (that's Chayevskyspeak— remember Bill Holden saying that in *Network*? Can't remember what he was adamantine about; maybe falling onto the edges of coffee tables). Oh! and Saul said he saw Jodie Foster at the Medavoys' and mentioned *Teorema*—we're using that as a temp title because we actually had legal with *The Stranger* and *The Visitor,* neither of which I was crazed about; I promised Grosseck dinner at Ginza Sushiko if she came up with something groovy—the Jode Girl wasn't familiar but seemed intrigued when Saul synopsized (Saul synopsizing is a scary thought). Worth a follow-up, so I'll call. Jodeth and I go way back, as in Way Back Machine. Saul pitched her as *diractress*: not sure she has the helming chops but could wow as the Stranger—if she'd just stop being *Jodie* . . . . Meanwhile (back at the L.A. Farm), Shelby's sneaking the script to M, though I'm not sure she's right; our girl's *got* to have Terry Stamp's slick menace. Jennifer Jason is, as always, a judgment call . . . somehow I'm bored—though Katherine's *obsessed.* JJ seems wan, *non?* Art-house outré? E, I think we need to have a casting bull session with some of your mean faggot friends, OK? Saul is pushing L but L's not *stately* enough, she's sexy but it's dizzy, off-kilter sexy—and *so* young. Sigh, shiver, yawn. Woe is me::::::::::Out of all the dentists in the world, why oh why did Oberon Mall have to go see *that* one. So horrible! Donny told me he thought it was weird that I went to the hospital but *fuck him*::::::::::Think I'm going on a three-week fast—Vidra's gonna walk me through it. She said it's *amazing,* after a week you're like *high* the whole::::::::::Lunch at the Ivy with Shelby, who's casting *Teorema.* One of the women she works with had a little boy over the holidays, born blind. The mom's my age—forty-three. Oh God! It almost extinguishes any hope I have. Every day I have to face the possibility, the growing *reality,* that I will go to my grave childless. In that very real sense, my films have become my children. If I sound pretentious or maudlin, then just kill me—but don't eat me . . . *at least never during lunch in this town again!* My only wish for the New Year is that *Teorema* has big blue eyes, a fat pink butt and an earsplitting yelp when it slides out the chute. By the way, E—where the hell am I staying in Park City? Do you know?

Sight Unseen
Letters to My Firstborn
by Sara Radisson-Stein

My darling Samson . . .

I wanted to put down in words how much I love you. I'm so glad we gave you that name—you'll need all your strength in this terrible, wonderful life. I'm sitting beside you as I write; the faintest of light falls on your marzipan cheeks. You're the sweetest plum, and sleep so soundly; still, I'm afraid the scratching of my pen will wake you. Perfect boy! I stare into your eyes any chance I get—to become familiar with them, to make friends so there's no fear, no estrangement. You won't need them, to know me—you feel me within as I felt you all these months. One of those monsters said I was "in denial." People should go to prison for using that phrase. This Adult Child Monster—she's infertile, that's all she ever shares at the meetings—wondered how I could say you were a perfect baby. She wants me to hang my head and weep so we can all be losers together and guzzle Prozac with our Starbucks Frappuccino. But you're perfect as could be, perfect as you wanted. If you had no ears, would you be "less" than nor-mal, "more" normal than a blind boy? Who makes the rules, Samson? We do, that's who.

*

Shelby came to see you today and cried 'cause you're so beau-teous. I told her I wanted to work, *needed* to work on some-thing wondrous. I'll blow a fuse if I have to go back to Warner Bros.—I've had it with *Blue Matrix* and "Vorbalid" cattle calls, the well-oiled casting machine that chews up sad English actors, and others who had no right leaving the New York stage. (Well, Hassan was an exception, but Hassan would be a star even if the DeBeers commercial was the only thing he'd ever done.) *Teorema* is *such* an interesting project! It's my time now, time to get off the TV treadmill—it's been a grand office party but I stayed too long and began to hate myself a little the last few years (till there was you. *There were bells . . .*). But don't let Daddy hear that, Mama's just having a kvetch. You won't tell him, will you, little Boy Blue? One day, I'll be a pro-ducer. That's why I want to pick Phylliss Wolfe's brain—*what* an interesting lady. The real deal. She's got style to burn and rots of crass (as our Chinese friends might say). Well look at you, you're smiling! Did you like that? Was that a funny joke Mama made? Are you the smilin' Chinaman? Or is it some-thing you ate?

*

. . . warm winds dancing leaves around the pool and Jeremy's worried I'm not sleeping enough. I always awaken just after four, long hangover from the earthquake; guess that makes you one heck of an aftershock. There: I've changed you and kissed you and turned off the lamp . . . *do* wish you could see the moon throw its pastel spotlight on your dad like he was the dead-drunk ringmaster of Beddy-Bye Circus. Hurry, hurry, step right up, see the silvery chest hairs where you nestle your buddhahead. You know, if I put my ear to your (Buddhist) temple, methinks I can hear the bones grow.

You're asleep now. You know, you look like something God threw together for a booth at eternity's science fair. I'll risk kissing your dark lids . . . they tremble like abandoned nests. You stir and suckle (that's okay—I shake and bake). O Samson, my Samson, of what do you dream? Surely it's not that you had eyes, that much I know.

Then I won't dream it either.

*** *The Thief of Energy* +++
Portrait of a Masseuse/////////////
by Gina Tolk

. . . after rubbing Donny Ribkin, I took a stroll on the Via Rodeo and made purchase of several cigars at Davidoff's of Geneva; Helen Hunt was there and I told her how much I enjoyed her work. Afterward, the woman showed me a humidor at a cost of thousands—I demurred. I will give the stogies to the agent on my next appointment. Donny Ribkin's hard-on is full-blown now before I even begin; he is in my web. The first time I rubbed him it was the night before his mother was entombed. I could feel the residue of her on him like blue smokey tentacles, pulling him into the Earth. The raccoons saw her energy and came close. Donny said they were her friends—they were loaded with her energetic droppings, which they gleaned from foodstuffs she left for them on the patio. I like his energy; it's orange in hue and looks like kelp—or sleepy eels—floating on the surface of a pinkish coral reef. (Agents have good energy that they generally misuse.)

Bought a red leather daybook from Francis Orr and have started to write again. Mustn't forget I have *always* written and consider myself a Writer by definition above all else. Perhaps (I don't think I am deluded, at least not in this case) my story may eventually be deemed fit enough to film by the likes of a Gus Van Sant, a Jane Campion or a Tim Robbins. My saga *does* resemble a latter-day *Shampoo,* with elements perhaps shying toward Polanski, or so I am told. (I'm compelled to note I am writing with a stunning, rather bulbous Cartier silver pen 'appropriated' from a client with a vast collection. There is a blue jewel of some sort on its non-writing end, I believe called a Cabachon. They don't make this particular one anymore, or so I am told, and I noticed coincidentally that in Francis Orr's glass display case, one was there among the paperweights at the price of twelve hundred and seventy-five dollars. I would say I definitely got a deal!)

Since I was a girl at Horace Mann School in Beverly Hills (one of the 'Four Sisters' of the Beverly Hills elementary school system: Beverly Vista, El Rodeo, Hawthorne and Horace Mann—the latter being the poorest; Hawthorne and El Rodeo with the most star-studded scions), I remembered being lauded for my literary efforts. My story 'The Drought' was deemed 'Best Written' . . . the short, gripping tale of a primitive village that underwent a terrible onslaught of drought. This was in Junior High; I was, I would say, the tender age of eleven. The story was only five pages long. On its penultimate page the rain finally came, the ironic 'twist' being that it *would not stop*. And the village sank under, so the final sentence told us, as in ancient times! This morbidly effective divertissement was of course written under the spell of O. Henry and Bret Harte (and even, perhaps, *The Twilight Zone*), whom I greedily admired. I uncovered the pages of 'The Drought' recently, and while it is somewhat Hemingwayesque, one clearly would not necessarily associate it to being written by a child of that age. I have since progressed to more sophisticated authors, Jane Smiley, Stocker Vidra, and Gogol's *Dead Souls*—not to say I don't indulge in the occasional Grisham, Koontz, Straub, Crichton or Krantz (sounds like a law firm)—but this latter quintet, only in bathroom or den. I will *not* have them in my bedroom, because they sully. My saga will cover the Early Years of my life, with special poignant emphasis on the death of my sister, Wanda—this will beautifully set the stage. There will of course be discussion of the subsequent, infamous kidnapping (which marked me indelibly); I will discuss and share my apprenticeship in the art of massage and festively detail my subsequent acquired intimacy with celebrities on the calibre of Jodie Foster, Laura Dern and Whoopi Goldberg. How I took from them, and gave, too.

As I began this process, I had the desire for a professional person to be available as a bellwether or anchor. I set sights on the famous psychiatrist Calliope Krohn-Markowitz, but the doctor would not see me. I know from furtive Filofax peregrinations that she is currently Laura Dern's ongoing therapist (I snuck a look while Laura was in the ladies' room, post-Massage); and that Julianne Moore saw her for a three-week crisis, impromptu. Alas, a sad commentary, but in the pecking order of this town one must be a luminary in order to be seen by certain rarefied psychiatric types—très pathétique! I *did* talk to her, Calliope finally calling back after several days, apologizing for her tardiness, which was thoughtful if slightly rehearsed, as if covering bases in a routinary fashion. I told her stupidly that I had read various flattering profiles of her (*Vanity Fair* and *Mirabella*), and when she appraised I was an 'unknown' (I said I was a Miramax executive—first thing that came to mind. It wasn't enough) she referred me to one Dr Erica Miller at the NPI. All this before I could even ask if her lesser husband could see me in her stead. (He sees his own patients in an adjacent guest cottage—or so I am told by the *Mirabella* profile.) Haven't yet decided which course to take re: whole therapist notion. Lie low awhile. It is inevitable it would be a helpful tool, in conjunction with a working journal—the 'Journal of a *** Thief +++ of Energy.' Perhaps I will call Dr Erica Miller after all. In therapy, which will enhance and focus my telling of this tale, I will discuss the Men/Women/Clients in my own life; growing up poor in Beverly Hills (shit happens); the death and subsequent kidnapping of my sister Wanda; and slowly building to the Great Rip-off—how *Beverly Hills 90210* was appropriated from me by Mr Jeremy Stein and Mr Darren Star; how *The X-Files* and Mr Chris Carter will too have their day in court. How I let that happen, because I wasn't a shark, and am ignorant of shark-like ways.

I know if I can massage Julia Roberts or Sandra Bullock (I have already been recommended by Laura to the latter—now there is only 'one degree of separation' between Sandra and myself!), one of them will eventually agree to play the *** Thief +++ on-screen.

Hello, Columbus

To: SHARKEE@CLS.OHIO-STATE.EDU (STOCKER VIDRA)
FROM: DOLPH@AOL.COM (KATHERINE GROSSECK)
Dearest Sweetest Sharkee (AKA Stocker Vidra, AKA Mi Vidra Loca, AKA Charlene the Tuna),

Miss you SO bad—the Dolphin misses her Shark. (Starting my period; miss your cotton-pickin' mouth.) *Hate* you for going away to teach; live for our time together. The ban on phone calls *so* Victorian . . . and so *mmmmm.* You're my e-mail fatale. Who ever thought freaking Ohio would be an erogenous zone?

Phylliss told me all about how you're going to do her memoir. Mercy, I got steamed (mercy of a rude steam)—a writer's jealous pang, a mercenary, knee-jerk thing about anyone thinking they can put pen to pencil, that it's so fucking *easy*— but more, thinking about the two of you stoned, doing slow migration 'crost a six-mile-high dark empty plane, with Greek chorus of Stepford stewardii in the wings. Hopes to Gawd there warn't no hanky panky committed in dem aisles (dose lips, dem aisles). If so informed, Dolphina wilst surely speak her Greenpeace then swim away. Holy moly! the sacrilege I would have committed between the stretchy, stained headrest tombstones of those vacant seats . . . oh well. Comfort at least to know I'm the only one who takes your Red Eye, *really* takes it, salty cyclops, anytime, anyhow, anywhere. Jeepers creepers, where'd you get that peeper, anyway?

Did you know my ex has been helping Phylliss with financing on *Teorema*? (He was the one who put her together with Oberon Mall before the, ahem, dental mishap; I still think that's bullshit cover for drug-induced coma.) Have the sneaking suspicion he's doing it to somehow still be *involved*—Donny needs to know there's some kind of connection between us, even if it's indirect. He's *very* fucked up, Vidra. I've heard weird rumors about him that I'm trying to confirm. I think his mother dying unhinged him; this thing he has with me *totally* relates back to her. He always tried to be low-key about Serena, but I think he was . . . *obsessed* somehow. Oh God, did I tell you his father's supposedly back in L.A.? That is so *freaked.* This old guy, trying to flog his zombie franchise! I think it's been a bit too much for Donny the Rib.

Adored your short story; envy your facility, freedom, mastery of the form. Loved "Desi"—it was Phylliss, through and through. All the nuances, conversational rhythm and then some—Phyll would shit in her DKNY! You're so good, you scare me, Sharkee . . . I get lost in your sentences the way I get lost in your cunny (and other places). Sometimes I'm angry at *les mots* for seeing more of you than I do (lately, anyhoo). I get possessive of your participles and subjugated by your future-perfects; your prose poems make me tense. Here I sit with my big dumb screenwriter crayons: "EXTERIOR. HOUSE. DAY."'s and "INTERIOR. AUTOMOBILE. NIGHT."'s. Retardo. So you're Susan Sontag and I'm Kathie Lee Gifford. Uh, like, I can deal. Goddammit girl, I want your fin inside me NOW. I'm a good Ethel Mermaid and I go where I'm kicked (splash, splash). I wannabe your C-food (cock)tail. I yam what I yam what I yam: Sharkee's Machine.

Showbiz update: UTA keeps saying I'll be nominated for *Imitations,* but I don't want to think about it. The studio's supposedly gearing up for a big push behind Emma, so maybe I'll leech along. On the *Teorema* front, Phylliss heard about a young director (woman) who's showing a film at Park City called *Janie Wong Eats Cum.* (Promising title!) Her name's Pargita Snow (heard of her? Hard name to forget) and she's actually a known painter in NYC (kiss of death?). That was enough to make me instantly loathe her—you know your Dolphin Lung-Grin can be a heartless bitch—when I heard she hadn't done any rock videos, not-a-one, I softened. Phylliss said Pargita is supposed to be a combo of Jane Campion and Q. Tarantino and that sounded hot but I've since been puzzling over what the fuck it *means.* (How 'bout Wim Wenders and Nora Ephron? Martha Coolidge and Todd Haynes?) Once we get a directress, Ms. Wolfe has convinced we'll nab our lead. I'm pressing for Jennifer Jason (as are Saul and Shelby) but Phyll's oddly resistant. Says whenever JJL appears on-screen, the audience begins a "tacit countdown to the rape"; that's glib and unfair—sometimes the Wolfe sound-bites more than she can chew (which makes for best-sellers, lucky you!). An unknown isn't being ruled out, if we can get exotic ingenues for the kid parts and a coupla international art-house heavies to play their folks. Shelby talked about reuniting Harvey Keitel and Holly Hunter; I thought that was a *way* cool idea. Anyhoo, Phyll's a soldier and a schtarker, every inch the sweet-fanged kike depicted in your towering prose Inferno!

Wish just wunst in a while you'd let Dolphina take care of you: let her book us some time at the Doral Saturnia—or SST to Gay Paree for a super-luxe R&R wkend between the sheets at the Montalembert (don't Frette). We could yacht to Capri for some clam (aw shucks. Nothing like a little sexual molluska-tion). Come on, Sharkee, what they pay me is *obscene,* so why not do obscene things? Seriously, Veed, whenever I give you things or even *want* to give, you resent it. . . . I understand

and respect your reticence and independence but sometimes I think you carry it too far. Par example, the Jag. I know I should have gotten something more practical, something you could drive from L.A. to the University—like the old Town & Country Wagoneer you had your eye on. Well okay, that one was my big boo-boo. (My heart was in the right place; wish your head was.) I *see* now the error of my ways, and *why* I did it; it was obvious I didn't want you to go! So I got you something old and delicate and elegant and temperamental, like the Dolphin herself. So the damn thing sits in storage like Donny's damn Impala, waiting. I take it out for a spin, once a month. Just like my hole(s) . . .

Been re-reading the Keats letters.

Going to the Ivy again with Phyll (seeing too much of her lately) for lunch. It's full of fags, meaning everyone in the Business. I call it the H-Ivy!

Maps to the Stars
by Kim Girard

Often, at the strangest moment {usually smack in the middle of reciting the Specials}, my mind toggles back to Vancouver and the friends and family I left behind; and I am temporarily sidetracked by that sinking homesicky feeling—penny dreadful! After five months, I was certain I'd be more inured. Today was a bad day in that regard. First thing off, I spilled sauce on my slacks and had to work the whole shift like that which I HATE; I cannot tolerate being unkempt, especially for the public. Kevin wouldn't let me go home and change. I don't know what he has against me. Coupled with the fact one of

my heels is coming unglued and my cuffs were GRAY because
the stupid dry cleaners could not find my other blouse—well,
I almost broke down right there during an order. {No, Diary,
it didn't help that I'm majorly PMS.} Instead, I had to swallow
my emotions and focus on the matter at hand: the Soup of the
Day {I'm trying to make that Soup of the Night. Jabba says the
tips are so much better}.

   Jabba's a complicated, VERY interesting girl who's lived
a hard life—I feel privileged in comparison. Yet she's far
beyond me in street savvy and SO beautiful, she looks like a
combination of ALANIS MORISSETTE and that nurse from
ER. She was almost given the lead in *Showgirls* or so she said;
and I choose to believe her. I WILL not be cynical, like so
many of my fledgling compatriots. Jabba's real name is Molly
and she apparently took her nom de stage {a cute and exotic
conversational icebreaker} from STAR WARS {CIRCA 1977,
1980, 1983}. Another interesting detail about Jabba is that her
father "is-was" a "personality." CHET STODDARD, according
to her, was a relatively famous talk show host in the early
seventies. I've run this past Kevin and others and indeed
they knew the name. That impressed me because GARRY
SHANDLING, SHARI LEWIS, KELSEY GRAMMER and one
of the FOO FIGHTERS aside {I saw them at Von's, within a
one-week period!}, this is my first "personal" connection to
somewhat of a blueblood. She said she doesn't talk to her dad
much {"not because he molested me, which he didn't," which
I thought was a peculiar way of phrasing}. Jabba has modeled
and lived in Europe—my first REAL friend since I came to
this town.

   And now, without further ado, it's time for . . .

GIRARD'S LIST—PANTHEON OF THE ELITE!

With this New Year, I restate my goal: to forge a career in
the vein of the following: MICHELE PFEIFFER, UMA
THURMAN, LAURA DERN, ANDIE MacDOWELL, SANDRA
BULLOCK and LINDA FIORENTINO. {JULIA ROBERTS, you
MAY return to the List in coming months but I CANNOT for
some reason relate to you just now {{could it be the dream I
had of you and your brother, ERIC? He was falling from a rock
and you would not extend a hand—would not let bygones be
bygones}}. I DO love you for your camera-beauty {{you are like
the ceramic white-and-gold plastic horses I kept on my bureau
as a lonesome child}}, your regal independence and ability to
unapologetically command a male star's fee so important to
all of us working {{and unworking!!}} actresses. Did I mention
your quirky taste in men, which is exactly MINE? For me,
LYLE is neck and neck with TOM WAITS. I know you were
meant for each other and hope you will find your way back
again; it is hard to be strong in the ceaseless glare of Media;
love is always better the second time around.} If I fail to achieve
in my own trajectory as artist, surely it will only be for having
set my markers too high—of that, I cannot be ashamed.

You'll Never Eat Me During Lunch . . .

Park City exhausting but worth it. *Janie Wong Eats Cum* was
beyond anything I'd hoped for (title refers to gang graffiti;
Nexus had to censor and will release as *Janie Wong*). Funny,
fierce and made me cry—three days in the snow with Pargita
(Snow): she's the one, the one, the one! And, E, the most *unbelievable* thing is I actually own a painting of hers! As Orson

Welles said, it's all true. I evidently moved into her loft in the East Village about a hundred years ago, inheriting a canvas she left behind in the fury of decampment after her split with Kelvin Grotto. He, the Mad Collagist of NoHo. I remember finding it in the closet—Pargita said she *deliberately* left it but I kind of doubt that—E, you will never believe—it's the oil on the wall of my study. Haven't you seen it? Do you know what it's *of*? It's the image of the accompanist—the piano player standing at the window in Pasolini's *Salò*! You know: the pianist goes over to the window and you think she's taking a break or something but she just steps out to her death, walks into the air like a sleepwalker. Pargita Snow left it and I've always hung on to it. Not too bizarre. I offered to return, and she refused. Made a few calls—it's probably worth about twenty-five thousand. She is *obsessed* with Pier Paolo and was planning a movie of his life called *The Agony of P3*. She tried to get Malkovich interested and you know, I think he'd be great for the dad. Serendipity doo-dah! Kismet and kizz me too, oh cum-drunk Janie Wong! The girl is *wild*. Smoked tons of hash (been twenty years) and went midnight range-riding with Oliver Stone and a horde of Nexus execs (I call 'em "Nexex"). Heard all kinds of gossip: like Arnold Vega's fucking his fourteen-year-old stepson! (Put that in your Prince Albert and smoke it.) *And* . . . that while she was making her documentary, Gaby Silverman masturbated a prisoner—a multiple murderer, no less! Did some masturbating myself, won't say with who:::::::::Here I am again. Boy, some cliffhanger. You won't get it out of me; let's just say he's famous and young enough to be the son I never had . . . and *you*, sweet guy Friday, would gleefully rim Al Sharpton after a marathon run for a chance at *thirty seconds* of tongue-in-cheek with unsaid paramour. Oh what the fuck, it's Cat Basquiat. There, I said it. Now, unstick your tongue from the floor and keep typing. Sez he wants to see me when we're back in L.A. but there's::::::::::Eric, do I have a Calliope today? That new pill is giving me cotton mouth. It's called Zoloft; Katherine Grosseck's on it too 'cause she's been having love problems— that's right, with my very own editor. (Not too incestuous, this town.) She calls it "Zoloft, been good to know you." Don't you just *love* it? That's why she's a writer and I'm a talker. Or am I?

Hello, Columbus

To: SHARKEE@CLS.OHIO-STATE.EDU (STOCKER VIDRA)
From: DOLPH@AOL.COM (KATHERINE GROSSECK)
Am cut to the bone. What did I do to invoke such rage? That was a *love* letter, anyone could see! The only "hidden agenda" was how I hate that you're in Ohio, Vidra—hate being apart. Staring at the stupid laptop for hours, wondering where I went wrong, pathetically looking for my hidden agendas. So *tired* of being the victim . . . sitting here with my Wheat Thins, Cherry Coke and Percocet, Powerbook a gray grave, headstone scrolling its digital glow-in-the-dark epitaph. Does that make you happy? Isn't it obvious that I feel *nothing* toward Donny? And I was teasing about Phylliss. Hanky-panky with Phylliss Wolfe? Jesus, Vidra! "Dolphina will swim away" was flirty and frolicsome; to you, it was a "passive-aggressive doomsday scenario." Hel-*lo*? *Are* you seeing someone else? Kinda sounds like it, no? Like you're looking for the egress. If it's true, Vidra, let me know; I'll stay on my perch awhile before climbing down. Tough finding trapeze work these days.

Sight Unseen

MEMO: To Oceanspray Strongboy Sam

NBC's doing Daddy's series, *Palos Verdes*. The announcement buoyed him—for a few days, we were a happy TV family again. He snuggled you. But now he's back to five A.M. workouts and coming home so late. Did you know your daddy was cross-eyed when he was just a tiny boy? They corrected it with surgery before his teens but I think Jeremy actually feels he "passed something on," though the doctors say there's no connection *whatsoever*. One of those crazy macho things—he's convinced your sightlessness is on account of his weak genes. We both went and saw a therapist, Mitch Markowitz, recommended by—guess who?—your godmother, Holly Hunter (who's coming all the way from Warsaw to see you soon, ya know). A *very* empathetic man. There's evidently a long waiting list (he's married to a famous "shrink to the stars") so we were lucky Holly got us in. Sure helps having a godmother who's an Oscar winner. Ain't nothin' but a g-mother thing! Jeremy was uncomfortable being there and I thought he (Dr. Mitch) did a bang-up job at setting him—setting us *both* at ease. I think he'll draw Daddy out of his shell.

Wouldja like to be in motion pictures? Or do you just want to swing on a star? I'll be taking you on casting sessions soon—to give you the lay of the land. Shelby says I should wait awhile but I'm feeling housebound and want my Gregor Samson to see the world. Gregor Samsa was a big old bug. Phylliss Wolfe hired a director for *Teorema* named Pargita Snow. *Par-gi-ta Snow*—isn't that strange and lovely? Seems I'm the only one who never heard of her; then again, I'm the only one with a big butterscotch ball in her lap, too. Holly's dying to meet you, did

you know that? She might have to go to Boston first, though—
maybe she'll bring some baked beans for the Beanbag.

Hello, Columbus

To: sharkee@cls.ohio-state.edu (Stocker Vidra)
From: dolph@aol.com (Katherine Grosseck)
Crying for two days . . . Pink Dot keeps delivering blue ice
masks. Haven't left the house—all dressed down, with no
place to go. Dreamed I was in the hospital (for some reason, it
was the Writers Guild) and they were tying me to the gurney.
I asked why and they said because of your "restraining order."
My dreams always did tend to lean toward the literal (litto-
ral?). Have you forgotten St. John's, Vidra? You said you'd kill
yourself if you ever hit me again. You promised and you never
reneged . . . but can't you see, Vidra, how this is the same? Out
of *nowhere*? It's been so wonderful—until now. I'm beat up all
over again—

> Now I am your mother, your daughter, your brand new
> thing—a snail, a nest. I am alive when your fingers are.
> So tell me anything but track me like a climber for here
> is the eye, here is the jewel, here is the excitement the
> nipple learns. I am unbalanced—but I am not mad with
> snow. I am mad the way young girls are mad, with an
> offering, an offering . . . I burn the way money burns.

That's Anne Sexton.

To: sharkee@cls.ohio-state.edu (Stocker Vidra)
From: dolph@aol.com (Katherine Grosseck)

The Dolphin lies at the bottom of her tank, tangled up in blue fisherman's net, with her Dolores O'Riordan. *Does anyone care . . . Does anyone care . . . Does anyone care . . .*

*** The THIEF of ENERGY +++

A two-hour, in Benedict. A mid- to well-known screenwriter named Katherine Grosseck. It seems apparent, from *Buzz* magazine and other gleanings/cullings—and copious ads in *Variety* and *The Hollywood Reporter*—that she is more than likely to be nominated for an Academy Award for *Imitations of Drowning*, the filmed bio of Anne Sexton (poetess) that starred Emma Thompson. Not very many people saw it (including me!) but I told her I loved it anyway. No harm done. They are all such egoists, but pretend to be humble. They'd never ask, 'Oh really? Which part did you love' instead taking your comment as one of countless myriad laurels thrown at their well-deserved feet. I think she's an important person for me to connect. I told her I wrote, and she seemed interested rather than on the dismissive. She's cute (gay, I am sure) and I think with some money reserves, but maybe saving it for the Big Purchase because the house, though rustic, is a tad dilapitated. There *is* a creek, though, and the most beautiful old green Jag in the Garage—two flat tires. I want it!

She screened her calls during the rub, and one came in from Jodie Foster—I egregiously pantomimed if she wanted me to leave the room but she shook her head so I kept on. She put it on the speaker. I think she got off on that, like people do—you know, playing the pragmatic syabarite mogul in front of me, Gina Tolk, lowly flesh kneader. (It made me think of *I*

Love Lucy when Lucille Ball was rubbing John Wayne. Wanda and I watched that together, a lasting, laughing memory of my beautiful sis.) Katherine and Jodie were talking about some script, obliquely kissing each others asses (they wished), that predictable, always fascinating Tinseltown dance. Later, I circumlocuitously asked what she was working on, and she said, 'A few things.' She wrote something new called—I don't remember the name, but it was Italian adaptation. Carte blanche, I asked if she knew those from the creative side of *Melrose Place.* She didn't, she said. She asked why and I said some of them were clients. I further inquired if she knew anything about *Palos Verdes,* newly created by one of the architects of *90210* and *Melrose,* named Jeremy Stein. She said she was 'confined' to features and I sensed it wasn't the appropriate moment to pursue—her energy suddenly diffused, becoming straggly—and I hoped she didn't take my query as too much the grievance-based non-sequitur. Though she could not have known any details as they were not forthcoming! I'm glad not to have continued in the line of questioning re: Chris Carter, forty-year-old executive producer of *The X-Files*—or wife Dori, too, a scenarist.

Last part of rub was intense. Took as much energy from her as I could, and it just drained and drained, like venom from a snake. I took energy from her sexual organs—maintaining professional propriety at all times, I firmly pressed down on the lower stomach close to Pubis, while telling her to breathe deeply. I think too she was loaded. I know I could have done stuff to her but would like a possible mentor-like relationship so didn't want to indulge any hijinks; they tend to backfire. By maintaining pressure, I believe I gained access to areas of her discipline (film structure, dialogue, arc of character) that will be useful, even temporarily, as it is tapped—pure, without extraneous neurotic bullshit she carries around in daily life. She was relaxed afterward and pleased enough to make another appointment. She is entering my webb.

Amazing brillant brainstroke! I was about to call Erica Miller (the NPI referral) but instead rang Doctor Calliope Dolittle Starfucker back and left word with her secretary that I was Katherine Grosseck! Gave my cellular and she called back within the hour. Said she loved *Imitations of Drowning*, can you believe it? Physician, heal thyself! Dolittle Starfuck went on to make it clear she 'is still Donny's therapist' and me being the slow wit that I am took a while to catch on that this was possibly a reference to a former relationship. (Donny Ribkin? Could it *really be*? OHMYGOD!) I disguised my voice slightly—suddenly worried she and the 'real' Katherine had spoken before; a worry soon dispelled—snuffling and saying I had a cold, I was entering the Canyon blah blah yakkety yakkety. It was a 'natural.' Made appointment for three pm next week! Her office is near an R$_x$ on Roxbury with a coffee shop within that I love called 'Mickey Fine.' I saw Charles Bronson there once, when Jill Ireland was still alive (a handsome man who walked like a panther). I think I could have helped by rake her energy. She was so beautiful and in such pain.

You'll Never Eat Me During Lunch . . .

Eric, you're gonna *love* this. Went to a benefit with Cat—oh! he told me this crazy thing about River Phoenix. He said that guy from *The Donna Reed Show*—Paul Petersen, isn't that his name?—I'm serious about this—Paul Petersen started a support group for washed-up child actors. Because so many of them are fucked up?

And a few months or weeks or whatever before River died, Paul and his group actually stopped by River's house to do an *intervention* because someone saw him shooting up in the bathroom of a club. I don't even think it was the Viper. Try to imagine some over-the-hill *Brady Bunchers* at your door like a post-pimple passel of Pentecostals! It's enough to make *anyone* OD.

Now where was I? Oh yeah. So we go to this benefit, me and Cat, which was good because I saw Jodie Foster there and (thanks to Saul) she already knew about Pargita being hired for *Teorema* and had even talked to Katherine. E, remind me to call Saul—Shelby says she talked to Keitel and he's *mightily* interested in working with Holly again, if we can make the schedule fit. I think we only need him for three weeks. So . . . after the benefit we go back to Cat's house in Sunset Plaza, which is like anal high-tech with token grunge messiness::::::::::::the CD system's plugged into his Mac—the album covers actually appear on-screen! He put on Mozart's "Requiem"; can't get away from *Teorema*. All the hot, hep young things dig Pasolini and he lobbied, very sweet and humble I might add, to be the Son. Well, if he's serious, we're definitely a Go. I sort of smelled this coming in Park City:::::::::I tried to talk to him about Oberon Mall but he buttoned up. I really think he must have loved her but he can't go to the hospital to see her because it's too much like when he had to go sit with his mom. (She died last year, ovarian cancer). Anyway, we get into this long rap about how he misses her (the mom). Poor, sweet kid. He told me that when the agency called with his first million-dollar offer—that Dustin thing that never happened, *Homeless People*—when he got the offer, he took his mother to Dominick's and they got drunk. At the end of the night they made out! Isn't that fantastic? I mean, he's so guileless.

If you talk about this, E, you'll be jailed and castrated (not too much of a leap). But seriously, you cannot discuss this with *anyone,* even if they're terminal—and I know that means most your friends. So he's telling me about his mother and then he starts to cry and within like twenty seconds he's licking my pussy like a tiger cub: his tongue is *serrated.* He begged me to stay but I left around three. Go figure::::::::::Zoloft makes me so sleepy I actually have to cut it into fours. Hard to believe a sliver of whiteness could make a difference (and it doesn't seem to. Not yet, anyway). Calliope says I'm depressed but it's an "agitated depression." Oh really? If I'm so agitated, how come I feel like Phylliss Epstein-Barr? Shit, there's the phone. Gotta run. Nexus calling—

Maps to the Stars

I read in THE HOLLYWOOD REPORTER about a project called TEOREMA, a remake of the film called TEOREMA {CIRCA ?} by an Italian: P. PASOLINI. I'm going to Blockbuster on my break to rent it {I called—they actually have it}. The article implied that CAT BASQUIAT was possibly one of the actors to be slated—I think he is amazingly beautiful and have been in such sympathy for him since the death of his mother, RIALTA LOPEZ. (CAT's stepfather is Mexican.) PEOPLE magazine said they were thisclose. With the tragedy that struck his girlfriend, OBERON MALL—well, it was a terrible year for this multi-talented {and extremely well paid!} manchild. {That was mean of me.} I am going to pursue the TEOREMA audition—I have always wanted to work with a foreign director, particularly MERCHANT-IVORY Productions. {EMMA THOMPSON is an ideal, she was so wonderful in IMITATIONS OF DROWNING,

110 BRUCE WAGNER

a role of a lifetime—and now an AWARD-WINNING WRITER, too! {{SENSE AND SENSIBILITY {{{CIRCA 1995}}} }}. I haven't included her in the PANTHEON because I am selecting domestic actresses only, to keep the list manageable, NOTE TO EMMA: Get Thee Back to Kenneth!!!} There should be no limits to our dreams.

*

A red-letter day: I have just been offered a position at the popular restaurant Sweets, which is partially owned by the powerful ICM agency! Jabba and I are going to the Monkey Bar to celebrate. We hope to run into Mr. JACK NICHOLSON, who, as owner, is a frequent booth sitter.

   We went to visit her mom and I think that depressed her, as it would have anyone. Lavinia is grossly overweight and a "rager," to boot; I'm surprised she hasn't had a heart attack {or two}. The house is unbearably humid because she is always cold so that the heat is on constantly. It smells of sweat and cake mix {and did I detect urine?}. When Lavinia went to the bathroom, Jabba led me back to a former maid's room where a tiny television was connected to a VCR. A cassette of one of her father's old shows was on the screen! It "is-was" called THE CHET STODDARD SHOW. Evidently they were bitterly divorced some years ago and this is what the poor woman does all day—namely, watches the soap opera of her life, as if suspended in animation. I find this so sad. Yet, at the same time, as an actress it is quite the character fodder. It is something that could only happen in Hollywood. We went to an NA meeting after and I asked Jabba about her dad. She usually sees him around the holidays and said if I didn't go back to

Vancouver, maybe we could all have Turkey Day together. I
told her I would really like that {which I would}. She said she'd
take me to meet her grandfather next, an apparent recluse who
lives by the HOLLYWOOD SIGN and once wrote for Mr. BOB
HOPE. Another Hollywood story, no doubt. What a melancholy, magical town this town can be.

*

TEOREMA {CIRCA ?} is a VERY strange movie! It's about
this GORGEOUS man {TERENCE STAMP, who I'm not that
familiar with but do know had a marvelous comeback in
PRISCILLA, QUEEN OF THE DESERT {{CIRCA 1994}}}. He
seduces an ENTIRE FAMILY—the maid, the son and daughter, the mom, even the dad! That's the ENTIRE plot and it is
VERY VERY sick! Then he goes away and the family, who have
each grown dependent on him, sexually and otherwise, goes
BONKERS. The young girl has to be hauled away in a strait-
jacket and the dad takes his clothes off in what looks like a
Europe version of GRAND CENTRAL STATION! Even Jabba
thought is was SO crazy! The mom picks up this guy on the
street and sleeps with him in a motel then drops him back
off—he's like a common street HUSTLER!—then right away
picks up two more guys and they make love to her in a DITCH!
I can't believe they're actually remaking this!!! I am trying, by
hook or crook, to get hold of this latest screenplay version,
maybe through one of the mailroom kids {ICM, of course}
who come in for drinks—these kids are not to be sneezed
at, look what happened to Mr. OVITZ and Mr. GEFFEN.
According to VARIETY, TEOREMA will feature a WOMAN
in the part originally limned by Mr. STAMP—a BRILLIANT

frosh outing for ANY ingenue. Not sure which I'd be reading for: the visitor {originally played by Mr. TERENCE STAMP} or the daughter. I'm nervous because the lead role may be too demanding for my current skills, but why not shoot for the moon? Though they may demand a "name." {Unfortunately, I'm afraid this role is tailor-made for LINDA FIORENTINO, the Comeback Kid! If I went up against Ms. LINDA and lost, I'd still feel proud—the best woman would have won. Now, there is someone who has been through the Hollywood School of Hard Knocks and it shows, in a most provocative way. {{I'm NOT being catty, Diary}}. 1985 was her year: from AFTER HOURS {{CIRCA 1985}} to VISION QUEST {{CIRCA 1985}} to GOTCHA! {{CIRCA 1985}}, she was a rocket poised to be launched. {{Did anyone see SHOUT {{{CIRCA 1991}}}?? I haven't. She is supposed to have co-starred with TRAVOLTA, no less—and look what happened to HIM!!! A lesson for us all}} But that rocket had to wait until 1993's NOIR blockbuster THE LAST SEDUCTION {{CIRCA 1994}}. If I could be given the opportunity for ONE such performance, I would rest my case as an actor and gladly retire.} {KELLY LYNCH would be good to team with LA FIORENTINO—they would be SO HOT together, making THELMA AND LOUISE {{CIRCA 1991}} look like a DISNEY!!}

Hello, Columbus

To: SHARKEE@CLS.OHIO-STATE.EDU (STOCKER VIDRA)
FROM: DOLPH@AOL.COM (KATHERINE GROSSECK)
Your Sharkee-ness . . .

Burning incense in your absence. Long, hot baths, letting the water flow inside. Smiling to myself as I soak—my cunny

smiles and when I dry her off, she winks. She declares the day
you appeared unannounced at my door to be hereby christened
the Day of the Dolphin. (I call it Columbus Day. Oh! Hi! Oh!)

Let me set the scene—again: I'd just gotten a massage and
was about to start a fresh crying jag. Thought the sound of your
cab was Gina, the masseuse (trailer park material, that one),
leaving. Heard the key in the door and my heart along with it:
fump-*fump* fump-*bump* fump-*bump*: fell into your arms and you
took me, raped me, made me whole again. Fucked me so long
and so hard I cried and came and cried for two long days and
nights and only now can catch my breath *I love you so fucking
much, Vidra.* I am at your mercy, beaucoup—wham bam, merci
'dam. I will *never* do anything to make you question my love
again; I won't be flip about that—about anything else, not that.
I love you unconditionally, there is *nothing* you can do to change
that, I will be waiting in supplication, until I die. The bruises on
my tits look like giant blue flowers, garlands for my vows. I wear
the plug you gave me to meetings and lunches—and at home,
thanking the messenger when he drops scripts at my door,
thanking the world as I walk around with a dumbass smile, a
Manchurian candida, shark fin broken off inside. I empty myself
in the toilet only when you say . . . you have me in line, on-line
and every which way: you control the horizontal, you control
the vertical. Do not attempt to adjust your RoboCunt/zombie
anus, your biggest chocolate flan. I am Sharkee's machine—

Sight Unseen

Precious Little Beastie Boy . . .

Holly Hunter and Hassan DeVore visited today and the
two would not let you go; I think some of those squeeze

marks will be permanent. (They were in the first play I cast, eight years ago.) Holly and I were in tears—took about a thousand pictures. You should see how you look in Hassan's arms: like the whitest of mushrooms growing on his chest. You are the Fat Sacred Mushroom from the Planet Zelda. Hassan brought a *Blue Matrix* mobile and pinned it to the playroom ceiling. He knew I'd hate it but it did provoke ten minutes of whooping-cough-like hysteria. Holly brought you the softest, fuzziest cub I ever saw from FAO Schwarz (we'll make the pilgrimage soon, I swear I swear). We tried to name it and Holly said if you were a Rod, we could call it Rod Steiger (don't feel bad, I didn't get it either)—as in Rod's Tiger. Ho ho ho. She's funny that way, your g-thing. Instead, we named her Lily.

After Hassan left, I told Holly I was writing these letters and showed her some, and we cried some more. Don't mind me; Mama's a big wuss. Hol was telling me about a school for the blind she read about in *The New Yorker*—some famous Indian writer went there. She thought maybe it was in Alabama. Her assistant's going to get us all the info. I dunno; it *does* seem a little TV-movie-ish. Hey, not a bad idea—could be Mama's premier production! Who could play me? How about Amy Madigan? (I can just see the article in *People*.) I *do* like the idea of moving, though. No riots or earthquakes in Alabama, huh. Least not till *we* get there. Did you know Grandma Willy's coming out to see you any minute? That's right. She would've come sooner but she was so sick and now she's all better. Cheese Whizikkers, you're a popular guy. Holly even wants to show my letters to her friend, a big editor at Grove Press. Everybody wants a piece of my buddhaboy. Have to quit now. Jeremy's home.

Goodbye, Columbus

TO: SHARKEE@CLS.OHIO-STATE.EDU (STOCKER VIDRA)
FROM: DOLPH@AOL.COM (KATHERINE GROSSECK)
Looking for production offices. Can't get it straight whether
Cat's for-real on board but Phylliss is milking it for all it's
worth. More power to her, I say. I'm changing the name of my
corporation. What do you think of Method to Her Sadness
Productions—too pretentious? Pargita's a hoot: you have to
see *Janie Wong* when you get back (you are coming back, aren't
you?). I'd send you a cassette but I want to see it together.
You'll like Parg—she's kind of a cross between Nora Ephron
and Wim Wenders. Just kidding. Her favorite phrase of the
week is "zero-wannasee" . . . as in "Do you want to go to the
Batman screening?" "Nah. I have zero-wannasee." She's lobby-
ing PJ Harvey for the Stranger, isn't that too fantastic? When
you're back we'll have Boys' Night Out. With Harvey (no rela-
tion to PJ) and Holly practically set, we're just about green—
could start early as June.

How's Phylliss's book coming? Does she actually have a
deal? Is she sending tons of pages? She's coy with me about it.

Maps to the Stars

Jabba's working nights at Planet Hollywood and is determined
to marry ANYONE who is involved with it, financially! I've
heard there are many, many investors, not merely Arnold, Sly
and Bruce. I'm concerned she's drugging again—she always
seems to have an "allergy" when we go out SNIFF SNIFF. Life
at Sweets is sweet; making MUCHO DINERO {I'd rather be

"making DE NIRO"!!}. Flirted tonight with PETER WELLER and HARRY DEAN STANTON {he's so old! but charming. And he sings at the VIPER ROOM with his own band!!!}. More importantly PAUL SCHRADER has come in. For the uninformed {namely YOU, Dearest D.!!}, PAUL is the famous screenwriter of TAXI DRIVER {CIRCA 1976}, CAT PEOPLE {CIRCA 1982}, RAGING BULL {CIRCA 1980}, etalia. He's casting an ELMORE LEONARD movie and gave me his card! Interestingly, PAUL is married to the warpy, wonderful actress MARY BETH HURT, who shined in THE WORLD ACCORDING TO GARP {CIRCA 1982} and recently limned JEAN SEBERG.

My life is very full!

STATEMENT OF PURPOSE AND INTENT

To change my professional name from KIM GIRARD to KIV GIRAUX {pronounced Juh-ROE}.

Goodbye, Columbus

To: SHARKEE@CLS.OHIO-STATE.EDU (STOCKER VIDRA)
FROM: DOLPH@AOL.COM (KATHERINE GROSSECK)
. . . consolation calls all week for not getting Oscar-nodded. Thank God for the WGA and Spirit awards, they're the ones that count (so I keep telling myself). Somehow it's embarrassing to care but less so than pretending I don't. One day (hopefully), I'll be in the who-gives-a-shit group, smack-dab where *you* are—when you get the MacArthur at age twenty-nine, what other group is there? You *are* the big genius: genus *Sharkay*.

Those rumors I heard about Donny were true: he's fucking (and getting fucked by) boys, Phylliss Wolfe's assistant, for one. You heard it here. Zowie yikes & jeepers. Gonna wind up with a rollicking case of AIDS, that kid is. So sad—not the gay thing, always had intimations of that, I *liked* that fearless, adventuresome thing about him—but how *lost* he is. Like this sad day player out of Sade (or Bret Ellis): the walking dead, just like his dad's old movies. Fuck. Now there's a frightening legacy.

Trying to read Proust again—still can't get beyond the hundred-page mark and that's *so* frustrating, Veed, because I really do love it. There's definitely some weird glass ceiling thing going on (or is it the floor?). Now, listen up, says Jayne Wayne (I'm sure you know it—reminds me of the way you write) . . .

> When we have gone to sleep with a raging toothache
> and are conscious of it only as of a little girl whom
> we attempt, time to time, to pull out of the water,
> or a line of Molière which we repeat incessantly to
> ourselves, it is a great relief to wake up—

*** *The THIEF of ENERGY* +++

Saw Calliope K-M (the incredible shrinking starfucker) for the first (and last) time and actually bespoke of disappointment over not being nominated for an Academy Award! I should win one myself. My plan was to discreetly absorb the energy she takes from her pet-celebrities, a la Robin Hood. While in the waiting room, I put several magazines into my Prada bag—a *Vogue* and *Marie-Claire;* I know these periodicals had been scanned by Laura, Julianne, Demi, Juliette and countless others (I can absorb minimal amounts from their exudate); once inside, I bespoke the murder of my beloved sister, Wanda, and my subsequent kidnapping by the distraught man barely recognizable toward the end as our Father. Calliope seemed to listen with great concern. Then! Mrs SangFreud of a sudden smiled, rather prim yet cantankerous too—nervously, it seemed—I saw her energy spasm then irradiate, like small animals do (i.e., the old Ribkin woman's raccoons) as she suddenly asked, 'Who are you?' Just like that. I feigned surprise but she was insistent, challenging, alleged I was *not* Katherine Grosseck and began calling 911! I hit her cashmere chest with a paperweight and bolted. Her breath was knocked out. I still have the purloined curio: a beautiful Lalique turtle with multi-faceted shell. Oddly enough, I believe all the energy I was after may well have been harnessed in the paperweight itself, because it had obvious talismanic power, hypnagogic, having sat on her desk for God knows how long, each patient (famous or not) obsessing over and gazing at, greedy of her possessions, *focusing* upon. The energy released and absorbed by the blow to the aging, fashionable chest has, in a fell swoop, accomplished a goal I'd intuitively thought of achieving not for three to five months from this day, at least. Triumphant!

*

After long wrangling of logistics, I have accomplished but another goal—a rub with the consummate thief Jeremy Stein. Here is how I achieved: I positioned myself near his home when he left for work. I engineered it so to be gliding by in the Mustang as he pulled from the driveway. I made sure the massage table was highly visible—top down, in backseat, much as a boogieboard might be placed. I was clean and fresh-scrubbed and said I was late for a rub, giving a classical pre-ordained 'wrong address' which he said must be *south* while I, mistakenly, was on the more expensive *north* side. Banal and alluring conversation ensued. He said I was up early for a rub. I told him I had many clients who demanded I be available on the twenty-four/seven. This, purposefully yet without innuendo. He said that was unusual and I said, not really, that is how we do it in New York where most of my clients hail from. Such as who, he asked, and I said, these things I do not discuss—with a smile, so that it was friendly and benign and alluring. He asked for my card and I knew he was in my web. Jeremy Stein is, of course, creator of *Palos Verdes*, a position he achieved by his skyward rung-by-rung climb on a ladder positioned in my groin. (Chris Carter and *X-Files*, you are on my back burner: 2good 2be 4gotten.) I am hard at work determining how close the inimitable Mr Stein was to the original *90210/Melrose* core group—i.e. Mr Darren Star & cabal—who ran roughshod over innovative concepts stolen from the diary I kept with my beloved sister, Wanda. Perhaps Stein & Co. were in cahoots with the beleaguered man who was ostensibly, but did not resemble toward the end our Father. Must sift fact from fiction. All the energy I've worked so hard to buttress/harness has helped me come this close. Keeping our appointment, I came to Mr Stein's sprawling ranch-style home only days later and masturbated his cock, his wife was in the other room—an unexpected occurrence, happening without effort or constraints, baby crying all the while, Mother shushing and cooing, so Jeremy and I knew she would not disturb us, even if she did, the way I managed it, stroking under sheets, all actions would not have translated to the eye as vulgar or illicit. Hope I didn't come off too much the 'pro'; I wanted him to believe this was a somewhat blushing rarity. He, like so many husbands of women with newborns, was needy that way. A calculated risk from my end, considering the high stakes, but time is running out and Jeremy Stein is a player in my own tragic opera bouffe. His penis is long and pretty, unmarred by the marbleized years-old accumulation of herpes scarring that characterize 'the Donny Ribkin shaft.' As in my first session with the agent, Mr Stein mirrored thus and was hard mere moments into rub and stayed that way, it jumping like a flag on a dog at a dogtrack! I let him go like that nearly an hour until touching and he came a subsequent gallon, the irony being, milk fed to baby not far from where where JS's own curdled 'low-fat' dribbled onto paunch! He made another appointment of which I know he will keep.

Sight Unseen

Holly Dearest,

Wonderful having you here—Samson loved it so. Ain't he somethin'? Hope this gets to you before you leave Wales. I think that's where Jan Morris lives; she's the glorious travel writer who used to be a man. Did you know I was there for my honeymoon? Wimbledon, then Wales . . . all that sand and Victoriana. Jeremy and I saw *The Naked Gun* at a theater there, can you imagine? Leslie Nielsen's big with the Welsh.

I was *so* thrilled your friend enjoyed my letters. Ashamed to say I hadn't heard of Stocker Vidra until you mentioned her but promptly ventured to Borders and picked up *Bleek Haus.* (They didn't have *The Brontë Reader and Other Novellas,* the one you recommended.) I sat with my latte and read. Your friend has a beautiful style that is difficult to penetrate; I'm not the reader I once was. Which one of her novellas did you option? I loved the picture of her on the back. She reminds me of a young Germaine Greer, but more delicate-boned. Whatever happened to Ms. Greer? Maybe she lives in Wales with Jan Morris.

It's fascinating she's also an *editor* at the place that publishes her work—that has to be high on the list of writers' fantasies! I'm flattered someone of her intellect and reputation could find late-night scrawlings to my dream-guy of any interest *at all*. Are you sure she isn't indulging you, Holly, just a little? Because of the friendship you share? Her work seems so experimental and I'm wondering why she'd be drawn to something so . . . You said Vidra thought the letters were a potential "publishing phenomenon." In the wee small hours, the ego starts primping and preening, trying on clothes for Charlie Rose; wondering if someone might please slip the galleys to Julia or Jodie or—yech! See how little encouragement it takes? Funny having the letters "out there" too—makes one feel a little *nekkid* . . . not the panic-public nakedness of a dream, though, at least I don't *think* so. Sorry I'm being such a wet blanket, I really *am* thrilled, Holly, you've got to know that. It's just that I hope the whole enterprise won't be construed as, I dunno, *morbid*. What I'm really saying is, I don't want to get self-conscious and start editing myself with an eye toward a Book. (See how nutty I am? The Sara Radisson you've never known!) Maybe I'll keep writing on this parallel track and the book can be our correspondence intercut with "Letters to Samson." Do you like that idea, Hol? You'll help keep me sane. It'd make a neat little safety valve, if you're game—' cause there's so much I *can't* put in Samson's little missives . . . things only for you, godmom and galfriend true-blue.

How can I bear telling him his father doesn't want to hold him? Dr. Mitch says I should let it go, that Jeremy will "work through it," and I hope he's right. But how do you "work through" abandoning your ball of butterscotch, your firstborn, your Life? And how do I "work through" his cold contempt, bordering on the sadistic? How does Samson "work through" all the crap Jeremy's sending his way through the ether? He can't help but pick up on it, as a sentient being—that he's blind, Hol, makes him even more so. He'll "work through it" . . . through the door and out of our lives. And I'll slam it shut behind him. Why, Holly, does he hold sightlessness against him, against *us*? We don't even sleep in the same room anymore. When I brought Sam to the *Palos Verdes* production office, Jeremy hid away in a meeting. I know now he is *embarrassed,* insane as that sounds! Oh, Holly, I *hate* him for this! You saw Samson! Is he something to be ashamed of, or stigmatized by? To discard with a wince and a shrug? The horror of it colors my life. But I will not let it. I cannot.

Sorry to dump on you—see, that's what you get. A funny thing happened on the way to best-sellerdom: Holly got slimed!

P.S. I'm a free woman! I gave Warners my walking papers and Shelby said I'm *in*. Adios to the Vorbalidian System—up, up and away, warp speed! Isn't it wonderful to be working together? Can't wait for rehearsals to begin. Harvey Keitel's back from Copenhagen, mid-week. Anxious to start working soon.

P.P.S. What do you think of the title *Sight Unseen?* Overused? And *please* don't tell Vidra what I said about her writing; I really think she is an amazing talent. Too exquisite for lowly me to apprehend, that's all. XXX OOO

Maps to the Stars

Kiv Giraux here. I've become embroiled in a minor soap opera at work. I share my shift with a girl named Ursula from San Diego. I think Ursula's trying to be an actress but she never quite comes out and says it. She's pretty but a little gaunt, reminding one of Sondra Locke. She has a daughter named Tiffany. I get the feeling Ursula is of a spiritual bent because of her frequent talks about camping trips and outings taken in the past with families that don't seem to quite be Christian but have a New Age leaning. She's encouraged me to go on a "study" weekend based on the teachings of a book of URANTIA that she brings to work and keeps in her purse. {She hides it from Rodrigo because he hates that, he's probably the most UNSPIRITUAL being on the planet. Not that Ursula would get on a soapbox or anything, she's not that way. She's really very smart.} URANTIA, she said, is actually about the planets themselves and our relationship to them. There may be some UFO stuff in there and that makes me leery. It's all very California—and very Hollywood too, by default!

Anyhow, all the mucky-mucks from ICM come in and that would include a red-haired gentleman named Donny Ribkin, who is, I believe, a veep there. {In Hollywood, VEEPS are as plentiful as actors and screenwriters {{sounds like something on a UFO: VEEP! VEEP! TAKE ME TO YOUR AGENT!!}}.} Donny is MUCHO flirtatious, which certainly isn't unusual— ALL agents and lawyers are, with some more aggressive than others. Donny got a hold of my home phone (Rodrigo the manager gave it to him) and started calling at very late hours, I might add. He's a very seductive man who has been through the ringer; his mother recently passed on and that really tore a hole in him. We talk for hours and sometimes don't even say anything—or much, anyway—just like high school {don't be jealous. Diary! I will ALWAYS luv only U}. He will be the first man I have dated in L.A. {if it comes to that and I still don't know if it will though it's pointing in that direction}. Trying hard to play my cards right and hope that doesn't sound too contrived—don't want to appear "available" and let me tell you, that's a struggle! Donny is an extremely powerful man, accustomed to getting what he wants. "WHATEVER DONNY WANTS, DONNY GETS . . . AND LITTLE GIRL, LITTLE DONNY . . . WANTS YOU!!" When he said he could easily secure an audition for TEOREMA, I could hardly contain myself. {He's old friends with its producer, Phylliss Wolfe.} And now, I must move my story along: I was having a drink with him at Dan Tana's {no, we still haven't done anything yet, not even really kissed} and suddenly, from out of the blue appears Ursula Sedgwick! And she is LIVID. It seems they {SHE and DONNY!!!} have or HAD something GOING and Ursula FOLLOWED Donny to Dan Tana's from the agency—a bit weird. I didn't like being put in that position at ALL, because I would NEVER have agreed to see someone who was still seeing someone—"as IF," as ALICIA would say. According to Donny, it was a fling that ended months ago and I tend to believe him. It's not like they were married or anything. The next day at work, Ursula wasn't there and Rodrigo said she was sick. He didn't smirk, so I'm pretty sure he doesn't know what happened, unless Ursula the Sometime Drama Queen told him, which is more than possible. She can be quite the loose cannon. Ursula hasn't been back all this week and I think she's pretty much moved on to greener pastures. I hope she finds something even better, jobwise, for the sake of Tiffany—the child's the part I feel bad about. I have no other reason to feel guilty, not that I even do over that because there is no just cause. Though the incident HAS left me feeling a notch on the scarlet side {AS ALWAYS!}. It shook me a bit but if that's as choppy as the Hollywood waters have got so far then I have to count myself lucky.

Footnote: ACTING SCHOOL RULZ!!!!! MUST go to Samuel French and pick up Tenn. Williams play, *Small Craft Warning* {?}

GIRAUX'S LIST—PANTHEON OF THE ELITE

I wanted to write about SANDRA BULLOCK but I think I may be too tired. I am asking you, dearest Diary, to forgive my brevity. SANDRA is on a Cinderella trajectory and does not need my help, of that I can assure. She is a dream story for all of us who struggle. We must not forget that before the brilliant blockbusters SPEED {CIRCA 1994} and WHILE YOU WERE SLEEPING {CIRC 1995} there was WHO SHOT PAT? {CIRCA 1990}, THE VANISHING {CIRCA 1993}, THE THING CALLED LOVE {1993} and LOVE POTION #9 {CIRCA 1992}. Sandra reminds me of MARISA TOMEI, in that both have such changeable looks—like well-tanned chameleons, they go from blue-collar "broadiness" to Audrey Hepburn delicacy without a hitch. Sandra's nose and mouth sometimes remind me of LAURA SAN GIACOMO {SEX, LIES AND VIDEOTAPE {{CIRCA 1989}}. Sandra is legendarily loved by film crews {frequently dating members thereof but not promiscuously}; a notorious junk-food junkie {that's because her mother, a German opera singer, was a health nut. Sandra has been known to slurp Fresca through licorice straws}; and, I believe, is receiving twelve million $$$ for her next outing. I hope one day she gets over Tate {Donovan} and finds her Prince Charming. {Probably someone on the camera crew! That's

what Holly Hunter did!} {TWO IF BY SEA {{CIRCA 1995}}
will do her no harm.}

You'll Never Eat Me During Lunch . . .

Taping this on the plane back from Illinois. Wish I hadn't gone
to the funeral. Good to see Mom, though. Calliope talked me
through a lot of it, long-distance. I am *such* an asshole. Better
watch out or she'll fucking fire me. Even therapists have their
limits:::::::::Airline food *never* gets better. There's a Billy Crystal
movie on. God, how I hate him. What *is* he? :::::::Think we're
over Kansas—a mid-air collision with Dorothy's house would
be a beautiful thing. That'd be a busman's holiday; the house
already fell down on me. Father died the day I arrived. Three
years since I'd last seen him—cancer made him all gray skin
and sharp bones. I kept a distance from the bed. *Carrie* kept
going through my mind, the part at the end when Amy's at
the grave and the hand reaches out to grab her—just looked
under my seat with a shiver, then remembered the sonofabitch
wouldn't be caught dead in First Class:::::::::Donny Ribkin's on
the plane, coming back from the John Hughes thing. We talked
about Obie. (She was supposed to leave the hospital but now
she has pneumonia.) He wanted to know what was happening with *Teorema* and I said Nexus wasn't involved anymore,
that the Gisela Group was financing. Hopefully. Then he gets
this creepy agent look on his face and says he heard one of
the major Gisela partners was *murdered* in Milan—someone
just told him that on the Airfone! E, my life is *insane*! I remain
cool, awaiting a vacant phone. Of course my credit card won't
work so I borrow Donny's, oy vay. I call Saul who isn't there
but his assistant says it's all over CNN:::::::::Vidra's gonna be

pissed. She's a mercenary cunt—likes the personal shit to off-set ShowbizWorld and thought the funeral would be great for some poignantly savage musings on the Bad Father (has any-body actually had a *good* one?). Maybe I need to get home and, uh, process::::::::::To the Spirit Awards, with Cat-boy. Our very own Katherine won for *Imitations!* We—Katherine, Pargita, Becky Johnston, Holly and husband, Buck and Gus and like fourteen others including this Hungarian animator Gabor (as in Zsa Zsa) and his girlfriend (a *total* match for Polanski and Sharon T—she's Jeanne Crain's granddaughter. Never mind, you're too young) limo'd to the Sunset Plaza digs where we talked cybersex (yawn) and Luddites (yawn yawn), drank Stoly and scarfed cups of microwaved cioppino while I called my shrink from the media room and wept. Upped my Zoloft to three-quarters a tab.

You'll *love* this: after I'm off the phone, Katherine tells me she got this call from the police because some psycho *impersonated* her (why hasn't anyone impersonated *me*, E? That hurts). This crazy girl went and saw Calliope, pretending she was Katherine—and assaulted her, physically! The motherfucker assaults my shrink! *Definitely* a new wrinkle in the stalking game. I instantly phone Calliope back to commiserate and she said she was fine, just bruised. I don't know why she didn't tell me—guess it's too pervy a thing to start talking about, therapist-to-patient especially. Plus, Calliope never talks about her life. It made me feel so shitty and weak, this stoic brilliant woman in her *sixties* actually getting fucking *attacked* and there I am calling from planes, trains and automobiles, *whining.* I literally puked when we hung up, hard knees on those hip cold green Spanish tiles. Thought of my father the whole time. Nice, huh?

Cat came in, very sweet, to hold my clammy brow—I'm not even sure if his friends know we're doing it. We're not demonstrative, we're furtive. Hotter that way. Here's a little bonus for you, E, 'cause you've been such *good* dog: he likes it when I lick his butt. It tastes like Equal!::::::::::Katherine was loaded and flirting heavily with Pargita—seems they're about to have a scene (if they haven't already). I think K's actually pissed Vidra never phoned congrats for the Spirit Award, though K denies. Unfortunately, her award won't help a rat's ass if the Gisela pyramid goes all-fall-down. First Gucci, now Gisela . . . is the Vatican behind it or what?

Hello, Columbus

To: SHARKEE@CLS.OHIO-STATE.EDU (STOCKER VIDRA)
From: DOLPH@AOL.COM (KATHERINE GROSSECK)
Tupac Sharkee . . .

Never got the flowers—did you send them to the Studio or the house? We were *very* drunk, me and Buck and Becky and Parg, trolling Cat's garden in the moonlight, and Phylliss wasn't in the best shape, either—I couldn't *believe* she called and woke you up like that. Worse, that she didn't come find me posthaste. Oh, did I tell you? When I walked to the podium at the Spirits, the plug gave a tiny tug and I thought it was you, calling long-distance. I'll show you the tape and you'll see the funny smile on my face.

A week of deaths. First, Phylliss's father—as you know, there was no love lost. The piece of shit molested her until she was nineteen; I'm sure it'll be in the book. She told me how he took her to see *La Strada* when she was twelve—I thought that was pretty intense. How she related (natch) to the Giulietta Masina character, Gelsomina. Right when Anthony Quinn's killing the acrobat (I always thought it was so weird it was Richard Basehart), Phylliss's dad is feeling her up! She told me this after I got her drunk at Club Bayonet. The irony being, *La Strada* is the reason she wanted to make movies (her production company is Gelsomina Films). Did you know she hung with Fellini during *Don Juan*? That's how she met Sutherland— Donald's been in three of her movies. Then one of the Gisela "principals" was murdered, in Rome; we're not yet sure if this is a problem vis-à-vis *Teorema*. (Aren't I compassionate?) Still think Penumbra is something we could step into, worst case scenario. Phyll will find a way. Lastly, Pargita's dog got run over by a unicyclist on the Boardwalk. Cindy Sherman gave it to her and Parg sobbed for three days, inconsolable. Finally dragged her to Jones, where Rosanna Arquette soothed, her own mutt having been eaten several years before by coyotes the night she broke up with Peter Gabriel.

Doing production rewrite for a Jodie movie (she's acting only); it's fast and will put major loaves on the table. If *Teorema* gets pushed back, I'm looking through the trunk to see if there's something I can do for cable. Maybe direct. It's shoot or be shot.

I wasn't comparing you and Proust, Vidra. I thought you'd love the quote. It honestly did remind me of the way you metaphorize. Thought we were moving out from underneath our "moon of misunderstanding" but there still seems to be a sliver hanging over our heads, by just a thread. Be gone, foul silvery strand—can't wait till morning comes. In the meantime, may God praise little girls and Molière, and dolphins with big ol' toothaches . . .

P.S. I think Phylliss and Cat Basquiat are actually fucking. (But you probably already know this. Don't editors know everything?)

Sight Unseen

Baby Boy Blue . . .

Casting begins next week for *Teorema* . . .

Holly and Phylliss took us to a "Church of Religious Science" called Agape. They pronounce it uh-*gah*-pay—I think it's Greek but don't know what it means. The "tent meeting" is in a big warehouse on Olympic, across from that restaurant, the L.A. Farm. It was *fabulous!* It's non-denominational, though one can't help notice the preponderance of beautiful, upscale blacks and folks from the Business too, like Dyan Cannon and Ben Vereen (both live in Malibu; he looks very well). Services opened with a half-hour meditation, which we missed. Then there were announcements and music, and everyone sang a song like it was summer camp and there was such refreshing politesse: special ushers made sure there were seats for all. A handsome Reverend Michael came onstage to speak and the words rushed out so fast he sometimes got them wrong but no one seemed to care. He's black and one of the founders. He'd just returned from India and spoke in such a charming manner, I was instantly taken in—serenely disentangled. The Reverend said people were always asking if there was life after death but what they should be asking was, Is there life *before* death? I liked that! I could tell that *you* liked it too, precious 'shroom, and so did your soft Lily the lion-girl cub; she purred while you smiled through her whiskers. And yes, you listened *very* intently to the sermon—I had an eye on you while we recited the affirmation, now pasted to your crib:

I AM A RADIANT CENTER OF DIVINE PEACE!

I EMANATE ONLY VIBRATIONS OF PURE LOVE AND INFINITE
JOY!

I LIVE TO CO-CREATE WITH PURE SPIRIT ALL THAT IS
BEAUTIFUL!

I AM HERE TO EXPRESS ORDER AND HARMONY IN A MOST
UNIQUE WAY!

THIS DAY I ELIMINATE ALL THAT WOULD ENCUMBER MY
EXPRESSION!

I LET GO OF ALL FEAR, DOUBT, AND RESTLESSNESS!

I DECLARE THAT I AM WONDROUSLY SUPPORTED BY PURE
SPIRIT!

EVERYTHING ALWAYS WORKS TOGETHER FOR MY GOOD!

I LIVE FOR GOD IN EVERY AREA OF MY LIFE!

I NOW GIVE THANKS AND LET IT BE!

AND SO IT IS! AMEN!

Saw Hassan and Rubie there as we were leaving and promised
to have brunch. Hassan is kind of a minister there; Agape has
its own school and you can learn to become a Practitioner—a
kind of reverend, yourself—in what they call the Science
of Mind. There's an entry-level class: "Core Concepts and
Meditation in Universal Principles." It's a fifteen-week course
(forty-five hours), and Mom just might do it!

*** The THIEF of ENERGY +++

Jeremy took me to the Ivy, then to the Peninsula. I waited in
the bar while he arranged a room and a cute old man said
he wanted to put me in the movies. His energy was brittle
and spongy; desperate like the old sometimes are, and used.
He introduced himself as Bernard Ribkin, quickly adding

that his son was 'the ICM chief'—with this, I just about fell off my chair. I revealed nothing, of course, playing it close to my gorgeous Mi$$oni vest. Then Jeremy appeared and curtly nodded in such a way I couldn't linger; his peremptory fashion brooked no protest or rejoinder. I had wanted to bring grandpapa into my web, for future usage, but was forced to regard the encounter as a fleeting energetic omen rather than something immediately exploitable, in any kind of pragmatic utilization.

Jeremy likes that my cunt is pierced. He's so horny, and demands I recount sex stories. The old man Bernie put me in mind of one. I waited for Beluga to arrive before setting the stage—I ate scoops while JS smoked the crack. Then I began to relay. I told him how when I was seven months pregnant, I was meeting my husband in Costa Rica. An American sat next to me on the plane. It was night and everyone slept. I let him feel my belly. He was a little drunk. He said he was fifty but I suspect closer to sixty or more. He was a pilot himself, for TWA, on vacation. I let him rub the belly and feel for kickings. He had grown children of his own. When he saw the ring (on my finger! not below), he made a big thing about it tho it was a simple band. We talked awhile about being married, him with the predictable divorces and romantic longitudes and latitudes for someone his age. He focused on the ring some more and I let him take it off me. He tried it on his pinky but it wouldn't fit, joking that now I was a single woman, and he took the same pinky with my ring on part of the way and rubbed my belly some more, then under the blanket and further until he was high on my thigh, then under the panty, then on the hairs and in my pussy. (I, of course, was not yet pierced and suspect few were. This was, notably, some years in the past.) He slid the ring in and I had my eyes shut, and further until teasing the anus, fat nail-bitten finger wet from my juices, he put the ring in rear and front ends alternatively, all the time talking about my kid and what I was going to name it and that I was going to make the best mom. Normal coffee-counter talk. I was afraid the ring might come off in there. Then he asked about my husband and how we met, how long we'd been together, our hopes and dreams and I told him he (my husband) was meeting the plane and more fingers went in and he asked again who was meeting me and I told him my husband— he made me say it more, 'my husband, my husband,' and I did, and the old pilot sighed and shook, cumming heartily. Jeremy liked that story. He'd done beaucoup coke but still came a gallon, me masturbating him only. *Larry Sanders* was on, in muted tone. His mood changed without warning and he told me about his blind baby boy and cried. He has asked for another girl to be there. I will call Jabba—I heard she is out of jail, and clean; her energy will be *containable*. I know I cannot give him the HIV, because I do not give energy, I only take.

Sight Unseen

Oh, Hol. He's seeing someone . . .

Samson and I are with Joi for a few days, at her house in Hermosa. (I plan on calling you after I write this; need to set some thoughts down before I hear your voice and fall apart.) Joi is involved with the Agape Educational Ministries, Sacred Order of Agape Practitioners. Her husband's a film editor— lanky, loopy Cedric—and they have about a hundred cats, mostly strays. Turns out we have lots of friends in common. (The long arm of *Blue Matrix*.) We met that time you and Phylliss first took me to Sunday services. Joi teaches Meditation/Breath Awareness and is getting me into the choir, which I *know* will be therapeutic. Though just now, I'm feeling beyond therapy. (Wasn't that the name of a play? And weren't you *in* it?) And, Hol, please don't tell Phylliss what's going on—I know you wouldn't. I'm just so paranoid and *shaken*. Humiliated! Not so much by the affair but—oh, Holly, I'm crying . . . He's been sleeping with someone from his show, that's all I know. When he told me, it was like hearing gossip about a distant cousin. *Not* the man I married, Hol—he doesn't even *look* like Jeremy, he's venomous and distorted, and the *baby knows:* Samson is, as all children, a fine and delicate receptor.

I really think his behavior is at this point pathological, exacerbated by a steadily growing drug intake. He'll have to find his own bottom, but I won't be joining him. Interesting too he now refuses conjoints; did I tell you he'll only see Mitch alone? At least he's still going, but I can't imagine that will last. Though, it is, I think, the only thing between him and a total loss of control. Mitch has made it clear that Jeremy's lollapallooza of a mid-life crack-up would have come with or without baby, sightless or not—but I don't believe it, Holly! I will not submit to it! He is the worst coward, and I will *not* move back into that house, under *any* circumstances! We will stay in a hotel and be perfectly fine, Samson and Lily and me. There's more than enough money, God knows. I always made sure of that.

Mother wants us home in Minnesota (Jeremy in Hazelden!) but I like the gypsy life with my Oceanspray and platinum AmEx—what more could I need? I'm growing stronger each day, Hol. I really do believe you see what you're made of in the midst of great challenge. Jeremy's learning what *he's* made of; that's his own private hell. I will not let him drag me down. . . . "Practice Random Kindness and Senseless Acts of Beauty"— the un-chic bumper sticker Joi has on her Saab. I've heard it for years, haven't you? I used to scoff at its saccharine poetics. But now I see the *sensefulness* through the whimsy—and that's what I'm going to do: praise and celebrate. *I am here to express order and harmony in a most unique way.* That's what they say at Agape. Ain't no lie! Long live positive anarchy and sweet disturbances!

I'm glad you like the *Sight Unseen* title (I like it too, though I still think it may have been used once too often. What are Vidra's thoughts?), with *Letters to Samson and Holly* going right under. I know you object, but that's Author's Prerogative, no? You are now an officially titled person and as such, eligible for your very own ISBN. And this you shall have, with great pomp!

Maps to the Stars

This was the first movie audition I have been on and my stomach was in TOTAL eclipse. I prepared as much as humanly possible, including a session in Malibu with my acting coach {seventy-five dollars that I didn't really have}. We painstakingly went over motivation, sense memory, breathing, etalia. As it turned out, the monologue was different from that on the "sides," having been taken from the wrong "draft" {I'll get the hang of these terms one day!}—"sides" are what they call the scenes they hand out to the actors *beforehand* the audition, because of the impracticality {not to mention the producers would never allow it} of giving out complete scripts during the casting process—although they probably DO give you a full script if they like your reading and have you on callback. As I said, the monologue I prepared was from the wrong "draft" (to my dismay) but the casting person let me read it anyway. She was friendly and accommodating. Little did anyone know that Donny Ribkin has been a PRINCE, having leaked me the ENTIRE KATHERINE GROSSECK script BEFOREHAND.

The casting offices are on the Twentieth Century-Fox lot, in makeshift bungalows. I have been on that lot only once before, as part of the catering corps for a Children with AIDS gala. On that day, I met AARON and TORI SPELLING and much of the cast, crew and executives of MELROSE PLACE. Sara Radisson-Stein, the TEOREMA casting person, told me the bungalow is just temporary, "until we get all our money." I suspected as much from the start because they seemed to be actively casting other things while I was there, such as PICKET FENCES. {I was hoping to see DAVID KELLEY and MICHELLE but that they would even be there was naive on my part. Guess I'm still the majorly starstruck Vancouver girl.} Sara put me at ease. I expected the director and producer etalia would be there {naive me again} but that is apparently not the way it works. Even Sara isn't the main casting lady; SHELBY BURKE is—and she wasn't there at all! There's a very important pecking order: it seems the lowlier, more unlikely people to be cast {little me} come in to read for Sara. If Sara sees someone she likes, you're invited back to read for her again. At that point, you may even be asked to read for Shelby Burke and you may read for Shelby three or four times before she asks you to emote for producer and director. That's the way they do it—like salmons flopping upstream are we, we poor actors.

Anyway, I read the sides she gave me several times {I'd rate my performance a solid B, which isn't bad} and Sara was patient and helpful, having me read a bunch of different ways. The first time, I was way over the top and she made me pull back and modulate. Her baby was there and wouldn't stop crying. Finally, she just brought it in and I really didn't mind. I think I may have earned a few points there but haven't a clue I'll be called back. On the way out, I asked if CAT BASQUIAT was still starring and she smiled and said, "We hope!"

*

Made love with Donny last night . . . O Diary, I don't know whether it was a mistake—SIGH. I didn't want him to think sleeping together was the "prize" for getting me the audition— that would be SOOOO Hollywood. He told me how JACK NICHOLSON once told him the difference between him {JACK} and WARREN BEATTY was that JACK would fuck warm mud and WARREN would fuck cold. I wasn't sure why this bit of wisdom was relayed at that moment in time. I wanted him to stay the night but he couldn't because he had to be on a plane for PARIS in the morning. I wish he would have asked me to go with him, as HARRISON FORD did SABRINA {CIRCA 1995}.
    Saw CAMERON DIAZ today, on the Promenade.

*** The THIEF of ENERGY +++

Congratulated Katherine on her Independent Spirit Award. While setting up, I asked if she might eventually, at her own discretion and convenience, peruse some pages of *** The THIEF of ENERGY +++ (she, slightly loaded, as usual). KG was sweet about it. I think the fact I softened her by being obeisant, and that I am a so obvious 'nothing'—and that she is gay and I am to her a possibly gay woman or at least interested in the permutations—made it easier to be cordial. I didn't want her to feel tied, so effortlessly changed the subject and saw her sparkler-like energy gratefully expand and release. I caught it and grew stronger. I will *not* give her pages that discuss taboo things: stealing from clients, ect. Only violent/quasi-poetic passages pertaining to Childhood Lost: i.e., the drowning of Wanda and my being held prisoner by the hardly recognizable man who once called himself our Father. Too, I would like her to read passages pertaining to my career as an autodidact. When I drew close to her pubis, Katherine said the lights were bright and I lowered. MTV was on, without sound, Mariah Carey. I concentrated on ass muscles and she started to subtly gyrate against the table. I kept molding the muscles and she expelled air (from her mouth!) and moaned, continuing the circular pelvic movement. I took liberties to spread the cheeks apart to reveal the tiny craterstink of asshole—obvious, I think, to her, what I was doing—then wider, as if to display medically to George Clooney but I think she would have preferred Julianna Margulies)—she moaned more. Though I never touched genitalia or asshole, Katherine climaxed; I was careful to absorb the cushion of energy like a shockwave through the air. When I was through, we fooled around approx, fifteen-twenty minutes, kissing and kneading and her ejaculating into my mouth, I milking her energy, and soon she was like a snake that had no more venom to give. She gave me much and I know I will see her again she is in my webb.

You'll Never Eat Me During Lunch . . .

Teorema is dying. There, I said it. Plus five other Gisela Group projects that appear to be moribund as a result of Mr. Chief Partner's untoward, karmically ominous demise. Penumbra may step in—so says the sage and dyspeptic Saul—and Nexus too. I'm not really holding my breath. It's starting to feel like a circle jerk (don't get excited, E). Where's Dawn Steel when you really need her? Probably at the Post Ranch Inn, thinking up bad book titles. Me, I'm gonna suck on Zoloft and go *Agape* till the storm passes::::::::::Saw Donny Ribkin (Angel of Death) at Bar Marmont and he said he ran into the ex, who it seems is doing a hush-hush rewrite on the Jodie picture. It gets better: evidently, Jodie's having second creative thoughts about her director, and Katherine has introduced her to . . . yup, *Pargita Snow*. If this is true, I think it's rather weird Katherine didn't tell me. I know people have to eat but there's such a thing as candor. I mean, does everyone out there know something I don't? As far as Katherine—as far as *any* of them know—we could be shooting *Teorema* in four months! What right does she have pulling Pargita into a seductive fucking situation that could potentially jam her for a year and a fucking half? Those *dykes*. Everyone talks about how fucked up *men* are but women'll slit your throat every time. I'll fix 'em::::::::::Forgot to mention I'm pregnant. You *heard* me, E. *Yeeeeee-Haaaahhhh!*

*** The THIEF of ENERGY +++

Late for rub with Katherine Grosseck. (Amusingly titillating that I was her simulacrum in the office of Dr Calliope Starfucks, she not even *aware* until the last moment. A reportage was not forthcoming in the papers, not even the *Beverly Hills Courier*. I am certain, though, police were contacted. I have zippo to fear—I touched nothing to leave a print, save magazines and paperweight, which were taken along.) I rang Katherine's door but she did not answer. It was a tad open; I entered the cool darkness. Chrissie Hynde on low somewhere. My pulse sped automatically, remembering how it felt to break and enter: electric dizzy beautiful feeling you can do no wrong, you are energetically impervious to all and do not waver. I thought of taking things and knew I would not. Tho I must say it is continuously fascinating to note my *primal desire* upon entering rooms emptied of people . . . to *rob*! Then I heard them, and walked back and saw: Katherine and (female) friend on floor of room where she takes her rub, naked and wildly going at it—*so much energy* I became still and closed my eyes to bank on it like a hawk on currents/ eddies of furnace-like wind, she saw me and whispered, 'We'll be through in a minute,' unexpected and clinically disarming. Her friend laughed, I thought it a laugh then it became more gurgle then giggle, a smear on the other's face the color of eggplant, I knew it was blood and sensed they did not want my (overt) involvement, only (covert) witness which I am sure was planned, at least by K. Grosseck. I was fine with that. My rub then proceeded approx, twenty-five minutes later (non-sexual, I may add, KG being spent, with the other busying herself in the kitchen quasi-domestically, then disappearing altogether). I was able to gather much energy from the room and post-orgasmic body(s).

Hello, Columbus

WESTERN UNION FSI
DALLAS TX 75238
TDDA SANTA MONICA CA 52 05-06 0428P EST
9515709990473101-1

JODIE REWRITE KILLING ME. REQUEST PERMISSION TO COME ON DECK. SQUAWK SQUAWK, POLLY WANTS A CRACK PIPE. POLLY WANTS TO PICK UP PHONE, HEAR VOICE OF VEEDRA. PRETTY PRETTY PLEASE, WITH STOCKER ON TOP? IT'S JUST THAT I WRITE ALL DAY AT THE STUDIO AND WANT TO HEAR YOUR VOICE TO BE ABLE TO PICK UP THE PHONE. REQUEST ONE–TIME WAIVER. COME OUT, COME OUT, WHEREVER YOU ARE. EVER THINE, CHARLENE THE TUNA–FORK (CATCH OF THE DAY) MGMCOMP 23:35 EST

Maps to the Stars

Two weeks of utter Hell but I know the LADIES OF THE LIST had their share of setbacks between triumphs.

I was fired from Sweets and am tempted to file suit. I was just beginning to feel comfortable there—not cocky—and that was my mistake. ALWAYS the mistake of the inge-nue, but I'm not by nature a guarded person. Donny cannot be of help; we've been playing phone tag and now he is in South Africa with famous BISHOP TUTU. Not that he would have lifted a finger. He's been remote since we "did" it and I know now that I erred. Live {love} and learn. {SIGH.} I have {innocently} dated some Sweets regulars and while that may have been a misjudgment, it certainly wasn't a terrible or unusual one {because NOTHING HAPPENED and anyway, this was NOT the reason of my "dismissal"}. I went out with HARRY DEAN TWICE {he invited me to one of his shows at the VIPER; he has a nice voice and the effect, particularly for someone of his age, is quite impressive. DAVID CROSBY came in the middle of the show, looking much like he did before the transplant—fat and Cheshire-smily. {{His wife and baby were there and the baby had tiny earplugs.}} } I also dated {ONE TIME} a guy who works for MADONNA'S production company {so he said} and {ONE TIME ONLY and NEVER AGAIN} a television producer/writer who called out of the blue to say we'd met at the Children with AIDS event on the Fox lot. {I'm sure Rodrigo gave him my number. More to come}. According to this VERY RUDE gentleman {how was I to know?}, I am the spitting image of DOROTHY STRATTEN, the STAR 80 {CIRCA 1983} girl. Not the first time I've heard that and it's always very flattering. If only I could find my PETER BOGDANOVICH. {SIGH.}

Jeremy Stein—that is the ONLY and LAST time, Diary, I will EVER write his name—took me to a party at CARRIE FISHER'S. {He is the one who said we met at the Fox lot event but I did not remember. Now, I know why.} I could not BELIEVE who was there. I kept running to the bathroom to write down names so I wouldn't forget {they must have thought I was doing drugs, just like my "date"!}: RICHARD DREYFUSS, CANDICE BERGEN, BETTE MIDLER, STEVEN SPIELBERG, ROSEANNE, NICOLE KIDMAN {TO DIE FOR {{CIRCA 1995}} }. She was SANS Tom because of his MISSION: IMPOSSIBLE {CIRCA 1996} publicity chores. {Did you know, dearest Diary, that this lucky twosome will be soon be working with MR. STANLEY KUBRICK in what VARIETY calls a "tale of obsessive love and sexual jealousy"? Can't wait!!!} Nicole is a very gorgeous, funny lady and TALL TALL TALL—I think TOM is the one she must mean when she says "THROW ANOTHER SHRIMP ON THE BARBIE!!!" Interesting to note MIMI ROGERS is no slouch in the height department either. {I have seen pictures of TOM's mother—she and MIMI look like twins!! how VERY Freud-like.} HARRISON FORD and TOM HANKS were there and BARBRA STREISAND {!!!}, SEAN CONNERY, JENNIFER ANISTON, SALLY FIELD, MERYL

STREEP and WARREN {his name is MUD in my book!!} with ANNETTE {I was thinking of adding her to the PANTHEON but her power, sadly, has been usurped by marriage. Gosh and golly though, is she classy—the epitome of *Town and Country,* of whose cover she recently graced}, MIKE NICHOLS, SEAN PENN and BOB DYLAN—all in one house at the same time, and THOSE were the ones I RECOGNIZED!!

The PERSON WHOSE NAME I WILL NOT AGAIN MENTION was kissing me in front of everyone and pawing my chest and I kind of pushed him because it was so embarrassing and CARRIE {a brilliant elf, in ARMANI black} made a joke about testosterone levels at his expense, I don't remember exactly what, but it was a rebuke, as should have been under the circumstances. The TO-BE NAMELESS PERSON laughed, as did the others, and from then on ignored me. Around half an hour later he grabbed my arm while I cordially chatted with the talented and underused RITA WILSON (NEE HANKS), forced me to a corner and said, "you fucking {C-WORD}"—so hideous. SALLY FIELD and RITA saw all, and MIRA SORVINO and KATE CAPSHAW too. I was SO SICK I went to the bathroom and cried but could only retch. I could see through the window to the front of the house—the valets were bringing THE NAMELESS PERSON'S car. He left!!! His action greeted with a mixture of shame and relief. I walked down the hill crying and there was ED BEGLEY JR. and ROBERT DOWNEY JR. and newlywed DON HENLEY of EAGLES fame. I sensed ROBERT wanted to say something kind {I waited on him once at Sweets; I don't think he remembered} but was such a mess I just kept walking, afraid as I drew nearer the gate wouldn't open and I'd be stuck there, ogled at as the party-crashing whore of all time. {At this point, I was crashing in reverse.}

Luck would have it that a car came in off the street and it was ALBERT BROOKS {who I LOVE—he caught me in his head-lamps and looked at me funny} and I kept walking, trying not to burst into tears. I went down Coldwater all the way to the "pink palace," and continued down RODEO DRIVE until I reached the Japanese-owned Regency Beverly Wilshire {site of PRETTY WOMAN {{CIRCA 1990}} }. I saw limos up the street—PLANET HOLLYWOOD. I went to see Jabba but they said she wasn't working there anymore. I took a cab home and had the best bubble bath then cried myself to sleep.

You'll Never Eat Me During Lunch . . .

Grosseck and Snow killed my movie. Pargita is directing Jodie's film; they start shooting in less than three months. I'm not speaking to either and trash them everywhere I can, any chance I get. If a director isn't found in two weeks, the jig is up. We'll lose Harvey, and Holly too. Saul is desperate, even suggesting I direct (don't laugh, E, it's too heartbreaking). Saul thinks we should ditch the Usual Indie Suspects and go for Milos or Phil Kaufman. (Script's out to Larry Clark.) Saw Jodie at Zev Turdetaub's, who may put up some money. Told her I was going to sue the *shit* out of her director and hoped court appearances wouldn't interfere with their schedule. Jodie played dumb—one thing she's never been accused of—and I can't blame her. It ain't *her* problem:::::::::::Bless his heart, Dr. Donny R gave me Demerol pills left over from his cancer-dead mom. As you already know, I'm mixing them with coke. And I thank you for your concern, Princess E, but please do not call 911—yet. The Dark Prince of ICM told me a *hilarious* story, which I herewith include to earn my advance (gotta zing for my supper, right?). He represents a screenwriter with AIDS. The writer sells a script to a Big Director. It's not quite a go, but you know not bad, a script in active development, boxed blurb in the trades bla bla bla. Sells it for three hundred-something. Anyhow, the guy's had AIDS for like twelve years, asymptomatic. He's in the closet about it. Finally he gets CMV, one of the Big Three opportunistic infections. Maybe there's four. Or *five,* what the fuck do I know. CMV attacks the retina, right? (I've learned more over the years about all this than I care to know.) Eventually you go blind but not before they stick a thingee in your chest, so when you're at home you can infuse yourself with this cell-killing shit that sort of holds back the tide till you drop dead. Sorry, E. I know you already know all this but Vidra doesn't. Or maybe she does, for all I know she's Queen of fucking AmFar. Am I slurring words yet? Anyway, the screenwriter decides to come out of the closet, minimally. Tells his mother he's Positive—she lives in Akron or something. Mom *completely* wigs. She calls the director. "Please!"— she's crying—"you have to make my son's movie, he's dying of AIDS!" So the director calls the writer, who (of course) says, "Rumors of my death have been greatly::::::::::

Maps to the Stars

Dearest diary, I must speak my peace, at least to you. Here, then, is how I was fired.

It was a Monday night {the busiest, with the most celebs} and CAT BASQUIAT was there with an older woman. CAT has been in a number of times {once with ROBERT DOWNEY JR.} and is always very gracious and open, much like the many profiles of him infer. CAT and his older lady friend sat in a back booth in my section. {I thought maybe she was his agent or manager} and were very into themselves. He left the table and when she gave me her VISA, I noted the name on the card to be PHYLLISS WOLFE—who I immediately connected with the article in THE HOLLYWOOD REPORTER as producer of TEOREMA. Naturally, I said something—perhaps that was inappropriate, perhaps not, but in this town I hardly think so. She seemed pleased to be "recognized." I told her I'd auditioned for the role of the Stranger and even went so far as to rent the movie upon which their project was based. She was friendly but I wisely took my leave before the inevitable Awkward Moment. By the time I returned with the credit card slip they were arguing, with unexpected VIOLENCE. CAT slammed his fist on the table and Ms. Wolfe seemed badly shaken. I felt a kinship to her and was actually worried he might strike out, and though he isn't that kind of person at all, one cannot tell—THAT was my crime. I very LIGHTLY said, almost joking, like a schoolmarm, "Alright, let's settle down," and that was when Ms. Wolfe glowered at me {if looks could kill} and MR. BASQUIAT said quite cockily to "go clear a table." Which I did, and gladly. It was so clear they'd transferred their problems onto me as a classic scapegoat. People are majorly crazy!!

To make a long story short, the next day Rodrigo calls to say he must let me go! For WHAT, I say and he says "soliciting jobs from clients"!!! OH MY GOD. Can Ms. Wolfe and MR. BASQUIAT be so PETTY? To vent their anger at ME, who struggles the way they have struggled before me? To laugh at my hopes and my dreams? My goal to star {or co-star} in TEOREMA was perhaps unreal, but now, it is dashed like so much driftwood. Diary, I cried and cried and for the first time thought of returning to B.C. But then I took a deep breath and went for a long walk on the Santa Monica pier. I thought of the story I read in the *Times* about the man who hand-cuffed himself and jumped off the end, the man who was rescued by passersby who just happened to be HEIDI FLEISS and DR. STEVEN HOEFFLIN, MICHAEL JACKSON's plastic surgeon {they were dining at the chic IVY AT THE SHORE}—what doesn't kill me will indeed make me stronger. I will take the blows, gladly, but will NOT be defeated. I'll have no regrets along the by-way, and be able to hold my head up high and say—I did it MY WAY—

Sight Unseen

Boy, you're getting greasy! You're just about as juicy as a big old Fat Burger. Make that a Sloppy Joe. Know what I'm gonna start calling you? Minnesota Fats, that's what.

Today, we moved to g-mother Holly's guest house, just around the corner from your pal Diane Keaton (Mommy helped cast one of her *China Beaches,* way back when). Holly and Janusz said we could stay indefinitely but I think a few weeks sounds about right. We were burnt out on Hermosa, weren't we? Too much sun and in-line skatin' fun. Time to enter our *Day of the Locust* phase, Burgess Meredith tromping wheezily through the hills, exotic drinks at the Garden of Allah and all that— plenty of old contract player ghosts in Beachwood. Hol's doing a movie for DreamWorks of all people so she's here a week or so then off to Texas for two months. A *very* cozy nest we have here, extremely cosi fan tutti, very Holly and that's why it feels so right. We have our own little bougainvillea'd porch; you can hear the plashing of a terra cotta fountain over the pool (little rock angels holding their wee-wees just like you do).

I have *plans* for us, Oceanspray, *big* ones! We're going to take a train ride to your grammie's!—*up* to Portland—*chucka chucka chucka chucka*—*over* to Idaho—*chucka chucka*—Montana—*chucka chuck chucka*—North *Dakota*—*chucka chucka chucka chuck* woo-woo-wooooooooooooooohhhhhhhhh! Won't that be heaven? And I promise: you will have the *biggest* Fourth of July of your life! (Minnesotans do it right.) You've never seen a backyard like Grandma Willy's. We'll hop in her great big cotton-candy bed and I'll write messages-in-a-bottle while you gurgle prayers and salutations to St. Cloud (that's where Grandma lives and where Mama was raised—St. Cloud, Minn.). Say, won't it be wonderful to publish in Braille? Wunnerful? Marvelous? Or do you not have a single thought in that beauteous, will-o'-the-wisp head?

You'll Never Eat Me During Lunch . . .

Abortion three days ago. Cat left for Europe just before. On All Bloody Eve we had a long drug-den-to-SST chat (as long as SST chats can be) that culminated in the *achingly* tender offer to send Chelsea, trusty chore whore, along to the clinic (yes, E, I'm being serious). I politely declined::::::::::Know who I dream of every night? Sara Radisson and her blind baby boy. I—oh God, I . . . shit::::::::::Eric, do you—I really need you to start looking at places I can—do you know about the Doral Saturnia? In Florida? Because I really need a place where I can chill—there's just too many people I know at the Canyon Ranch::::::::::Shelby said Sara's husband left her—alone, with a sightless child! Motherfucking *cock*suckers. Did you know all fetuses are female until a male hormone's introduced? Men are fucking *anomalies, mutations*::::::::::E, why did I do it? What was I fucking *afraid* of? I just want to die! Calliope says I didn't—because it's—directly tied to my father's rape. The fear of bringing a baby—another girl—like I'm some *breeder*—goddammit goddammit goddammit! It's all so . . . so *boring* and so *fucking tragic.* I'll be forty-four in six days, six hours and twenty-nine minutes. Twenty-eight. Twenty-seven—how I hate this life:::::::::blind babies again, chasing me through fields like in a horror film. They don't run, though, they glide or they fly, like fruit bats. No emotions attached, mercifully. I don't wake up screaming. Maybe that's the problem.

Maps to the Stars

On Sunday, spoke to Mother and did NOT tell her I was let go. I didn't want her to worry needlessly. She doesn't have an inkling of how this town operates; nor should she. They miss me but I reiterated how I said from the beginning I'd give my sojourn in the City of Angels a full year. I'll stick to my guns. Daddy respects me for that but it's easier for him all around because he's stronger than Mom. She hinted they might come out here to visit and that'd be fine as long as it doesn't interfere with auditions, acting class, etalia.

On the Sweets front, I keep turning it over in my mind {seem to have more time to do that lately}. I KNOW there's probably much more under the surface "to be revealed." What I was told by Rodrigo is most likely the proverbial tip of the iceberg. If I wanted, I could find out what REALLY happened, POLITICALLY. The Incident with MR. BASQUIAT and Ms. Wolfe may just be more of a tempest in a proverbial teapot than anything else, a smoke screen, if you will. It's more than possible Tammy was to blame—the malicious bitch from O.C. who thought I was flirting with PETER WELLER {AS IF he was going to marry her!! Besides, he's NOT my type—like JAMES WOODS, he's too thin-faced and INTENSE}. She is a majorly "ho" and had it in for me from Day One. It may also be I somehow became the sacrificial lamb in a ritual bloodletting of which Ursula Sedgwick was but the first casualty. HARRY DEAN has been the sweetest and most understanding, inviting me to sup at his beautiful home high on MULHOLLAND DRIVE. He's starting a new DAVID LYNCH and said he could get me a "meet." It's so refreshing being with someone who has made it on his own terms and is not a BULLSHITTER. HARRY DEAN was genuinely outraged at my being let go and is thisclose with one of the investors. He offered to throw his weight around, talking to Rodrigo at the very least. But I told him no, don't intervene. I don't wish to use him in that way—HARRY DEAN is a genie and I refuse to waste a wish on something so petty. But I will ALWAYS be thankful for his kind offer and concern. He cooked kickass gumbo and I cried some more and HARRY DEAN held me and told jokes and we sang songs and he didn't even try anything—what a gent!!! A true friend. I kissed him good night on the mouth, though. He had earned that.

*

Jabba is working at a club in Century City called BAILEY'S TWENTY/20 GENTLEMEN'S CLUB. I interviewed today and all looks well. It's topless during lunch {with lap dancing} and is frequented by famous attorneys and their clients, plus a host of top TV executives from the ABC Entertainment Center across the way. It's a safe and very unsleazy environment—site of the old Playboy Club. There is also minimal, well-heeled street traffic—the Shubert is there and Harry's Bar, etalia; it's quite the complex. The dancers are all gorgeous and taller than NICOLE KIDMAN CRUISE! At lunch, I counted twelve, on three different stages all at once. I can live with showing my breasts {the pay is high}—all one has to do is flip through HARPER'S BAZAAR or VANITY FAIR ads, etalia, to see NADJA and AMBER and CLAUDIA and KATE doing just that. Women have been baring breasts since time immemorial; I'm certainly in good company. {DEMI RULZ!!!} Jabba made a joke that her father the talk show host was a "regular"—and I believed it. I hate being gullible.

Hello, Columbus

To: SHARKEE@CLS.OHIO-STATE.EDU (STOCKER VIDRA)
FROM: DOLPH@AOL.COM (KATHERINE GROSSECK)
House bare of you now. No, I wasn't with Pargita while you moved out your things. Would it really have mattered? And who is feeding you information, Vidra, is it Phylliss? Is that why you got her a book deal? To buy yourself a spy?

Not even sure why I'm putting down words . . . sweet habit, I suppose, downloading my conscience-ness to you, somewhere in the Columbusian gridspace. I still feel the plug, like a phantom limb—I took it out this morning . . . now all your Tender Buttons are gone, removed for evidence. I'm sequestered and police yellow-taped: Katherine Grosseck Unplugged. Still not sure why I did what I did—the calculus of how it happened (Pargita)—or who I was with you—or who I am now—maybe I'll go see my "impersonator's" shrink. Ha! There's a movie idea for you. Everyone has a double who

gets therapized because no one has the time—and the doubles
get better! At least somebody does.

TO: SHARKEE@CLS.OHIO-STATE.EDU (STOCKER VIDRA)
FROM: DOLPH@AOL.COM (KATHERINE GROSSECK)
Heard a great country song: *Turn around slowly, walk straight
back to me, nobody has to get hurt*—

The doctor's bag sits in the middle of the den like a sadistic
alligator-skinned aunt—I knew what was in the box the second I saw the R. Crumb girl from UPS. It's out of the cardboard
nest now, and I'm afraid of what's within. I don't want to hurt
anymore, Sharkee, not today. I bought it for you in Paris, at the
flea market, remember? Then Proust's grave in the rain and
all that sad lover's jazz—funny little flower shops by the Père
Lachaise, ridiculous chalk portraits in Montmartre; late afternoon shoeboxes on folding tables by the Seine, each filled with
Genet and Colette and Novalis . . . and Stocker Vidra. I was so
proud and so happy. Here I am with my maudlin slideshow,
gushy and inane—circling the bag like a predator who's lost her
stomach. Mementos inside, my heartbreak piñata: return-to-
sender things, old love letters (mine) and chloroformed smells:
you'd send back blood and cum if you could. Oh Vidra . . . I'll
postpone the inventory just a little while, so until then: more
Percocet and wary circling of the Trojan whore's radioactive
goods. If I gathered the courage to march right up and, peering
in, found it empty—would that be better or worse?

*** The THIEF of ENERGY +++

I found Jabba through her mother, who still lives in the same
peculiar garish house in Mount Olympus Estates. As I knew

that Lavinia does not answer her telephone nor does she return messages, I paid a visit. Mount Olympus is a very strange community, forgotten and anomalous. Lavinia remembered me as she remembers all and everyone she has encountered; that is her curse and her bane, her reckoning. The house is neo-Grecian in motif but is run-down, as are many in that now anachronistic, desultory neighborhood. I hear there are Persian drug dealers living large on the Mount but perhaps that is slander. Lavinia is a heavy drinker (sounds like the start of a limerick) and, like many alcoholics, particularly women, has not aged well. She is fat and looked like a giant (stubbed) toe, with psoriasis to top it off. She rails against her ex but, to the point of bathos, watches tapes of *The Chet Stoddard Show*. I could hear it from behind the door as I peed (too, grabbing Tylenol #3s which are so old as to probably be ineffective); she lobs obscenities at this handsome Talking Head—so clearly obsessed. Whatever gets you through the night; I am certainly not one to talk. (That is a detail—haunted watching of the old show—*The 'Ex' Files*—I sorely wish could be worked into the filmic version of *** *The THIEF of ENERGY* +++) She said Jabba was there not too long ago and gave me her home #. All this, luckily, without my having to expend much. In fact, upon sight, I deliberately erected (à la the Vorbalids) a discrete Wall of Energy so as not to be tainted by her needy, blowsy, volatile energy demands. Her strands looked like frozen wine-colored urine, rubbery too—ironically suitable for web-weaving. Crappy, weak-looking people like that (often obese) are usually more dangerous then they appear.

Jabba was in jail five months then got clean (she's dirty again, haha), going to AA, NA, the whole caboodle. She lives in Jew World on Fairfax (near Erewhon) and dances nightly at a club in Century City. We went to the Beverly Hills Hamlet and caught up. It seemed as if she was marshaling her energy, emotive yet otherwise leery around me, not very giving rather into a mode of lambent self-preservation. In short, reticent, and I, respectful of that—having been there. I told her about Jeremy and because she would like the money and possible TV connections (still trying to be the Great Actress), the three of us went to dinner at Sweets. Johnny Depp was there and Andre Agassi, Ellen Barkin and someone from *Friends*—I have not watched that. In the middle of all this, funnily enough, was James Earl Jones and that was apropos because of Jabba (him being the voice of Darth Vader). I thought I would run into someone I had rubbed, but alas it was not to be the case. Some of Jeremy's overseers and agent-like colleagues trooped by the table with chagrin, to say hello. (He is represented by ICM—Sweets being a veritable hotbed of aforesaid crowd.) Mr Stein thought he was so hip to be seen with the trashy whores.

Well it seems Jeremy has missed a *lot* of work, critically so, one colleague brought him to the bar for a heart-to-heart while Jabba and I were otherwise engaged, attended to by the remnant crew of ten-percenters. They are just like pimps! Every once in a while I overheard Jeremy say: 'Sara has the baby now,' and 'She is a wonderful mother,' ect. And that is to his credit but I know he's weasling just the same. He is exceedingly grateful the baby is out of his hands responsibility-wise, knowing he isn't fit to be a dad at this juncture. I went to the ladies' room and was immediately buttonholed/ waylaid by one of the confessors who took me aside (before heavily hitting on me) and said, half with reproach, I should be mindful of Jeremy's substance intake because he didn't look

so great. Like I am the nurse. I wondered whether this colleague was attempting to posit a legal threat; energetically, I
could not read him.

*

When we got home, of course Jeremy's dick wouldn't work
so Jabba and I messed around, with him smoking the crack.
(Too bad James E. Jones wasn't in attendance!) He burned
a giant hole in the Laura Ashley comforter and the smoke
alarm went off and he thought that to be funny. Because I was
fairly loaded my guard was down; I could not resist bringing up the theft of *90210* ect. and Jeremy became *furious*—not
helped by the fact Jabba said I was now 'tripping' and not to
be indulged. She can be a cunt when so desirous. He became
so eerily unhinged/mixed-with-defensiveness that it was obvious my theme had merit, and did strike more than one nerve.
I quickly skimmed (aloud) the essential curricula vitae: [a]
that I myself had attended *Beverly Hills High,* this Jabba would
attest, having seen my yearbook and photo within; [b] that I
am an award-winning writer, albeit it on a student level; [c]
that I had a long, well-documented interest in and aspirations
to the Television Arts & Sciences, not to mention the Literary;
and [d] that I had as the *coup de grace* long ago submitted my
'Story Bible,' featuring an ensemble piece skewered toward the
young which happened to emanate in locus from the most
maddeningly obvious place on this earth (so obvious no one
ever thought of it but myself and Wanda) for looming Gen X
faddish involvement and piqued global interest (Wanda and I
had soared so far ahead of the curve)—*Beverly Hills High School*
and environs. Myself, having lived on South Peck for many

years with Wanda and that man who in the end, ect, ect,—
90210 was even our zip! I had within the purloined proposal
speculated adding the five digits as suffix to said locus to create a certain panache, personal-/individualizing. There may be
no record of the latter extant. Alas, Wanda is not here to join
in corroborative oral history.

I said everything in my précis—the existence of which was
ludicrously disclaimed upon written inquiries to Mr Spelling's
offices. All this time while '*90210* tripping' Jeremy grows
angered, I see his energy swell and become dirty yellow—like
toffee that is rotten, his denial fueled my own flames. For I
knew he had worked under Mr Spelling at that time, albeit a far
lower level, and may easily be the one to have come across the
stolen sheaves for his own wiles. Too, he knew Darren Star,
the then-unknown scriptwriter, of this I am aware through
research. Throwing a lit candle at me, JS said, 'get out,' and I
did, leaving Jabba on the futon in front of the fire to baby-sit
his flaccid knobby penis.

I coolly ransacked the house for themes and items to
appropriate. In the Master Bed, I took jewelry which could
only assume belonged to Sara. From what I have gleaned, she
is a strong woman and the jeweled items, tho of lesser value
I assume than the ones she chose to take with her, will prove
useful re: vestiges of energy I might choose to absorb. I continued my perambulations, taking favored power objects: custom
pens and stray coins, then: to the baby's room. I took a mobile
which hung above the crib (with poignant irony, for I knew
the baby was blind). It was of the *Blue Matrix* genre and will
serve as a potent 'power object.' I heard Jabba call my name
as if in panic. When I returned to the living room, the scene
was most bizarre—Jeremy having a seizure (crack-induced).

There was blood on the sheets from a minor gash on his head where he fell. Breathing was stable, as, I assumed, were other vitals. I told Jabba to gather her things, which she shakily did. I pretended to call 911 to soothe her (I had already deemed it unnecessary). Now, if there is justice, I will create a *new* show: and call it *Beverly Hills 911!*

You'll Never Eat Me During Lunch . . .

Out of the hospital and into the fire. Well, E, you're a real trouper: thanx for holding down the fort while Mama had her nineteenth nervous breakdown. I know you've been holding down *something,* nudge nudge wink wink. By the way, your visits were wonderful. You're a very good boy and I've decided *not* to fire you. For now.

I am *so* tired. *And feeling so upset . . .* Did you know Gene Tierney had a complete collapse when Aly Khan wouldn't marry her? Went into the nuthouse for *a year and a half.* (Had to have one hell of an HMO.) I read about this in *Vanity Fair,* while confined amongst detoxers and wannabe crazoids::::::::::Oh, Eric . . . serves me right for being so blasé about losing the baby. That's actually what I tell people, isn't that sick? I pretend I miscarried, I tell *myself* that. Oh God . . . Everything came home to roost. The stuff with my father—one morning I just couldn't get out of bed anymore. You saw what I was like. They say I didn't talk, not for a whole week—*me!* I still sent Vidra tapes but they were blank (my own version of the typewriter shtick in *The Shining*). Scared the tits off her. But she was my only link and I think she knew that. I *never* experienced pain like that in my *life,* never thought such pain existed, was possible. Not in this realm, anyway. Bill Styron knew what he was talking about (his daughter Susanna came to see me, so sweet).

I think once Vidra saw I was going to be okay, she was secretly thrilled about the Big Depression—I was having it *for* her because boy is she due. And it's good for the book, you know. She actually said, "Write your way out of it!" Real rah-rah Iowa Writers Workshop crapola. But you know what they say: what doesn't kill you scares the freaking *shit* out of you and possibly damages you for life! That you laughing, E? Hope *someone* is . . . probably you and God. You know, you were the only person I wanted to see. The only one who wouldn't judge me. Calliope loves you too; I told her all about your visits and the variety of hilarious contraband smuggled in. *And* the Show and Tell! When I described your Prince Albert, she smiled this ridiculous affectless smile of total generational befuddle-ment::::::::::It's good to be home but I need to work—and soon. I've got two hundred and thirty-five thousand dollars to my name and it don't feel cushy as it might have a few years ago. Oops—time for my meds. *"Zoloft, it's been good to know you . . . Zoloft, been good to—"* I make the housekeeper walk them over in a tiny little paper cup, while I'm in the "dayroom." (Gettin' nostalgic for that ward, baby)::::::::::*I'm Taping as Fast as I Can* . . . and catching up on lots of reading: the Tarkovsky book, Elmore Leonard, *Primary Colors*, the Vidal memoir . . . came across Sexton's *To Bedlam and Back*, inscribed by Grosseck, no less: "For Teorema and the Wolfe, these 'Notes Toward a Final Polish.' " Fuck you, Katherine. And polish *this*. Message last night from Cat, the machine said four A.M.—::::::::::The part that was so strange was how I remembered *everything* about my father, how it came back so vividly—suddenly I was *there*, I could *smell* it, smell *him*—sitting with the bankers in that

Nexus meeting, watching it like a movie: heavy steps coming
to the door, asking if I'd bathed. I'd say no and he'd say the
water was drawn. Always a bubble bath, like that would make
it all better. The sound of his shower in the master bath as I
sat and soaked and shivered, numb; I could hear it through
the pipes. When the pipes would stop, so would my heart.
A few minutes later he's mixing a drink at the wet bar, swiz-
zle-stick and chink-chink of ice. Honey? Out yet? Come on
now, you'll wrinkle like a prune—standing at the door watching as I climbed from the tub, hunching to cover myself . . . .
leading me by the hand to bed. My bed. Once the phone rang
when he was about to start in and it was Mother. He used my
pink Princess. She was in Denver and they talked ten minutes
while I lay there nude, dreaming of Richard Basehart, Father
rubbing my neck as they spoke, hand drifting down to brush
my nipples, then between my legs as they finished up—"I
just looked in on her," he'd say. "She's asleep"—she must have
asked to talk to me—goodbyes and I love yous as he turned
me over . . . Sleep well, darling. *And hurry home.* E, why did
the Fool have to die?

   In the shadows of my room I became Gelsomina and my
father, Zampano, under the circus tent. You know, as a girl, I
had a funny gift: when I went on planes, I could hear any song
I wanted in full orchestral accompaniment, plain as day just
beneath the drone. I could do the same with people—when it
was half dark, I could make them look like anyone, anyone in
the world. So I saw the Fool on his tightrope and wished with
all my heart he would stop being a dys-functional harlequin
with a death wish and that he would rescue me. The thing of
it is that when I got older, I came; Zampano made me come. I
never forgave myself for that::::::::::Oprah, book me!

Hello, Columbus

[FedEx LETTER] My lawyer's sending galimony as a way of saying thanks for the good times (I'm sure you'll accept). We did have some, didn't we, Stocker? By the way, if you intended to hurt me with your prank, you really screwed the pooch. When I told Calliope you shit in the doctor's bag, she was charitably restrained; I don't think she ever liked you. Said your "compelling infantilism" was a "Polaroid of Self-image": feces in a pretty package. (A cry for help? But wouldn't Sharkie cry for kelp? Alack, Tupac Sharkee is no more . . .) Everyone else I tell—and I do tell everyone—says you're just a sick puppy. Really, Stocker, I expected something grander. A barbed word, a faux-Proustian paragraph or maybe a short story lobbed my way. That probably comes later. You might like to know the doctor's bag has been assiduously cleaned and relined. Pargita now uses it as a script-tote; girl takes it everywhere. We're going to Paris for the weekend. I told her I'd get her a new one but she's adamant on keeping yours. Says it's to remind me never to take anyone's shit again. That's what my lover says . . .

Maps to the Stars

Work at Century City's BAILEY'S TWENTY/20 GENTLEMEN'S CLUB is good, clean fun!! And yes, dearest Diary, I AM keeping it from Mom because it would HURT, needlessly so—NO WAY would she understand this is merely a fuel stop on the road to the proverbial pot o' gold. {Unfortunately, she'd consider the whole event to be a very large, very PROMINENT billboard on that road—a PERMANENT one at that!} Here's the interesting part {to ME, anyway}: I'm a better performer {that way, on stage} than I ever imagined. The first few days I took a mild tranquilizer—"Zanax," I believe. Who is it that sits around and gives drugs their funny names?—which JABBA gave me because I was MAJORLY nervous and afraid to drink, in case it would show. Now I'm at my ease. You know, there's nothing really SEXY about it, CERTAINLY not the classic image I had of the "live nude" dancer. The appreciative crowd is well heeled and well behaved—it's a "Gentlemen's club" after all. We do lap dancing {a SERIOUS tease} and the Gentlemen have for the most part been respectful. {If they get frisky, you just have to work around it {{and I DO mean AROUND it!!!}} } Gratuities are good {BIG TIPS abound!! Close your ears, Diary}. On off days, Jabba and I try out routines. This week I danced to ANNIE LENNOX, BJØRK and R.E.M. I try to do something a little DIFFERENT—instead of the girls who use "Proud Mary" or "Purple Rain" {although "When Doves Cry" is a personal fave}.

Ursula's dancing here now {!!!!} and we got past our rough spot and have become friends. We DO seem to have lots in common {Donny Ribkin notwithstanding. I think she's still in love with him. Somehow he doesn't come up; a topic I think she'd rather avoid {{I, myself, wonder what "The Donnie" is up to}} }. EXCEPT that my father wasn't a shit Marine bastard. The terrible things people do to their children! {SIGH} Ursula and I talk about how we'd like to write a script together, a REAL one about dancers, something that is true and NOT tawdry like SHOWGIRLS {CIRCA 1995}, for a woman to direct. {We're supposed to go see JANIE WONG {{CIRCA 1995}} tonight, to feel the director out {{a woman}}.} I plan to write a role for myself and LAURA DERN. LAURA's the type of girl I grew up with: excelling in school, with no more ambition than to be a court stenographer. That's why the IDEA of LAURA is so important: because wonderful things can happen {and DO} to ANY of us. There's probably a thousand people out there who knew her back then and now kick themselves, wishing they had her life. SUCH interesting choices: SMOOTH TALK {CIRCA 1985} and those strange LYNCH films {I might have been a little more discerning, but in the career long view, of course, LAURA was wise}; RAMBLING ROSE {CIRCA 1991} and, of course, JURASSIC PARK {CIRCA 1993} which INSTANTLY placed her among a select PANTHEON: that of the BILLION-DOLLAR FILM. {I can't help thinking what a wonderful 1-2 punch it would have been if STEVEN would have let her play a victim in SCHINDLER'S LIST {{CIRCA 1994}} }. LAURA'S a dark horse who has triumphed, her triumph perhaps greater because she doesn't have MICHELLE or JODIE'S proverbial looks. For example, her face becomes gargoyle-like when she cries but that is something that—in the long view—helps, I think, with ACADEMY AWARD NOMINATIONS. She'll never be a "beauty," yet when one reaches a certain Level, all's forgiven—God merely amends the Beauty Book, redistributing it to the public so that not only are one's physical flaws glossed over but they are actually made into new "standards" as part of one's reinvention. SANDRA BULLOCK and her interesting body, case in point. One wakes up one day and says to oneself, "Well—but . . . she was ALWAYS beautiful—why couldn't I SEE??" BECAUSE THEY ARE MOVIE STARS, ALL MOVIE STARS ARE ESTHETICALLY BEAUTIFUL, whether "conventional" or Classic. {I'm HOPING that is true, for my time is soon ta come!}. This, I think, has become a rule of thumb. LAURA has further triumphed because of a Mom {DIANE LADD} who I am sure adores her even though she strikes me as a bit of a competitive/crazy—I'd LOVE to be proven wrong. {I myself would opt for the relationship JENNIFER JASON LEIGH has with hers—from out of which came GEORGIA {{CIRCA 1995}} .} Moms are hard enough AS IS, so again, hats off to LAURA D! Dad's {BRUCE DERN} a professional runner, moody, someone probably off doing his own thing a lot when not brooding on career tailspin. {I don't know why, but I'm thinking of the sensuous MADELEINE STOWE, who reminds me of MARLEE. I always wanted to see CLOSET LAND {{CIRCA 1990}}—I'll tell Ursula to ask if Blockbuster has it when she picks up EXOTICA {{CIRCA 1995}} {{EXOTICA takes place in a strip club—we're viewing it as part of our Research}}. I saw MADELEINE's hands in close-up in a VOGUE once and they were large and unwieldy—her worst feature.}

Sight Unseen

. . . they wanted me to postpone but I went to the hospital anyway. "I'm going through with the divorce." He cried and I felt nothing. (His stroke was mild and the doctors say recovery will be complete.) Holly, what an empty, monstrous feeling that is you can't imagine. He isn't anyone I remember being wooed or loved by, or marrying, or dreaming dreams with. Honoring and obeying . . .

*

I wanted to thank you—*we* thank you for the gift of these last weeks in the sanctuary of your home (Samson and I play *Sea Hunt* in the pool every day in front of the angel-grotto. I call him Lloyd Little Britches). I'm absolutely *delirious* about Vidra's offer; we will make a beautiful book. It was lovely to meet her, though she isn't in the best frame—but I guess you know all about her breakup. Small world, isn't it? And *Teorema* was such a wonderful project. . .

We're going to stay in town awhile, until affairs are in order—a lump settlement is in the works. I don't want our future pending on the vicissitudes of this man. Until all's quiet on the medical/legal front, Samson & Co. may be cordially reached at the Bel Air Radisson (the people at the desk treat me royally—they think I'm an owner!) Call me! Kisses to you and your Polish Prince.

*** The THIEF of ENERGY +++

A dream last night: I was going to lie in wait for Jeremy Stein but Darren Star intervened. 'It has been true all along,' he said, looking like the famed Minotaur of old, 'that you have been terribly wronged. But my child the time for vengeance has not yet come. Jeremy *was* involved,' he added, 'tho not at the level you think. You have done well in taking his energy but now must save yourself for the internecine struggle ahead. In time, the pupil will outshine the teacher.' I felt a warmth toward Darren I never imagined conceivable. Spontaneously, we floated above the sidewalk outside Philippe Starck's Hotel Royalton, site of the inaugural party for *Central Park West*. Mariel Hemingway's arm hooked in mine—how beautiful she looked. 'Gina, let it go!' she informed. We were suddenly high above the city where the lights shone with individual brilliance and myriad lives played out their destinies amid apocryphal opulence and squalor. We strode on wisps of cloud above the

Brooklyn Bridge—traversing the stars, a miracle of joy. As we circumnavigated the glowing Xanadu of the Hamptons below, I began to weep large, perfectly formed tears that resembled diamond pendants. 'It is your father, Gina!' Mariel said. 'It is *him* who has stolen from you and him you must defeat. We will help you. But the battle is not here, Gina! The battle will be elsewhere.'

Thus will conclude Book One of *** *The THIEF of ENERGY* +++.

SIX MONTHS LATER

Kiv Giraux

They are available on certain satellite venues (one called the "Adam and Eve" Channel and another called "Spice") and are NOT XXX, as private parts are NOT shown. {Camera angles are such that offending areas remain "teasingly" out of view— MUCH more intriguing than your garden-variety porn, of which erotica quotient is somewhat "nil"}. I've done three to date: *Sleepless in the Saddle, Pulp Friction* and *Dirty Squealers* {a "film noir" motif}. By and large, the production people I've met are friendly and supportive—just folks. The thesps are uniformly intelligent and might I add EXTREMELY hygienic, more so than your average blind date!

Due to my "girl-next door" looks {that I'm a fresh face in the field doesn't hurt}, I find myself somewhat in demand. That's a nice feeling in this town. I've also been told I'm a hot commodity, oddly enough, because I'm SANS tattoos. Seems since so many Yuppified-types {do Yuppies still exist? Yes, I'm talking to you, Diary, so stop yer yawning} subscribe, the

producers prefer the "Vancouver Virgin" look to the more cli-
chéd, standardized "Biker Chick." Lucky me.}

I have to say I did much soul-searching when this
opportunity arose—as always, in my darkest hours, the
LADIES OF THE LIST helped see me through. Actresses
have always worked beyond the pale; countless members of
the PANTHEON have bared breast AND pubis. Altogether
my new venue is not too far a cry or leap. In the meanwhile
I am getting FANTASTIC experience with set, crew and
camera—I'm quite comfortable around a soundstage, my
"in-house" knowledge and professionalism growing leaps and
bounds, and that's an INVALUABLE BLESSING. {I CANNOT
fail to mention the extraordinary "case" of TRACI LORDS,
though my work in this medium will NEVER approach the
explicitness of her early "non-pro" limnings. TRACI's certainly on a SUPERB trajectory. Her manager said in an interview that because of her work on MELROSE, she'll soon be
presenting on the EMMYS—from there, it isn't too far from
handing out an Oscar or two {{meaning STATUETTE!!! I am
SO TERRIBLE!!!}}. Just LOOK at the depths from which she's
come {{TROY CAPRA, director of *Dirty Squealers,* showed me a
tape TRACI did at age fifteen or thereabouts. It was the MOST
SEXUALLY EXPLICIT I have ever SEEN, with TRACI giddily
vaulting from one stiffened member to another as if in a Sexual
Olympics. WAY SHOCKING!!}}

*

I've kept in touch with HARRY DEAN and he promised to
introduce me to a number of well-connected cronies in the
legit film world. {ROBERT EVANS is high on his list.} He's

been supportive and non-judgmental and I adore him for that. He even came to BAILEY'S and we lap-danced, as a kind of a joke {I'll soon be working there no longer}. Afterward, he tried to tip me and that hurt. I told him I didn't want his money and I know HARRY DEAN felt bad with his FAUX PAS. Upon occasion, I still frequent the MONKEY BAR, VIPER ROOM and Sweets. The last time I visited my old place of employment, Rodrigo comped me drinks and the bartender {new there} recognized me from the Spice Channel! My first taste of the kind of standard adulation so common and everyday for LADIES OF THE LIST—Diary, I swear, as you're my witness—I'm on my way to the Pinnacle of the Elite!

*

Jabba and I have become roommates. Troy helped us move this weekend {he, director of *Dirty Squealers* and stage plays too numerous to mention. We've been seeing quite a bit of each other lately} to a tall apartment building on DOHENY, near SUNSET—a stone's throw from the ROXY. I cannot WAIT to walk from room to room, I LOVE the smell of new-paint and hygienic emptiness, so magically HOPEFUL and filled with promise. I can finally bring out Mother and Father; it will be plain to see I am truly making it on my own terms. I have become a Hollywood story! The doorman told us GOLDIE once lived here during her ascent {MUST include this effervescent dynamo in my next installment. Forgive me, GOLDIE, for I know not what I do! And by the way, may I borrow your husband?}—as did JAMI GERTZ, THERESA RUSSELL {an interesting anomaly; I wonder if NICOLAS ROEG is as old as HARRY DEAN}, LISA EILBACHER, COURTNEY COX and DAPHNE ZUNIGA. Also KIM CATTRALL {a

fellow underappreciated Canadian, especially in TICKET
TO HEAVEN {{CIRCA 1981}} }, PHOEBE CATES {KEVIN, I
adore you!} and SHERILYN FENN. What a pedigree! From
this aerie, Troy and I will plot our assault on Hollywood in
all fields, anew! As Troy says, "The world is our keester." {I
love his sense of humor.} All joking aside, I remain Sincerely
Yours—and with no regrets . . . *Kiv Giraux.*

GOOD MORNING: Boothing at Sweets were whitehot
thesp Kiv Giraux and helmer Troy Capra. In case you didn't
know, Troy and Kiv are thisclose. They've just completed
their fourth feature together and next month Kiv begins
her second book of **The Pantheon** series (St. Martin's), "a
comparative study of starlets of the Fifties: starcrossed,
middling and those destined for the Pinnacle." **The
Pinnacle?** Congrats, Kiv—looks like you're already there.
{Okay, Diary, so I went a little over the top. But it's my
DREAM and DREAMS should have no limits}

CALLING ALL ACTRESSES! Helpful Tips from Kiv:

HELPFUL TIP #I: Don't smoke—it yellows teeth and skin and
creates lines around the mouth. HELPFUL TIP #2: Keep lots of
plants in the house. They help you sleep and even aid your
disposition. Talk to them and stroke them while you water
and feed! "Plants are people too" is a neglected truism. HELPFUL

TIP #3: Don't forget to water YOURSELF. If you have a problem you can't resolve, by all means seek short-term help from a therapist so as not to have that problem fester. HELPFUL TIP #4: Don't let the bedbugs bite!

Phylliss Wolfe

Communion at Women in Film luncheon with the Usual (premenstrual) Suspects. Jodie's movie is deep in post; Katherine G just finished directing a sapphic short about a scripter and experimental novelist (write about what you blow). Wants to arrange screening for Griffin and yours truly—because, I know, she thinks I have pull at Sundance. Pargita heard about the Sarandon thing and was all over me like a cheap muff-diver. Not a word on *Teorema* until the end:

PARGITA
(AVEC LINDA HAMILTON/*T*2-LIKE RESOLVE)

Let's just do it, Phylliss. It'll be *so* fucking hot. It's *time.*

KATHERINE
(MYSTICAL/HEARTFELT)

She's right, Phyll, you *know* she is. We *have* to.

PARGITA

Why aren't we in post on *that,* instead of *this?* Why didn't it *happen?*

KATHERINE

Hey, did they ever find out who killed the Gisela guy?

I flashed a wan smile at the Sisters Quim, hating myself for that. Said "Yeah, we'll kick it" or some such rah-rah hip-hop horseshit. Holly Hunter was there and looked fabulous—Christ to Hell, I wish I was Southern::::::::::Dating again and it's flat-out weird. Does something to me *hormonally;* I go on these absurd little fantasy-jags. Like I'll be cleaning out my closet and suddenly start thinking, "Gee. Hmmm. I wonder where women store their bras while nursing?"::::::::::Pregnant again by fall, or bust! But who shall I turn to, when nobody seeds me—a butcher, a baker, a Jewish dealmaker? I *do* know she'll be a girl-child, willful and green-eyed and gorgeous. And I'll tell you something else, E. If she wants to join the circus, I *will* say yes, yes, a thousand times Yes. She will be the epic child of sky and of strada, my child and no one else's::::::::::My *Gelsomina.*

Katherine Grosseck

To: SNOWITE@MSN.COM (PARGITA SNOW)
FROM: KGB@AOL.COM (KATHERINE GROSSECK)
    Lovely Pargita Meter Maid (AKA Her Snow Whiteness) . . . What the fuck am I doing here? I mean, besides going to dailies and jacking the director's ego. Well, that's what I get for exec-producing. *Hate* Toronto, always have. The only thing good about it is Leonard Cohen, and he's from Montreal, n'est-ce pas? Though I have to say the movie's looking good. Laura Dern is some kinda wonderful. (Did you ever see *Smooth Talk,* the thing she did with Treat?) Anyhow, Laura saw *Janie Wong* and *flipped* when I told her we were an, ahem, item. It's kicky being on the street with her—she's mobbed by kids because of *Jurassic.* Laura is *really* smart and apparently

heard all about you from Jodie, which had me freaking for like maybe a second. (Did you and JF ever make out? Oh, never mind.)

To: SNOWITE@MSN.COM (PARGITA SNOW)
FROM: KGB@AOL.COM (KATHERINE GROSSECK)

Writing you is almost good as sex—in my head, I call it "flesh crocheting"—must be Cronenberg's influence. (We had dinner with him and he's sweetly super-normal. Long live the New Flesh!) I like how you never write back 'cause you're the Big Nonverbal Image-whore. Did you know that I'm wearing your plug? Well, I am. My very own Snowmobile—Her Snow Whiteness's Eighth Dwarf . . .

To: SNOWITE@MSN.COM (PARGITA SNOW)
FROM: KGB@AOL.COM (KATHERINE GROSSECK)

So *unfair* you're in Rome and I'm still here. When what I really want to be is . . . *stuck in the middle with you*. I wanna buy a castle for us in Ireland—in Cunnymara, by the sea. Do that whole resident tax thing and live there six months each year like the big bohemian lezbo artists we are, would you like that, Geet? I wonder if Cheryl sold their place when he died, did you know the Michael O'Donoghues? They had a castle in Connemara. Galway, I think . . . I could finally read *Finnegans Wake* and we'd paint and make movies and go on cliff-walks and get sandblasted by scary Celtic winds. Oh my Pargita—*Oh my Pa-pa* . . . I ride your clit on the cardiac rapids—me, sure-footed, obedient pack-mule of your canyons. The Snowmobile is deep within: I wear it for ATM and groceries and teeth-cleaning—all the sweet mundane Muzaky chores of everyday life. There I stand at the twenty-four-hour

Ralph's, on line at the cashier, a stab and a shiver while the pimply Latina says *Have a good one.* Do you know how I fall to sleep at night? I imagine myself flying to Italy, snuggled in First Class booties, slipping into ROMA/AMOR like a burglar, spy in the house of Love. Racing up Spanish Steps, heart in mouth . . . then *your* heart in mouth, copper arms again, splayed under mine, those fingers I dream of gripping the iron headstand, all your smells an altar. I turn onto my stomach. Your hand with those fingers, those rings I gave you, moves up thigh to cork—Eighth Dwarf out, yanked from dreamy sleep, then out *I* come and nod away in the arms of Manchild—sure beats the shit out of counting sheep.

You won't believe this. Laura and I had dinner with Dana Delany and we were talking about how we want to write this book on all the kinky massages we've ever had. I tell them about the time that girl Gina walked in on us—do you remember? Gina Tolk? With the Sheryl Crow mouth and the white trash New Age vibe? How she used to pull out this big frog paperweight and sit it between my tits like some crystal succuba? So Laura brings up the thing about me being impersonated (she heard about it from Jennifer Jason—they both see Calliope Krohn-Markowitz, the shrink who was attacked) and suddenly Laura goes *Oh my God!* She says Calliope has a glass menagerie of paperweights she keeps in the office and Laura's favorite one—the *frog*—was stolen by the girl who assaulted her! We *screamed.* (It seems a few weeks after the attack, Laura asked where the paperweight was and Calliope told her what had happened.) So Dana says we have to call, like, *now.* We leave a message for Calliope and she phones us back in twenty minutes. I describe the masseuse physically and the shrink says it sounds like her so we actually call the police, on a conference! Me and Dana and Laura and Calliope and the LAPD! Isn't this *fantastic?* Make a great script: *The Women* meets *The Hand That Rocks the Cradle.* You know, if they arrest her, she just might slander us on *Court TV.* "And what did you see when you entered the room, Ms. Tolk?" "Why, the screenwriter—Ms. Grosseck—eating the shaved holes of the director—Ms. Pargita Snow . . ." "And where were they positioned, Ms. Tolk?" "The *holes?*" "The ladies." "Why, on the bloodstained futon, counselor." "Objection!" "And what was the condition of the futon, Ms. Tolk?" "Objection, Your Honor! The futon has been described!" "Overruled! Answer the question, Ms. Tolk . . ." "Could you please repeat—" *"What was the condition of the futon?"* "Objection!" "The futon!" "Why, it was—" "Suh-STAINED!"

Gina Tolk

In these moments, I think ruefully of my sister, Wanda, and how she suffered at the hands of the man who was (and had never shirked from claiming to be) our Father. Wanda and I played out our roles: the casually heartbreaking children of Charles Laughton's masterful *Night of the Hunter*—spectral yet corporal. But that is another movie *entire* and another magical saga too, riven with tears and with blood. For in *** The THIEF of ENERGY +++ Book Two it will be revealed that Wanda was I and I was Wanda; and that I drowned her to save myself. This is the story I had cogently wished to unfurl within the confines of a professional, i.e., Dr Calliope K-M, plaintiff. But I will tell it alone, without help—this is as it should be. Perhaps there is time now. It may stand as a eulogy for a little girl lost at a tender age, too tender to be sanctioned. For you see,

Wanda is a part of me I could not revive under any sort of gentle ministrations—the part that succumbed to the bountiful travesties committed upon her by the putative Father who is long dead. Mariel has told me I will meet him soon on another plane in Time and Wanda will thus be vanquished. Mariel has discussed the 'kidnapping' in evenhanded tones, applauding me for my sanity-saving ruse, her knowing Voice joined by others whom I have rubbed; their energetic Mass has let it be known. The Voices are deafening and fruition is near.

I left some personal things with Jabba for fear they would be confiscated—the paperweight long since buried. I could not let them have it. I predict thirty days of hospitalization maximal before imprisonment on theft charges, ect. As I am giving my best 'nutcase' show this will be an indomitable time (and has already been) to recoup energies squandered in the meaningless dance with Society's snitching celebrity *goons*. To think Laura and Dana had to do with my demise is a cruel, mesmeric twist worthy of a future literary gambit—I will try to begin its saga, as I have kept my fat Pilot 'Explorer' pen and delicate leather notebook, a talisman purchased at Barneys New York the day of the Assault.

I called Jeremy and asked for a loan and he went off on me. It was well worth it—I received energy over phone, such was his outburst. 'You took my wife's jewels, you krazy cunt,' ect. This, all he could muster, he is a TV hack, lest we forget. He yelped about pressing charges (a slight slur from the stroke but he is no Chris Reeve: he is *completely* capacitated). We both know there is no way he ever will—I have too much to tell. I am wiling away the time working on my set piece, a sitcom earmarked for CBS, *Sybil's Place,* based on the life of society matron Sybil Brand, whose name graces the women's jail. I hope it will not be confused with *Cybill* and, too, hope to get clearance from Mrs Brand herself once I am transferred to the jailhouse. She seems to be a generous lady and I am counting on her benevolence in this matter; she clearly enjoys giving those incarcerated a leg up. *Sybil's Place* will be exempt of the high camp, rough-hewn edges of your usual female prison soaps and, too, will bridge the world of high society within which Mrs Brand has always traveled so effortlessly. (I read in the *Beverly Hills Courier* that she is ninety-something and hope she doesn't succumb before giving her legal/energetic blessings.) The show as conceived is a winner and I am prepared for the usual uphill battle and ultimate vindication on all fronts. It is a show for DreamWorks or perhaps Brillstein-Grey, the Jews behind the *Larry Sanders* success.

*

This is truly the time of the 'event horizon,' part and parcel of the Black Hole concept—the 'event horizon' being the rim of such like a waterfall drop—the exact point where life and matter, *all* energy, is sucked in and Time, with a capital T, ceases. *That* is where my energy is now. Willing and joining with the cessation of all Time.

*

Energy on the ward is good. I am rubbing some girls here (non-sexual) to acquire vestigial strength for court and psychiatric appearances; too, for sleepfulness, waking vigilance, ect. There are a few pregnant ones and I seek them out for their double energy—getting to them before they become too big and muster out to Sick Bay (I am the starship healer). I must draw energy for the next Great Battle—that against Carsey/ Werner and/or the perpetrators of *The X-Files*. Mr Chris Carter and family will soon be in my web

Sara Radisson

Hell and bejesus, it took a while but we are finally Minnesota-bound. We have a first-class sleeper car with a jiggly bed and our very own shower and toitie. I cannot tell you what it's like to be rocked asleep by the clickety-cluck-clacking, with you, the Quiet Storm, in my arms (you, the I of my storm.) We awaken at the witching hour and stare out the looking-glass window at the silvery world. Then it's dawn and because I give Max the porterman twenty dollars a day, he is *very* good to us and brings hot tea and helps with baby's things. Max serves lunch and dinner in our room, unless we choose to take it in the white linen'd dining car, with its perfectly polite passengers and their ambient, holy Middle American murmur-talk, the glass dome like some kind of church—isn't that right, Samovar? That's what we call you when you have on the furry hat Grandma sent. Boy, is she gonna be glad to see *you*!

Most of the Dining Car People don't even know where we stay: they must think we fall asleep somewhere in the cruddy, high-backed seats with the riff-raff—if they knew how pampered we were, they'd be *so* jealous (sad thing is, most of the bedroom suites are empty because they're so expensive). . . . After we're fat and sassy from our grub, we stroll below and find the door to our floating room. We lock it behind us, then nestle in for the night and Maxwell brings hot chocolate if we want. Aren't we the luckiest people in the whole World Wide Web?

Don't you ever let anyone tell you anything else. You are my sun-
shine and my dreams, my heavy-lidded night-blooming orchid,
all I ever wanted, all I ever need, and I made you long ago: you're
positively antediluvian, and younger than springtime too.

I ordered you with those damn infinity coupons, I did I
did—sight unseen.

Book 3

A GUIDE TO THE CLASSICS

Zev Turtletaub

The black steward kneeled and stroked the drowsy superstar. "She's the *best*. Aren't you, Mimsy? Aren't you the *best*."

Mimsy lay on her seat without a yap while Zev Turtletaub got sixty pages of the Reavey translation of *Dead Souls* under his cinched Kieselstein-Cord belt. The trim, hairless producer loved this character Chichikov: a con man, replete with idiosyncratic servant and driver, traveling from town to town buying up serfs—"souls"—expired ones, that is, from well-off farmers and gentry still forced to pay census on their dead. But why? Because if Chichikov acquired enough names (so went his reasoning), he could approximate a wealthy landowner, a "man of a thousand or more souls." Or something like that. If his motives weren't quite clear, neither were Don Quixote's. Zev was convinced there was a movie in it, an AIDS opera that would make *Philadelphia* look like the HBO cartoon it was.

Even in first class, pets were prohibited from lolligagging outside their pissy plastic enclosures. Yet this was the famous star of *Jabber* and *Jabberwocky,* the just-opened *Mimsy* and upcoming fast-track sequel, *All Mimsy*—the cabin being only a quarter full, an exception had been made.

"You're *so tired,* aren't you, Mimsy-girl?" The steward massaged the skin of the languid superstar's neck, bunching it up then letting go. "Mimsy-girl looks *so so tired.*"

The phlegmatic pooch had indeed overexerted himself at *Mimsy's* New York premiere. As if to mitigate a stressful itinerary, he'd shacked with Zev in the producer's capacious hotel apartment. Mimsy loved the Carlyle. Life being what it was, there came a hitch: the studio jet was down and they had to fly back commercial. Bit of a bore.

On the way to the airport, Zev got the bug to hit the legendary Gotham Book Mart. He was greeted by a tidy tree farm of authors he'd never heard of, and that was surprising, because if Zev wasn't a great reader (didn't have the time), he definitely considered himself au courant. He scanned the major *Reviews* from cover to cover, and the lit rags too—he loved the ones with poisonous intramural letter exchanges the most. There were droves of people at the Turtletaub Company whose only job was to ferret out writers before they were hot, textual soldiers who did nothing but read galleys and talk to book agents all day long. Still, there was nothing like going through the stacks and sniffing out quarry oneself. Example: a short while after whizzing past the pale cashier, Zev purchased the thirteen-volume Ecco Press edition of Chekhov's short stories, arranging for them to be FedExed to L.A.—within five days, each tale would be "covered," i.e., broken down re: plot, characters, updatability. Like a high-brow predator, Zev stood at the register, flipping through tides—Roberto Calasso, Cormac McCarthy reissue, Penguin Henry Green—then grabbed a volume his sister had always pushed on him . . . Nikolai Gogol's *Dead Souls.*

"Anything I can get you, Mr. Turtletaub?"

Your mouth around my dick came to mind but the producer asked for cookies instead; he loved the warm doughy meltiness of a front cabin chocolate chip. The steward had a rock-hard bubble ass—no Princess Tiny Meat was he, of that much Zev was certain.

A month ago, the important passenger chanced across an article in a magazine that had seized his imagination, worrying it ever since. It was about a service that arranged for persons with AIDS to get cash advances on their life insurance. It seems that within the HIV community, brokering this kind of deal had become somewhat of a cottage industry, a vulturine shadowland of the quick and the dead that Zev Turtletaub instantly saw as the stuff of potentially great drama. A towering character already floated at the edge of his mind, a dead zone Music Man, a millennium Willy Loman, and the more he dipped his beak in Gogol's fountain, the harder it came into focus: that character was Chichikov. Who could do such an epic theme justice? A LaGravenese or a Zaillian—he'd go after talent first. Zev would talk to Alec Baldwin. Tell him this was Academy Award time, *Elmer Gantry* meets *Inferno.* It was big, it was very big, Zev could *feel* it. The man who threw a Jack Russell terrier into a troika of projected half-a-billion-dollar-grossing comedies would soon be known for something else, entering his middle period with a classy, unexpected *Schindler's List*–like crossover coup. The beautiful part being the template was there in his hands, pages lightly smeared with fuscous-fingered bile—*Dead Souls.* The stage was being set for the perfect Zeitgeist melodrama, a work of high, elegiac art that wouldn't be afraid to make money, the frisson being that Gogol was public domain. The rights wouldn't cost dime one.

He winced at the thought of his sister; she'd call his vision hubris and hate him for his efforts. Aubrey Anne was pretentious that way. He remembered when she came to the house a few years ago and Douglas fixed them a wonderful lunch by the pool. Aubrey spewed patented zingers and made diggy little looks, then announced she had AIDS, just like that. The producer felt spiteful and disconnected. He couldn't wait for her to leave.

Locking himself in the restroom, he vomited on the descent—a septic torrent of cookies, hot fudge and shrimp, scotch and filet mignon, salad and steamed veggies, potatoes au gratin and a dozen bags of peanuts so sweet they had made him shiver.

It was raining in L.A. The steward draped the coat on his shoulders and Zev slipped him a card. Gogol and Mimsy tucked in armpits, he nodded suavely at his fellow passengers—Katie Couric, Brian Dennehy and the agent Donny Ribkin among them—and debarked. The driver waited at the gate. He took Zev's Il Bisonte bag and walked eight paces ahead. Down the escalator and through the tube, Aubrey Anne nagged at him. A brainy type, she'd always been mad about the Russians. He could see her scrunched on the sofa, see the covers of the books with their yellow college USED stickers, her four-eyed face buried in Lermontov, *The Idiot,* Turgenev—and another one that stuck in his mind: *This Fierce and Beautiful World.* He loved that title but never remembered who wrote it. Oblomov? Maybe. One of his soldiers would find out.

Troy Capra

(Kiv Giraux lies on a blanket, sunbathing. The lawn is green, the sky powder-blue. She is topless. Troy interviews her from OFF-CAMERA.

While they talk, his lens drifts languidly over the anatomy: legs, tummy, breasts, smile. Zooming in, dallying. No abrupt movements . . . casual and conversational. A supered title: THE FOXXXY NETWORK'S STARSHOT #10—XXX-FILE GIRLS. *The short, popular segments, dubbed "Starshot Skinscapes," usually run between feature films on the twenty-four-hour Adult Channel but lately have been airing in MTV-like blocs of five. They have an informal, documentary feel, brainchild of Troy Capra. The fresh, improvisational style and home-movie look have made them a hit with viewers)*

Tell us about yourself.

(*smiles, deep breath*) Okay. My name is Kiv.

Kiv. That's unusual. Very pretty.

Thank you.

Where from?

Vancouver.

Beautiful place. Lots of television production up there now.

Maybe I should go back!

We don't want to lose you just yet. That's close to Seattle, isn't it?

Vancouver? Uh huh.

Home of the Grunge.

That's right. Kurt Cobain and many others.

Lotta rain up there.

I'm a rain person.

Tell us how you got into the adult-film business, Kiv.

I was working as a dancer—in fact, I still do, between auditions. It's something I enjoy.

Bet you're pretty good.

I think I'm fair. Until a few months ago, I'd never even *seen* one—an X-movie. Then I started going out with someone—

An actor?

He was an agent.

Uh oh. Name?

. . . that shall remain anonymous! (*laughs*) He had a satellite dish—

Still seeing him?

No! It didn't work out.

Not a big enough dish, huh.

(*smiles*) That's partly true.

Most agents have that problem.

And how would *you* know? (*laughs*) He was actually very nice. For a while there, anyway!

You were saying . . .

Well, he subscribed to some of the satellite channels that show adult films, soft-core. You don't really see very much.

Uh huh. And you liked watching these Disney-type—

(*laughs*) I wouldn't say they were quite Disney. But everything was pretty much left to the imagination—in that sense, they were actually very erotic. And very well done.

Make mine medium rare, thank you. Now, is that the Spice Channel? (*Kiv nods*) And when you and your friend watched this, was that kinda like foreplay?

It did get us in the mood. But then he showed me the *other* channels—

The FoXXXy Network . . .

And they showed *everything.*

Oops! Rear-entry time.

Right—yes—*everything.* I was amazed. They showed home videos, too. People who got it on and sent in tapes.

That's hot.

Suddenly, it was like . . . the whole world is into adult filmmaking.

The whole world is watching! Remember that? Welcome to the kinky Global Village. Tell us more about the home videos.

Some were really sort of gross but some were *very* hot. Because you'd see couples that you usually don't see, in professional productions. Petite girls with these really big guys—

Big in what way?

Tall. (*laughs*) It's more real, because that's what life is like—not everyone has these perfectly matching bodies.

You said petite girls. You mean, chest-wise?

Petite in general. Like, little Koreans—and white girls too—with these big, hairy guys.

That's attractive.

(*laughs*) It was *real*. They were like "the couples next door"—people didn't care how they looked and I thought that was great.

You're not one who's lacking in the chest department, (*she tweaks a nipple with her long red fingernails, screwing and unscrewing; it stiffens*) Wow, look at that.

They're very sensitive. (*she does the other one*)

I'm getting sensitive myself just watching. So, Kiv: all this channel-surfing put you in the mood . . .

I guess you could say that, Troy. I certainly got curious.

What are you into? What turns you on?

Men. I'm really into men.

Have you done a film with a woman?

Not yet. But I haven't done very many movies.

If you did, would you prefer a petite?

You mean, chest-wise?

Uh huh.

Someone smaller-chested than buxom, yes.

I'll put your order in right away, (*she laughs*) Well, how about Singapore?

Singapore is *great*. I *loved* working with her in *Dirty Squealers*.

So you'd feel comfortable doing Singapore.

More than comfortable!

Or being done by.

Mmmmmm. In fact, while we were shooting, I was kind of disappointed you never put us together.

I'll have to give myself a thousand lashes with the wet noodle. If it's good enough for Ann Landers—

And she's really sweet, Singapore. Not at all competitive. She's just so great.

Speaking of erotic channels . . . would you mind taking off your panties? (*Kiv smiles as she removes them*) That's beautiful. (*CAMERA PUSHES IN CLOSER until her bush fills FRAME. It has been shaved in the shape of a heart*) Hey, it's Valentine's Day. Move over, Edward Scissorhands.

I *loved* that movie. I think Tim Burton is a genius.

Did you do that yourself or did you have any help?

Just a little, (*smiles*) A little help from my friends. (*laughs*)

What kind of acting have you done, Kiv?

Mostly stage. Various productions in Vancouver. But I came to Hollywood so I could get experience in front of the camera. (*CAMERA ZOOMS on bush*) My plan is to cross over, like Traci Lords—

She's not doing too bad, is she?

I'd love to do a series—something like *Friends*—but I'm also pursuing low-budget film work with interesting directors like Quentin Tarantino and Robert Rodriguez. But I really enjoy theater work and might be doing a play soon, in Burbank.

Beautiful downtown Burbank.

It's Chekhovian—*The Cherry Orchard.*

I think you mean Chekhov. Chekhovian is the name of my grocer. *The Cherry Orchard . . .* that's where farmers grow virgins, huh. (*How had this happened to him? Years ago, he'd staged* The Seagull *in Topanga with Will Geer.*) Kiv, do you think your work in adult films will hamper you? Lotsa prejudice out there.

For sure. But I point to Traci Lords as an example of how nothing can get in your way if you're really motivated. I look at what I'm doing now as a preparation for film. It's a legitimate tool.

"Legitimate Tool"—I like that! Can I use that as the title for my next film?

I think that when my time comes—

I'd love to watch your time come.

—(*laughs*) that I'll be able to make that transition. Things are different than even ten years ago, especially so as we approach the fin-de-siècle.

The huh? The who? The what?

It's French.

I didn't know you were bisexual—I mean, bilingual—

(*laughs*) It means "end of the century."

(*Of course, he knew what it meant*) Can you touch yourself, Kiv? (*She does. CAMERA PUSHES IN for EXTREME CLOSE-UP*) That's great. You know, you're a cunning bilinguist.

(*JUMP CUT to CLOSE-UP of Kiv's face, sometime later. Still the green lawn and blue sky, suburban ratcheting of distant sprinklers. Kiv moans, biting lip dramatically. CAMERA drifts down to breasts, jiggling against her athletic arm. Follows until we reach wrist and flailing hand with long, lacquered fingernails. Then a MEDIUM SHOT of Kiv as a muscular long-haired surfer in Speedo briefs ENTERS FRAME from b.g.)*

Chet Stoddard

The housewife in toreador pants had been squinting at him from the moment he walked in. When Horvitz introduced him, the woman went nuts.

"Chet Stoddard who had the talk show?"

"That's right." Oh Christ, he thought. Why hadn't he used an alias?

"I *knew* it!"

"Isn't that something," said the husband.

"Great memory," said Chet with a Dick Clark smile.

"He doesn't tell me *anything,* this guy." Horvitz smiled too, but a little awkwardly. He didn't like surprises, especially at the beginning of a pitch.

"That was *a good show.* We *watched* that show, didn't we, Kenny?"

"Yes, we did," said Kenny, matter-of-fact. "You were one of the first guys to go into the audience."

"That's right," said Chet. "With the long microphones. They called them shotgun mikes."

"Shotgun mikes!" Kenny effused, turning to his wife. "I *remember* that."

"*We're* not going to be on a talk show, are we?"

"Not even an infomercial," said Horvitz, taking over the reins.

"Not today, I hope," said Marion. "I'm having a bad hair day."

ViatiCorps helped the terminally ill cash in their life insurance, providing the option of "accelerated benefits." The debt-ridden former personality dropped by for an interview, then signed on as an "independent seller's advocate" trainee. Kenny and Marion Stovall were glad to have a nominal public figure in the house. Somehow, it made the investment more of an adventure, and less of a risk.

"How did you become involved, Chet?"

That was the dentist.

"Well, I do a lot of fund-raising," he lied. "Walkathons, benefits. I met Stu at the carnival."

"For children with AIDS."

"I keep wanting to go," said Marion, demurely glancing at her mate, "but somehow we never make it."

"I think," said the dentist, "you have to be invited. They don't take people off the street . . ."

"We're hardly 'off the street,' darling."

"Oh I think we can wangle an invitation," Horvitz said. "They had a tremendous amount of celebrities this time around."

"Great turnout," said Chet, the sudden civic bureaucrat.

"Tom Hanks and his wife, Rita, always make an appearance. They're good people. Gee . . . who was there? Jerry Seinfeld, Marcia Clark, Jay Leno. *There's* someone who'll give you a run for your money."

Chet rolled with the punch. "He's got a helluva car collection. But I was an unlucky man this year—got trapped in a ring-toss booth with Sharon Stone. It was sheer hell." The dentist asked if the star wore panties and was promptly swatted by his wife. "Let's just say that with or without, she arouses some fairly basic instincts." Everyone laughed as Marion went for coffee.

"Anyway," said Horvitz, "Chet liked what we were doing and wanted to come along to see how this thing works, on a personal level."

"I hope that's not too much of an intrusion," Chet said diffidently.

"Hell, no," said Kenny, "but I warn you: by the time you leave here, I *will* be your dentist."

"Kenny, stop it!" cried Marion, from the kitchen.

"You have to promise to bring in a photo for my Wall of Stars."

"It's a deal."

Horvitz dug in. "Kenny, your profession certainly hasn't been untouched by this terrible disease and its attendant controversies."

"We certainly have been."

"As you know, there's a lot of lip service given to 'awareness.' What's wonderful about ViatiCorps—and its database of professionals like yourselves—is that you and Marion can do something concrete, something *tangible,* to ease human suffering."

"That's what's so appealing," said Marion, bringing in the tray. She looked to her husband, then added: "To me."

"How exactly does it work?"

"Simplicity itself. I have a client who's perfect to wet your feet with."

Horvitz reached for his satchel, and Chet passed it on. He sorted through documents, grousing about life as a "great paper chase." Then he found what he was looking for: a Polaroid of a wispy-haired man in his forties. Chet knew the picture had been taken by a nurse who supplied ViatiCorps with leads on the dying, for a percentage.

"He's a costume designer. Has a T-cell count of twenty-two."

Marion looked pained as she examined the photo. "Is that very bad?"

"It's not great."

"What's a normal count, Stu?" asked the dentist, with alacrity.

"It's a little arbitrary, but as a guide or indicator, that's about all we have. The government defines full-blown AIDS as anything under a hundred T cells." Marion screwed her eyes and nodded. "You and I may have six or seven hundred. Funny thing is, you can have *nine* hundred and *still* be on your way out."

Ken shook his head. "That's insidious."

Marion tucked now shoeless feet underneath her and studied the photo; Chet noted a passing resemblance to Sally Field. "What's his name?"

"Philip Dagrom. He's actually fairly well known for what he does. He was working on *Blue Matrix* up until a month or so ago. I saw him on Friday. He's pretty much clinically depressed."

"Who wouldn't be?" said the dentist.

"He doesn't *look* all that terrible," said Marion, grimly fascinated. "Don't they usually have those spots? What are they called?"

"Kaposi's sarcoma. Phil's had everything *but* KS. Now, he's losing his sight."

"Real science fiction stuff, isn't it?" Chet chimed in.

"It's diabolical, believe me," said Horvitz. They made a fairly decent tag team. "But Phil's a fighter. We're still looking at an expectancy of three to six months—don't quote me now!"

"Was he an addict?"

"No, no. A hemophiliac—also gay."

"Wow," said Marion. "Double whammy time."

"I've worked on hemophiliacs."

"I always wanted to know," said Chet, "how you fill a cavity in that situation."

"*Very carefully!*" laughed the dentist. "What kind of insurance does he have?"

"A two-hundred-thousand-dollar policy. We can get it for maybe sixty cents on the dollar."

"We give him a hundred and twenty thousand," said the dentist, "which ultimately nets us—"

"You become eighty percent beneficiaries, with ViatiCorps retaining twenty."

"Receivable upon his death."

"That is correct. And that is subject to federal tax, not state."

"Why did he wait until now? Pretty soon, he won't be able to enjoy himself."

"That's the risk they take. Maybe he didn't need the money, Kenny—until now. Or maybe he was just in denial. You have to understand there's a *finality* involved in the selling of a policy."

Marion bounced up. "I've got *great* pastries from Mani's, sugar-free—muffins, too. Chet?"

"Love some."

"Then follow."

Chet brought his coffee with him. On the way, he amended his observation, telling her she looked like a young Mary Tyler Moore. She seemed to like that.

Back in the living room, the dentist was concerned. "Stu . . . if we do the deal, what happens if he lives a full twelve months—or more?"

"It's an inexact science, but I've got a pretty good gut. We'll also furnish a doctor's opinion so you know we're not whistling in the dark. Let's say, for argument's sake, he lives a year instead of six months. You'd *still* be earning twenty-three percent on your money."

The dentist nodded. "That's better than CDs."

"You betcha."

Chet chose a chocolate croissant while Marion poured a refill. She asked if he wanted sugar and he said, Just dip your little finger in there. Marion blushed; all in good fun. Gotta keep a hand in, Chet thought.

"Soupy Sales used to come on your show all the time," she said.

"He was marvelous," said Chet. "An early genius of the medium, like Ernie Kovacs."

"And those pie fights! Weren't those crazy days?"

"They certainly were. Good days."

They walked back to the living room and Marion replenished the cups. Horvitz was explaining how the couple could go in on a pool if they were leery of forking over the full amount.

"What will Mr. Dagrom do with the money, Stu?" she asked, then looked toward her husband. He was tucking into a bear claw. "If we buy the policy and give him the cash?"

"I understand he wants to take a cruise. I think he'd like to die in Greece. He evidently used to travel there quite a bit."

The dentist grew pensive. "I know this is a pretty big hypothetical, Stu, but let's say—for argument's sake—that out of the blue, a cure is found."

Marion was mildly embarrassed. "I don't think we have to worry about *that,* honey."

"No, I'm glad you asked," Horvitz said. "It's a good question, don't feel bad about asking *anything,* that's why we're here. Put it *all* on the table, so there aren't any surprises." The advocate clasped hands together as if in prayer, then placed them to his lips. "Even if a cure *were* found, and that's *highly* unlikely"—a glance at Marion—"from *everything* we know . . . the people we're dealing with are just too sick to be helped." His logic was irrefutable; the room responded with a moment of silent gravity. "What I'd *really* like to get you in on," he said, emptying a second pink packet into his coffee, "is an IV-drug user. Once you hand them the money, they tend to shoot it straight into their arms. Dramatically shortens their expectancy."

Bernie Ribkin

Bernie Ribkin sat at the outdoor table that overlooked the customer service area, scanning *Majestic Life,* the "exclusive lifestyle magazine for Jaguar owners." The alarm system on his Range Rover was out again.

Something about Bernie's body put the hex on electrical things. It had always been that way. When he pushed the arming button on his key ring, the doors wouldn't lock—or went haywire, locking and unlocking in seizure-like succession. Sometimes he could activate the system from hundreds of feet away; then again, he'd be standing right at the door and nothing would happen. There were other problems. Much as he loved the way the car looked, the interior was chintzy. The dash and environs continued to shed whole plaques of poorly glued walnut lookalike. The plastic burl on top of the gearshift popped out in his hand and a cheap husk of passenger seat molding kept crapping onto the carpet. You could literally see the masking tape that held it in place—and this was supposed to be a new car. Each day brought another hassle. Like Wednesday, when the key froze in the ignition and Bernie had to be towed all the way to Santa Monica. He was over by Western at the time and wasn't thrilled.

Once semi-famous for a series of zombie films made in the early seventies, the producer was desperate to re-enter the Business. He had traveled the world for twenty years and the money was nearly gone. Now he'd come full circle, back to where it all began. He would have to reinvent himself—Christ, it'd been done before by lesser lights then he. If the concept was right, he could strike gold again. He had just paid fifteen hundred dollars in corporate filing fees: Bernard S. Ribkin was the new President and ceo of Scramblin Entertainment, Inc. He loved the ballsy, mischievous allusion to Spielberg. Made the broads laugh. (Next time, he'd do Scream Works.)

The best part about a Range Rover was that if towing was needed, you simply dialed an eight-hundred number and they came in about twenty minutes with a giant flatbed to cart you away. Bernie was towed three times in five months, once when he stalled on the Sony lot—an ignition thing again— and another, when the hydraulics jammed at Le Dome. All told, the car was in the shop around eighteen times in the year he'd owned it. Buying it had been one of those impulse things. He went to the showroom in Beverly Hills and wrote out the

check, fifty-five thou, high-roller style, that's the way Bernie
always did it, bigger than life. He used to play the tables like
that in Vegas, back in the days with Serena. One bet, twenty-five grand, win or lose. Then walk away.

For months, when the thing acted up, Bernie didn't seem
to care. He came to view his forbearance as a sign of mental
health. Why fret? His way of saying "fuck you" to the car and
its sundry hissy fits. Besides, it was the other fellow's nickel.
If repairs took a few days, they got him a loaner. He paid only
with his time. The ritual of service relaxed him. He came in
early, got his cup of coffee, flirted with the cashier. Sat at the
customer table outside and worked the cellular. Watched the
bored Fendi ladies cruise by and make the servicemen jump
through hoops.

Bernie enjoyed the shop's wide, clean driveway and the
men who emerged from glass hives to diagnose and schedule.
They wore white lab coats and studiously entered the producer's complaints into a computer. They had carefully manicured
beards and were even outfitted with sterling Anglo-Saxon
surnames, courtesy of their supervisors. Bernie didn't mind
the subterfuge, as long as its aspirations were first-class. For
shorter repairs, an obsequious Mexican in a Jaguar Polo shirt
shuttled him back to the Edith-Esther, his apartment house off
Burton Way. Yes, the producer perversely admitted, he sopped
up everything about the place, even the part when he paid his
bill and a "porter" was paged to bring down the just-washed
car. Like checking out of friggin Claridge's.

He sat there trying to come up with a Concept, a twist
that would buy admission to the game—horror again?—or
something like that crazy *Pet Detective* he'd seen on cable.
His mind kept drifting to the car. The producer had bought

English before and knew all the problems; he just couldn't see himself in a Lexus. But then the air-conditioning fritzed (twice) and the seat belt snapped and the window jammed and the hood wouldn't pop and the dash CHECK ENGINE light stayed on three months and the sunroof wouldn't sun and the engine hummed, hideously augmented through Howard Stern (because of the power lines, said the men in white smocks: "It happens with all cars"), and the hatch door wouldn't hatch and Bernie replaced brake pads thrice the first six months ("because the car is so heavy," said the men). Often, they fetched him from the Edith-Esther at the end of the day with great apologies because the mechanic discovered a part was needed that wasn't in stock and would have to be UPSed "from the East"—assuming the mystical East was in possession, which was never certain because by the time they requisitioned, the East was usually already closed. A "part" might take three weeks to arrive. When the alarm system went code blue (fifth time), Bernie sat in the manager's office to show he meant business. The smocked men coaxed it to work but along the way uncovered something grievously wrong with the pistons, a good two-to-four-week job—warranteed, of course. That was the day something turned and Bernie saw himself as the pawn of a bunco repair syndicate, an addled mark, juicy as a widow. They had singled him out. He couldn't help but wonder: would these men actually have the gall to tell Zev Turtletaub the reason he couldn't listen to the news—literally could not hear the commentators through a banshee of revving engine interference—was because of the fucking power lines? Maybe they would.

So Bernie got the name of a law firm specializing in lemons. He paid a small fee and completed a form relating the lengthy, redundant history of repairs. After a week or so, a paralegal called to say they didn't think he had a case just yet—the legal hitch being, none of the recurring problems were deemed dangerous. Bernie's inventory described a minor, exasperating potpourri; alarm-system shorts, freon glitches and frozen ignitions—a nuisance, to be sure, yet a far cry from your chassis dropping out on the four-oh-five like the surgeon's wife's a month before (Jag) or the realtor doing sixty on Fountain when the brakes spontaneously seized (Land Rover). The would-be litigant was encouraged to document future repairs.

Maybe he'd just sell it and take the loss—around thirty K. He could drive around in Donny's Impala, who the fuck cared? Life was too short. Even now, after all he knew, he combed the *Recycler* for Jags. Sell the Rover for thirty, buy something old for fifteen. Ride around in stone class with pocket change to boot. Bernie had that "classic" feeling again, always the same: the "blow-job Bentley" Serena hated, the little MG that knocked out his teeth, the murderous Mini—the Jensen, crapped-out at Cyrano's, overheated at Romanoff's—the XKE, puttering from Perino's, stalled-out at Schwab's . . .

That's the way it was in this English life.

Zev Turtletaub

"Hey, cunt."

"I'm sorry?"

That was Taj, the relatively new Assistant.

"What happened to the *Dead Souls* coverage?"

"What did you call me?"

Shortish hair in tight curls. The kind of preppie skin that mottled pink when he blushed or got cold or evinced outrage. Fear quickly soured his breath.

"A gaping, shit-contaminated hole."

"I am *leaving* here!"

Ellen Wiedlin, a Microsoft attorney from the Bay Area, enjoyed hearing brother Taj's colorful stories of that alluringly neurotic industry, the Movies.

"You're not going anywhere!"

"Let me *out*—"

"Give me my coverage!"

Taj hadn't yet told her about office hijinks. He wanted to give it a little more time before he asked if she thought . . .

"You're *crazy*! Get out of my—"

"I thought you went to Harvard."

"What does *that* have to do with anything?"

"I thought you could *take* it. Oh! Gonna fold up your cards? Pick up your jacks and go home?"

"I did *not* come here to be ridiculed and abused."

"Really! Listen, Princess Tiny Meat, that's what Hollywood's *about*—abuse. So don't give me your bullshit dignity speeches, because you sound very Ridiculous Theater. You want to *learn*? You want to be a *producer*? I asked you a question!"

"I—I don't know!"

"*Please* don't cry. Here's a Kleenex, like we're on Ricki Lake. If you don't want to be a producer, then what the *fuck* are you doing here?"

"I thought that—I thought that—"

"Why are you wasting my time?"

"I'm *not*—I—I *do* want to . . ."

"You do want to *what* . . ."

"To be—a producer!"

"Goal! He scores! He whores! Three points! Okay. Now that we've established what you're gonna wish for when you rub the lamp, let us negotiate the amount of *genie shit* you will suck through your pretty little mouth to get there. You're upset. Why? Because you have an ego. A good producer *has* no ego. A *great* producer *pretends* to have one, a very *big* one. You are not a good producer—you are not an *anything*. All you are *today* is an assistant manqué. Do you know what 'manqué' is, Mr. Hah-vehd?"

"Yes, I know what manqué is." Defiant.

"That's a good Hah-vehd boy. You're an assistant *manqué* because of your fucked up ego. But I'm going to give you a chance because I don't *care* about you. If I *cared,* you'd *stay* a shitty assistant except eventually—maybe—you might drop the manqué. I'd make you into a *great* assistant. Is that what you went to Harvard for?"

"The reason I—"

"Shut up. Donny Ribkin called and pitched you—*that's* the fucking reason. Donny Ribkin is a *great* agent and he's also a good friend. I owe Donny Ribkin. Donny Ribkin had a very bright assistant who didn't seem to know his own mind. This very bright and wonderful assistant thought he wanted to be an agent. But one day Very Bright and Wonderful changes his mind."

"Donny always knew I—"

"Shut up. Very Bright and Wonderful *thought* he wanted to be agent but as it turned out, fickle feckless Princess Tiny Meat announced he'd rather be a *producer.* Mommy, I want to be a producer! Lots of time wasted on both sides. Because this is not the *Hahvehd* Romper Room but the real world. So be it. These things sometimes happen. Youth is wasted on the young—and the hung. Because Donny Ribkin is the sweet and thoughtful and gracious guy he is, he calls friend Zev. And, because friend Zev owes him, he takes on your very smart and wonderful, very hairy ass—stop crying *now*, fucked up cunt! Real producers don't cry, understand? I am going to take a giant shit on your head! Did you think the world was a Ron Howard movie? What is your *fantasy* of apprenticeship to a 'successful' producer?"

"I d-d-d-didn't *have* a fan—"

"Freaky stupid *bitch*. *Liar*. Everyone has a fantasy. Did you think you'd be at DreamWorks sipping cappuccinos with *Steven*, 'shepherding' pet projects? Associate Producer: Taj 'Cunt' Wiedlin! Executive Producer: Taj 'Wet Hole' Wiedl—"

"Stop it! Please . . . stop—"

"This is your wake-up call, you cunt fart."

Zev brings Perrier to the trembling assistant. The smallest of small bottles. Taj takes it but doesn't drink, futzing with the cap instead.

"What *is* your fantasy?"

"I would like—I . . . I-I would like to produce a major film . . ."

"Well, thank you for sharing." Pause. "I can help you make it real." Pause. "You know, you're just like my sister—you think you're hot shit cause you've read Dante." Zev swigs from his own little bottle and stares. "Do you want to call Donny and tell him what a bad man I am?" Holding the receiver in the air. "Do you want to call Mommy and cry?"

"I—I don't— . . ."

"I'll puke in that Harvard mouth."

"Oh God."

"Fuck that ass so wide they'll call it the Harvard Yard."

"Pl-pl-plea—"

Time to get back to the business at hand. "What happened with Dustin?"

Taj tries to shift gears. "He . . . he—his office said he w-w-wasn't able to—"

"W-w-w-w wasn't able to w-w-w-*what*?"

"He he's w-with his children. For . . . for uh for the next two weeks."

"*Shit*. Find out where—unless of course, you're quitting on me."

Screwing up all his courage and dignity now. "I'm going to *stay*! God*dammit*—"

"Oh who cares. Did you read *Dead Souls*?"

"I-I-I did . . . my Powerbook was, uh, something isn't—"

"Your Powerbook's broke. There's a metaphor."

"I—I took it. It's fixed now."

"I want coverage in the morning."

"I'll do it—I will. I'll I'll—I'm sorry. I didn't—it's just—no one ever talked to me that . . ."

Completely bored with this. Looks in the mirror, sideways. Bald pate; fluff and flex the swollen quads. Liking the way he looks today. Svelte. "Well, good. Why don't you order some food in from the Mandarin." On his way out now. "Smile," he says to the bludgeoned Ivy Leaguer.

"I—I-I-I can't."

"Come on . . ."—Taj manages a trembly grin—"*there* it is. And there it is again!" A bigger one this time, Elvis twitch receding, face splotched pink. "You're cute when you smile, like the *Northern Exposure* kid. God, those eyebrows. Who has eyebrows like that?"

"My m-mother."

"Scary." Taj starts to laugh, too hard. Zev is charmed. "Why are you laughing?"

"It's just so . . . *absurd.*"

"Yes, it is. Absurd you were going to throw away the *only* fucking mentor you will *ever* have in this town. You were going to throw out your *life*—and trust me, you *will* have one, a *major* one, if you watch and listen—you were going to throw all that away because someone called you a cunt. That *is* absurd."

"Sorry to interrupt," says another nervous helper, popping head through door, "but Alfred is here."

"That would be the nigger steward. Hmmmmm—fly the friendly guys of United. Mimsy helped me score."

"You met him on the plane?" Shyly conversational.

"You know, you're a real dumbo. I said *steward,* didn't I? *United,* as in *Airlines?* God, you're dumb." Taj downcast again, Zev cheery. "He's got a great ass. I call it the black box. Get it, Dumbo? It's the only thing that survives his affairs."

Chet Stoddard

The dentist's wife was an exception. Not too many people recognized him anymore and that was a blessing.

He used to look like his letterman homeboy from Wayne State, Chad Everett. Chet 'n' Chad, gridiron buds. People thought they were brothers. They came to Hollywood and got jobs parking cars at the Luau on Rodeo Drive. Those were prehistoric days, when the street had a leafy small-town charm—nineteen sixty-two. A twenty-four-hour coffee shop at the corner of the Beverly Wilshire was always good for star-gazing: Broderick "Ten-Four" Crawford and Phil Silvers, Nick Adams and Frank Sutton (Sarge from *Gomer Pyle*). One night after work Chet smoked some reefer, walked to the hotel and plunked himself down in a big booth where Tony Curtis was holding court. No one seemed to care. He chatted up a redhead, the roommate of Curtis's girl. Her name was Lavinia Welch and she was a secretary at the Morris Agency around the corner. Her father, a writer for Bob Hope, was a client there. She was nineteen years old.

They started dating and Lavinia pushed him to go on auditions. He won bit parts in *The Sons of Katie Elder* and *Follow Me, Boys!* and a recurring role on *Rawhide*. Lavinia wanted to marry, but Chet was still sowing wild oats. When she caught him in bed with her room mate, they split up. He spent days and nights drinking and playing pool at Barney's Beanery, back when the place still had a FAGGOTS STAY OUT sign nailed above the door. The barflies, especially showbiz fringers, knew Chet from his television work and accorded him real-actor status. He moved nearby so he wouldn't have to drive—he'd been busted twice for DUI. That was okay too, because all the sluts and fine ladies liked driving him home.

He found his way back to Lavinia. His career foundered— cut from *The Wild Bunch*, Chet never worked as a film actor again. After they married, the father-in-law helped buy them a house in a new development called Mount Olympus. That was fitting because Lavinia—new husband and new digs, high above the glittering city—really did feel like a God in Heaven.

Severin Welch was eccentric and charming and rolling in TV money. His wife, Diantha, a frustrated ballerina, had

hard, elegant bones. (Chet never saw her eat anything but little red potatoes.) Having in-laws was easy because his parents were dead, and he missed that presence. Severin lived
in the old Beachwood Canyon house to this day, a prisoner
self-imposed—gone off his nut long ago. Maybe Chet would
call and visit. He could get the number from Lavinia, if he
dared; she was nuttier than her father. Talking to his ex had
a way of throwing a person into toxic shock. While Chet was
at it, he'd get their daughter's number too—Jabba, she called
herself now—another call he'd never make.

He remembered a time long ago, the first day of summer.
Diantha threw Severin a surprise party on his birthday. Chet
felt free and easy; out from under. Things hadn't turned out
the way he'd expected—they never did, not for anyone. From
the backyard, the HOLLYWOOD sign looked impossibly, hilari-
ously near. Jack Cassidy and Shirley Jones were there and the
TV producer Saul Frake. At dusk, Chet and Jack smoked a
roach by the pool and everyone played charades. The new son-
in-law was a hit. When the game was over, he launched into a
Tonight Show improv, sitting on the diving board introducing
Jack as his first guest. The actor had just finished shooting
Bunny O'Hare and Chet asked if there was any truth to his
"reputed long-term affair with Ernie Borgnine." Saul Frake
laughed so hard he broke a blood vessel in his eye.

Two weeks later, Frake called. He wanted to know if Chet
would be interested in hosting a talk show. Chet thought it was
one of Cassidy's pranks, but Saul paid for a test and Jack was
gracious enough to replay their expurgated poolside shenanigans for the camera. Saul convinced the network boys they
had something special and they bit: four months later, The
Chet Stoddard Show debuted. In the first week, guests included

Bobby Rydell and Judy Carne, the cast of *Don't Bother Me I Can't Cope,* Dionne Warwick and Karen Valentine, the ubiquitous Joey Bishop, dancer Larry Kert, a Lloyd's of London man who insured anything, the Ace Trucking Company comedy troupe and Eartha Kitt. *Medical Center's* Chad Everett dropped by and they cut up old times with clubby, rollicking pregonzo repartee, a Rat Pack of two. Chet was quick and telegenic, but after eighteen months the show fizzled. By then, he'd already bought a Cobra for the hooker who supplied him with coke. At the final taping, he announced Molly's birth, then flew to Vegas and lost sixty thousand dollars in forty minutes. When Lavinia came to get him, he fractured her skull with a chair during a blackout.

They divorced. He stayed in town to be close to his daughter. Somewhere around nineteen seventy-nine, he free-based himself into a heart attack. When Chet recovered, he returned to Michigan—those were the go-go years of detox, and he found his niche, becoming a paid counselor and proselytizer for the cause.

Now he had returned to the city that once held so much promise—and, somehow, still did—to pre-sell the bones of the dead.

Troy Capra

He took Kiv to a production of *Ghosts* on Santa Monica Boulevard. It was a while since he'd been to a play and Troy was flooded by memories of his own "life in the theater."

The drama teacher at Beverly Hills High was an occasional character actor in films, and when Troy enrolled as a freshman, some of the students already had agents—everyone felt more or less poised for stardom. It seemed like a birthright.

Alumnus Richard Dreyfuss was a beacon. Troy was still in elementary school when word spread through the district like a flash fire that one of their own would soon appear on *Bonanza*. Like a distant cousin, he rooted him on through the years: *The Graduate, The Young Runaways, Two for the Money,* then *American Graffiti* and *Duddy Kravitz, Jaws* and *Close Encounters* and *The Big Fix,* an Oscar for *The Goodbye Girl* . . . and, of course, the quirky *Inserts,* where Richard portrayed a faded director, reduced to shooting porn. There was irony for you.

Troy acted in college but his real joy was directing. The first thing he did professionally was three Feiffer sketches at a tiny stage on Wilcox. Then, Kopit and *Krapp's Last Tape, The Sandbox* and *Oh Dad, Poor Dad,* Murray Schisgal and *Small Craft Warnings.* Did that almost ten years. While Troy churned them out in Hollywood's Little Theater ghetto, Richard was busy making a comeback in *Down and Out in Beverly Hills.*

It was nineteen eighty-eight and Troy was getting bupkus for a community-funded production of *Guys and Dolls.* Toward the end of the run, one of the male dancers told him a "film" he was acting in on the weekend had lost its director—would he be interested? What kind of film? A student thing? Not exactly. There was nudity. Oh. I see. Troy knew a bit about cameras—and there was a thousand dollars in it. He needed the money. But more than that, Troy reasoned, he needed *experience,* to know what it felt like to "carve up space" with a camera. What difference did it make what he was shooting? He'd been trying to break into film directing for years; if this was how it was going to be, he'd just let it ride. Everyone had different points of entry, pardon the pun—that Troy Capra's was X-rated would become a famous factoid, a talk show anecdote and nothing more.

At curtain, they went backstage to find the producer, an old friend. Troy used a pseudonym in the adult world; none of his former colleagues really knew what he'd been up to all these years. When he did run into them, he painted a vague, glamorous portrait of himself as diehard vanguardist, peripatetic artist-in-and-out-of-residence, the kind who directed *Uncle Vanya* in a Bronx crack house or accompanied Susan Sontag to Bosnia to "put on a show." Kiv drew in excited drafts of backstage musk, at home with the gypsies. As the couple rubbed past players from tonight's drama, Troy nodded to each like a priest to his flock. The actors—needy, optimistic children that they were—could only hope he truly was a Higher Power.

Familiar laughter emanated from one of the dressing rooms. Poking a head in, Troy discovered his old acquaintance—and the paroxysmal Richard Dreyfuss himself, gulping with psychotic hilarity. The visitor was embraced, and introductions, including the radiant Kiv Giraux's, made all around. Richard had an open, vibrant charm, unlike other celebrities Troy had met. He was very much *there*, genuine and unguarded, charismatically earnest; one got the sense he'd bare his soul to a stranger, particularly one met in the homey ministry of Theater. He made eye contact with everyone—maybe that was a seduction, a trick of largesse learned long ago—but Troy chose not to be cynical. At least part of Richard was "performing" for Kiv, and that was only natural since she was the only woman in the room, and stunning. Even so, the actor always struck him as the sort who needed to seduce the men and win them over before polishing off assorted wives and lovers.

When the producer was called from the room, Troy and Kiv had the actor to themselves. Richard talked shop and generally effused in his high-voltage way while Troy's heart pounded, waiting for the best moment to insert the business of their alumnihood. He finally ventured how they'd almost been classmates and the two men bandied old teachers' names, resurrecting a few campus scandals. Kiv asked what he was working on, "currently." Richard said he was preparing for *Medea,* in La Jolla—"Des" was coming back to mount the six-week run, which they might do as a film, with "Des" directing. When Richard asked what he did, Troy said he directed too. The star nodded respectfully, without further inquiry—no need. Backstage, all were brethren.

*

At Planet Hollywood, Troy was solemn. Kiv talked about *Close Encounters* being her favorite film and how blown away she was to have met him. How funny he was. She fantasized Richard would become their new best friend, that he was the sort of person who'd be eager to help their careers—help Troy direct a movie, anyway—especially since they went to school together. How he was someone who was naturally simpatico because he'd had so many highs and lows himself. Troy let her talk while David Caruso posed for pictures with the tourists. What a hellhole.

On the drive back to Studio City, her hands were all over him but Troy felt far away. When they got home, Kiv pulled him to the bedroom but he was like a stone. He watched her with the dildo, then wandered out the sliding glass door to the redwood balcony. It was drizzling and the Valley glistened and blinked like a rhinestone cape, from the black MCA building to the Sepulveda Dam. In five years, he would be fifty. He had sixteen thousand in savings and was around forty in debt. No filmography to speak of, no fans, critics, flack, manager, agent or life. There was only one option and it came to him like a pop epiphany: he would write and star in a one-man show. The piece would be called *Adventures in the Skin Trade* (he was sure Dylan Thomas wouldn't mind) and Troy would lay it bare—the obscenity of his failed ambitions, the dead end that had become his life—filming the whole carefully scripted catharsis onstage. Then he'd arrange a meeting with Richard to tell him the truth, what kind of director he *really* was, a bona fide pornographer, before handing the startled movie star the fresh, revelatory cassette. Who knew what might happen? Troy had the feeling this was just the kind of dark thing the actor sparked to. Maybe Richard's production company would climb aboard for distribution. Troy could remember *Swimming to Cambodia,* so threadbare, so *nothing,* made on less than a shoestring. Ditto Bogosian.

A sense of fate and purpose invigorated him. The smell of wood burning in the crisp air shook him down deep: an old, arcane melancholia. He thought to himself, *I will get out alive.*

Troy wandered back to the bedroom and stood in the door, watching Kiv's frenetic hands ride the humming thing that snaked inside her—for an instant, she seemed like a crazed Great Mother assiduously following the devil's pronouncement: *for each thousand thrusts, a child will be saved.* He slid the door shut behind him.

Bernie Ribkin

Bernie sat in his weensy Hollywood office, staring idly at the latest Range Rover repair printout.

The bungalows were filled with kids (music-video production companies) but the rent was cheap. The girls had tattoos and rings through their tummies—through their friggin *eyebrows*—and Jabba said you-know-where else. Maybe he should get one, Bernie thought, right through the nose, like a fuhcocktuh bull. Why not? At seventy, he felt like a gangbanger. He still wanted to mix it up, leave his mark, make people notice. Do not go gentile into that good night.

But Jesus H, if you weren't in the Club, you could forget about it. The studios were spending eighty, ninety, a hundred million a picture like nothing, and that was before P & A. He remembered a story in *People*: "The shoot was agonizing. Though he was earning fourteen million dollars and living in an eighteen-hundred-a-night oceanside bungalow, Costner looked, says one extra, 'like he needed a hug.' " Somebody give *me* a friggin hug like that. But these men weren't dumb. They had their formulas. They had their New World Order MBAs with their scorched-earth policies—a show that did fifty million in the States could do another hundred and fifty in Europe. He saw the full-page ads in the trades, trumpeting unimaginable grosses for movies he'd never even heard of. Europe! Europe! Europe! Were they talking about the same Europe? Because *his* Europe, the *Ribkin* Europe, was dry as a zombie's ass. All he wanted was three—three million lousy dollars—but how the hell could he step up to the plate? He'd have better luck pinning a murder on O.J. If only he *knew* somebody . . . with his son a honcho at ICM, no less! A Senior Veepee who hated his guts! That made him crazy. But that's life, like Sinatra said.

Hollywood didn't make movies anymore so much as big-screen novelties and reruns of the Baby Boomer TV hit parade. Kibitzing at the Peninsula Bar with a Showtime exec, the decrepit producer concluded his only hope was to auction off the three films comprising his *Undead* opus—it was Bernie's job to connive some Young Turk into having a go at the campy, mothballed omnibus. Miraculously, he still owned the series; he could thank Serena for that. What a head for business, marvelous. Bernie would give himself six months to raise studio money. Donny might be badgered into making some connections just to get the old man off his back. If the majors didn't bite, Bernie would go cable. The Showtime fella was talking about the splash they had made with those American International re-dos a few years back—Sam Arkoff was no dunce. Cable felt like a slam dunk, but Bernie had to explore his feature options first. Cable was a fallback.

He was almost drunk. He parked in the underground garage and listened to the idling engine—something was in there, different from the piston sound. Kind of a ping. Or maybe a pong. He stepped from the car and pushed the lock-and-load button on the key ring: nothing happened. Again—nothing. It kicked in on the fourth try, securing all doors. As he walked to the elevator, he saw a dark figure weeping by the Dumpster. He stopped and stared. He thought it was a homeless person, then recognized her and softly said *Hello?* The woman braced herself against the bin and heaved with cartoonish agony.

"Are you all right? Did you hurt yourself?"

She was a neighbor. It was the first time he'd said a word to her in ten months of living there.

"My baby—"

"You're upset. Can I talk to you? Can we talk a moment?" She nodded, childlike. "I'm Bernie—Bernie Ribkin, from two-oh-seven."

"I don't want to live. *I do not want to live!*"

"Of course you do, darling. Let's go inside now. Do you have your key? Darling, do you have your key? Is it in your purse there? Let's find your key and I'll take you upstairs. Let Bernie take you upstairs. You're upset. Stop your crying. Is there someone I can call, darling?" She turned and faced him head-on, helpless. She was formidable, mega-uterine, her head a stone-carved monument to some corybantic race long dead. He surprised himself by putting his arms around her. "What is it? Darling, it can't be that bad."

She blurted out the tale of a paralyzed daughter, and when she told him her name—Edith-Esther, same as the building itself—Bernie put it all together: this was the bereft mother of Oberon Mall. The condolent producer invited her to his apartment, where she poured her heart out over Frito-Lays, non-pareils and Snappled Absolut. She could really drink. He called her Double E, and that made her laugh.

She reminded him of Gala, an old lover who kept horses in Chatsworth—both women smelled of stables, leaf and menses. Bernie felt sorry for this dappled gray mess of a woman, this rueful roan oak. Edie (he settled on that) said the terrible thing was that in brainstem injuries like her baby's, the extent of damage was impossible to assess—doctors were reduced to using the patient's tears as a crude gauge of awareness and mental competency. The somewhat jaded old man found that detail haunting.

Bernie walked her up to four-ten and they exchanged numbers. She told him he was a courtly man. She wanted to show him her computer "when the place was clean." He had already turned to go when Edie asked if he would come see her baby: today, *now,* or at least in half an hour or so. She held his arm and begged him to walk over—they were that close to Cedars. All we have to do, she said, is pick up the cake before we go, around the corner at Michel Richard. Edie asked him again because she didn't have it in her to go alone. If they could just pick up the cake; she already had the candles. Today was Obie's birthday.

*

Late Friday afternoon, he went to see Jabba. She was dancing at Little Kink's, a club in East Hollywood.

They met when he first came to town. Bernie picked her up on El Centro and she gave him a blow job but it didn't work so well. He gave her a hundy to have lunch with him at Musso's. She was impressed with the old man and his Range Rover. He was coy about what he did for a living, and Jabba thought for sure he was a Player—they had their little game. Nice for Bernie's ego. He saw her every couple of weeks like that, usually for lunch or a movie. They never did anything, but he always slipped her a hundy.

This time they went to Locanda Veneta, a chic Italian place on Third. Jabba's skin was broken out. Bernie pointed to a man sitting with his back to the kitchen.

"See that guy? Billy Friedkin. He directed *The Exorcist.*"

"He looks like a dentist."

"And *The French Connection,* ever see that? What are you doing to yourself, you look like hell."

"Thanks."

"Are you eating right?"

"I'm fucking depressed."

"You don't have the right to be depressed. You're too god-dam young."

Jabba glared, deciding whether to spit in his eye. She looked over to see what Friedkin was up to, then took a fork and farted with her food. "I need money."

"Join the club."

"Fuck you."

"*Work* for a living." Bernie was afraid she was going to walk. Her head caromed between Friedkin and the front door.

"Why don't you put me in one of your pictures?"

"I was going to."

"Bullshitter."

"My movie fell apart."

"Such a *bullshitter*! I can't *believe* this—*you*, like everybody else!"

"How am I a bullshitter, Jabba?"

"You're not a producer, you're not an *anything*—"

"Tell me how I'm a bullshitter, you little punk!"

"All right—I'm leaving." She rose but he stopped her.

"Give me the decency of a response. I *had* a picture—and that's no bullshit. There was a nice part—"

"Oh, *fuck* you," she said wearily, sitting back down.

"Would you lower your voice?"

"You're sad, you know it? Mama!" she shouted, as two or three heads turned. "Mama, he's gonna put me in pictures!"

The veins in his temples swelled like candelabra. "You want me to prove it?"

"Is that Burt Reynolds?" she asked of no one in particular as a nondescript man swept through the door. "That's not Burt Reynolds. *Every*body's a bullshitter—"

"Do you think I lie, Jabba?"

"No. You just bullshit."

"I go out on a limb for you."

"Oh right. Put your life right on the line."

"I'll show you. Then you'll think twice about the kind of crap that comes from your mouth."

He paid the check and Jabba said she just wanted to go home. Bernie took her arm and steered her across the street to Cedars. He told her Obie Mall was the star of his picture and he'd been struggling to find a replacement. Jabba only started to believe him when they reached the room. His heart was pounding, and he searched his pockets for stray tranquilizers—nothing. He made her wait in the hall while he ducked in to make sure Edith-Esther wasn't there. The private nurse smiled and said he'd just missed her. The nurse toweled the Big Star's chin and said, "Well, who's the popular girl? Mr. Bernie's back to see you, but he didn't bring a cake." She left the three of them alone.

"Oh my God," said Jabba. "It *is*, it's *her*."

Bernie sat in the nurse's chair and held Obie's hand. "It's okay," he said as the agitated Big Star's eyes bugged and darted about. "It's all right, your mama will be back."

Jabba took in the catheter bag and said, "It's *piss*." She'd never seen a hospital room this big—crammed with flowers, a humidifier, a "wave" machine, VCR, giant New Age crystals and all kinds of expensive-looking knick-knacky things. There was a whole table filled with nothing but framed photos from better days: Obie and Clinton, Obie and Courtney, Obie and Travolta. R.E.M. played softly on a CD boombox.

"Can she hear me?"

"Of course she can."

Oberon made clicking noises from her throat as Jabba moved closer. She'd lost weight since the stroke; an elegant satin "healing" cord—gift from Meg Ryan—fell loosely around a tiny, protuberant wrist.

"You're a great actress," Jabba said, chapped lips brushing the ear of the spasmodic icon. Bernie stood and smiled nervously at the nurse as she re-entered. "I think maybe we'll go," he said. "She seems tired."

"Hurry and get well," Jabba whispered as the nurse took over. "I want to work with you someday. That would be my greatest honor in life."

Zev Turtletaub

Zev and the boys out by the pool, talking cock. Alfred the Steward long since airborne, black box and portable flotation device intact. There's Yon Koster, the trainer who wrested muscle from the liposuctioned abs and flabby arms of a classic endomorph: Zev, with that unwieldy, oddly over-developed, dressed-for-success praying mantis thorax, like Jeremy Irons's in the third *Die Hard*. There's Moe Trusskopf and friend, one far-out looking "Lancelot," whose true name—Rod Whalen— suggests (sez Moe) an honest-to-God nom de porn.

"You never told us about Flyboy," said Moe.

"Stout, dark and uncut."

"Like a Guinness."

"On the nose."

"You mean the head."

"MTV should do an 'Uncut.' "

"First, Seal, then Tom Petty."

"Seal'd with a kiss."

"Flyboy had about the biggest hole I have *ever* seen. You could drive a Bronco through that urethra."

"An attractive image."

"A slow-speed chase to the bladder."

"Who's got the biggest straight dick?"

"Oh no!" Moe posed like Munch's *Scream.* "Not *this* again."

"Jimmy Woods."

"It isn't straight, it's crooked."

"How would you know?"

"Into the Woods!"

"Oh please. No one's ever *seen* Jimmy Woods's cock. It's like the Abominable Snowman."

"The Abominable Blow Job."

"Lisa Marie Presley in action."

"Paula Abdul."

"Celine Dion."

"They say Jim Woods is the Milton Berle of our time."

"He sleeps standing up 'cause it's like a kickstand."

"What about Brad Pitt?"

"Didst thou dare invoke Princess Tiny Meat?"

Everybody laughs as Douglas brings hamburgers.

"It *can't* be huge, he'd be too perfect."

"Tom Cruise."

"Oh yes. And L. Ron Hubbard's another one."

"Birds of a feather . . ."

"*Fock* together."

"They say Hubbard was hung like David Koresh."

"What about Timothy McVeigh?"

"No! Alfred Mullah."

"Who's Alfred Mullah."

"You know—the federal building."

"*Alfred P. Murrah!*" Howling with glee.

"Isn't that it? The building that blew up?"

"All those militia guys are way hung."

"What about Cat Basquiat?"

"I don't talk about my clients."

"Uncut?"

"Definitely unplugged."

"We can remedy that."

"The girl can't help it."

"There's an executive at Buena Vista with a tiny penis. We're talking nub. He scores with chicks who want to get fucked in the ass but were always afraid. It's like a big toe going in."

"You are so full of shit."

"Uh, no, the toe is."

More laughter as the boys dig into burgers. Moe asks Douglas if there's ice cream. Moe wants a sundae, then asks for a malted. Asks about available sherbets, hankering for a peristaltic treat. Something easy to upchuck. Would he still like the sundae? Zev says forget it. Alec Baldwin calls from Amagansett and Zev takes it inside.

"As for your nubby Buena Vista friend," sez Moe, "some say the ass is half-empty, others say it's half-full."

Guffaws as Zev enters the house. Taj has arrived from the office. Zev motions him into the library, then picks up.

"Hello there."

"Hiya, Zev."

"You are *such* a good boy to call me back on your holiday."

"The career never sleeps. Desperately seeking material."

Zev snaps fingers at his assistant, motioning him to come near. "Caught you on the Stern show."

"Oh yeah."

"You were fucking hilarious."

"Howard makes it easy."

"He becomes your *straight* man. I can't believe it—Howard Stern, a fucking straight man! Helluva trick."

"I *feel* like a trick. My agent said you had some brilliant project."

Zev, sitting now, puts a hand on the helper's ass. Taj backs away, but the producer pulls him back by his A/X belt, grimacing with anger. Zev spins him around and Taj stands still for the remainder of the call, buttocks in front of Zev's face.

"I've never been more excited. This is Academy Award time, Alec, I'm serious."

"You're giving me a boner."

"It's my AIDS movie. I know that sounds crass."

"Is there a script?"

"I'm talking to Mamet and Zaillian. And, would you believe, Arthur Miller."

"The lightweights."

"I'll make this brief, 'cause I don't want to hector you."

"Hector away. You know, you should *get* Hector—Babenco."

"I love Hector but he's erratic. Here's the premise, okay? Well, not the premise-premise, but the context: *If you have AIDS and need cash, you can sell your life insurance and collect the money upfront.*" A thumb bisects Taj's thigh, stopping at the back of the knee.

"Your office faxed me the article."

"Did you have a chance to read it?"

"Very dark—but *very* interesting."

"You know, I always wanted to do *A Face in the Crowd* with you but instead of the music thing, I wanted to set it in Werner Erhard–land."

"I love that. I never knew you wanted to do that."

"For *years*. You were gonna be this con who scams the human potential movement—a dysfunctional *Music Man*! But one day I woke up and the whole 'inner child thing' felt passé—"

"Tell that to my wife."

"And how is the most gorgeous woman on earth?"

"She's great. So the character's one of these insurance guys."

" 'Viatical settlement advocate'—that's what they call themselves. He's down-and-out. Bad karma, like Newman in *The Verdict*"

"I loved *The Verdict*. Where does it go?"

Cradling the phone on his shoulder, Zev puts both hands on Taj's ass, gently spreading cheeks beneath loose fabric. "He gets involved with an activist, a woman who's HIV. Sandra Bullock."

"Your sister's an activist."

"Yeah, Aubrey."

"How's she doing?"

"Fine. Well. Tough lady."

"I saw her at the Hard Rock thing in New York. She looked great."

"This is my gift to her."

"I'd love to work with Sandra. She's terrific."

"Together, you're *perfect*. There's a medical conspiracy thing going on, like in *The Fugitive,* only a thousand times subtler. I thought of this because I asked a hemophiliac how he got AIDS and he said, 'I got fucked in the ass by seven major drug companies, honey!' "

"That's so great."

"I'm really waiting until we get the writer on board, Alec. I just wanted to feel you out, because to me the character is phenomenal, a classic, towering. It's cosmic Elmer Gantry. Would this sort of thing appeal to you, Alec? Because I can't see anyone but you, you'd be brilliant. I just need to know if this kind of guy—a hustler, a parasite who slowly, painfully has his eyes opened to human suffering and comes out from the thing . . . *transcendent*—I just need an indication it's an arena you might like to explore." Zev slides a finger down the pallid crack and Taj jerks away. The producer contemptuously shoves the assistant toward the desk, where he nonchalantly fiddles with some papers.

"Absolutely. But the article . . . the article isn't based on a book—"

"No. The article is an article. What I want to do is graft that information onto the superstructure of *Dead Souls,* an extraordinary nineteenth-century Russian novel—"

"Right, I know. Tolstoy?"

"Nikolai Gogol. But you win the literary consolation prize."

"Howard Stern would have known."

"Howard Stern would think it was Stephen King. Now, when am I gonna see you? When are you coming to L.A.?"

"Jesus, never, I hope. I'm kidding. Probably three weeks."

"Do you want me to send the book, with coverage?"

"What's the coverage," he laughed. "Cliffs Notes?"

"We broke it down. But I don't want to overwhelm you."

"I've been known to dip into a tome or two. I'm halfway through the new Roth—*Operation Shylock*. Fucking fantastic."

"You'll have book and coverage tomorrow . . ."

"Bell, Book and Coverage."

". . . and if you have *any* thoughts or questions, call me, Alec, anytime, day or night. Okay?"

"You are the Monsignor."

"And thank you for your patience."

"Thank you for your interest. I'm always flattered, Zev."

"You flatter *me*. It's time we did something together."

"*I flatter you, you flatter me*," he sang, while Zev laughed. "*We both flat-ter too ea-si-ly—*"

"Goodbye, you nut."

"*Too ea-si-ly to let it show . . .*"

"Is this a concert?"

"Later, Zev."

"My love to Kimberly."

Zev hung up, rubbing his crotch as he ogled his minion. "Hel-*lo*. Anyone *home*? Ground control to Major Taj!"

"I . . . I haven't done the last fifty pages—of *Dead Souls*."

"Why not?"

"I had—so much other work."

"Come here, silly wabbit."

"Please . . ."

"I won't bite. I might suck, but I won't bite."

He came closer. Zev grabbed the hips and reeled him in.

"Please don't."

"Finish the coverage," he said, fumbling with the belt. "I really want to know how the thing ends." Zev unbuttoned

the fly, pulling the pants down with the aloofness of a tai-
lor—or sailor. "It doesn't seem to be heading toward a resolu-
tion. There's an essay in the back by the guy who wrote *Lolita*.
Maybe you could cover that too."

Taj felt like a child—he wanted to urinate as the under-
wear shimmied down, hammocking at knees. Bloodless lips
fastened around him and the assistant lost balance. Zev's
hands clapped around his rear, steadying. Taj toughed it
out, hardening in the hothouse mouth, watching the smooth
skull, noting moles, veins and fissures from afar like the book
of aerial shots he flipped through at Super Crown: *Above Los
Angeles.*

Chet Stoddard

That night, he went trolling for HIVs at a Narcotics Anonymous
meeting in Van Nuys. Horvitz told him those were good places
for leads. Some were restricted to sero-positives, but they were
easy to crash—no one asked questions. Chet watched and listened, attuned to money woes. Not everyone had life insurance. Finding out who did was tricky, especially if you weren't
infected yourself; one didn't want to be tagged a policy-chaser.
Sussing out candidates was dicey all around. Though he used
an alias, eventually some trivial pursuiter was bound to know
him as Chet Stoddard, boob-tube relic. Winding up on the
"Where Are They Now?" page of a tabloid wasn't a pleasant
prospect, "ONE-TIME TALKER FULL-TIME HAWKER: ADVANCES $$ TO
WALKING DEAD."

The meeting was lower-scale than Chet would have
wished. Lots of bad news bears: sour prison faces, weepy
dementia heads, remorseful crack bingers and the usual
quota of self-important alcoholics—smug vampires who felt

less hopeless hanging with the pozzies. Whenever they stood to speak, you could feel the room's fatal contempt. Around mid-meeting, Chet realized there was a halfway house next door and that explained it; a pissy, policy-poor crowd if he'd ever seen one, hard-core wraiths who took the RTD to get their methadone. Still, you never knew when that stuntman (Aetna) or production designer (Prudential) might stand and share. Expect the unexpected, Horvitz always said.

Luckily, he remembered the party. Someone started a group for heteros with AIDS and tonight they were having a shindig. Chet fished in the glove compartment for a flyer given him by one of his viatical co-workers: Oakhurst Drive, south three hundreds. That was Beverly Hills, over by Olympic—Persian World. No mansions but sure as hell no halfway houses, either. Sounded promising.

The modest two-story home was probably in the eight-hundred-thousand range. The canapé-eaters were nicely dressed, to be sure, and none had the Look except one—a swarthy, charismatic man with thick Yves St. Laurent glasses, a stylish cane supporting sinewy legs and a tell-tale girth that betrayed (to the trained eye) a set of diapers. Emblazoned across his T-shirt was: I SURVIVED THE HOLOCAUST MUSEUM. He was holding court, in the middle of one of those comically anarchic HIV riffs featuring Mothers in Denial, Sado-Healthcare Worker Mayhem, Brides in Dementia on Their Wedding Days and other assorted gruesomely hilarious phantasmagoria. A black-haired boy ran twittering circles around him, mummifying the monologuist with imaginary streamers, like a maypole.

Chet was about to knock at the bathroom door when a woman in a crazy miniskirt emerged.

"This is the hour of lead," she said, looking straight in his eye. "Remembered, if outlived, as freezing persons recollect the snow . . ." He smiled and she went on, very dramatic. "First, chill: then, stupor. Then, the letting go."

"I like that."

She held an arm toward the toilet, like Vanna White. "You are free to wash—I'm through vomiting."

He found her in the backyard a few minutes later. Her name was Aubrey and this was her house. She had black hair and twinkly green eyes.

"How long have you known?" she asked, out of nowhere.

How long have you . . . His mind stuttered: she assumed he was HIV-positive. Chet scrambled up the slick rock of her question—the Question of all Questions, it seemed—trying not to fall into the swallowing sea. "Six months."

"You're a virgin."

"You?"

"Seven years, eight come May. What do you do?"

"I work at the Holocaust Museum." It was supposed to be a kind of joke.

"No shit, the Wiesenthal? What do you do there?"

"Acquisitions."

"Well, that makes you the perfect host—for this party, I mean." She nodded toward the diapered man, expostulating poolside. "Did you see Ziggy's shirt?"

"Pretty fuckin' funny."

"You're not going to sue, are you?"

She was swept away by new arrivals and Chet milled around, waiting for her to get free. He'd used his real name and was glad about that. After a while he decided to leave, thinking the time they had in the yard was as good as it would get—tonight. On the way out, she slipped a card into his pocket. He didn't look until he was in the car.

<u>TRYSTS & CONFABULATIONS</u>
Aubrey Anne Turtletaub
(310) 555-1722

Troy Capra

Troy worked feverishly on *Skin Trade* while keeping an eye toward potential venues, Equity-waivers where he might rehearse and film the performance. The idea of shooting on an "X" soundstage came to mind, but Troy dismissed it as too "on the nose."

The plan was to film ninety minutes of written material honed at private showcases—technically, a no-brainer. The key, as always, was the writing. The autobiographical vignettes had to stand alone yet be of a piece: a child's sudden recognition of the sacred, mystic ordinariness of a winter morning; a twelve-year-old boy, marooned in a body cast after being struck by a car, spins tales of chivalry; the sightless cello teacher who set Whitman to music; tender agonies of first love and the eeriness of first death—his bookish father's, from lupus; mother-son healing on a magical trip to New York, the smell of subways and Broadway and Mother's Arpège. Troy wanted to pierce the heart of things, to learn, if he could, how it was he found himself—three quarters of a life undone—onstage at this precarious benefit, this fund-raiser for his soul.

If he kept it honest, he couldn't go wrong—that's why he decided to begin with a skit of himself directing porn, in pantomime: stooping to invisible actors as he held camera on shoulder,

zooming in, panning flesh, cajoling, extolling, a clockwork artist under the fiendish, ticking cock of a come-shot. A naked and
bravura opening for the performance of his life.

*

He made Kiv call the actor a week after they'd met. A week felt
about right—a week wasn't pushy. Troy wanted to play out the
connection, keep it alive until he could sit with the star and fill
him in on *Skin Trade*.

When Richard asked if she and Troy were an item, Kiv
said, "Off and on." Very high school—very Beverly. That's
what Troy told her to say and they fought about it but Kiv
finally agreed, in the name of Troy's career. (She couldn't resist
adding, "Mostly on.") They were supposed to get together for
coffee, but Richard was going to England for a few weeks and
wouldn't be able to see her till he got back. She was somehow
relieved. Before they hung up, the actor asked if she'd ever
been to London. When Kiv said no, he said she should come
along. She just laughed and so did Richard, in that famous
way. She wondered if he was serious.

A few days before Richard was due home, Troy called the
office. He was close enough to finishing *Skin Trade* to lay the
groundwork for drinks. If they could just meet somewhere—
Orso's or the Grill or the Ivy—he'd bring the actor up to speed,
dropping the completed script in his lap. He knew that without Kiv, there was little chance Richard would even return his
call; maybe that wasn't even the case. What was he expecting
from the star, really? Financial backing? Hosannas and cama-
raderie? How could he benefit from pimping Kiv? By becoming
Richard's friend? (The pseudo-friendship of a dealer.) Maybe

his needs were that simple. Where was the rule that said he couldn't be Richard Dreyfuss's friend?

"Hi, my name is Troy Capra. I met Richard at a play . . ."

"Troy?" asked the astonished voice on the phone. "It's Betsey—Blankenberg!"

"Jesus! Betsey? How *are* you?"

"I'm *great*! How are *you*?"

"Fantastic!"

"This is *so funny*."

"I didn't know you—you work for Richard?"

"No, I'm *stalking* him. I break in every few weeks and answer the phones."

"For how long?"

"Oh God. I've worked for Richard four *years* now."

"It is *such* a small world."

"He *told* me he ran into you—he said he saw someone from Beverly."

"He couldn't have remembered—"

"He barely remembered *me* and we went *out* together!"

"I didn't know that! But *how*? He was gone by the time we—"

"*Way* after I graduated. Long, boring story."

"So you just *work* for him now."

"What can I say, I like the bastard."

"Well, that's fantastic. Are you married?"

"Divorced with children. You?"

"No way."

"Tell me what you've been *doing*, Troy Donahue—with your *life*."

"I'm still directing theater—"

"I *knew* that—I mean, you've been doing that for *years*. But I don't see plays anymore, unless I'm in New York. Even then, I'm not really a big—*I'm so ashamed!*"

"I do stuff all the time, you should really come."

"I'd love to *see* you."

"Tell me when. But the reason I was calling was . . . Richard and I met at this Ibsen play and we talked about getting together—"

"Let's see . . . he was supposed to be back on Saturday but now he has to go to Dublin, for a *wake* if you can believe it. He *should* be home the fourteenth, but I know he'll be crazed that first week."

"Can we pencil something in for the twenty-first?"

"Uh huh. Will he know what this is about?"

"Uhm, yeah. When we talked, he asked—"

"That sounded horrible, didn't it? What I meant was, if there's an agenda, sometimes it's good that I know so I can remind him—who knows *what* manner of jet-lag we'll be dealing with."

"*Adventures in the Skin Trade*—the performance piece I'm working on."

"*Great title.*"

"I'm just about done and—"

"Super! You know, you guys should really *do* something together, Richard *loves* the theater. He's doing *Medea,* in La Jolla—"

"He mentioned that."

"With Des McAnuff. It's going to be *so wild—Medea* meets *Sunset Boulevard.*"

"Set in Hollywood?"

"It's called *Medea Madness*. Medea marries this great director. When his movie goes in the toilet, he leaves her for this Sherry Lansing–type—and you know what happens *next*!"

"Sounds intense."

"Practically the whole second act is a murder trial—it's, like, this great *commentary*."

"Have they found someone for Medea?"

"That's what's so great: Des reversed all the roles. *Richard* is Medea!"

"You're kidding."

"Isn't that fantastic?"

Bernie Ribkin

Sitting on the deck chair in his Polo shorts, mezuzah sweating in the snow of chest hairs like a tiny gold traffic light, the producer scanned the printout:

CAR HAS NO REVERSE GEARS. DIS ASSEMBLE SELECTOR SHAFT MECH FROM INSIDE CAR. INSPECT SHAFT AND FORKS OPERATION, R&R GEAR BOX TO REP REVERSE LEVER AND SLIPPER PAD, CH SHAFT POS & GEAR FOR DAMAGE AND OPERATION ADJ REVERSE PLUNGER-BLEED HYDRULICS.

REAR BRAKE LIGHT IS OUT. REPLACE R/STOP LIGHT BULB

WASHERS ARE NOT WORKING. PARTIALLY REMOVE WASHER RES TO CK FOR KINKED TUBE, CLEAR JETS AND ADJ SPRAY

He glanced from the mechanical litany to the ocean—a gorgeous day in the Colony. No one wrote about the fabled enclave anymore, at least not like they used to. The place really used to get the hype. To this sandy Eden, Oberon Mall had come home.

The beachhead was stormed: squadrons of physicians rallied by Rear Admiral Trott, round-the-clock nurses, major and minor domos, ensigns and assholes, commodores, captains and petty officers first class; guerrillas and partisans; shock troops, domestic and culinary; nutrition and therapy corps; cadres physical, emotional and respiratory; voice coaches and snipers, channelers and chanters, WACS and wackos, dune-crawlers, bush-fighters, gossip-mongers and mercenaries; engineers of kitchen, pets, pool and bath; astrologists and masseurs, mediators and meditators and just plain groupies; paraplegic cheerleaders (a sexy stuntgirl among them) and sundry tear-streaked Big Star pre-approved dropovers. Visiting Oberon Mall had become anecdotally correct.

All this against the ceaseless crashing of waves. Bernie thought that was probably calming to the Big Star, in the amniotic sense. It was to him, anyway—he never slept this well in town. The air, the mood, the everything was better. He even cut back on Halcion. Edie invited him to stay in a guest room for long weekends. Edie was in love: so be it.

CK FOR EXHAUST NOISES. REPLACE STUDS FOR BOTH EXHAUST SECURING CLAMPS W/DAMAGED THREDS, REPLACE MUFFLER CENTER MOUNT

CUSTOMER REQUESTS THE "ROYAL CROWN" SERVIC. PERFORM SERVICE AS REQUESTED

THANK YOU FOR ALLOWING US TO SERVICE YOUR VEHICLE

The producer anchored the Rover printout with a gin glass, squinted over the water and stood. He set out with his huaraches and Dunhill, a crusty pioneer.

Gulls hung in the wind like mobiles. The old man walked barefoot to the water, sand warm as memory. A sweet, unclassifiable scent cudgeled his being. The scent became a feeling, the feeling an image: a Baltimore yard, nineteen thirty-two. White-hot and wickedly bright. He was seven years old, younger than his rich first cousins, whose house looked like a bank—the property took up a full city block. Aunt Janine built them a two-story playhouse that rivaled the apartment Bernie and his mother lived in downtown. June hated her sister for that. The boy had only visited a handful of times; this would be his last, during a short period when the feuding sisters attempted rapprochement. (Their animosities sprang from money, of course. Janine wouldn't give them any.) The aunt, in black taffeta and pink parasol, served cookies and cider and he remembered with a shudder June's embarrassment when she called from the sidewalk for him to come, Bernie clinging catastrophically to Janine's traumatic skirts, miserable and blind, cousins laughing at first, then queerly gawking as a servant pinched the boy's neck to get him off, like a crazed, distraught pet. Poverty didn't become him, even then.

What would he do with Edith-Esther Gershon? he pondered, luxuriously rhetorical, even jaunty, amused and heartened by the strange and generally positive turn of events, for it wasn't *a bad* thing that she loved him, no love could ever be, even if—He sidestepped a frothy, impetuous little wave that rushed at him with the pep of a Pekingese. As Bernie bent to scoop a sodden card, a cantering Labrador spattered the cuffs of his shorts.

THE ARTISTS RIGHTS FOUNDAT
DIST GUISHED BENEFAC S

J. PA L GETTY, KBE

TEVEN PIELBERG

USTAINING FOUNDERS

ENNETH BRA AGH	*SYDNEY POL*
AMES & LINDA BU ROWS	*IRWIN WINK*
ORMAN JEWISO	*WRITER GUI, WEST, IN.*
RBARA & GARR MARSHALL FA LY FOUNDATION	*BUD YORKIN*

Just then, three shirtless, wiseass men were upon him.

"Hey! Aren't you Donny Ribkin's father?"

Bernie blinked. "I certainly am."

"Pierre Rubidoux. We met at the bar in the Peninsula." The tall blond extended a hand. "Showtime."

"My watering hole," said the old man. "I hope I was civil."

Pierre introduced the others, whose names the producer didn't catch. The bald one had a massive shoulder tattoo; the other was around six-five, with a half-dozen studs in each ear. He was smoking a joint. Bernie tucked the bottleless *Artists Rights* message into a pocket.

"Your son's a helluv'n agent," said Pierre. The bald one belched, then laughed indiscriminately.

"Taught him everything I don't know. Say, you and Donny didn't go to school together, did you?"

"No, we didn't."

"He grew up with a Rubidoux—Jesus, I think it might have been a Pierre!"

"I know two other Pierre Rubidouxes. We get each other's mail."

"The mother was Clara," he said, irresolute. "You're not related?"

"Not that I know of. Were they from Toronto?"

Bernie shrugged and turned to the others. "Are you fellas also with Showtime?"

"We were, but now we're homeless," said the bald one.

"Now," said the giant one, "we're PWAs."

"Forgive my slightly fucked up friends," said Pierre.

The bald one began to sing. *"We had fun, fun, fun till my daddy took our T cells away!"*

The giant exploded with laughter, then lit out after a Frisbee. The bald one overtook him but the Lab got there first.

"Do you live out here, Bernie?"

"No, I'm visiting with a friend," he said, resisting the urge to name-drop. "But I'd *like* to—certainly on a day like today." The others rejoined them, tailed by the foaming Frisbee-mouthed dog.

"Bernie produced all those *Undead* flix," Pierre called out. *"The Waking Dead, The Walking Dead—"*

"The Mister Ed . . ." said the giant.

"I *loved* those movies," said the bald one, circling back as the giant waded into the tiny swells.

The producer repositioned his extinct corona. "We had lots of fun."

"You know," said the bald one to Pierre, "you guys should remake those."

"Love to do it for ya," Bernie said.

Pierre scrunched his face. "They *did* that already—with those rock 'n' roll zombie pictures."

"That was, like, fifteen *years* ago," said the bald one. Bernie was starting to like this guy.

"What do you *care,* Mr. Showtime?" said the giant. "Those were *bullshit.*"

"Maybe," said Pierre.

"It'd be fucking *fantastic*," spat the bald one, all marijuana breath and missionary zeal. The giant tore Frisbee from muzzle and threw it to sea. "Man, we fucking *loved* that shit. We used to go to midnight shows in Westwood—"

"At the Plaza," said Pierre, warming to the concept.

"The days of Lew Alcindor."

"Lew! Lew! Lew!"

"Who owns them now?" asked Pierre, donning his business affairs hat.

Bernie got a pang of heartburn. "Me, myself and I," he said, rotating the cigar on the marbly mucous membrane of his mouth.

"No shit," said the giant, indifferently.

"Didja make a bundle, Bernie?"

"I did fair-thee well, fair-thee well."

"I'll bet. Donny Ribkin wasn't the son of no slouch."

"How do you know Donny again?" asked the proud father.

"I was at ICM five years."

"Well," said Bernie, "it was nice meeting you boys." Better not to pal around too long.

"Call me, at Showtime." They shook hands while the others peeled off without saying goodbye. "I can rent those, right? *The Undead*—"

"Sure can. Blockbuster has 'em. You can get 'em anyplace."

"Vaya con Dios," said Pierre, flashing a peace sign.

"Don't you mean *Viacom*?" he bantered. The executive laughed, then ran ahead.

Bernie dreamed this and the dream had been delivered, lapping at his feet like so much mother-of-pearl. That was the omen. To hell with the Studio Shuffle, he would sell *The Undead* cycle to Showtime without lifting a finger: the world was still magical, vivid, ultramarine. The world still held treasures for the likes of Bernard Samuel Ribkin—now hopping wood steps, scrubbing sand from ungainly feet, the fragile, knobby creepers of a courtly old player who'd seen a few things. He was hungry and wondered about dinner. Then a shiver of the abstract washed over him, and for an instant the mysterious seaboard of his destiny was illumined; but Edie's second-story shout reeled him back to mundane shores and he lost what had been seen as quickly as the thread of a reverie.

"Old Man and the Sea!" she cried, leaning from the window of her room, smiling like there was no tomorrow. "Old Man and the Sea, do you love me?"

Zev Turtletaub

Taj sat in the bath and visualized the article from that day's *Reporter*, a front-page piece about the Turtletaub Company's "hefty slate": a musical remake of a Spencer Tracy movie called *Dante's Inferno*, planned for Broadway; two films already in the

can and soon to be released—a Robert Redford and a Martha
Coolidge; *All Mimsy,* a sequel to *Mimsy,* a spin-off of the hugely
successful *Jabberwocky* chronicles; an unnamed Holocaust
project with Richard Dreyfuss, plus the potential filming of
a yet-to-be-announced Dreyfuss stage vehicle; an upcoming
feature to be written and directed by David Mamet, with songs
by Mamet and Sondheim; *Middlemarch,* to be adapted by A.
S. Byatt and directed by Stephen Frears; three bestsellers—a
romance, a policier (for Dustin Hoffman) and a dysfunction-
al-family drama—in active development; an animated film of
a tale from the Brothers Grimm by the director of *A Nightmare
Before Christmas;* a remake of *The Four Hundred Blows,* directed
by David Koepp, the *Jurassic Park* scribe; *Charlotte's Web,*
by the *Jabberwocky* writers; an unnamed story by Poe to be
helmed by actor Anthony Hopkins; a remake of Pasolini's
Teorema (with producer Phylliss Wolfe attached, Turtletaub
serving as exec producer); and a teaser about *Uncle Wiggly in
Connecticut* that vaguely implied J. D. Salinger might possibly
have agreed to expand and adapt his original story. This, of
course, was untrue. To his utter dismay and delight, the name
Taj Wiedlin had been invoked as "associate producer" in the
very last paragraph of page seven in connection with a "fast
track" adaptation of Nikolai Gogol's *Dead Souls,* for which no
writer or star had been set. Mr. Turtletaub called it "a priority
project, a labor of love."

The guest-house tub was empty. Taj wore a mask and
gag, his wrists and ankles tied with leather. He could hear the
voices of the party outside. The associate producer laughed
through the gag as he imagined his mother stumbling in to
find the toilet. She'd been visiting from Chicago and had only
just left to see his sister, in Walnut Creek. He took her to

City Walk and Rodeo Drive and the Ivy; Cybill Shepherd and
Sarah Jessica Parker were there, but not together. His mother
didn't like the way Taj was looking. He was too thin, she said,
too "drawn." They bought a ton of groceries at Gooch's and
she packed them away while he sat at the kitchen table and
smiled. When she asked if he was having "girl trouble," his
mind kinked up like a hose—for two seconds he thought she
was hip to his errant faggotry. When Taj realized her earnest-
ness he laughed so hard that if he screamed, he was certain
the frequency would shatter her heart. Yes, he vamped, he had
fallen in love but the girl wouldn't love him back. *Then it wasn't
meant to be. Do I not know my son?*

He was cold. He went over the details of the *Reporter* article again. There it was on the mindscreen—Whole Document,
Cursor here, Cursor there, Pg Up, Pg Dn—and it warmed him.
What he really needed was a tape of *Dante's Inferno;* as yet,
Taj had only read a précis in *TimeOut*'s movie guide. Spencer
Tracy played a "ruthless manipulator" who opened a carnival
featuring the eponymous ride. The nineteen thirty-five film
was supposed to have a spectacular "vision of hell" sequence
that was technically ahead of its time. It was all so drolly
ironic—in college, *The Divine Comedy* happened to be Taj's
favorite book; he even learned Italian to apprehend its beauty.

More voices outside as the party grew. Taj shivered. He
thought about the Harvard years and hummed a little dog-
gerel. Then it came back, inexorably. On the outskirts of Hell,
the poets heard lamentations. Virgil tells him,

> . . . *Questo misero modo*
> *tegnon l'anime triste di coloro*
> *che visser sanza 'nfamia e sanza lodo.*

"Such is the miserable condition of the sorry souls of those who lived without infamy and without praise." In that snowy collegiate world—the dormitory of his own soul—Taj already heard his voice rise up unaccomplished to take its place in the infernal suburbs, a sad tenor among the meritless Dead, their complement unworthy of Hades proper.

A door opened. Voices. Men laughing. Splash of a Hockneyesque dive. Taj prepared to bolt—he hadn't agreed to this. If Zev was accompanied, the associate producer would thrash and bloody himself, make a ruckus . . . The door closed, separating them from the sounds of the world. Zev was alone. He made a few calls, but Taj couldn't hear. He hung up, rummaging in a drawer before coming to the bath. He smoked a cigar. His breathing was heavy, labored. The producer sat on the toilet and defecated. The air grew musty and fetid. Zev puttered in the other room, casually talking on the phone again. He came and stood over him, breathing calmer. Taj felt the mouth at his groin like a fish feeding on aquarium bottom. Then, mouth skirted nipple: hovered over belly while a stertorous groan scared Taj half to death: and gilded him with throw-up. The producer regurgitated a warm rhythmical hail of egesta that put the rookie in mind of Jeff Goldblum in *The Fly.* Zev finally off his knees, washing at the sink. Cigar relit. Dreamy party voices through the door as he leaves, locking it.

Taj shifted in the puky tub; he would endure. Tomorrow, the rewards would come—Prada jacket from Maxfield's, vintage Rolex from Second Time Around, thousand-dollar gift certificate from Burke Williams—he was generous like that. Maybe Zev would bring him along next weekend when he sailed to Catalina with Dustin and the kids. Such a gift was precious and intangible, an investment in the great career unknown.

Taj Wiedlin, Associate Producer.

This was his time. He would live it with infamy and with praise.

Chet Stoddard

The dentist and his wife finally took the viatical plunge. When Horvitz brought the cashier's check to Philip, the dying costume designer, Chet went along.

The bungalow on Cynthia Street had a Grecian façade. An Abyssinian slept through its sunny sentinel. Ryan, Philip's roommate, showed them in. The house was clean and bare, low-budget minimalist: in the living room were a few Noguchi lamps, a tulip in a tall vase and the requisite Mapplethorpe photo book. It sat on a low boomerang table like a stage prop.

Philip lay in a hospital bed, neck craned back, eyes closed, mustachy open mouth. A male nurse smiled at the visitors, lowering the volume of "The Flying Dutchman." *The closest he'll get to Greece,* Chet thought, *is inside a fucking urn.* The lids fluttered and Philip coughed. Totally blind? Ryan handed him a glass, guiding the straw to his mouth.

"I knew you were awake," said the roommate. "He always pretends to sleep."

"The Great Pretender," Philip muttered, clearing his throat while lifting himself up on sharp elbows.

"Stu and Chet are here," Ryan said, pitched a little louder. "Looks like you won the lotto."

Philip smiled broadly. Horvitz asked how he was doing. The lucky policy-seller coughed while Ryan answered for him.

"Not so good."

"Not so good," Philip echoed rheumily.

"Yesterday was better."

He closed his eyes as the roiling clouds of a coughing jag loomed, then passed, chased by merciful winds. "Yesterday was *definitely* better." Cued by Ryan, the others laughed. "As David Bailey said"—eyes opening again—"there is nothing uglier than the sight of four men in a car. Well. Maybe four men with Kaposi in a car."

"Forgive him," said Ryan, with mocking affection. "He slips in and out of dementia."

"Why, pastor! You *must* try Dementia, the new altar boy— I've been slipping in and out all day! It's *heaven*."

"Now listen, my son—"

They went on like that until more cough clouds overtook their cabaret. "He might have pneumonia," said Ryan, sotto voce. The elder viatical rep took this opportunity to remove an envelope from his attaché case. Upon Philip's convulsive recovery, the roommate placed it in hand.

"Mr. Horvitz brought us a little check."

"Checks and balances," said Philip, with that mustache smile; it made Chet forlorn. He fingered the paper. "Well, this is glorious. We must call the limousine company, at once."

"When do you leave on your voyage?" asked Horvitz.

"Friday," said the roommate, somewhat skeptically.

"Will you manage?" Chet thought his boss's grave, stagy modulation had belied the euphemism.

"Better believe we'll manage," said the plucky invalid.

"Big boys don't die," Ryan said.

"And white men don't jump—but boy, do they Gump."

"So wish Jason and his Argonaut well."

*

Just before dessert, Aubrey Turtletaub took a fistful of pills from a Kleenex. She pressed each to her lips as if to divine a code word before letting it pass—admitting them one by one, with slow, steady intimacy while Chet confessed. Well, half confessed, because there was no way he was going to discuss his short-lived career as a rising viatical settlement advocate.

He said that a Narcotics Anonymous buddy told him about her party—Chet knew it was for positives only, but hadn't been deterred. Aubrey smiled mordantly and called him a "singles night bottom-feeder." Shamefaced, he apologized for misleading her on his HIV status. It's just that he got so flustered when she asked, *How long have you known?*

"How many years did you say you've been sober?"

"Four. Going on five." That was the truth.

"People tend to get squirrely around that fifth chip," she said. "I know I did."

"I still feel like a jerk."

"You just didn't want to disappoint."

"Maybe. It gets a little twisted. You did dazzle me, though—I guess that was part of it."

Aubrey smiled; she liked that. "Sure you're not one of *those?*"

"What do you mean?"

"Oh, there was a chick who hung around forever—we finally had to tell her to fuck off. She was *desperate* to test positive, had no *life.* A huge chick—five-two, two-fifty. She was a *wall.* Her old man taught jumping. Parachuting. He was pretty strange himself. She started taking his AZT when he died. I mean before, *before* he died! She was always asking people for their Zovirax, so we finally said, *Here, bitch!* Everyone has shit-loads of Zovirax. And she's *still* testing negative—although I heard she was pregnant by some hemophiliac, so maybe she'll get her wish. I know I sound terrible, but there's for sure some fucked up people in the world."

Chet eyed the last of the pills. "They *do* look sort of appetizing. Mind if I—"

"Go right ahead," she said, without missing a beat. "This one'll put hair on your liver."

On the way back to Oakhurst, they drove to Roxbury Park. He'd been to AA clubhouse meetings there. Aubrey pointed to an apartment building with a Frank Gehry penthouse floating above the trees like a tiled post-modern elysium. Chet never noticed it. They walked in the darkness and sat on a bench in front of the lawn where retirees did their Sunday-bowling.

"I was married. He was a lawyer. We weren't rich, but he did okay. You know, the Tom Hayden type, public-interest. We tried having kids, for six years—nothing. That turned out to be a good thing, though, I guess. It ended. He has two now, boy and a girl. Then I met this guy through my brother. I wasn't really looking. My brother works in film, does *rather* well. Anyway, this guy was an editor and I wound up apprenticing. It felt good. I never really had a vocation—God, that sounds dumb! 'Vocation.' White-trashy. But I *liked* editing. That sounds dumb too, I know. I guess what I *really* liked was the idea of cutting something together, having to make *sense* of something, be in that kind of control. *Some* kind of control. I decided I was going to 'edit' my life. Hey, why not? Naturally, I fell in love with the man who was teaching me. Women are like that." She laughed. "Jake—the editor, that was his name—he was a sweet man and I was needy, to put it mildly. Sexually, I was *starved*. Not to mention emotionally. I mean, at this point if it wasn't for the fertility stuff—having a kid became an *obsession*—I don't think my husband (the lawyer) would have ever *touched* me. And most of the ways we tried, he didn't *have* to! I mean, it was bad. I got pretty out there for a while. Anyway, we divorced. I got pregnant right away with Jake—of course, right? He was *ecstatic*—I mean, Jake was. Am I confusing you? I look back and . . . Jake used to sweat at night, I mean sweat a *lot*. I thought it was just the sex—he was *so* attracted to me. There was never a question about that . . . and I just wasn't thinking in any other terms. This was a good, gentle man. Never used drugs. Zephyr was negative—that's our son—so *something* went right. Jake got sick a few months after Zeph was born. Six months later, he died. Wanna see something?"

Aubrey searched her pocketbook while the wind gusted the trees outside the designer aerie. She stuck a snapshot in his hand.

"Isn't he beautiful?"

"I saw him at the party."

"That's my Zephyr."

"Beautiful boy."

"My American Zephyr—we named him after a train, you know."

*

When Chet got home, there was a message from Horvitz. He turned off the machine; he would listen in the morning. Then he'd call and quit—death takes a holiday. He fell fast asleep and dreamed Aubrey was a guest on the old talk show. The theme was "People Who Have Recovered from AIDS."

Troy Capra

Troy got a curious phone call from Quinn, the gaffer.

They'd worked together on scores of X-rated productions and Troy planned to use him for lighting on *Skin Trade*. An occasional performer, Quinn saw most of his action off-camera—as a bisexual pretending to be straight, he was a crossover hit.

Quinn was eager to talk about a recent "scene" with Moe Truss kopf, the well-known celebrity manager. They had been joined by Trusskopf's beau, a studly stud and nicely knight with the moniker of Lancelot who happened, in actuality, to be none other than the famous Rod Whalen. Ring a bell? Troy blinked, trying to place the name. Quinn reminded him of the young dancer in *Guys and Dolls* who gave him his big directing break.

"Jesus, how do you even remember that kid?"

"You told me about him. I became a fan of his work. You forget I'm an aficionado."

"I thought he'd be long dead."

"Just long."

"How did my name come up?"

"I made the connection. You know, I never forget a pretty face—especially one I've sat on."

"Don't start talking like a queen. Please, Quinn, not you."

"Listen, I got this idea, right? You have a copy of that, don't you?"

"A copy of what."

"Your first film! Come on, Troy, I *know* you."

"I may have it somewhere."

"You *have* it, Troy. What was it called?"

"*Up in Adam.*"

"*Up in Adam!* Right! Okay, here's what's happening: Trusskopf *really* wants to see it—he's like, been *looking* for it, right? He's *burning*, he would *kill* for a copy. And the kid is, like, game. I said I'd talk to you and arrange a little screening."

"At the Directors Guild. Have it catered."

"You should *do* it, Troy. They're having a party Sunday. We should go over with the tape."

"*You* go over."

"This could be good for you, Troy."

"Yeah. I can have a scene with Moe and Curly."

"Moe Trusskopf's a *heavy*, okay? And he's *smart*, Troy, he'd *like* you. You'll like *him*. The movie's just an entrée."

"And your dick's the aperitif."

"You want to do *Skin Trade*, don't you? I mean, you want to exploit it, right? To be in that position once it's done? Just get into a *conversation* with him, Troy, and tell him what your plans are, right? Or *whatever.* You don't know where this shit leads, he could fucking *sign* you. Tell him all your theatrical bullshit, he's *from* that world. And he *knows* all those guys, he knows *everybody,* right? I'm telling you, man, you should do it."

*

On Sunday afternoon, Troy and Kiv looked at houses. That was her idea, because with the expense of the coming show, there'd barely be money for rent let alone four-point-four million for a shanty in the Bel Air hills. It was only practice, Kiv said—she wanted to know what it felt like to be a "lady of the Pantheon." Besides, convincing the realtor she was "a nouveau" was a good acting exercise. Driving through the West Gate in his near-jalopy of a Mercedes, Troy felt uneasy. He already had a pretend life.

She was starting to nest (that's what the house-hunting game was all about) and Troy wasn't happy. Kiv slept in his bed most every night now. She sipped morning cappuccinos and went on about sofas and ottomans, trying to impress with her thrifty, no-nonsense ways. She called him honey a lot and stroked his head as she stared into space, theorizing about drapes—muslin or parachute?—then off she'd go to a hard-core shoot. It was everything Chet tried to avoid, to shun, to cast off: the pornographic Middle Class. Soon they'd be on Sally Jessy Raphaël with the other porn couples, expounding on the Lifestyle, sugary and witless.

His muffler echoed through the streets like the canned laughter of an old *Beverly Hillbillies*. He made the mistake of idly recounting his conversation with Quinn, and Kiv was all over it. Quinn was right, he'd be stupid not to "play along for the connections"—she wanted to go to the party too. By the time the realtor hove into view, grinning like a moron beside her billion-dollar BMW, they had almost come to blows.

Champagne wishes and caviar dreams! The woman smelled a fish but kept a stiff upper lip throughout the tour. The house, former residence of John Huston, George Harrison, George Hamilton and Roger Moore, recently rented to Tom Arnold for thirty-five thousand a month. Their guide proffered a lavish binder stuffed with magazine profiles. Not a room had been spared the photographer's lens—the master bath itself lovingly showcased in Diane von Furstenberg's big book of celebrity loos. A guest house sprang from the villa's cunningly designed gardens like a hallucination, stupendous enough to briefly lift Troy's grim, vindictive spirits. It looked like a

gargantuan Roman column snapped off at the center. The thing
even had windows. The realtor called it a "folly," the replica of
a house that stood in a forest outside Paris; the owner made
the commission after seeing a photo in *Architectural Digest*.
As Troy approached the surreal structure, Kiv's hickish oohs
and ahhs broke the quixotic spell. With great annoyance, he
walked to the car and waited.

"Feel better now?" he asked, venomously. They were back
in the car, rattling down the hill. "Feel *rich*?"

"Fuck you!" Kiv started to weep. A minute later, coasting
round a turn, she told him she was pregnant.

"Oh shit," he said, pulling over to a fiftyish woman selling
maps to stars' homes. The vendor made a move, then held her
ground.

"I'm *having* this baby, Troy!" she sobbed. "I've had *too*
many abortions, I can't *do* that anymore. Troy, I *love* you—"

As they reached Sunset, he thought of jumping ship—
making a mad dash, but where would he run? Back to the
folly, to be swallowed by the rabbit hole. There had to be a
rabbit hole—

"We can be so *happy*, Troy! So happy . . ."

He laughed and Kiv shot from the car, storming across the
Boulevard in a haze of tears, beating him to it. It was just like
a movie, except there wasn't a pile-up in her wake. And—the
movies again—Troy gave chase.

Bernie Ribkin

Edie was a big creature who bellowed when they made love.

It was strange, but something about her, something
chalky and carnal, took him back to those whitewashed yards
of Baltimore. His cousins' faces floated up as he rode the pale,

doughy, mole-flecked country of her flesh, smelled the cooking of ancient neighborhoods in her hair, saw dreary storefronts in the bone beneath her breast. Under her arms were trolleys and hydrants; nipples conjured washtubs and linoleum; her long, flat fingernails, the dirty birds of a public park. Her face, during the act, looked stylized and anguished. She was like a powerful wrestler, scissoring the air with broad, indefeasible strokes. Her eyes were the deepest brown he'd ever seen, and when he looked within, Bernie saw himself as a boy standing tentatively in a sawdust-strewn saloon out of *The Iceman Cometh,* heard the chink of billiard balls until they shooed him away, running home through wind that tore open his cheeks; had only to smell the gray-white hair at Edie's temples to summon tracts of sidewalk, *his* sidewalks, their spidery cracks, graffiti and Crayola'd arabesques evoked by a whiff from the tough, translucent seashell of her ear—had only to nuzzle an eyebrow to step on the burnt-yellow lawn of the downtown house where he once lived. Edie's teeth were bad (the warped and splintered sun chairs of the falling-down porch where his mother waited) but the breath was always fresh.

How did they banter, Bernie and his new girl, when in bed? Something like this:

"That was lovely. Thank you."

"You're a very strong girl."

"You're a very strong man."

"Are you Polish somewhere in there?"

"In where?"

"In there. Somewhere."

"I am *not.* No, no, I don't think so, no."

"You look a little that way. Jesus H, I schvitz with you. Lemme get a towel. I'm schvitzing like I got stuck."

"A big patch of hair."

"I'm the stuck-er and you're the stuck-ee."

"Did you know you have a big patch of hair on your back?"

"I'm the Cabbage Patch Kid."

"Right there, Bern. It's very funny and sweet."

"So I've been told."

"Oh? Who told you? I don't like that, Bern."

"It's from the skin graft."

"Mister Liar. You didn't have any skin graft. Bullshitter. And who told you you had a sweet funny patch?"

" 'Cause I'm part Apache. Didn't you know I was part Apache?"

"Don't make me dislike you."

*

Out at the beach, Bernie felt the years drop off. He kept his own room ("for propriety," Edie said) but didn't think that would be for long. It wasn't like they weren't of age, for Jesus H. Soon they would shack up properly—for all he knew, next week they'd be honeymooners. The more things change, the more things change, just like they say. He'd never balled a schizophrenic before. He kept waiting for her to tell him Janet Reno was sending radio signals to her tits, but it never happened. Never even had the decency to crap in her panty hose. The only evidence of malady was a few fat bottles of pills in the medicine cabinet and the occasional puzzling affect. He'd lived with far worse.

Edie wasn't beautiful but it didn't embarrass him to be with her, either. He was no Larry King, he laughed to himself, and that said a lot right there. They didn't socialize too much, anyway, confined for the most part to the paralytic duchy of fallen Big Star daughter. Until he found Edie, the producer hadn't realized how tired he was. He was through hunting and gathering. What had it ever gotten him? Edie had money and twisted Tinseltown tenure—if this was the end of the line, he'd rise to the challenge. They would marry and attend galas, photographed for glossy Westside society pages, at table with Roddy McDowall, Sybil Brand, the Robert Stacks, and Mr. Blackwell. May we present . . . Bernard and Edie Gershon-Ribkin.

He stepped from the bright, claustrophobic elevator and stood in the hall, unable to move.

Someone sat by his door. It was sinister because the bulb above had been unscrewed.

"May . . . may I help you?"

As Bernie edged toward him, the man gripped knees to chest and began to sing. "*Papa, can you see me?*"

"Donny?"

"*Papa, can you hear me?*"—High camp, from the lower depths.

"What's the matter with you?"

His son looked wild-eyed and spent—as if, lashed to the prow, he'd survived an epic storm only to become transcendently unhinged.

"Donny, what *happened*—"

Was he drunk? The agent held out some smallish books, strung together by a schoolboy's cord, and laid the leathery bouquet at his father's door, smug as a toastmaster. "Returned from whenth they came," he said, lisping. Or some such nonsense. Then Donny drew forward and Bernie met the hairraising eye. His progeny stank—the interregnum smell of a soul dethroned and demonized. Bernie shook, though staring at this boy, his own, he felt nothing; as in a morbid children's story, he was man become a tree, bosky fingers avulsed and outspread, evicted legs a quivering snarl of loamy, snaky roots. As Donny swept past, the old man felt the waft of kingly cape, the regicidal blow.

The agent entered the lift and Bernie waited for the doors to close. (If only they could be sealed forever, the box thrown into space like a tomb.) He picked up the strap, reindeer of books attached, and went to his room. There he remained for a number of days, oblivious to even his gigantic lover, who fussed over his general health and prayed for his restoration to the world.

Zev Turtletaub

Zev and Phylliss Wolfe went to see Donny at the Westwood Hospital. That's where she'd been for *her* breakdown. Phylliss hugged the nurses and the inevitable "old home week" comment was made. Zev joked that it was more a "busman's holiday" for him.

Donny was drugged and uncommunicative. Phylliss's Joan Rivers routine and Zev's dealmaker gossip fell flat. When the agent became accustomed to their presence, he made a few shy, touching efforts at normalcy. They talked about buying art, then Donny resurrected an old piece of business about *All Mimsy*—something handled weeks before. Phylliss prattled about the beloved canine getting the power table at Mortons and the agent loosened up. It was smooth sailing until Donny said he possessed the name of the man who was the architect of the race war that would bring down ICM, leaving the city in shambles. "Dresden will look like a brushfire." He took a crumpled get-well card from his pocket and unfolded it. On the cover was a "Far Side" style drawing of a priest, saying, "I am here to administer your 'last rights.' " Inside was a list: the right to remain in bed, the right to moan and complain, the right to get well. "So get well, all right?" A small window shade of paper was pasted on the blank side, opposite. Underneath was a handwritten inscription: "You so crazy!" Zev lifted the flap, uncovering a photo of Donny's mother clipped from a society magazine. There was a crudely drawn devil, its red-pencil cock invading Serena's mouth. The card was unsigned.

*

"What was *that* all about?" asked Phylliss as they drove to the studio.

"I'm not sure."

"Did you *see* that? Oh my God, who would have sent it?"

"Probably Rubidoux. Though it's hard to believe he'd be that vindictive."

"Ruby who?"

"Pierre Rubidoux. He used to work at ICM, above Donny. I think he represented Oberon for a while."

"Where is he now?"

"Showtime. Does very well."

"What happened?"

"Donny's Mozart and Rubidoux is Salieri. They grew up together, went to school at El Rodeo. Donny was the popular one. The girls were always after him, loved by all the teachers—you know Donny. Pierre was a rich kid, a techie. A fine mind, but people weren't drawn to him. They had this life-long entanglement. You know, Donny came to ICM *later*. Of course, Rubidoux had to leave when his old nemesis became the superstar—El Rodeo all over again. Donny isn't blameless; it takes two to tango. He told me the whole story once and the details, the *dovetailing,* are exceedingly weird. It's an SM folie à deux, a bad *Night Gallery.*"

"Were there *good Night Gallerys?*"

"Oh, and you'll love *this:* Rubidoux's been married three times—"

"And they were all with Donny."

"*Before.* All three."

"Sounds like a homo thing."

"But this is the *best*—this is the part I want to make a movie of Rubidoux's mother was a sleepwalker. I think she was an epileptic. The husband would wake up in the middle of the night and have to go find her—by the pool, in the kitchen, whatever. One night, Bernie—Donny's father—is driving home. He turns a corner and there's this gorgeous woman walking down the center of the street, in a nightgown! He's got this funny little go-cart English car, a Mini-Cooper, and he slams on the brakes, but not in time. And he *hits* her—"

"Oh my God! She doesn't *die*—"

"Yes! Donny Ribkin's father killed Rubidoux's mother!"

"No!"

"I think that they were sleeping together. That was the implication—Donny's. Bernie was supposedly drunk. But they don't convict because—*newsflash!*—she was walking down the middle of the street at two in the morning and it was dark."

They pulled onto the Sony lot and rolled toward Joan Crawford's old bungalow. Phylliss was smiling in disbelief.

"Donny's father goes to see a shrink 'cause he can't get the image of this statuesque woman staring at him as he rolls over her out of his head. So here's how he 'cures' himself: he raises money and makes this cheap horror film called *The Undead*—"

"Donny's father *produced* that?"

"Yes!"

"*The Walking Dead?*—"

"Yes!"

"Zev, stop it! I do not believe this!"

"He makes *millions* off these movies filled with dead women walking in the middle of the road in their nightgowns! And in the first one—there's, like, three or four—the guy kills them by running over their heads with his little English car! Isn't it fantastic?"

Bernie Ribkin

The old man was nervous about the meeting. No reason to be, he told himself. Either Showtime wanted to make a deal or they didn't. He swallowed a few Halcions, just to take the edge off. Bernie wondered if he should have at least consulted an attorney. He didn't know any attorneys. There'd be time for that, after the offer. Think positive.

He sat in his den, watching the Range Rover off-road instruction cassette. The car had been trouble-free for a few weeks and Bernie figured it might be a good time to learn how to four-wheel. The guy on the tape looked like George Plimpton. When he came to a creek, he stepped from the car, measuring its depth with a branch. Then he forded— Rover'd—the stream, neat and civilized. The narrator mentioned a driving academy in Aspen where one could master off-road techniques "the rather exceptional way" before caravaning across the Continental Divide. That's what Bernie would do, when Showtime closed the deal. Spend a few weeks in Aspen, learning the art of rough-terrain navigation. Maybe work in a little romance—the rather exceptional way.

As he drove to the Burbank offices, Bernie distracted himself with the diaries. Had Donny found them under a mattress, or had they actually been willed? Serena would have her revenge. The pages chronicled his extramarital dalliances—and her touchingly improbable devotion to the Cantor Krohn, a love that grew unforeseen from platonic to unbridled and undone. The congregant's idyll was cut short when the hangdog producer announced his syphilis. Serena had by then passed the scourge to her lover and Krohn to his wife, who fled in turn to her parents in Queens. The Baritone of Beth-El followed, as did Serena in confused desperation—characters in a Preston Sturges nightmare. And that is where, delirious with guilt, the singer of psalms shot himself through the mouth (temple left intact). His colleagues had much success with a face-saving tale of subway homicide. Those were happier days, when a secret was still a secret.

*

Aside from Mr. Rubidoux, there were two others present—an inhouse lawyer named Fred, a fan of the *Undead* series who'd lingered after an unrelated meeting just to shake the semi-legendary schlock-meister's hand, and Denny, a shiny-faced boy of voting age who Bernie was shocked to learn was a Veepee. Everybody in town was a fuhcocktuh Veepee.

They kvetched about how the business had changed, and Bernie thought that mildly comical, as no one in the room looked over thirty-five. Nostrils dilating, Pierre rhapsodized about Donny Ribkin. When asked if they were close, Bernie lied—then got a twinge of paranoia. What if the exec decided to call the psychotic, vituperative agent just to shoot the bull about Dad? That didn't really seem to be an issue; in his current state, Bernie doubted his son would be at work, let alone returning calls. Another possibility was that Donny's condition might soon go public. Though there wasn't anything in the papers yet, Bernie had to admit the boy was bound to hurt someone, or himself, unless he found help—fast. He hoped that wouldn't happen. At least, not before a deal was in place.

"Bottom line: Showtime's willing to give you two and a half million for the rights. How does that sound, Bernie?"

The old man smiled, trying to be cool. The muscles around his mouth went into spasm and he coughed, to cover. All he'd expected was an option at a token amount. He was glad to have taken the pills.

"For all three pictures—" He coughed again.

"That is correct. But here's what we need: we need you to come on board, to produce this at a price."

"You've done this before and you've done it *well*," said Denny the Boy, self-assuredly.

"The more things change, the more things change," said Bernie. His Sinatra ring-a-ding mode.

Denny the Boy turned to Fred. "Who said that?"

"Travolta," said the Attorney. "*Look Who's Talking Too.*"

"What do you think, Bernie?"

Pierre bore in on him, shining the light of a batty grin.

"I think it's a beautiful thing," said Bernie, smooth as a Hillcrest *macher*. "You know, I was doing this when 'cable' was something you sent over the wire. What price are we talking?"

"A million-five, with an eighteen- to twenty-day shoot."

"For each?"

"We only want to make one. A kind of condensed version of the three."

A million-five and a twenty-day shoot. Sounded reasonable. Of course, he'd been out of the game awhile . . . but these men were professionals. They wouldn't be suggesting impossible numbers. Yet the two-and-a-half-million-dollar acquisition-of-rights fee didn't add up, in light of the budget. He asked Pierre to reiterate, and the executive said the money was an advance against distribution, foreign and domestic. That made sense, but Bernie didn't want to open his mouth too much. He'd sort it out with the lawyers.

"I don't think any of this is going to be a problem, gentlemen. I'm Bernie Ribkin. I like to make movies."

The sweet rustle of assent; then Pierre grew solemn, like a minister at a sticky theological crossroad. Fred and Denny stared at the floor. "Question, Bernie: do you think you could make it for *under* a million?"

Truth was, Bernie didn't know. "Pierre, tell me," began the scat and softshoe. "What kind of approach are you going to take? What I'm saying is, how do you . . . does Showtime have an idea how they might want to approach the property? With this material—"

"Maybe something like *Tales from the Crypt.* Classy, but not taking itself too seriously. Something that can be sexy, funny and gory, all in one."

"*Creepshow,*" said the Boy. "Remember that? Leslie Nielsen?"

"Did you know Ted Danson was in that?"

"And Adrienne Barbeau."

"Jesus," said Pierre. "What ever happened to her?"

"Hunger commercials with Sally Struthers."

"She had some *very* serious tits," said Fred the Attorney.

"Well, they're in Ethiopia now."

"Sally and Adrienne? Or the tits?"

"The tits stayed here. They just signed with Gersh."

"I think it's important to come up with a franchise-type narrator," Pierre said. "Someone like the Cryptkeeper to tie it all together—he'd be our link, our tentpole."

Bernie nodded. He'd seen *Tales* a few times and thought it was cute. "Okay," he said. "I got it. I got it. That's fun."

"Now, Bernie," said Pierre. "I want to ask you something point-blank. You don't even have to respond."

"I'm seventy-two years old."

"I was not going to ask your age," said a smiling Pierre.

"You look fucking *great*," said Fred. "Doesn't he?"

"I would never have guessed you to be seventy-two," said the Boy.

"I'll tell you my secret: I like to fuck. I don't fuck too well—but I fuck every day!"

The men laughed.

"Bernie—" Pierre began, "—and remember, you don't have to answer this *now*." He inhaled deeply. "Do you think you could make our little movie—at least submit a budget—for four hundred thousand? With a ten-day shoot? I mean, down and dirty."

How could he deliver a budget without a script? They used to shoot 'em in a week and a half, but that was thirty years ago—without unions or permits. If the movie took place in one location, maybe . . .

I'M LOSING YOU   263

"I don't know what four hundred thousand gets you, Pierre. And it depends on the script, we don't have a script! I need to do some investigations." He turned to Fred the Attorney and smiled cockily. "Four hundred thousand. Does that rent you a honey wagon these days?"

"Here's a hypothetical," said Pierre. "If you can do this show—because this is the way your two and a half million would be guaranteed *up front*—if you can do this show for a hundred thousand dollars, a three-day shoot, no frills, no bullshit, *bam bam bam*—"

"You're kidding. Are you kidding?"

"I'm not fucking kidding, Bernie. You would not be in this room if I was kidding."

"You mean like a video thing—"

"Feature film."

"It's just that—"

"A hundred thousand dollars, Bernie. Three days."

"Yes!" cried the Boy. "I *love* it. Come on, Bernie. They made *Clerks* for twenty-nine thousand and change. *El Mariachi* was made for *seven!*"

"I have to go," said Fred, ill at ease. Again he shook Bernie's hand. "I have an appointment."

The room shrank precipitously when he left. Bernie felt woozy and reprimanded himself for taking the Halcion. "Three days!" He rocked in his chair, sweating and grinning like a hooked grouper.

"It's definitely do-able," said the Boy. "We'll get you great people. Some killer kids. We'll get you the kids from *Kids*."

Pierre retreated to his desk. "If you put your mind to it, Bernie, if you work out the logistics, I'm convinced you can shoot this with a Steadicam in forty-eight hours."

"A one-day shoot would be the ultimate," added the Boy. "I'd like to make a string of these—a series—each shot in one day. Film-school style."

"Think about it. Any way you slice it, we have a deal. Congratulations! Cups of borscht and crackers all around. I'll have business affairs draw the papers and get you half your advance—one-point-two-five, you can buy a lotta kippers with that, Bernie—soon as I see a budget. Cut a check the same day. If you don't think you can do this, *be honest,* huh? Because I'm committed to this project and we'll have to find another way."

"I know it's rough," said the Boy, patting the producer's shoulder. "But every picture we do is like this. It's always a nightmare."

The old man stood and made his way to the door.

"Think it over, you scary old cocksucker," said Pierre, embracing him. "Mr. Piece of Shit Roadkill."

"A one-day shoot!" said the Boy, jumping around like the circus had come. "I love it!"

Chet Stoddard

IMMEDIATE CASH FOR THE TERMINALLY ILL

We are committed to advising terminally ill people who seek financial assistance by selling their life insurance policy.

The transaction is quick, easy and confidential. See new places, see old faces. Do something you've always wanted to do. Take care of business—or pleasure.

LIVING WELL IS THE BEST REVENGE

We know the effect of stress on the immune system and do everything we can to minimize your effort.

Generally, the viatical companies pay between 40%–80% of policy face amount, paid in a lump sum by wire transfer or bank check. The purchase price is based upon size of policy, cost of ongoing premiums, life expectancy, etc. and must meet the following criteria:

> 6 mo. to 4 year life expectancy

> Policy face value from $10,000 to $3,000,000 (lower/higher amounts are considered)

> Policy is beyond the contestability period of—

He sat in the outer office, scanning a ViatiCorps brochure. Horvitz appeared behind the girl at the desk, waving him back.

"I'm sorry you're leaving us, but I understand. It's not for everyone."

"And I thought show business was depressing."

"Thinking of giving the talkers another shot?"

"Too many out there right now."

"Every time I pick up *TV Guide*, there's a new one. Where do they find these people?" He took an envelope from a drawer, handing it to Chet. "Your paycheck and . . . a partial commission from the 'dentist' deal."

"I appreciate that, Stu."

"Not at all. Keep in touch. If you change your mind, the door is open."

"I'll call you."

"By the way, Phil Dagrom just died. The costume designer."

"I'm not surprised. I thought he was going to die while we were there."

"No, he got *much* better—after we gave him the money. Happens all the time: the pressure eases, spirits rise. They get *better*. And Ryan—the roommate?"

"What about him?"

Horvitz smiled like a maître d' with no more tables. "He ran off with the money."

"You're kidding."

"With a lover. They get on a plane to *Paris*."

"Oh Jesus."

"And poor Philip dies forty-eight hours later."

"Did you tell the dentist that?"

He closed his eyes and gently shook his head. Did Chet think he had no finesse? "I told the dentist Mr. Dagrom died in Crete, in his roommate's arms, while the sun went down on a ruin. Hey! Isn't that what Jackie O called it when she gave Onassis a blow job? Going down on a ruin?"

*

Aubrey was subdued. He was desperate to touch her, kiss her. The timing was bad, she said. She'd been to UCLA that day for tests. Something was funny with her eyes. They dilated the pupils and made her scan a grid—she was certain it was CMV. If the virus was confirmed, she'd have to take medicine each day through a shunt. She was forthright and even-tempered except when it came to Zephyr. She didn't want the boy to see her around the house with a fucking permanent tube in her arm.

I'M LOSING YOU 267

Chet laid her shaking body down. She wet his face with tears and sex, and searched his eyes with the drama of the inchoately blind. He pulled off the condom but Aubrey made him put on another. She came in great, shuddering waves, and when Chet caught up, he hated that his come couldn't find hers, turning stickily onto itself, sheer pornography; he wanted to give her his best, a viscous magic bullet—to fuck her to life as she'd been fucked to early death. Once outside, he tore off latex and quickly wrapped their bodies in sheets, as if to preserve and protect—to cleanse—through an improvised classicism of the bedroom. Aubrey said, "I needed that," and laughed so hard she shrieked and gasped, pounding his chest with tiny fists.

Zephyr and the sitter were asleep on the couch when they came in. The girl quietly gathered her things, and Aubrey lifted the unconscious child in her arms. She trudged upstairs and tucked him in, then called to Chet from the landing. They went right to bed. It was a long time since Chet had a sleepover. He hoped he wouldn't snore or cry out from a dream.

His last thoughts were of the treasonous roommate, and not the girl he left behind: Ryan the apostate, the cockatrice *à table* at a swanky bistro, say, Le Voltaire, beneath what was once the master's house—supping on *canard aux cerises,* awaiting his lover's return from the urinal.

Wish Jason and his Argonaut well . . .

Troy Capra

The legendary personal manager was well known for his collection of large outdoor pieces. He walked them past a Nevelson, a flock of Lalanne sheep, a Schnabel table with some kind of metal figure in its center, an enormous bronze breast and, finally, the most peculiar of all: a phony garden populated by two male manikins, one young, one old, pants down around the knees, the latter humping a tree while the former fucked a hole in the ground. The figures were motorized; Moe flicked a switch and everyone watched straight-faced. He waved toward a Kienholz—more middle-aged men in suits without pants, standing around a barrel—but the sprinklers had been on and it was too far a trudge.

Rod Whalen's body was amazingly beautiful, a transformation casually attributed to years of power yoga. It was easy to see how a true collector might be stirred. Instead of desiring him, Troy merely wondered how muscles could look that way—gills seemed but a small evolutionary jump. They reminisced about that *Guys and Dolls* summer while a gang of pretty boys and fortysomethings arrived, including Zev Turtletaub and the dermatologist Leslie Trott. The producer escorted a handsome kid with tangled eyebrows and a cold sore: "Taj Wiedlin, my Veepee of Bedevilment." Troy shook hands all around. Maybe Quinn was right and coming here today would somehow pan out. He liked the queers well enough but rarely went to house parties. Wall-to-wall men had a way of throwing him into heterosexual panic.

When the guests disbanded for drinks, Troy cornered Moe for a little spin control. He told the attentive manager how he was in truth a theater director who'd conflated his labors in the adult film world into an epic monologue that he planned to film before an audience the very next month, with himself as star. Trusskopf said the idea was brilliant and demanded an invitation. He seemed sincere.

The director introduced *Up in Adam* as his "seminal work" and that got a polite laugh. The half-hour film took place in a barracks. It featured a raw recruit (Rod Whalen aka G.I. Blow) and a black drill sergeant (Sarge Large). For kicks, Troy had ripped off a favorite movie, *The D.I.*—he had the black get in Rod's face and shout, just like Jack Webb: *"Do you love me?"* G.I. Blow rejoined, *"Yes sir!"* Again: *"Do you love me?"* *"Yes sir!"* "I can't hear you!" *"I love you, sir!"*—and on and on, until Sarge Large barked, "Prove it, Mister!" At this, the room broke into pandemonium. Troy hung a few minutes, then went to find the head.

As he walked down a hall, Troy imagined big-bellied Kiv waddling after, realtor in tow, face flushed by desire of possession—house-haunted. He stepped into a vast neo-classical *salle de bain* with white-marble lion-pawed bath and tiny Bonnard. He lowered himself onto the bowl, staring up at a recessed fixture. He imagined a Spy Shop camera hidden within; cued by infrared beam, Troy's naked ape image might at this very moment be supplanting the shopworn *Up in Adam* players. In a bit of funhouse high-tech horseplay, the partygoers were actually watching him shit and he'd never be the wiser.

He decided to explore, treading softly toward the cavernous master suite: twenty-foot ceilings, majestic savonnerie, Louis XIV armchairs in suede and leather—a Johns and a Clemente, and a Haring painted on a vast tarp. There was a life-size sculpture of a man that soon revealed itself to be the true flesh figure of Moe Trusskopf, head turned upward like a poet translating the clouds. Kneeling crotch-level was the bedeviling Mr. Wiedlin himself. Troy slunk off as the latter's coughing began, like croup in a clinic of the damned.

When the director returned, most of the audience had dispersed to kitchen and patio. Only three or four diehard cinéastes remained in quiet attendance of the acrobatic enlisted men—Quinn among them, thigh welded to a married attorney's. The acne-pitted Dr. Trott stood in a corner shoveling down canapés, regaling Zev Turtletaub with radioactive gossip, indifferent eyes only occasionally drifting to television screen. As Moe resurfaced *sans ami,* the houseman answered the door and a great whoop rose up: there was Richard Dreyfuss. Betsey Blankenberg brought up the rear with a party-hopper's fatuous grin. The bantam latecomer embraced Moe and Leslie and Zev, then sat up close to watch final maneuvers with boyish impunity. "You know, I've never seen one of these," he said, squeamish fascination turning to horrified glee.

Betsey shook her head indulgently.

"Oh my God!" he gasped. "Is that *physically possible?*"

"I thought you knew," said Moe, deadpan. "This is a CAA training tape."

Richard laughed like hell and the room started filling up again.

Troy assessed his options from the kitchen. He could make an end run for the Kienholz, but wasn't sure of an easy alley exit; probably worth investigating. He cursed himself for not having parked on the street. He was certain to be boxed in, probably by Dreyfuss.

The door opened and a server came through, followed by his old chum Betsey. There was nothing for Troy to do but take her by surprise—a pain-free moment suspended in time, like after you catch a finger in a door. She stood back, trying to work the equation of why he was there, unable to factor "gay" as an answer. He leapt in and told the truth, more or less, a blue movie done long ago for money, Moe's boyfriend, yadda yadda, and was halfway into the *Skin Trade* rap when Dreyfuss came in, searching for nosh. Betsey reintroduced them, but the actor nodded as if meeting him for the first time.

"Great flick," said Dreyfuss, incognizant of the director's presence. The server merrily prepared a Fiestaware bowl of Spanish olives. "Needs a new title, though: how 'bout *Full Metal Jack-off?*" He cackled as someone shouted his name, and then he was gone.

The air was stale from the innocent snubbing, and Betsey's awkward failure to make an assertion. It would have been so easy to reference the alma mater—her loser-detector must have gone off. Troy asked what brought them to the party. Betsey said they were filming the La Jolla *Medea,* with Zev's company producing. People noisily poured in and Troy excused himself, telling her she should have a look at the art in the backyard. It would blow her mind.

He went out front to the circular driveway—blocked in, as he suspected. Just then, Moe appeared and offered a cigar. Troy declined.

"Don't know why I still smoke—some kinda throwback. I don't even enjoy it. Freud got cancer of the palate, didn't he? That's all I need. 'Moe, the lower jaw has to go.' Jesus! Cigars are 'hot' again. I know four guys want me to join their 'smoking clubs,' I'm supposed to pay twenty-five hundred a year for the privilege. Know what I read in some fashion magazine last week? I think it was *Vogue*. It said: 'Black—the new white!' Black is the new white, isn't that *brilliant?* You know what? Pretty soon, it *will* be. Black-white, in-out, hot-cold, who dictates? *W?* The *gangs?* Bill Gates? And I'm the one who's supposed to *know!* I'll tell you something: I don't have a fucking clue . . ."

"It certainly is mysterious." He felt dull and vocational, like one of the caterers.

"Troy, I have a question for you. Would you make a movie for me? I know you're busy with other projects—"

"A movie?"

"I'd like you to direct a little film, for Zev's thirty-fifth. Do you think you could do that for under thirty? With, of course, something for yourself."

"Thirty thousand?"

"No, thirty *million*. Of *course* thirty thousand! I'm not *that* rich," he said, laughing. "Who you been talking to?"

"What kind of film?"

"It should be *totally hilarious*." Troy asked if that meant X, and the personal manager nodded. "This could be a *classic*. What I want to do is find actors that *look* like the people in his life—and someone who looks like *Zev!* That'll be the hard one—but maybe not. Maybe we can use masks or something. You *know* a lot of these people, don't you? Are they any good, these actors? I mean, when you give 'em lines? And we need a *dog,* a dog that looks like Mimsy! I don't want anything illegal—but I want it *crazy*. Think you can do it, Troy?"

Zev Turtletaub

Taj sat by the pool with the writer profiling Zev for the "Calendar" cover. The frothy ethnography—part *Day of the Locust*, part *That's Entertainment!*—was a sexy Sunday staple, its recipe tried-and-true: a breezy, somewhat cynical day-in-the-life of a mogul of the moment (one who played by his own rules, of course) that included brutal and/or sybaritic anecdotes, unhappy childhood bits with foreshadowings of the

"inveterate dreamer" (quotes from grade school teachers preferred, along with fuzzy photo of the buck-toothed, incipient
Barnum surrounded by classmates/future losers); a little false-
starts/years of failure/turning-point shtick, with obsequious
and/or borderline libelous quotes from even more famous
friends and traumatized unnamed sources re: the Subject's
lavish generosity/pathological niggardliness and longtime
generally-rumored-to-be-lithium-treated bipolar moodiness;
not to forget his onetime political aspirations and current
Major Contributor status; slight pause for some *What Makes
Sammy Run?* pop psychologizing, with REVENGE/FUN/ART/
SPIRITUALISM/FOR THE HELL OF IT alternately speculated
upon as the Grand Motivation; rounding off with the seems-to-
have-slayed-his-demons number, a tip of the hat to Hedonism
("One cannot deny that in this singularly serious world, he
is having, well, yes, dare we say it? Fun") and a quick dip
into the Subject's perennial bachelorhood and sexual ambigu-
ity . . . topping the whole concoction with a creaky allusion to
"Rosebud." In between, the columns garnished by newfangled
City Walk/City of Angels/City of Quartz observations; quotes
from Adorno; nonsensical Internet forays.

The assistant-cum-associate-producer, who had toyed
with reportage himself, couldn't believe he once envied the
kind of sweaty, Polo-shirted schmuck who sat across from him
with a ThinkPad and a glass of Steven Seagal cabernet. He was
temporarily at his mercy; the guy was probably livid at Taj's
good fortune and could easily portray him as a kiss-ass wimp.
He'd be careful not to mention Harvard—why add fuel to the
fire? While they waited for Zev to arrive, the stringer busied
himself with deceptively ingenuous interrogations, his stab-
in-the-back smile dominating like a rogue fart.

Two years from now, Taj thought, *my name will be on seventeen hundred screens and you will be trudging to the Royalton whenever Joe Marginal Icon blows into town.* He maliciously finished the "Calendar" piece in his head:

The producer wanted to know why the fax in the Bentley was on the fritz. "Doesn't anything in this fucking car work?" His driver smiled, accustomed to the employer's colorful imprecations. On the tarmac, the Gulfstream waited to loft him to azure skies, to the London premiere of *All Mimsy.* He would dine at the palace with the Queen Mother. As he mounted the steps, Mr. Turtletaub turned, his face breaking into the trademark, toothy grin. "Who would have ever thought that the Mother of all Queens was not to be found on Fire Island?" Minutes later, he was where he belonged, where as a boy he dreamed he might be, far from the dirt and disorder of the world—where he could lay claim to his rightful title in a palace of his own that hung in the sky: *Emperor of the Air.*

They talked about the Turtletaub Company slate and the writer asked about the Salinger adaptation. Taj was coy. He knew Zev wanted to give the appearance to the press that the reclusive author was involved.

"I read you're going be associate producer on *Dead Souls.*"

"Uh huh."

"*That's* an interesting project. Will it be period?"

"Contemporary."

"It's been a while since I read the book, but I can't imagine—the man buys *peasants,* doesn't he?"

"The core of the book—the conceit—will be the same."
Taj instantly regretted using that word; the writer would use it
against him: "Everything else is quite different."

"The same but different." The journalist smiled, savor-
ing the Wonderland doublespeak. "Is there a screenwriter
attached?"

"We're talking to one or two people."

"And the 'conceit' is—?"

"It's actually Zev's—Love in the Time of AIDS. It takes
place in the viatical settlement industry. Those are the people
who—"

"I did a piece on that," he said eagerly.

"The protagonist is a salesman—they call them 'sellers'
advocates.' He's kind of a down-and-out. He becomes this—
merchant of death. And suffers the consequences. It's also a
love story."

"Wow. That is *very* compelling. Very cool!"

Mimsy arrived with her trainer. The journalist amused
himself with an impromptu interview: how much was a bitch
like this worth? did she have a shrink? how could he be sure
this was the "real" Mimsy?—surefire fodder for the Nathanael
West sideshow angle. When the photographer came, the
"Calendar" boy made him take a Polaroid while he mugged,
shaking Mimsy's paw. "I will treasure this," he said, watching
it develop. What a wag.

*

Zev was on his way to the pool when the phone rang. It was
Hobson, the AIDS specialist. The doctor had dreamed of
building a luxury hospice and healing center in Ojai; when

they met at a benefit, Zev expressed interest in seed-funding. Hobson was calling to say—in confidentiality—that Aubrey Anne had been admitted to a hospital in the Valley for what her doctor believed was an allergic reaction to CMV meds complicated by a flu. Zev asked if his sister was dying and Hobson said he didn't think so. The producer thanked him and they spoke a moment about the hospice. Then Zev went to meet his hagiographer.

The producer hadn't been told "Calendar" wanted him photographed with Mimsy. "Oh Jesus. Another shot of me and the dog? Let's do something more original, okay? Is the piece about me? Or the dog? Or is it about me *and* the dog?" he asked, not expecting an answer.

"It's your call!" said the writer, delighted at the auspicious first encounter—the producer as godhead orchestrator of his world. "Your call, absolutely!"

"We've taken thousands of pictures already." He bent to kiss Mimsy's crown. "Haven't we, girl? You won't be upset with me, will you? No, I didn't think so."

Chet Stoddard

Aubrey wouldn't let him come to the hospital. When he called, she gasped like someone who'd just run a marathon. *"How! are you! Can't! talk! call! back! how! are! you! do! ing! Can't!—"* Her diapered friend Ziggy occasionally picked up the phone and that's how Chet got his information.

She had a horrible rash, he said, a side effect of the drug taken intravenously for her eyes. And she was out of breath like that because she probably had bronchitis—the docs had ruled out PCP, a viral pneumonia. The minute he got her home,

Ziggy was gonna do his alternative thing: ayurvedic eyedrops and hydrogen peroxide baths, ganoderma, schisandra and white atractylodes, ligustrum and licorice. Toad's breath and baby-tooth if he had to.

Chet felt her weight on him at night. He carried her during the day, too—like the fat lady he read about in *Star* who strapped on her invalid husband before morning chores. Why this mawkish preoccupation, this neediness, this profound yearning, this nostalgia for what they nearly were? Why now, why *this* woman—merely because she was dying? Obscene. Yet, as Chet told himself he loved her, the question cuffed his ear: how was it he hadn't gone to visit? He hated hospitals, spent too much time there recovering from too many battles lost. Days of infamy. He remembered the blur of visiting hours with a shudder, friends and flunkies come to view the perpetrator in his habitat. Aubrey was different that way. She wasn't cowardly, spiteful or ashamed; she wasn't a neurotic with a death wish. Yes, there was the thoughtful moment Chet reasoned she'd want her privacy, but in a few days his delicacy showed its color of fraud. After a week, he still hadn't gone. He went to bars and flirted instead, nursing drinks like a jilted man, telling himself lies: he and Aubrey were on the brink, they'd yet to arrive, tragic miscarriage of love, one of those curves life throws, all they'd needed was one more week for that animal bond. *This time we almost made our poem rhyme . . . didn't we, girl?* A few times, just before last call, he drove toward the hospital—if he went to her now, Chet feared he'd be as unrecognizable to her as she to him. They'd crossed over. Turning around and heading for home, he still reserved the right to call it love. *This time we almost made that long hard climb. Didn't we almost make it . . . this time?*

He kept calling her room—he knew she wouldn't answer—and Ziggy didn't seem to mind. Ziggy didn't judge. They would be doing a spinal tap soon because Aubrey lost some muscle coordination. The doctors wanted to check for cryptococcal meningitis, a fungal infection that swelled the brain. It was shoptalk for Ziggy, inventory and nothing more. Voices subdued, they lollygagged on the phone like teenagers with crushes on Death—guides to the Holocaust Museum.

Zev Turtletaub

Aubrey was sedated so she wouldn't panic during the MRI. They were checking for brain cysts and put you in this tunnel—she didn't like enclosed spaces. The Valium or whatever it was let her drift; a lozenge in a cylinder, she woozily returned to the scene of old crimes.

She could remember visiting a brewery, when a girl—was it Schlitz? It rose up in the Valley like an Erector-set Oz. You toured the place from a tiny tram and Aubrey'd had that fantasy ever since: life as slow monorail past the blown-out landscape of memory, forgotten landmarks of the dead. From her people-mover perch, the child saw middle-class phantoms in seats ahead and behind, safety bars pulled down around laps; polite, curious, hygienic, each watching its own diorama unfold against the autumnal Muzak of remorse, chilled and tender, fragrant with burning leaves and failing light. In adolescence, fantasy honed to futuro-utopian: naked Aubrey lay within a clear, impermeable tube—emerald cities rising in the distance, floating sci-fi brewery palaces—snaking its Grand Tour past lantern-fish-filled ocean floor, then forest primeval, wind-scarred dune and glaciers that cracked apart like thunder, transecting volcano heart and hurricane eye, through pasture pure, plains and prairie; and there, Aubrey—fantasy further evolved—now icon of Woman, chosen representative of this blue planet, itinerary no longer encompassing the rooms and rude basements of suburbia (the basement where Zev did the things he'd done)—no, that was centuries ago—but the galaxies themselves. She floated like a cork inside her crystalline conveyance, trajectory set to Infinity. If only the cannon of Magnetic Resonator would shoot her through the Big Top, to the spray of stars beyond.

Something brought her back. Cold in the tube. Why was she going through with this Easter cyst hunt? Why wasn't she arranging for her child's protectorship in the world, after she was gone? *Because I am a whore.* Nothing could stop her death, yet like all cowards she submitted to the asinine men and their pain machines. Instead of building a palladium for Zephyr, ensuring his safe passage, there she was in the bowels again, Zev's basement again, all the useless old torments. Ziggy (what a madcap) had already told her the treatment for lesions was medieval: skull shunts, with medication poured right on the brain.

She flinched at images of past entombment, Zev binding her first, Zev the chthonic destroyer, coat wire on skin, chest constricted, heightened neighborhood sounds around her—syncopated bark or channels turning, warbly ice cream truck melody—resurfacing at Cedars, Valium waning, trying not to panic because once you did you may as well lose your mind. Zev left a hose to breathe through, but she always worried about the mice—Aubrey thought she could blow one out to Kingdom Come if she had to, like a Pygmy warrior. But sometimes mice were so hairless-pink and tiny-toothed . . . if she panicked, the little girl might faint, tube fall from mouth. She invented ways to calm herself—a precocious repertoire of meditative skills—recalling techniques while the MRI did its loud work: isometrics of prayer employed years back, stuck in the hole of the basement at six thirty-three North Rodeo—

A technician said they were almost done; help was on the way. Aubrey took that as a crazy cue to skirt the crevasse, ice pick in hand . . . down she went to the cellar again, back to the pit he put her in beneath the removable concrete slab, hanger-wrapped like a cut-rate martyr, left sometimes overnight, urinating into the ground like a plant—once a week for two years and no one ever knew . . . not Mama dying and Father insensate from ECT . . . taxiing home from the private Westwood clinic, couldn't even remember his own name. In the dark hole, house sounds gave comfort: heater coil and toilet flush, wooden creak and water-rush through pipe.

The orderly wheeled her back to the room.

It was only when she saw her brother waiting there, rising from his chair in a blue bat-sleeved Miyake coat, rising like a collector of dead souls, that she knew: he would have her Zephyr when she was gone.

Bernie Ribkin

He knew the meeting hadn't gone altogether well, though he was foggy about the whys and wherefores. There were some problems, but what else was new. He didn't have a deal and he didn't *not* have a deal. Bernie already put in a call to an attorney Edie recommended, a *macher* at the firm representing her daughter. He'd let the lawyers set things straight. All in all, he was in good spirits. He felt "in play"—all was "do-able," as Denny the Boy had said. The old man would make it work.

Edie wanted him to move to the beach full-time, but Bernie didn't feel ready. This Showtime business had given him back his sea legs. He felt alive and on the ornery side. She took it in stride, enjoying his crustiness—called him her "fat old bachelor." She knew she'd win and that's why she didn't get riled. Edie was a handful but so were they all. They had good times together and it was nice because now it looked like Bernie might have a little something to crow about, to make her proud. He smiled to himself, alarmed at his own thoughts. Jesus H, maybe he was falling in love with the big bastard.

"I am so thrilled for you, Bernie."

"It isn't a lock, Edie."

"But they're *very interested*. Something good will happen."

"It seems so. But it isn't a lock and bagel. We'll see what the lawyer says."

"Did you phone Barry?"

"A few days ago. He hasn't returned my call."

"He's very busy."

"You trust him though, huh, Edie?"

"Obie *loves* him."

"Listen, Edie, there's something I need to get your feed-back on—artistically. An idea I want to run past you. I need a *hook* for this—to tie the stories together, see? That's what these kids talk about, it's all about the 'hook.' This Cryptmaster thing . . . you remember Alistair Cooke? English Alistair Cooke? Remember that—what was that show?—*Masterpiece Theater*. He came out in the openings and tied things together, you know, unified. See, that's what we're gonna do, that's what they want: to take my three little movies and tie them together. Unify and condense. That's the way they do it. Everything in a package. And what I need to find—this is my challenge—is a *device*—to *interlink*, something to grab people by the balls so they keep their rear end in the seats. And what I was thinking," he said gently, "and bear with me now, because the idea is still . . . fetal. What I was thinking is that Obie might play that role beautifully."

Edie smiled. "My Obie? I don't understand."

"Hear me out. First of all, I think it would be invaluable for her to be in front of a camera again—mind you, we're not talking tomorrow, either. But my feeling is that it would be more therapy than a hundred of these so-called gurus and healers we got trooping through there now. For Oberon Mall to feel the lights, the *tumult* of a crew again—it might awaken something. She's a performer, Edie. And she's still a *star:* for us to forget that does a terrible disservice. I think she *craves* that, *misses* that more than we could ever know."

Edie stared in disbelief. "What did you want her—what could she—"

"Now, I'm just starting to think about this. I'd set it up as 'Oberon Mall Presents.' It's three parts, right? Here's my thought. Those three parts are the dreams—or *nightmares*—of Oberon Mall. She'd be like a female Hitchcock: *very* classy, with Obie, it could never be anything but. We'd have an actress do her voice, you know, looped. A top impressionist. I'd hire the greatest cinematographer, someone from one of her movies. People would *beg* to work on this show, Edie, they would be *honored.* The *best* lighting people; the *best* makeup; the best *everything.* Academy Award people. You can trust me with your life, Edie—and so can Obie—to make her look more beautiful than ever. Because it will be a *totally controlled* situation."

Edie hurled her glass, striking him hard in the shoulder.

He stood and she fell upon him, pounding his stomach. The producer feebly raised a hand to ward off the blows.

"Have you seen her?" she bellowed. *"Have you seen my baby? She's having seizures!"* She struck him across the face, slicing open the skin with her ring. "She's in diapers! My baby is in *diapers!"*

She was sobbing now and Bernie lurched to his feet, toward the door. He couldn't see because of the blood in his eyes. Edie tackled him and they rolled on the floor. He broke free again and managed to shove her into the sofa, buying enough time to dash to the hall. From the stairwell, she roared like Godzilla.

It was only a few blocks to Cedars, yet by the time he made it to the lobby, the producer changed his mind about going on foot. He was having trouble breathing; it felt like a rib was broken. He rode the elevator to the garage and maneuvered himself behind the wheel. As the motorized gate dragged itself open, Edie appeared, pounding on the window with terrible force. He floored it and she tumbled harmlessly back.

The old man got a stabbing pain in front of Orso's and ran the car into a curb. A valet rushed over and Bernie said he'd only be a minute. The sullen Mexican saw the blood and retreated. Bernie looked in the mirror at the gouge on his cheek. He got a handkerchief from the glove compartment and held it there to stanch the flow. What would he tell them at the emergency room? Better to say he was mugged by a nigger than bitch-slapped by a shack-job. That's right—some shvug

in a hairnet, just outside the bakery where he got his regular almond alligator and coffee. Let me tell you, this is one
crazy old Jew who put up a helluva fight. Shvuggie's out there
sucking on a crack pipe with a split lip, fatter than the one he
was born with. You better believe it. And that's Bernie Ribkin
talking, cockeyed cowboy of the wild Westside.

"Bernie?" A familiar face peered through the passenger
window. "It's Fred—Fred Toschen."

"Hiya." Bernie managed a smile but it was awkward keeping handkerchief to cheek at that angle.

"Jesus, what happened to you?"

"Had some surgery—coupla stitches. Started to bleed
again. On my way to the doctor's . . ."

"Are you okay? Can you drive?"

"I'm fine." Who was this man?

"Look, I wanted to say how sorry I am about the other
day. If it was me, I probably would have punched Pierre out—
and that little a-hole Denny. But you were *great*. Anyhow, I
just wanted you to know I was *not* involved in their practical
joke. I was in that room as a *fan,* pure and simple." Bernie
beamed like a gargoyle, stifling a cough, afraid of the pain and
spewing of blood. "I don't know what it's all about, but Pierre
seriously has it in for your son, that's the *agenda*. It's like a
pathological . . . *grudge*. Something that happened when they
were kids—"

The producer was sweating, the pain in his chest unen-
durable. He started the engine.

The valet pulled up in the lawyer's car and Fred smiled
obliviously as he took his leave. "I know how you can get
your revenge. Go in there and say you can do it—tell 'em
you can shoot the thing in an *hour*! A sixty-minute shoot! Go

in with a budget and everything! I'll walk into the son of a bitch's office *with* you!"

The Range Rover jerked into the street. There was a jam at the crosswalk—wheelchairs heading for the clinic—so he hung a right to Robertson via Burton Way. Right again at Chaya Brasserie. A lung collapsed as the emergency room hove into view, and Bernie blacked out. The car jumped curb, hurtling toward the foot of the Thalians Mental Health Center steps.

A crowd of women watched curiously as the black bumper struck them down.

Troy Capra

It rained the night of the show. A goodly group of friends and invitees attended, but they lost around half during the performance. That was because technical problems caused the taping to take twice as long as had been announced.

There were cheerleaders and cronies from the Adult world and stage actor friends from the old days—now voiceover mavens grown round from the weight of the years. Kiv brought her room mate, Jabba, and wangled an agent, a casting person and a hotshot exec from New Line. She even charmed a guy from the *Reporter* into coming, on condition he wouldn't review if he didn't like what he saw. Missing in action were Sir Lancelot and big-ass Guinevere (they never RSVP'd). Troy hadn't heard boo about Zev Turtletaub's birthday reel and assumed it went the way of all flesh.

After the show he took Quinn, Kiv and Jabba to Tana's. Kiv wasn't drinking. When Jabba teased her, she came right out and said she was pregnant. Troy didn't mind. Everything was changing—no place left to run. He would ask Kiv to move in, officially. Soon he'd be editing *Skin Trade,* splicing together a new life. He might even land a festival: all Troy needed was an "audience favorite" award and distribution would be guaranteed. It didn't matter what happened now. Directing was the equalizer and he had his reel—he'd come into his own, leveling the playing field forever. Troy felt a keen sense of victory and knew it wasn't the Cristal or the coke Quinn slipped him in the grungy head.

Dabney Coleman sat in a booth across the way, Ellen DeGeneres in another. Troy belonged—a gladiator just like them. Kiv kept bringing it back to the show, giddily recounting each roller-coaster moment. From the winner's circle, Troy kissed her sober mouth, Kiv so happy, grasping his hand, moving it over swollen belly as across a Ouija board. They bussed some more, unnoticed by Dabney and Ellen, who, now bent in communion, shared secrets—gladiator lore—leaning together at the hinge of adjacent booths, opposing cameos charismatically shutting out the room.

Zev Turtletaub

Certain pointless vignettes crowded his Dilaudid-steeped consciousness. One was particularly cunning.

A few years ago, he dropped seventy-four thousand dollars at Maxfield's on clothes and jewelry, gliding from room to room, attended like a famous assassin (or murderous cardinal). At transaction's end, the owner's hauteur unexpectedly crumbled. "You're my hero," he said, ringing down the curtain on Zev's exotic fantasia. What galled the producer was that, for a moment, his native misanthropism flagged and he actually believed him. The ridiculous phrase—*you're my hero*—had recurred like a punishment ever since, compulsive and deracinated, cropping up for hours, even days on end. He sometimes playfully countered such importunacy by silently singing back, *We don't need another hero!* which echoed itself as well, so that Zev was doubly irked. He endured these petit mal sieges with a vague smile on thin lips that usually concealed flat, pearly canker sores, sweet to probing tongue.

The RN came to change his dressing. Zev refused to look at the wound. Flexor muscle and tendon had been torn away and would require a graft. It was too early to test positive for HIV; the concern, for now, was controlling the staph. Anything else was simply not a possibility . . . he would reject her AIDS as he had rejected everything about her, always: every doomed, sickly thing about all of them, from Mother's metastatic CA to Father's catatonic depression and cirrhosis-induced ascites, stomach fanning out big and hard as the Liberty Bell. The lurid pediatrician joked about Zev's floppy breasts (he was fourteen): *Your sister should be so stacked.* Aubrey heard their dad use that on him and Zev put her in her place to shut her up; that would be a hole in the ground. Everyone would have their hole. Eye for an eye, hole for a hole, every dog his doggie-do. Zev Turtletaub would puke the world—their world—then bury it.

His only thoughts were to keep the incident from the press; that possessed him, more than the pain. Leslie Trott came up with the spider-bite strategem, flukily believable—the culprit being a brown recluse at his rock-molded Moab canyonland cabin (were there brown recluses in Utah? He'd have an assistant confirm)—something that caused wildfire tissue necrosis.

In a week, his sister would be dead. He bit down on a towel while the nurse lavaged the macerated crater of bicep. What had Aubrey done with her son? He would find him, there was no doubt—he already had people looking. Zephyr was his charge. Raising him would be his duty and his joy.

Was not the boy named for him, after all?

Chet Stoddard

He phoned the hospital in Sherman Oaks, but Aubrey wasn't there. He drove by the Oakhurst house for almost a week, at different hours of day and night. There were no lights and nothing stirred. Chet revisited some NA/HIV meetings and was able to track Ziggy down.

The garden apartment was just south of Sunset, by the Virgin Megastore. The "infected faggot" cordially asked him in—that's what Ziggy liked to call himself. A burly volunteer from one of the AIDS organizations was just leaving. When he was gone, the shut-in held forth from the center of the living room, in trademark stand-up despot mode.

"Why do they send me this straight guy who can't clean? I'm sorry, but the straight guys do *not* know how to clean a kitchen floor. He comes and he sits, with his Ziploc'd tuna sandwich and his little apple. *A polished little apple!* My ultimate horror is that when I'm bedridden, this motherfucker's gonna sit there and read aloud from Marianne Williamson! I mean, what is he *doing* here?"

"I've been trying to get hold of Aubrey."

"She's in a world of shit."

"What's happening?"

"She's toxo: toxoplasmosis. Attack of the Brain Parasites."

"Oh Jesus."

"*Totally* crazy and half paralyzed and that ain't all. Her brother got rid of her."

"What are you talking about?"

"She took a fucking *bite* out of him! Isn't that the most *fabulous* thing you ever heard? Very Anne Rice—and lemme tell you, he is the *meanest* cunt on the planet. Zev Turtletaub, the Vomit King, ever heard? Zee very grandest of Grand Wazoos. Well, Aubrey Anne gave him a lovely going-away shove—and now he's on the funicular to Dementia Street and Diarrhea Way. As we speak!" Chet reached for a Marlboro and lit up, his first in eighteen months. "I know, 'cause I was *there,* right after it happened—before the parasites turned her into Sybil." Ziggy started to cackle. "She said she was going for his *neck,* but he backed up and fell or something and hit his head. So she *jumps* on him and takes a *huge* chunk from his arm—those *expensive* Yon Koster—sculpted arms—and then she *barfs* into his mouth! Oh God! Don't you just love it?"

The phone rang and Ziggy networked awhile. Whoever it was needed advice on whether to sue a hospital, healthcare worker, insurance company or possibly the government over some incident Chet couldn't fathom. As far as Ziggy was concerned, the details—petty, real or imagined—didn't seem to matter. It was *attitude* that counted. Attitude was agitprop; attitude was sacred; attitude was all. And today, "attitude" decreed that *someone* needed to be sued.

"What about her son?" Chet asked when he hung up. "What about Zephyr—"

"*Long* gone. Underground railway. Vee haff ways. Vee haff *connections.*"

"But where?"

Ziggy's jaw moved around, itching to blab. But the loquacious gadfly was mum. "Gone in sixty seconds."

Bernie Ribkin

DAILY VARIETY

Spielberg mom in close encounter; two critical

REX WEINER

Leah Adler, the mother of Steven Spielberg, was uninjured in a traffic mishap outside a wing of Cedars-Sinai Hospital, ironically named after the helmer.

Two of her companions were severely injured when a car driven by Bernard S. Ribkin, 74, leaped a curb, striking startled bystanders. The injured women are Holocaust survivors who Mrs. Adler was accompanying on a tour of the facilities. She is still expected to attend tonight's gala wrap-up for the International Artists Rights Symposium, of which her son is a benefactor.

Mr. Ribkin is the father of ICM Senior Veep Donny Ribkin.

Charges were not filed. The news that Bernie had been mugged and was desperately seeking medical attention when the accident occurred drew an outpouring of sympathy. Leah herself sent flowers and a note urging speedy recovery. "I know how terrible you must feel," she wrote, and went on to bemoan these violent times. The story was carried by a number of papers but none connected Bernie Ribkin with the *Undead* series from which he made his name. In some articles, he was merely referred to as an "elderly driver."

The battered producer suffered anxiety attacks for weeks afterward. He was worried the press might unearth skeletons, and brand him a menace. Years ago, they would say, a neighbor had been "mowed down" in a "strikingly similar incident"— that's the way those sons of bitches liked to talk. Always the conspiracy, always the something rotten. Jay Leno might even pick it up and make him a late-night laughingstock.

Bernie had real nightmares about Clara Rubidoux, and the constant harassment didn't help. Someone was papering his car with HOW AM I DRIVING? bumper stickers—it played hell with the paint—and he knew the phone calls were from her meshugga Showtime son. They were scary. There was more than one voice, doped up and guttural; maybe the whacked-out friends Bernie met that day in Malibu. The question was always the same, whispered at first, then distorted by reverb and repetition: "Mom too middle-of-the-road?" When the old man thought he recognized his own son's voice, he called ICM. Sure enough, the Senior Veepee was back in his office. Bernie was afraid to talk, convinced Donny was going to kill him.

The doctor prescribed more Halcion, but still he couldn't sleep. He took long walks at night to the Spielberg mother/son eateries—the touristy Dive! and Pico Boulevard's kosher Milky

Way—but never went in. He wondered if Leah had a boyfriend. Her husband (Steven's stepdad) had passed on a short while back. His name was Bernie, too, and maybe that was an omen. The old man started getting ideas. He'd lose some weight, get in shape. What might it take to woo a woman like that? Leah Adler seemed feisty and sexual, a gemutlich powerhouse—a pint-size version of Edie, without the torn synapses. Once, he even "bumped into" her outside the restaurant. When he said how much the flowers had meant, she looked at him quizzically. The old man had to remind Spielberg *mère* who he was.

But who was *she?* And where would he begin? This was no lonely schizophrenic who happened to live a few flights up—this was the gaudy, tough-minded mother of a billionaire, arguably the most powerful man in the history of the Business. She was probably a snob, with every reason to be. Let's say, Bernie thought, by some miracle he managed to get a foot in the door. What about his provenance of schlock? How could she even *introduce* him to her son? But maybe it wasn't so bad, maybe Steven never approved *any* of them and Leah kept her admirers hidden; or maybe the director just didn't care, long as Mom was happy. Could be all the boyfriends were geriatric schlocks, silver-maned fuck-ups and that was just her tacky friggin taste in men—with friends thinking it endearing and hilarious and loving her even more. Scramblin and Scream Works would get her laughing, and that was three-quarters of the battle. Once they were laughing, you were home to bed. Jesus H, maybe Spielberg was an *Undead* fan himself, the way Tim Burton was a freak for Ed Wood. Who knew?

Four in the morning. Bernie sat in the chair watching *Creepshow* on the cable. Leslie Nielsen was burying his wife and her lover alive in the sand of a private beach. Sets up monitors so the two can watch each other drown. Then Nielsen goes back to the house and settles in front of the TV with a drink to watch. Stephen King sure has a mind. Days later, the moldy couple has their revenge: swaddled in seaweed and very undead, they snatch him from bed and haul him to a watery grave. Jesus H, Nielsen was funny. The old man could split a gut just looking at him.

He tossed and turned for an hour, then got up and dressed. He figured he could make the Colony in half a day, by foot. What was the rush? The sun was just coming up.

*

As he passed the Beverly Hilton and ascended the luxurious ramp of Wilshire that divided the country club, the producer felt a surge of youth. His gait was steady and sure—the Bernard S. Ribkin Walk-a-thon was in full swing. He could go on forever. Like *Creepshow's* Ted Danson, he saw his body buried in the sand outside Edie's house and laughed aloud. She'd laugh too, she'd *have* to—and forgive. Laughter was three-quarters of the way. That's what he would do then: outrageous showmanship would save the day. He'd have to dig after dark, so as not to be discovered . . . chortling again at the image of those algae-blistered, stringy-haired zombies, an homage to his *Undead* if ever there was one. He'd send King a fan letter, thanking him for the tip of the hat.

At Beverly Glen, he was barely winded. Bernie thought about stopping in the Village for a cappuccino. No—he'd keep going until he reached the terrace of greensward that overhung Pacific Coast Highway. Watch the tourists before setting out to the Colony. There was a camera obscura over by the pier. Maybe he'd have a look.

And if Edie wouldn't have him, he'd walk straight to Santa Barbara, on to Pismo Beach and Morro Bay . . . Hearst Castle. He'd never been. Scale the cliffs of Big Sur to Henry Miller's cabin—Carmel, Salinas, Cannery Row. He felt the pull of Baghdad by the Bay: he would treat himself to a gourmet box lunch smack in the middle of the Golden Gate. By then his legs would be like salty pistons, unstoppable. He'd about-face in Marin and march all the way back down, to Baja or wherever the hell his fabulous old feet would take him.

He'd walk and he'd walk and nothing could stop him— nothing—because he was Bernard S. Ribkin and he was undead.

Troy Capra

Moe Trusskopf said he wanted the thing as "out there" as possible. Even Dreyfuss threw his two cents in: what Moe should do was a "triple-X *Medea*." The manager loved that.

Troy boned up on Euripides and wrote a quickie variation. It was kind of fun—one more anecdote for the next installment of *Skin Trade*. For our heroine, Quinn engaged a five-foot, two-hundred-pound chick who'd do anything, even fuck the Mimsy double (christened "Rimsy"), a furry-dicked compulsive copulator. A real pro, that one. As a bonus, the fat lady—"Zanzibar"—had just dropped a kid, so she could really squirt. Troy made Moe pay through the nose for that. For old times' sake, Sir Lancelot had a walk-on in the role of Johnny Depth, but wouldn't participate in any sex acts. Moe practically had to blackmail him to show some basket.

In Troy's rendition, Medea is married to the blond-haired Jason, a dentist-surfer with a hirsute crack known far and wide as the Golden Fleece (his scant bikini, the Golden Floss). He moves Medea/Zanzibar, Rimsy and their skinhead kids—the ever-resourceful Quinn "discovered" a set of nineteen-year-old twins at Plummer Park—to Hollywood to seek his fortune drilling celebrity molars. As fate has it, Jason falls in love with the first patient in for a cleaning, the famous producer Zevvy Girdleshtup. The boy who played Zev was a find, a buff albino whom they dressed in one of the producer's wiggier signature Gaultier leathers. Jason and Zevvy were joined in marriage and, as a "traditional Greek welcome to the bride," Rimsy, after having his way with the love-starved Medea, attempted sodomy upon His Girdleshtup with failed albeit jackhammer gusto. Meanwhile, Medea plotted her revenge, giving suck to the twins as she schemed, one on each teat, whilst the boys shook each other's martinis (real-life-brothers, to boot). Even Quinn was amazed.

*

Kiv dropped by during the shoot, looking beautiful. She was starting to show. She spent her days buying clothes for Jodie— that was the baby's name, after Jodie Foster, Pantheon queen.

She watched him direct the last scene, where Medea learns of her betrayal. There was no sex in it at all—Troy's last laugh on his employers. Kiv studied her love while he advised the actors, denuding their campy gestures and intonations, honing and paring, excising innuendo. This was the man who would soon direct marvelous movies, movies belonging to the world. Could no one else see? Inside the bubble of this drafty gray soundstage, focused and unbroken, burning bright, Troy made the best of the demonic hand he'd been dealt and for a moment, like a ghost schooner, this ship of fools lifted to the black starry realm.

Zanzibar, obese, lactating, borderline psychotic that she was, gave vent to a brassy, eerily moving rage that Troy sculpted with painstaking love. The crew fell silent—Kiv knew they had transcended this travesty, this gutter—human drama unfolding without cumbrance. There were no borders. This searing mystery wrought from language and emotion, unexpected majesty wrenched from horror, was Troy's doing, Troy's gift, the gift of her fiancé, father of her child. Kiv was so proud—pulling swatches of Kleenex from the box at craft service, holding them to her eyes like warm compresses. The tears rolled down her cheeks, stinging her lips. She wanted to go someplace far away for their honeymoon, maybe Cannes. She loved reading about the festival in *Variety*. She would sit on the terrace of the Hotel du Cap and answer their questions. *I am here with my husband,* she would tell them . . . *the director Troy Capra.*

She heard "Action" and quietly slipped to the stage to join him.

Chet Stoddard

Chet went to Circuit City and bought himself one of those little satellite dishes—a gift to himself. He surfed until he got to T3. The screen read:

THE FOXXXY CHANNEL—ADULT MOVIES
ALL DAY—THEATER 10
Rating: NR
Cost: $ 6.99
(plus applicable taxes)
Started at: 4:30 AM

Time Left: 3:15:26
(Press ENTER to purchase program)
(Otherwise change channel)

When the show came on, a number of things were happening. A hostess was interviewing a comedian called the Jokeman. At the same time, half-nude girls struck lascivious poses on ratty motel-yellow couches; folks at home could dial a nine hundred number to access live on-camera "one-on-ones" with favorites. The robonymphos pouted, preened and gyrated on the electronic auction block, tweaking nipples with red-lacquered pincers, working tongues like the village idiot in a Monty Python sketch. It was amazing to Chet that this could be someone's idea of a hard-on. The medley format was surreal: in a Frankenstein-stitched decathlon of carnival burlesque, the Jokeman ran his crude shtick while hopped-up, underworld yeomanettes, in varied states of bullshit arousal, feigned "mirth."

The camera discovered the girl at the end of the couch, and Chet got a start: it was his daughter, JABBA flashed on-screen in orange neon letters, like a game show's secret clue. She winked at the camera, crowing, "Jabba Dabba do!"

The last time he saw Molly was Thanksgiving Day, a few years back. She was on bail for possession and soliciting. He took her to the Sepulveda Velvet Turtle for turkey and all the trimmings. After, they saw Lavinia at the Mount Olympus place—what a mistake. She was sixty pounds overweight, housebound with a stress fracture. Molly nodded out in her old room while Chet endured the ex's diatribes and sophistic recriminations. It was two hours before they got out of there. He dropped Molly at a motel somewhere on La Brea.

The sweaty Jokeman stood before the camera like a boxer in a cheap interactive game. "A wife goes to her husband and says, 'I don't have any tits. I want you to buy me some tits.' The husband says, 'We can't afford it.' Wife starts crying. *'I want you to buy me tits!'* Husband says, 'Tell you what. Here's what you do. Get some toilet paper and rub it between your chest, okay?' Wife says, 'What'll *that* do" And the husband says, 'Well, it sure worked on your *ass!*' "

The camera panned to the couch, where Molly, hand inside panties, busied herself with the garish chores of simulated masturbation. She still managed to catch the punchline and laugh a beat late, a bad actress rehearsing for bedlam.

*

It was cold in the house. Chet found two dusty Placidyls zipped into a weathered shaving kit. He swallowed them and got into bed.

His thoughts turned to Aubrey's boy. He wished they were on the road together—why not? He always wanted a son. Where would they go? Taos, maybe, or Santa Fe. Some big beautiful place with chaparral. Orphans from the plague, they'd be, riders on the storm. He'd find work on a big spread belonging to Hollywood-types who remembered him from the glory days. Saul Frake probably had a ranch somewhere in Wyoming . . . Moab or Ketchum or Sedona—herds of bison à la Ted Turner. Or Chad Everett: an absentee landlord situation. Live in the caretaker's house. He'd take Zephyr everywhere, tutor him at home. There were laws about that. A boy didn't have to go to school if a parent taught him right—part of the Homestead Act. Together, they'd learn the way of the Hopi and celebrate winter solstice, whittling *tithu* for prayer and protection from rough things. They would honor his mother—

As the pills did their work, Chet grew warm. Tears lowered him like a soft rope into sleep. Holding fast as he fell, he begged his daughter's forgiveness. His sorrow had no bottom and, mercifully, upon his awakening, could not be recalled to extinguish the hopes of this savage new morning.

Zev Turtletaub

The "Calendar" article spotlighted Zev Turtletaub's ambitious adaptation of the Russian novel *Dead Souls*. The updated classic would limn the viatical-settlement industry, its grand scope being "love in the time of AIDS." The producer was furious and Taj was fired. Perhaps the recent hospital stay and surrounding events caused him to overreact, but the assistant should have known better. With certain projects, Zev's penchant for secrecy was legend.

More than a hundred people came to Aubrey's funeral—actors and activists, virus freaks, coffeehouse poets, people she had touched. All the men had yarmulkes bobby-clipped to their hair. You could tell which ones were sick; they stared into the open pit with sly know-how. Those who asked about Zephyr were told he was ill; assuming the worst, they fell silent. Zev read a Russian poem he picked from a sheaf his staff provided.

Of course, Zev wasn't in love with the editor when he played matchmaker, not for a long time (if ever). The end had been sealed when Jake began making demands—more work, more this, more that—simple enough, but therein the beggarly middle-class contract Zev so despised. *Gimme mine!* It

made his stomach turn. That was when he hatched the plan.
His sister fell under "more this, more that" and Jake was enrap-
tured when Aubrey agreed to give him her hand. Admittedly,
the announcement of betrothal heated the producer's blood;
once or twice a week throughout marriage, Jake watered Zev's
mouth, loving the whiteheads that ringed the jaundicey skin
of his wealthy brother-in-law's languid eyes—again, in hospital bathroom, awaiting Zephyr to be born. The producer never
worried about getting sick, because he didn't really have sex
anymore, not real sex, not for years. A month before marrying Aubrey off, Zev began to suspect his protégé: a six-week
siege of diarrhea (and thrush!) that Jake attributed to a taco
stand downtown. Food poisoning doesn't last six weeks, Zev
said. He told him to get tested but Jake got so upset, Zev never
brought it up again. Some people were like that—even at the
end, the film editor's denial was so great he told people he had
the Jim Henson Killer Flu. He was still convinced Zev would
give him money for a post-production house in Santa Monica,
a state-of-the-art facility by the sea. That was his Big *Baywatch*
Idea; everybody had to have one. It was easy for Zev to string
him along till the end, right through dementia.

The producer remembered how they'd first met, at a club
on Highland. He went to the toilet and there stood Jake, pants
around ankles, facing the wall. That was an anomaly, he later
said. Jake forever downplayed "running with the queers" and
maybe he was telling the truth, because marriage sure brought
out the hetero in him. How much did Aubrey know? She was
such a savvy, cynical girl; she'd *have* to have known, why else
would she attack him like that? But so late in the game . . . and
if she did know, when—*when* did she know? That's what Zev
idly wondered as they lowered her down.

In two weeks he turned thirty-five. Moe Trusskopf was throwing a big party, and Zev was actually excited about it. His production company was busier than ever; it was an expansive time. Now, he'd redouble his efforts on *Dead Souls*. They were closing on a writer and Alec would soon follow. Alec was perfect. Zev would dedicate the movie to his sister and start a foundation in her name—or a hospice in Ojai. He would buy her soul, fair and square. It was worth more dead then alive.

*

As they drove from the cemetery to his Santa Barbara home, the bulimic producer imagined himself as Chichikov, pulled along in a carriage by Selifan the coachman. There was a magnificent passage that closed Part One. Chichikov is skipping town and begs Selifan to speed up. As the horses go full gallop, their very movement elicits a rhapsody:

> Russia, are you not speeding along like a fiery and matchless troika? Beneath you the road is smoke, the bridges thunder, and everything is left far behind. At your passage the onlooker stops amazed as by a divine miracle. "Was that not a flash of lightning?" he asks. What is this surge so full of terror? And what is this force unknown impelling these horses never seen before? Ah, you horses, horses—what horses!

The traffic was light and he told the chauffeur to accelerate. Zev rolled down the windows and let the wind blast in. The driver was excited at what he took to be his powerful client's spontaneous, cathartic post-burial passion; it would be a memorable ride, something to tell his wife after work. He smelled a big tip.

"Almost a hundred!" shouted the driver, with glee.

"A hundred, a hundred! A hundred and ten!" screamed the producer. He was on fire. "A hundred and twenty! Troika, troika, troika!"

Russia, where are you flying? Answer me! There is no answer. The bells are tinkling and filling the air with their wonderful pealing; the air is torn and thundering as it turns to wind; everything on earth comes flying past and, looking askance at her, other peoples and states move aside and make way.

Book 4

THE GRANDE
COMPLICATION

Rachel Krohn

"It has nothing to do with *thinking*, it has to do with *knowing*. You should *know*."

They were lunching at the Barney Greengrass aerie, on the terrace that overlooked the windswept postcard of Beverly Hills—one of those crisp, automatic days that trigger nostalgic dominoes of déjà vu.

"He's happily married," Rachel replied.

The agent threw back a creamy neck and snorted. A Jewish star lay on her olive skin like a delicate inlay. "They're *all* happily married, that's *part* of it. They love going back to *Mommy*."

Rachel liked staring at her face; it was out of kilter, like a Modigliani. "He's not that way, Tovah. They just bought a big house."

"There's no way he's going to go from where he *was* to where he is *now* with the *kind* of money he has made in the *time* he has made it without *some* instant gratification, Rachel. Of the genital variety."

The women laughed. The subject was Perry Needham Howe, a television producer and UTA client who'd recently hit it "large." Rachel had worked as his assistant almost three years, not once catching the scent of adultery—not even a whiff.

"Are you PMS?"

"Why?"

"Because you always end up grilling me about Perry's sex life when you're PMS."

She was a funny, contradictory girl who'd become Rachel's best friend on the planet. Her father, Dee Bruchner, was a senior agent at William Morris; ever the rebel, Tovah defected to UTA, where she quickly corraled a group of young writers who cut their teeth on shows like *Larry Sanders* and were now creating hip, middle-of-the-road TV of their own—the Gary David Goldbergs of tomorrow. But Tovah was shrewd: she wanted a finger in *all* the pies, including a slice of Perry Needham Howe. She was "attracted to him physically," but that didn't explain her ambitions—most men were attractive that way. Her interest could be chalked up to good old-fashioned agenting, pure and simple. Tovah knew that pushing him toward the unexpected, seemingly oddball target—say, sitcoms or one-hours—was the long-haul thing that would keep him at the agency. Smart thing, too. Perry was cautious at first but already loosening up, flattered by her spirited attentions. Tovah told him she was going to push him straight through syndication, into Bochco country.

Rachel was forty-four and Tovah barely twenty-six—worlds apart, with worlds in common. The agent's family went to Beth-El, the temple where Rachel's father had been cantor. Tovah was still fairly observant. The mother, long divorced from Dee, became a Chabadist and met an engineer through a *shiddach*. Rachel, the prodigal Jew, loved hearing the details of an arranged marriage: how they weren't allowed to touch until they wed and how during courtship the front door was always left ajar, for modesty. "Orthodox Judaism is wonderful," the mother told her when Rachel went to Tovah's for Shabbat, "because there are so many rules and you just have to follow them. The rules do not bend."

"I visited the set of this miniseries," said Tovah, tucking into a sturgeon omelette. "A writer I represent. They were using black leopards—big, beautiful cats. Oh, Rachel, you would *love* them. There was this woman trainer there, *gorgeous,* with a leopard-skin belt! Like out of *Cat People.* There were all these warnings on the call-sheets: 'No children or menstruating women allowed on set.' "

"Then I'm safe." Rachel hadn't had a period in two years, not a real one, anyway. She was a runner and had always been irregular.

"I told you, just go see an acupuncturist."

"Maybe it's menopause."

"You are *not* menopausal, Rachel, I'm *sorry.* I *told* you who you should see, Watanabe, he's the *best,* Crescent Heights and Sunset. And *stop jogging.* No one even *does* it anymore."

"Tell me about the cats."

"These *cats* . . . once they're out of the cages, the trainers don't allow *any* movement, especially in the distance—their eyes go to the horizon, *right away.* It's veldt instinct."

"Oy guh-veldt."

"And little kids—the woman said the cats see kids as, like, a *meal.* So, she lets them out of the cages. I'm hiding behind the camera . . . she takes the *leashes* off and everyone gets quiet, I mean *dead,* a *very* weird moment. This giant gaffer looked like he was going to shit in his pants! Did you hear about that woman who was killed up north, by the cougar?"

"God, Tovah, you've really got the bloodlust."

"Someone at the agency actually *knew* her. In Cuyamaca— it was in the paper. It's a recreation area, a *park* where people *camp.* There's been *lots* of people killed by lions this year. Very Joan Didion."

"What happened?"

"She was jogging."

"Without a Tampax, no doubt."

Tovah shot her a "you're next" look. "It said in the article that the mistake she made was to *flee.* Well, *excuse me!* Evidently, they like to take their prey from behind—that part doesn't sound so bad. This ranger they interviewed said anyone confronted by a mountain lion should maintain eye contact, make noise and wait for it to leave. *Right!* I mean, that's what I do with my *lawyer!* But a mountain lion?"

*

They were supposed to meet at the track, but Calliope never showed. When Rachel got home, a message on the machine apologized for standing her up. "I hate it," said Calliope, "that you don't have a phone in your car."

When she was twelve, her father was murdered in a New York subway. The cantor's killer was never found. Calliope renounced Judaism and moved the family—Rachel and her brother, Simon—to Menlo Park. It was at Stanford that she began the metamorphosis into Calliope Krohn-Markowitz, renowned Hollywood shrink.

The children didn't fare as well. Rachel lived in colorless communes and volunteer clinics. In Berkeley, she ran daycares, shelters and co-ops, life an unsweetened wafer, sober and unsalted. Forty and unaffianced, she moved back to the Southland to study law for a time before dropping the thread. Calliope enlisted her in showbiz battalions, where Rachel won the Purple Heart for neurotic conscientiousness, lack of ambition and over-qualification. She felt close to superstar Mom but didn't see her much; admiring from a distance, like one of her magazine profiles. As for brother Simon, he was a lost soul, a burnt-out *tummler*—sometimes she wondered what there'd ever been to burn. He was kind of an exterminator and called his business the Dead Pet Society.

Soaking in a tub, candles burning, washcloth over eyes, she jogged along Angeles Crest Highway—a lion suddenly across her path. What would she do? Rachel shivered, imagining the last moments of a deadly attack. A long time ago, there was a story on the news about a woman who'd been killed while tracking Kodiaks in Alaska. Her final radio transmission was "Help! I am being killed by a bear." The horrific refrain stayed in her head for months.

Oddly, Rachel had forgotten all about a clipping she'd attached to the fridge some months back. She reread it before bed, with her muesli.

A woman on a camping trip in Mendocino stabbed a rabid cougar to death with a kitchen knife; her husband lost a thumb wrestling it off. "None of us panicked, to tell you the truth," the woman told a reporter. "But we moved swiftly." People were capable of stupendous things—that meant Rachel, too. It would *have* to mean her. And why not? She clung to the image of the woman, suburban, untried, hand on hilt of serrated blade plunged deep into the small heart of a dank hard-breathing thing trying to extinguish her life.

Perhaps Rachel would move swiftly when her time came—because something was stalking her, that much she knew. As a girl, running home from the playground at dusk, she pretended something was after her. There *was* something, her own soft shadow catching up with itself, frozen a moment, then melding, overtaking: no one ever told her shadows had shadows. It was upon her again after all these years, crazy Casper energy, flapping like the sail of a toy boat in a squall—shadow of her father's shadow—and the cantor's voice chased alongside, like a bogeyman.

The bogeyman of psalms.

Perry Needham Howe

Seven years ago his son died of a rare cancer and now Perry had something in his lungs exerting its mordant claims. The dead boy's sister, Rosetta, was flaxen-haired, pink-skinned and almost thirteen; had he lived, Montgomery (they never used the diminutive) would have been a dedicated brother of around sixteen, come June. Graduation days.

The doctors said in the first year of an illness like Perry's—"stage-four adenocarcinoma"—there was ninety percent mortality; after twelve months, a hundred percent. Chemotherapy might add six or eight weeks. When Perry asked how long the treatment lasted, they said, "You'll never get off it." You did the chemo until you died, what candid caretakers described as more a "leeching" than anything else.

Curiously, he didn't have much fight in him. The professionals translated that as depression, but Perry didn't *feel* depressed. He felt like one of those existentialist anti-heroes in the novels he'd read back in college—dreamily disburdened. Maybe all that would change, he thought, and in a few months he'd wake up screaming for Mommy the way pilots sometimes lose it when they go down. That Perry was asymptomatic didn't help him feel less surreal about his predicament;

blood-stool or a little double vision would have gone a long way. At least then, he could become a proper fatal invalid. As it was, the producer was living an ironic "television" reality. He even made a halfhearted stab at getting hold of kinescopes from *Run for Your Life*, the Ben Gazzara series where the smirking actor learns he's terminal. It was *The Fugitive*, with a Camus makeover—the one-armed man was Death.

A routine X ray showed nodules on the lungs. There was the usual hopeful speculation the little balls might indicate an infectious process such as TB or histoplasmosis, transmitted by an airborne fungus kicked up by the quake. Farfetched but within the realm of possibility. When the cancer was confirmed, his wife became obsessed with the idea the family had been exposed to something environmental. What else would explain two cancers hitting like that? The doctors said there was no connection, but they always said that—there was never a connection between anything. That they hadn't found Perry's "primary organ"—the point of origin—made it all the more heinously suspicious. Jersey raked over the past, when her baby was alive, searching for clues, tearing open old wounds with a monstrous fine-tooth comb.

After a decade in the Palisades they relocated to North Alpine, in Beverly Hills. Jersey had mixed emotions about giving up the house where Montgomery lived—and died—but it was time. For Rosetta, it was easy. She was getting hormones and any kind of break with the familiar foretold great adventure (you would have thought they were moving to Paris or England). The Antoine Predock trophy home—walls covered with Bleckners and Clementes—cost around four million. Across the way was Jeffrey Katzenberg's pied-à-terre; it was that kind of neighborhood. Lately, Perry had been looking to buy a "weekender" in Malibu, and the one Jersey liked best was a few doors down from the Katzenberg beach house. You couldn't get away from the guy.

A syndicated show about real cops made Perry Needham Howe very rich. He knew he'd gotten right place—right time lucky: in a nation of voyeurs, *Streets* was a front-row seat to the cartoonish orgy of crime that was the American nightmare. Imitators were legion, but Perry's half-hour was the mother of them all. Its simplicity couldn't be further distilled: cops chasing crooks in real time, the jiggling camera and panting, out-of-shape officers lent proceedings the kinky familiarity of coitus, without the mess—they even threw in the handcuffs. Cigarettes were smoked while spent, exhilarated fuzz offered post-bust blow-by-blows. Once in a while, if everything jibed, episodes had Emmy-worthy story arcs: like the one with the body in Hancock Park. An elderly bachelor had been murdered. His car was missing and a detective said it smelled like "sex gone bad." (A criminologist's phrase, currently in vogue. Perry heard a stand-up on one of the cable channels use it to define his marriage.) A local minister reports a call from a teenager in Vegas who confesses to the crime and wants to turn himself in. At the end of the show, the killer tidily appears at midnight in front of the Crystal Cathedral, no less—in the victim's Porsche. The minister asks the cops if he can say goodbye to the wayward hustler. "Just tell the truth," says Father Flanagan to the kid, like something out of a thirties meller. *Streets* could give *NYPD Blue* a run for its money anytime.

*

Perry was on his way to Club Bayonet.

He was meeting Stone Witkiss, the man who created *Daytona Red,* the early hotshot vice-squad hit. Stone and investors had pumped a few million into an old Mexican bar on West Washington, transforming it into a private wood-paneled oasis with a literary theme. Perry knew the preternaturally boyish Witkiss from way back—Bayonne, in fact—and enjoyed his company.

The place was packed. Steve Bochco and a few execs from UPN were at the bar and Perry said hello. Bochco complimented his show and that felt good. Cat Basquiat shared a table with Sandra Bullock, and Perry thought he saw Salman Rushdie in a far booth with Zev Turtletaub and Sherry Lansing. Stone gave him a hug and Perry followed him back. Along the way, he met Sofia Coppola and Spike Jonze, a handsome kid who made videos (Perry laughed at the resonance of the name). They liked *Streets* too.

The old friends settled into Stone's corner table.

"You look great. How's Jersey? Why didn't she come?"

"Rosetta's not feeling so well."

"Jesus, what is she, sixteen now?"

"Thirteen, comin' up."

"What does she have, the flu?"

"I don't know. It's a stomach thing."

"What does Jersey do, hold her *hand*?"

"Don't bust my balls, Stone, all right? Are you coming to the bat mitzvah?"

"Of course I'm coming to the bat mitzvah. What am I, a skeev?"

They talked like that awhile, back and forth, like old times. Then Stone hunched, discreetly nodding at a slender, well-dressed man in his early fifties.

"Guy's a *total freak*. Know who he is? Patented a computer thing—something to do with screens. Worth, like, *three billion dollars*. Just bought a house in Litchfield, next to George Soros, two hundred and fifty acres. Jesus, did you read about Soros in *The New Yorker?*" Stone ordered wine and stir-fried lobster, then circled back. "Anyway, guy lives in a thirty-room house in Palos Verdes. Contractor does a lot of work for me. There's smoke detectors in all the bathrooms—you *cannot* repeat this—with tiny cameras inside, so he can watch the ladies in the can."

Lesser lights steadily made their way to the table. The host looked a little twitchy. Wearing the hats of TV mogul/restaurateur was doing a small number on him; he hadn't yet found the groove. Funny, Perry thought, what linked them—from *Daytona Red* to *Streets* was a bit of a stretch, but Perry knew his friend liked to think he'd somehow smoothed the way. He respected Stone because he'd been through all the hype, glamour and insanity without cracking up. Perry wondered if he should fess up about stage-four. The moment passed and the waiter brought the wine. Stone sniffed, nodding his assent.

"I was talking to this forensic pathologist about Ted Bundy," Stone said, puffing on a cigar after the last visitors departed. "Bundy was confessing to *everything* in those last days—trying to forestall the execution—really blowing lunch. You know, they always talked about the 'long hair,' all the girls Bundy killed had long hair. The shrinks wondered who it was he was killing, over and over. Know what Bundy told this guy?" He hunched again, cocking his head, *intime*. "They never released this because it was too fucking hideous. You're gonna love it. There was a *simple fucking reason* behind the long hair. He liked long hair because—are you ready?—because, he said, it was *easier to get their heads out of the refrigerator.*"

The billionaire smiled as he edged past the table. Stone leaned over and whispered. "See the watch he's wearing?" Perry hadn't. "II Destriero Scafusia: what they call a 'grande complication.' Ask him to show it to you, he'd *love* it. Swiss— seven hundred and fifty components, sapphire crystal, seventy-six rubies inside. We're talking *mechanical,* nothing digital about it. I used to collect, mostly Reversos and Pateks; had a thirties Duoplan, Jaeger-LeCoultre. LeCoultre's *hot* this year. Loved the thing to death. But *this* one," nodding at the billionaire again, now at Frank Stallone's table, chatting up a longlegged girl with a huge mouth, "is the fucking *grail*— they call 'em 'super complicateds.' I mean, the fucking thing *chimes,* Perry! It shows the changing of the century on its face, the fucking *century!* I got a watch, cost me seventeen grand, a Blancpain *quantième perpetual.* Has a moon phase I used to adjust about every three years. And that's pretty good. But *this* motherfucker"—nodding to the freak again—"has a deviation of about a *day* every hundred years."

Just before leaving, he found himself at the urinal next to II Destriero Scafusia. A watch like that probably wound to the movement of the wrist; Perry shook himself and suppressed a laugh, scanning the ceiling for hidden cameras. The billionaire followed him to the sink. Had he been keener on inquiring after baubles, Perry might have asked for a look. He'd done enough of that over the years—everything had always been out of reach. Now, nothing was. Nothing, that is, but time.

Ursula Sedgwick

Ursula and Tiffany weren't homeless anymore. They lived in a house on one of the old canals.

Their neighbor, Phylliss Wolfe, was a producer who sold her Cheviot Hills home after having some kind of breakdown. She called it "Down(scaling) Syndrome"—movie projects were on hold so she could finish her book and get pregnant. She wasn't happy about the local gangs, but it had always been a fantasy of hers to live this way: in a writer's bungalow on an ellipsoid patch of grass still called United States Island. She christened the avenue Dead Meat Street because so many were dying of AIDS, or gone.

On Sundays, they went strolling on the boardwalk. Phylliss brought Rodney the dachshund, fearless sniffer of pit bulls; while Ursula and Tiffany had their fortunes told, she binged on cheap sunglasses. They shared life stories over time, shocked to have Donny Ribkin in common. Every little detail about the agent came out, including sexual proclivities—which Phylliss expanded to include the affair with Eric, her ex-assistant. Ursula blanched. It stunned her to learn Donny's father recently drowned in Malibu; that was someone he never talked about. But the worst thing was hearing he'd been hospitalized for a crack-up. "Hollywood rite of passage," Phylliss joked. "Don't knock it till you've tried it." Ursula felt sick inside. He was still her man.

She'd never met anyone like Donny—so smart and chivalrous and full of passion. If that's what Jews were like, you could sign her up for more. He scared her too, but men did, that was par for the course. He was the first lover to lavish any kind of gifts on her. At a time in her life when she really needed it, Donny Ribkin gave her a whole new way of seeing herself. They used to go "power shopping," buzzed on crystal. He got her an Oscar de la Renta at Saks, a seven-thousand-dollar strapless sequined gown, and there she was that very same night at a charity ball honoring *Forrest Gump's* Robert Zemeckis, the greatest night of her life, speed-grinding her teeth as she eavesdropped on Michael J. Fox and Meryl Streep and God knew who else, Donny's friends, their smiles like razors. Then he would brutalize her in bed, punching and choking her as he came, reviling her idiot faux pas. *How could you say what you said to Goldie?* Once he made himself vomit on her. But there was the other Donny, her "Sunday morning boy," who cried inconsolably for hours on end, begging forgiveness, tears from some faraway place like a sad, hip monster from *The X-Files*—the Donny who paid Tiffany's schooling and wept for his dead mother.

He could be cruel, but at least he wasn't one-sided. Ursula knew nothing but violent men, military father and brothers, men with just one side. The day came when she'd had enough, walked from the trailer park bloodied, holding Tiffany's bitty hand, living shelter to shelter, freeway to freeway, rape to rape, with only *The Book of Urantia* to grace and solemnize each day— the Book, with its Morontia Companions (trained for service by the Melchizedeks on a special planet near Salvington) and Thought Adjusters (seraphic volunteers from Divinington). She prayed with Tiffany for the Mystery Monitors to come, "who would like to change your feelings of fear to convictions of love and confidence."

There was *The Book of Urantia* and there was her daughter and then one day—off-ramp miracle—there was Donny Ribkin. Now, he shunned her. She still worked at Bailey's Twenty/20 and began each shift hoping the agent would drop in. The men she stripped for had his face; she made it so. One day it would come to pass. Ursula wasn't sure how she had turned him off like that—was it her homeless helplessness

that turned him on? None of it mattered. This alluring, troubled, soulful man had seen her at her worst and not turned
away. For that, she would love him forever.

*

"You need something to fill this black hole," Phylliss said.
"Donny Ribkin is a *panacea*. If it wasn't him, it'd be someone
else. *Something* else. Listen, he's no catch, okay? He's fucking
loonie tunes. Not to mention a probable health risk at this point.
So why don't you deal with your black hole?"

"Then what do I fill it with?"

"A sausage—a fat, hairy sausage with a 'Donny' tattoo."

"You're terrible," she said, laughing. She could still laugh.

"Have you ever heard of Eckankar?" Ursula shook her
head. "They call it the religion of 'the Light and Sound of God.'
The name's from Sanskrit—it means 'co-worker with God.'
But it isn't a Christian thing. It isn't an *anything*."

They said the odd word a few times together. Phylliss told
Ursula that she turned to the practice out of desperation: her
movie had fallen apart, and she'd suffered the death of a fetus
and father—how she'd gone to a hospital to heal but emerged
more shattered than whole. ECK reached out and stopped
her fall. Since then, it was the most important thing in her
life, bar none. "I've become a 'spiritual activist,' " she said.
"My New York friends are about ready to do an intervention.
I just tell 'em I want to have Yanni's child. Or John Tesh's, in
a pinch."

From what Ursula understood, Eckankar was less a religion than it was about dreams and soul travel and accepting
other planes. That was familiar ground. She was impressed

someone as cynical and sophisticated as Phylliss could have allegiance to a thing so radically ethereal; then again, with the terrible abuse Phyll had been through with her dad and all, you would *have* to let in something new, unless you wanted to go bonkers. When she brought up Urantia, Phylliss yelped "Dueling cultists!" and strummed an imaginary banjo, laughing her coarse cigarette laugh. Ursula said she had considered converting to Judaism as a way of winning Donny back—that sent Phylliss on a coughing jag. "You're the only person I know," she said, "who's more fucked up than I am." She invited her to Sunday morning worship services at the ECK Center. After a month of wheedling, Ursula gave in.

She wandered the sunny rooms at peace, as if having already dreamed such a place. Phylliss said those kinds of feelings weren't unusual—it meant the Eckankar Masters had been busy nudging you to the point where you had enough power to seek them out. As more people arrived, Ursula scanned brochures on "the ancient science of soul travel" and the soul's return to God. God was sometimes called Hu, pronounced *hue,* or Sugmad. Through a series of exercises that took just twenty to thirty minutes a day, it was possible to reach a supreme state of spiritual being. One was guided in this pursuit by the Living ECK Master, or Mahanta, who was descended from the first Living ECK Master of around six million years ago. (The first was called Gakko.) The current Living ECK Master, also known as the Inner and Outer Master, was a married man from Wisconsin named Sri Harold Klemp. His picture hung in a modest frame on the wall of the meeting room. The Mahanta's hair was thinning; there was nothing grandiose about him and Ursula liked that.

Around fifteen people gathered in a circle to discuss the morning topic, "The Golden Heart." Passages were read from a book of the same name, written by Sri Harold. It was a diverse bunch: an impeccably dressed couple, married fifty-two years, ECKists for seventeen; a carefree, homely, shoeless girl with a wide-brimmed straw hat; a heavy-set, dikey-looking nurse; a couple of friendly, formidable-looking black ladies in their sixties; and two or three fresh-faced professional men who might have been marine biologists or aeronautical engineers. One of them looked disarmingly like the Mahanta. They broke into groups of three. Ursula wound up with the old man and one of the churchwomen.

"The Golden Heart," he stammered. "Well, that's just another way of saying Conscience, isn't it?" He sounded just like Jimmy Stewart and it beguiled her.

When the lady's turn came, she said one day she found herself en route to an ECK convention in Las Vegas to see the Mahanta. "I said to myself, 'What are you doing?' Because I'd followed Jesus all my life and now here I was on my way to see Mr. Klemp. When I got to the convention hall, I saw a halo around his head—I knew pretty well then, I was on the right path. For me, that path is the Golden Heart."

The leader said it was time to chant Hu, and everyone closed their eyes. Ursula blushed as the voices raised around her, blending, fusing, overlapping—a celestial curtain rose behind the lids of her eyes, wafting so tender in the dark, and she knew what was meant by "the religion of Light and Sound." How could something so beautiful emanate from people so common and undemanding, people just like her? Yet there it was, irrefutable, like the whistle of a thousand trains, heaven-bound.

She cleared her throat and began, her voice a rivulet joining the stream that fed the Golden Heart.

Severin Welch

This man, seventy-six years old, in robust health and reasonable spirits, has not left his home in some fifteen years, initially because he was waiting for Charlie Bluhdorn to return a call.

That was the putative reason, now hidden somewhat by time's seductive sleight of hand. His name is Severin Welch, a widower who once wrote for Bob Hope; Charlie Bluhdorn, of course, being the legendary founder and ceo of Gulf + Western. Some decades ago, after indentured servitude to set-up and punchline, Severin Welch began a preposterously ambitious big-screen adaptation of the Russian masterpiece *Dead Souls,* set in the Los Angeles basin. Where else? It took a certain comic gall. Why *Dead Souls?* He'd read it in school, written papers on it. He once met a fellow at the Hillcrest named Bernie Ribkin. Horror was where the money was— that's what Ribkin said when Severin took him to Chasen's for a little interrogation; horror was the future. He told Ribkin about *Dead Souls* and the producer liked the title. "Just don't call it *Undead Souls,*" he smiled, chomping on his cigar, "or I'll be suing your friggin ass."

He worked the script ten years, finishing in 'seventy-five. Over at Morris, his then-agent—the still redoubtable Dee Bruchner—took a month to read, hating it. But Severin wanted Paramount to have first look and (back then) the client was always right. Dee morosely messengered it to a Yablans underling. Over ensuing months, the agent dutifully tracked the hundred-and-ninety-three-page ms. from suite to suite until it was the faintest blip on the radar screen, then no more.

Severin kept his day job, tinkering with *Souls* on weekends, a hobbyist possessed. Meanwhile, he wrote sketches for *Sammy and Company* and worked on specials: Mac Davis and Flip Wilson, and Hope's twenty-fifth anniversary, with a hundred guest stars—Cantinflas, Neil Armstrong, Benny, Crosby, Sinatra, Chevalier—those were the days. Aside from Lavinia's painful divorce in wake of her husband's nervous collapse (she somehow blamed her father for *The Chet Stoddard Show* fiasco), it was a ring-a-ding good time. Severin and the wife had dinner parties twice a week, and bought a place in Palm Springs on a course. He had just one complaint and it lay in wait at the end of each day: the gargantuan discourtesy of Paramount Pictures.

Months passed—why hadn't someone the decency and professionalism to respond? Because he was a television writer? That seemed bizarre. Chayevsky had been nominated up and down the street for *Network*. Didn't that ring anybody's bells? Didn't the Morris agency have any *clout?* Wouldn't it have been reasonable for Dee to phone someone up at the studio and say: "Listen to me! You have not responded and my client is angry. He is important to this agency and you owe him that courtesy. *Call* him—*now.*" If you don't like something, come out and say it. I want to *hear* about it, don't be shy, meet a guy, pull up a chair. Give it to me with both barrels—what doesn't kill me sure as hell will make my script stronger. That's the way Severin looked at it. Anything but the silent treatment.

Another year. Severin, with his golf and gags and pool parties under the HOLLYWOOD sign. He'd throw back a few, then go on a Paramount rant: if the script came over the transom, *then,* he said, *then* it would be something else. Whole different story. But *Dead Souls* arrived by the book, so to speak, through a powerful agency—and Severin Welch was an established writer! One of the wiseacres said he should stand in front of the studio gates naked with a sandwich board, and Severin thought that a swell idea, especially when Diantha bridled. It'd probably kill his agent, but hell, Dee was dead already for all the good he did—sitting on El Camino scratching his ass like a dull-wit stonewalling Buddha. The tragedy was, Severin knew it would be a perfect marriage—the studio that so handsomely produced *The Godfather* would be the ultimate venue for this multitextured classic. Knew it from day one but was forced to go elsewhere, finally persuading the agency to send the script to other majors. At least they had the courtesy to eventually express their disinterest. Or maybe Dee's secretary typed the rejection letters to get him off their backs. Maybe the damn script never left the mailroom—Severin didn't really know anymore. The whole rude, unseemly business had thrown him for a loop.

With dull awareness of his compulsion, he began to place morning calls to his agent, Mondays, Wednesdays and Fridays, year in and year out, urging him to appraise "the progress at Paramount." To keep his finger on the pulse. The first few weeks, Dee thought it another gag from the gagman, but as the inquiries persisted, the agent grew irritated, then angry and finally intrigued by the underlying pathology. It became something of a joke among Morris acolytes; when they saw Father Bruchner at the Polo Lounge or Ma Maison, they never failed to ask after "the progress at Paramount." Severin still made money for the agency, so his eccentricities were grudgingly tolerated.

From atop his hill, the television writer watched the bilious Paramount parade: *Orca, the Killer Whale; Bad News Bears Go to Japan; Players; The One and Only; Little Darlings; Going Ape!; Some Kind of Hero.* No wonder they'd been too busy to respond! It was like the marathon dance in *They Shoot Horses, Don't They?*—yet the band played on. He was rankled in some deep, unapproachable place. When his wife delicately suggested he might "talk to someone," Severin reacted so harshly that Diantha half thought he'd try fingering her as a Paramount spy.

Then one day in nineteen eighty-one, a Morris secretary called to say "there was movement." In measured tones, cryptic and grave, she told him Charles G. Bluhdorn himself was in possession of *Souls.* "Mr. Bluhdorn wished to give the script his personal attention," her words went. A senior agent at Morris who dealt exclusively with the chairman would be calling Severin with a follow-up. In the excitement, he didn't write down the name. He waited by the phone until six, finally calling Dee's office. No one was in. After a fitful night, he left messages with the switchboard "regarding Charlie Bluhdorn." He was on his way down to the agency when Dee Bruchner called back. It had been a few months since they spoke; work had been drying up.

"Severin, what the hell is going on?"

"I want to know what's happening with Bluhdorn."

"I don't have *time* for this crazy shit!"

"Someone called from the agency—"

"*Nothing's* fucking happening with Bluhdorn! Okay? Why don't you go see a fucking *shrink,* Severin? All right? How many years have we been doing this?"

"A secretary called, from the agency," said the client, undeterred. "She said Charlie Bluhdorn was reading my script."

That night, Dee phoned from La Scala. He sounded drunk and vaguely repentant. The whole thing was a practical joke, he said. When Severin asked what he meant, Dee said, "It must have been a joke." He reiterated his desire for Severin to seek medical help. "You really should," he said. "For Diantha. It's not fair to put her through this. You know, people love you, they really do. They really care." What the hell was he talking about? In the morning, the disbeliever reached Bluhdorn's office in New York but was rebuffed. He kept calling, and when Dee found out, he sent a telegram saying the agency no longer represented him and that Severin Welch should "cease and desist" contact or run the risk of becoming a "nuisance."

Came a gentle temblor in his head, a shifting of plates, and so it was decreed: the matter *would* be resolved by the definitive telephonic intervention of that high-flying commander, that Mike Todd of ceos, Charles G. Bluhdorn, whose imminent call was not open to conjecture. Severin withheld this magical revelation from world and wife; he wanted to live with it a spell, try it on for size, test its sealegs. Fear of missing the Call soon tethered him to the house. He might have laughed about such an arrangement—how could he have not, particularly after Bluhdorn's subsequent death?—but there it was, unreal yet present as the HOLLYWOOD sign. The occasional women's magazine had been perused, *Redbook* and *Reader's Digest,* but these were the pioneer years of phobic disorder: no clubby Internet or national network of like confederates, mystically moored by zip code demarcation and sundry voodoo Maginot lines. Diantha indulged his epic call-waiting best she could. When she died, swept away by the flash flood of cerebral hemorrhage, Severin could not leave the front yard, so missed the procession. Lavinia poignantly misunderstood, thinking her father unhinged, which he was, though not entirely by grief.

That the Call didn't come never disheartened, for its pre-
sentiment rang in his ears, an astral tintinnabulation like the
warm, flirty scent of a holiday roast; Severin, wrapped in a
comforter of acoustical yearning. Pink Dot delivered groceries
and laundry, and daughter Lavinia picked up the slack—thus
ensconced, the old fossil roamed the low-tech shagscape of
his Beachwood Canyon home, listening to his precious scanner, reading aloud from Thurber and Wodehouse, Gogol and
Graham Greene, anchored by his powerful Uniden cordless
and the entropy of the years. Did he really expect a call from a
dead man? No: after all, he wasn't crazy.

There was a piece in the *Times* about John Calley that he'd
read with great interest. The United Artists head had returned
to the business after years of lying fallow and was now in the
methodical process of sifting through studio archives—the
idea being to discover old projects, then revise, update and
order to production. They had stuff going all the way back to
Faulkner and Fitzgerald.

> "It's very much of an archeological expedition,"
> says Creative Artists Agency's Jon Levin, who has
> researched everything from old production logs to
> the memoirs of Hollywood legends. "There are only
> so many movies that were made every year, and a
> number of more scripts that were developed. So
> chances are there are good [unproduced] works."

It went on to say that because of rights issues and liability
concerns, boxes of unproduced scripts—some of which had
been donated to the AMPAS Margaret Herrick Library—now
resided at a remote storage facility for "things that are not supposed to be seen . . . a no-man's land." Severin Welch's *Dead*

Souls had to be out there somewhere, waiting. If you write it, they will come! And when they did (perhaps Bluhdorn progeny, that would be a nice, a fine irony), Severin would have a surprise: the work of the last five years, gratis. For the busy shut-in had been revising all along, retrofitting for these hard, fast times. The money boys would like that—it would save the expense of hiring a pricey rewrite man. Severin wasn't too worried about ageism. Charles Bennett (the initials alone were auspicious) had sold a pitch right before he died. Bennett wrote for Hitchcock and had to have been in his nineties. No, the tide was turning. Everything old was new again.

He sat by the pool with the scanner, monitoring car phone transmissions. That was illegal now, but Severin had no fear. He used it as a tool, plucking characters from the vapor, finessing dialogue, shoring up unsafe sections of his work. Writers were mercenary—had to use whatever they could. Originally, the old man's presciently "virtual" adaptation of the Gogol book submitted Chichikov wandering an antiseptic city buying memories of the dead. Now, as if in sly homage to Mr. Bluhdorn, it would be voices the man coveted instead.

Voices on the phone.

Rachel Krohn

On the first night of Passover, Rachel had a dilemma. She was supposed to go with Tovah to an Orthodox seder but now the agent was in bed with a fever, insisting Rachel go alone.

"But three hundred people!"

"It'll be *easier*. Less intimate."

"Tovah, I won't *know* anyone—"

"*No one* knows anyone, that's the *point.* It's skewed toward singles."

"I haven't been to a seder since I was a kid."

"There'll be *lots* of Jews who've *never* been to a seder, that's what this *is,* an outreach for singles. You want to meet someone, don't you? Then just go."

*

Rachel was in a cold sweat. For some masochistic reason, she arrived early, and because there weren't a lot of people yet, it was harder to hide her discomfort. She thought about leaving but remembered her pedigree: her father was a goddam cantor. Rachel Krohn didn't have to prove a thing to these people.

She mingled awkwardly, admiring the rabbis' long coats, very Comme des Garçons. A woman asked her to light a candle. Were candles lit each Sabbath night or only on Passover? She was clueless. She only knew you lit candles for the dead, though her mother never did.

Nondescript men in poorly cut suits approached, abashedly letting on how they were Fallen Ones, come back to the fold. There were South Africans and San Diegans, Australians and Czechs, Muscovites and New Yorkers, and a dance troupe from Tel Aviv—the girls were gorgeous. Rachel stared like she used to at counselors during summer camp, envying their tawny bodies and musky élan. Again, she felt like bolting.

She was targeted by a schlemiel. He was about to speak— the mouth opened, showing braces—when a rabbi bounded up and introduced himself as "Schwartzee's son." Rachel put a hand out but he demurred.

"I'm a rabbi, I don't shake hands! I don't mean to embarrass you. It's just a choice—the only hand I touch is my wife's. Let's just say I don't like to start what I can't finish!"

A woman lunged forward. "Then *I'll* shake it, I'm his *sister!*" She pumped Rachel's hand, exclaiming, "I'm not so choosy!"

Schwartzee himself appeared, holding a clipboard in such a way as to discourage the flesh-pressing impulse. He was coatless and wore Mickey Mouse suspenders. "Moishe Moskowitz," the rabbi crowed, thumbs tucked in each side, "for the children!" He checked off Rachel's name and was sorry to hear "my old friend Tovah" was sick. The rabbi's naked, musty breath evoked a weird mosaic of memory and sensation—of synagogue, family and dread. The doors to the banquet hall swung open and Schwartzee shouted after the guests, "It's fat-free, so enjoy!"

She entered the cavernous room in haphazard search of a table.

"Rachel!"

She spun around. Standing there was her brother, Simon.

"What are you doing here?" she asked, dismayed.

"I got a call from Schwartzee—there's something dead in the basement. Could be Lazarus! Or should I say Charlton Heston."

He wore a dark suit and looked thoroughly in his element—the Dead Pet Detective, born-again. Simon had left a slew of messages that she hadn't returned.

"You never called me back!" he said, oddly enthusiastic.

"I was going to. I've been real busy, Simon."

"I was just wondering if there was any way I could get with your boss."

"Simon, I've already told you, Perry doesn't *know* any of the *Blue Matrix* people—"

"Oh come on, Rachel! *All* those people know each other."

"That's not necessarily how it works."

"I have three scripts, okay? Can't you at least get *one* to your boss?"

"Simon, let's not talk about this now."

"Where are you sitting?"

"Not with *you*. I'm with about twenty people."

"Well, *excuuuussse meeeeee!*" She started to go. "Wait! What does a man with a ten-inch penis have for breakfast?"

Rachel was beyond ill will; she didn't even feel like leaving anymore. She had accepted her lot as among the condemned.

"Uh, well," Simon stammered, "let's see now. Uh, I had two eggs, toast . . . a glass of o.j.—" He cracked himself up as she moved away.

*

A blithe, bitchy couple sat across. The woman let everyone know they'd met during one of Schwartzee's relationship seminars at the Bel Air Radisson. On Rachel's left was an overweight, attractive Canadian called Alberta. Mordecai, the lovestruck schlemiel with braces, hovered breathlessly, too nervous to sit beside her; he took a chair by the great Province. The place beside Rachel remained empty, a sitting target for the requisite Elijah jokes.

After her father's death, Rachel's family joined the landlocked diaspora of the faithless. She had been so far and so long away from the water that the dizzying, chimerical ceremonies at hand made her feel like an ethnographer in the

field: symbolic foods on plate, the leaning to the left, naming
of plagues—boils, hail, cattle disease, slaying of firstborn . . .
like crashing a meeting of freemasons. Yet when she heard
the congregants' intonations and the indomitable old songs of
her father, her otherness burned away. Schwartzee's six-year-
old son (the fertile rabbi's latest) took to the stage and sang
a flitting, singsong prayer. Rachel blotted her tears with the
hackneyed inventory of images: Sy at the pulpit, mighty and
dour, a gray, businesslike Moses, neck vibrating like a turkey's
when he sang; huge white hands and slicked-back hair; fat
gold ring.

Schwartzee asked how many commandments were in the
Bible. Someone raised a hand and shouted, "Six hundred and
thirteen!" Rachel puzzled over that one during the ritual hand
washing. She asked Alberta about it.

"You're not really supposed to say anything after the
washing of the hands," the big woman said. "Until you eat the
matzo."

"Oh! I'm sorry."

"Sit in the corner," said Mordecai, leaning over to be seen.
"No matzo for *you* tonight!"

"It's *tradition,*" said Alberta, contritely. "I mean you *can,* but
you're not supposed to."

"Then I won't," said Rachel, unperturbed.

Mordecai shushed her, holding up an admonitory finger.
"Please reply in the universal sign language."

"It's all right—really!" said Alberta. "I just wanted to tell
you what was traditional." To her annoyance, Mordecai sang a
few bars of "Tradition" from *Fiddler on the Roof.*

"Schwartzee's seders tend to go till midnight," said the
woman across, to no one in particular. The boyfriend watched

the waiters like a hawk, making sure to get double portions. Timing was everything.

A woman in her sixties was ushered to the vacant seat along with edgy Elijah jokes from the hawk-eyed man, who clearly regarded her arrival as a threat to the food bank. Birdie was from New York and, as it turned out, a cantor's daughter. She ran a mortuary in the Fairfax district, a *chevra kaddisha,* or "holy society." Rachel remarked how difficult it must be to work in such a place, but the woman said it was "her greatest mitzvah." Birdie was a *shomer,* a member of a volunteer group that attend the dead before burial. She explained that *shomer* meant "watcher." Mordecai made a dumb eavesdroppy joke about "birdie-watching" and the woman tensed her lips in a bloodless smile.

Birdie's father died just last year, at ninety-five; it surprised her Rachel's loss had come so long ago. Spontaneously, the younger woman offered that he had been killed.

"What is your last name?" Birdie asked.

"Krohn."

She stared at her plate, then turned and looked at Rachel with a dead blue eye. "I knew your father," she said.

"You—knew—"

"Yes. My husband did his *taharah.*"

"His what?"

"Your father's *taharah.* The ritual cleansing—the prayers. He sat with your father before he was buried."

Perry Needham Howe

He took Jersey to all the black-tie benefits and still, hardly anyone knew. That's how he wanted it. He felt strangely invisible—imperishable, even—a dapper traveler incognito in the land of the living. He hadn't succumbed to the savage placebos that made one a bald vomit-machine: that would be sheer cowardice. Perry wanted to die on his own terms, not like some whore pretending to be a hero.

They went to the Bistro Gardens for the Hospice of the Canyon, an outpatient program in Calabasas for the terminally ill. Perry liked the irony. He cracked death jokes under his breath, but Jersey wasn't up to playing Mrs. Muir. A few friends knew, with his permission—like Iris Cantor, their great guide. Iris had networked them through Memorial Sloan-Kettering and was there tonight, along with the usual crowd. There were bevvies of doctors and nurses (Jersey felt like buttonholing Leslie Trott and pouring her heart out) and a monsignor, for show.

On Saturday, it was Suzan Hughes's birthday at Greyhall mansion. The former Miss Petite USA had married the perennially handsome founder of Herbalife. Jersey was active in the Herbalife Family Foundation for at-risk children, as she was in Haven House, Path, Thalians, Childhelp, D.A.R.E., Share, the Children's Action Network, the H.E.L.P. Group, the League for Children, Operation Children and the Carousel of Hope. All the "ladies who lunch" loved Jersey Stabile Howe's energy—and thought Perry was gorgeous, like a young Mike Silverman. Something of the Cary Grant about him. The tragedy of their son's death was well known and bestowed another, popular facet: they had the dignified weight of a handsome couple who had journeyed to "another country" and come back with slides for future tourists. The ladies spoke of Montgomery as one would an infantine lama, snatched from their midst to fulfill a greater prophecy—cosmic honors to which aggrieved parents must perforce acquiesce.

Jersey wondered what would happen when they found out about Perry; he'd be wasting away by then. The ladies might even revile her misfortune, secretly dubbing it over-kill. (That was a sick thought.) There was nothing to do but master the art of crying in public restrooms. She'd tough it out, *had* to for Rosetta's sake, her beautiful little girl. Jersey knew how to cope: she drank Kombucha mushroom tea by the gallon, washing down Zoloft and Ativan. To outlive one's husband and son! She perversely looked forward to the ladies' memorial attentions. For now, all she could do was natter about environmental carcinogens—leukemia in the suburbs, toxic seepage, government lies. And across the world, the doomsday cover-up of the corroding containment husk around Chernobyl's reactor number four.

Stage four . . . Reactor number—

The Bistro gardenias weren't completely sold, worried their young friend might be truffle-hunting too far afield. They were more at ease with orphanages and battered women, AIDS and oddball diseases. What chance did plain-wrap adenocarcinoma stand against pediatric exotica? Standing there between Vanna White and a bloated Charlene Tilton, Jersey watched her beautiful blue-blazered husband and blinked back the image of him stone cold dead. Guiltily, she watched the Tadao Ando–designed monolith rise before her: **THE PERRY** (AND JERSEY?) **NEEDHAM HOWE CENTER FOR EARLY DETECTION**. The betrayal was more than she could bear—how *could* she? There was Jay Leno and Steve Allen, LeVar Burton and Charo, Pia Zadora and someone from *Laugh-In* whose name she couldn't remember. Perry hooked his arm in hers and charmed the lot of them, all the while turning over the one thing that had possessed him since Club Bayonet: Il Destriero Scafusia.

*

Rachel contacted its makers, and the International Watch Company FedExed a cassette along with a small hardback catalogue. Within the latter was an inventory of prices—a "moon phase skeleton model" pocket watch available in yellow gold, at sixty thousand; a Da Vinci wristwatch, for over a hundred. There were Portofinos, Novecentos and Ingenieurs—and, of course, the rather modest looking eighteen-carat rose-gold Destriero, a grande complication that stood, très grande, at a cool quarter of a million.

The watch itself was crafted in the village of Schaffhausen on the banks of the Rhine. *Destriero* was the name given to a jouster's steed; one easily imagined such knightly trials unfolding hard by the medieval castle—built from plans designed by Albrecht Dürer—that overlooked the town. Just what *was* a "super complicated" watch? The voice on the tape explained a mechanism could only be classified as such if three elements came together in its movement: chronograph, perpetual calendar and minute repeater. Among collectors, "minute repeaters" were the most coveted. They were the watches that chimed the hour, quarter-hour and minute, an action originally devised for the blind.

Perry lingered over a bit of text: "Firmly secured inside the movement is a replacement century display slide, which can be installed at the end of the twenty-second century and will continue showing the correct year until the end of twenty-four ninety-nine A.D." Heady stuff, though he wasn't exactly sure what it meant. There were other details hard to fathom, such as the Destriero's unique ball-bearing-mounted "flying" tourbillon (eight vibrations per second) that was described as a kind of cage made of anti-magnetic, ultra-light titanium. The tourbillon was invented right after the French Revolution, its function being to improve accuracy by counteracting the earth's gravitational pull on the balance.

The catalogue ended with a flourish. "Fin de Siècle: The Grand Finale—This Is What Will Happen at Midnight on 31 December 1999. At precisely this moment, the most complicated wristwatch the world has ever seen will come into its own, as a multitude of functions start taking place simultaneously." The final paragraphs walked one through the horological ballet, ending with the changing of the millennium guard. "A figure 'twenty' replaces the 'nineteen' in the date display of the Il Destriero . . . and the twenty-first century since the birth of Christ has begun."

*

Tovah called, wanting drinks at the Bel Air. He opted for breakfast at the Four Seasons instead—that felt safer. He wasn't going to cry himself a river and he wasn't going to fuck his brains out behind the cancer blues. Not his style.

What she proposed was a "special project," a television movie about the remarkable life and death of his son, Montgomery. Perry felt trivialized, ready to be offended. Tovah stiffened. Then he laughed and the agent smiled.

"I hope it's all right, my—"

"It's fine. It's fine," Perry said, suddenly emotional.

"Rachel told me the story. I just thought it was so *amazing*."

"A lot of people did."

"And I wondered why no one ever—did anyone *ask* if you and Jersey—"

"I think Aaron and I talked about it. And Jim Brooks—we played a lot of basketball together. But I don't think Jersey and I were up for it. It really took the wind out of us. The idea of revisiting . . ."

"I'm sorry—"

"No no no. Maybe it's time," he said, tapping his glass with a fingernail. "Maybe it's been long enough."

Ursula Sedgwick

"She's not coming," said Sara.

"Shit," said Ursula, disappointed. "Why not?"

"Because," said Phylliss, "I'm a crabby cunt." She padded to the kitchen and retrieved a carton of Merits from the old Amana.

Sara Radisson was a casting agent who had worked on a movie of Phylliss's that never happened. There was money from a divorce. After the split, Sara took the baby and lived awhile with her mom in Minnesota. It was a hard time; Phylliss was going through changes of her own. When the producer discovered Eckankar, she ordered Sara to visit the Temple of ECK, in Chanhassen—right near her mom's place. Phylliss said that was no coincidence. There had to be a reason she wound up so close to the source.

Sara was a seeker. She found plenty of *chelas*, students of the Mahanta. She chanted Hu and was initiated on the Inner. One night, the ECK Master Rebazar Tarzs came to her in a dream and said it was time to stop running. The ECK Master (a pure blue light) said she should return to Los Angeles and complete unfinished business with two women she knew from a past life. When Sara awoke, Phylliss Wolfe and Holly Hunter hung before her like illuminated cameos. She got on the phone to Venice and the tears poured out in a stinging, soulful rush. Within a week, *Sight Unseen* had been sold to Lifetime, with Holly and Phylliss committing to star and produce.

"We *know* you're a crabby cunt. But you still have to go."

"I didn't even hear about this thing."

"I told you last week."

"My womb is tired and bleeding."

"So *that's* it."

Ursula was stumped.

"Phyll thought she was pregnant."

"By who?"

"Some Abbot Kinney bimbo."

"Is it serious?"

"Of course, it's serious. He's a selected donor."

"She means, selected at Hal's—from the bar."

"Is that safe, Phyll? I mean, has he been tested?"

"Yes, Mother. And I'm telling you," she said, hands to crotch, "this model has got to go. If Larry Hagman gets a new liver, Phylliss Wolfe sure as shit wants a new womb."

"*Annie, Get Your Womb.*"

"You need a transplant."

"The girl from *Baywatch.*"

"No! From *Friends*—"

"Amateur hour, baby. I need me a *professional* womb, a Meryl Streep–Mare Winningham model, industrial-strength. I want me a *litter.*"

"How many does Meryl have?"

"Four, at last count. Mare has, like, twelve."

"Meryl has four? I thought it was three."

"Don't quibble."

"Come on, Phyll, *please* come." Ursula rubbed her neck. "It'll be *fun*. It'll get you out of your mood. Pretty please?"

"You guys go. I just want to sit in bed and watch *Bewitched*. I have an inclination to see Dick York, pre-dementia."

"Oh all right," said Sara. "I guess *someone* has to baby-sit that big bratty uterus of yours."

"Damn straight. And that's 'cervix' to you."

Ursula gathered up her things. "Tiff, do you want to come with us or do you want to stay with crabby Phylliss?"

"Go with you!"

"See?" said Phylliss. "Kids instinctively know to shun a barren woman."

Sara asked if it was okay to leave her baby, and Phylliss insisted. "It's high time," she said, "that Samson bonded with Dick York. You know, a little imprinting couldn't hurt."

*

On the way to the ECK Center potluck, Sara talked about *Sight Unseen*. She was becoming another person, she said, and the book was part of that transformation. She talked about the divorce and what it was like to live with her mom again—the bond between mothers and daughters. Ursula reached back and grabbed Tiffany's bare foot, almost the size of her own.

"Are you writing the movie too?"

"No way! We're trying for Beth Henley—she wrote *Crimes of the Heart*. There is *no way* I could write a script. I could barely do the book!"

"Phyll's writing one too, huh."

Sara nodded. "We have the same editor. But Phylliss is going to have a best-seller—she's a *real* writer. Mine's just a compilation of letters."

"It must be so exciting! Is Eckankar going to be in it?"

"I'd *like* it to be but . . . Phyll and I are kind of at logger-heads about that. I just want it to be universal. I don't want critics saying there was anything—*cultish,* or whatever. I'm already thinking about critics!" She laughed, remembering how Phylliss said she wanted their "movie of the weak" to be special.

The Center was filled with kids and tons of Tupperware food. Sara pointed out seven H.I.s—Higher Initiates—those who'd been around ECK some twenty years and more. They were plain folk, down-home and grounded. Ursula talked to a writer who got turned on to ECK by his shrink, and a horse trainer from Rancho Cucamonga who married a non-ECKist. (He was into reincarnation, she said, so they got along just fine.) There was a shy young man with a bright smile—a boy, really—who looked a little ragged. Two of the H.I.s asked how he'd heard of the Center. Once they realized he was possibly homeless, they made sure his plate was full. Ursula was touched.

After a while, everyone sat in chairs and the cabaret began. The horsewoman read a poem about the Mahanta, then a trio sang songs about Light and Sound and Soul. The boy took a seat beside Ursula. A sticker on his shirt said HELLO, MY NAME IS TAJ. His knee touched hers and she moved it away, then moved it back. He smiled a bright, disenfranchised smile.

An H.I. who cheekily called herself "the Living ECK Master of Ceremonies" introduced a sketch called "Motorcycle

Man." A girl around Tiffany's age slipped into a makeshift bed onstage. As narration began, a bearded, friendly-looking biker roused her. The girl brushed sleep from her eyes and climbed on his back while he revved the high handle of an imaginary Harley. "Now this girl was visited every night by the Motorcycle Man," said the H.I., "and they cruised the city streets, then up to the sky. He told her many, many things. But every morning her parents wanted to convince her it was just a dream." The upshot being that when the child grew up, she realized the Motorcycle Man was none other than a Living ECK Master. After the applause and laughter ebbed—the girl was a natu-ral-born ham—the H.I. thanked "the father-daughter comedy duo of Calvin and Hobbes." Everyone knew that "Calvin and Hobbes" was the Mahanta's favorite cartoon. The sketch was taken directly from Sri Harold's parables, she added.

The afternoon ended with everyone chanting Hu. "Gather your attention in the third eye," whispered Ursula to the rag-ged boy. "Hold on to your contemplation seed."

*

That night, Tiffany stayed with Phylliss. Ursula turned around and picked Taj up at the place she said she would, over by the Center. He was waiting there like a kid, after school.

They went to Bob Burns and listened to jazz. Taj ate some more. He'd pretty much been homeless the last few months, he said, begging for change outside Starbucks and the twen-ty-four-hour Ralph's. She brought him back to United States Island and plunked him in a bubble bath. Then she lit the candle of her earthquake preparedness kit, slipped into a robe and put on Gladys Knight. Taj came to bed sopping wet, and she ran to get a towel to dry him off. He seemed perplexed, a dreamy colt, sweet and wobbly. He let her roll on a condom. She got on top, and when they were done, Ursula started to cry; she was thinking of Donny and everything, wanting out of her own skin. Taj got flustered. He said she was crying because of the transmitters in his mouth that made people sad when they kissed him. That scared her, but he laughed his bright laugh and she punched him. They wrestled awhile, then chanted Hu.

They lay side by side, listening to the carp of a cricket, close by. Suddenly, she was looking down, watching his tongue dig at her as she squirmed, arching back, hands trembling on the pommel of his head. The cricket was an omen that confirmed the fatefulness of this moment: just that day she heard Sri Harold talk on tape about the Music of God manifesting itself as flutes, chimes, buzzing bees—and crickets. Ursula was certain she'd met this boy in a past life. Sara and Phyll had a whole Victorian thing going, but Ursula sensed she and Taj went back much further. It would take some hard work on the Inner to find out just how far, but at least now the path was marked.

She shivered, lifting the boy onto her.

Severin Welch

Severin never strayed far from the Radio Shack scanner and its Voices. He picked his way through mines of static, listening to the agents and execs en route to power lunches; after midnight, pimps and drug dealers ruled. The choicer bits were duly recorded, then transcribed by his daughter, who still lived in the Mount Olympus wedding house on Hermes Drive. Lavinia made a meager living typing screenplays, and Severin was happy to throw some dollars her way.

The transcripts were returned and Severin pored over them, ruminating, sonic editor on high, scaling heights of cellular Babel, ducking into rooms of verbiage, corroded, dank, dead end—then a sudden treasure, odd heirloom, dialogue hung like chandeliers, illuminated. He held the sheaves to his ear and heard the dull, perilous world of Voices—the workday ended, seatbelted warriors homeward bound. All was well. Whereabouts were noted, ETAs demanded and logged, coordinates eroticized; half the world wanted to know just exactly when the other half thought it might be coming home. *On the one-ten—kids there yet?—called you before—love you so much!—trying to reach— taking the Canyon—couldn't get through—losing you . . .*

Severin thought he recognized Dee Bruchner amid the welter. *You tell that nigger,* said the Voice, *he closes at the agreed four million or I will spray shit in his burrhead baby's mouth.*

Had they always talked that way? He couldn't imagine Mr. Bluhdorn coming on like Mark Fuhrman. Not to worry—he'd use it all to stitch one hell of an American Quilt. These were the Voices of a dying world, no doubt. They needed a script to haunt, and *Dead Souls* was just the place.

*

"You look awful," she said, treading the doorway in a flowery perspiration-stained muumuu. Lavinia's skin was oily white, an occasional pimple pitched like a nomad's pink tent. She was turning fifty-three and wore a knee brace; the year had already added thirty pounds.

"Do you have my pages?"

"Do you have my pages! Do you have my pages! Don't you say hello anymore?"

"Hullo, hullo!" He stood and did a jig. "Hul-lo, hul-lo—a-*nuh*-ther opening of a-*nuh*-ther show!"

She scowled, lumbering to the kitchen to fix a sandwich. Thank God Diantha wasn't around for this. His wife had been so fastidious in her person, so immaculate—proprietary of her daughter's fading beauty.

"Have you heard from Molly?" He risked a diatribe but couldn't help himself. It was a year since he'd seen his granddaughter. Her birthday was coming up.

"Molly *died*, Father, remember? Molly died and *Jabba* took her place. That's what she calls herself now—Jabba the Whore!"

He took the transcript from the counter and sat back down with an old man's sigh. "Such a tragedy."

"Since when is it a tragedy to be a whore?"

"Don't, Lavinia. Don't talk like—!"

"A whore and a doper. A jailbird, Father! She should die in prison, with AIDS!"

"Lavinia, she's a sick girl."

"*I'm* a sick girl! *I'm* a sick girl!" She pointed to a purplish knee. "I'm in *pain*, Father, *twenty-four hours a day*. I didn't *choose* that! Jabba the Whore lives in a world of her own choosing."

"So do we all."

"So do we all! So do we all!"

"That knee of yours is in bad shape because of the weight."

"Oh, that is a *lie* and if you want to talk to my chiropractor, Father, he will tell you. So do we all, so do we all! Would you like me to call him?" Severin wearily shook his head. "You can talk to my acupuncturist too. And if you really want to know, which I'm sure you don't, the weight on my knee is a cushion—"

"All right, Lavinia. It's a cushion."

"And the moral is! If you *don't* know what the hell you're *talking* about, *don't* offer opinions! The great So Do We All has *so many* important opinions! God, do I *hate* that."

They moved to Los Angeles in 'forty-three and Severin bused tables at Chasen's, working up to waiter. A quick, funny, ingratiating kid. He made his connections and eventually scored with the regulars, free-lancing bits for Red Buttons and Sammy Kaye. Then he met Hope and sold a few gags to the weekly radio show. They signed him full-time—but he'd always have Chasen's. Took Lavinia there on her tenth birthday, still had the snapshot: slender girl in a party dress wedged between him and Diantha, George the maître d' in his monkey suit on one side, Maude and Dave sidling in on the other, smiling from the blood-red booth like royalty. One of his old customers wheeled in the cake on a copper table—Irwin Shaw. He respected Shaw, a real writer, a book writer, that's what Severin wanted to be in his heart of hearts. He tried and failed a dozen times before deciding to do the next best thing; adapt a classic for the screen. A novelist by proxy.

"And don't you forget: Jabba the Whore was made from *his* seed."

"Who?" he asked, riffling pages, not really listening. Severin tensed; too late—fell for it again. He was a player in a grim sitcom, a straight man in Lavinia's little shop of horrors.

"Who! Chet Stoddard, that's who!"

"Oh Christ—"

"Don't you *oh Christ,* don't you dare! For what that man put me through? Did you *know* that my *jaw* will never mend? Never mend: do you even know what that *means?*"

"It's a long time ago."

"Tell it to my *jaw*! Tell my jaw how long it's been! I go to Vegas to *rescue* him and that piece of shit *punches me out*! At Sahara's, right in the casino, hundreds of people!"

"All right, Lavinia—"

"Don't *all right* me and don't *Oh Christ*! The bone could have gone to my *brain*. Do you know what kind of *headaches* it has caused me? The *migraines*, Father? Do you understand how *demeaning*?" She began to weep. "With the *pain* and the *police* . . . the *humiliation* in that desert town. And not *even jail*, they dried him out in a *luxury* hospital, flew him back first class! If it wasn't for me, his show would have gone off *months* before it did! I *schmoozed* for that man! With Saul Frake *pawing* me, his *tongue* in my mouth, I could *vomit*. Father? Would you please give me the courtesy of an answer?"

Severin poured himself a drink at the wet bar. He felt like an actor doing a bit of business.

"I'm a good person! Why has this *happened* to me? What has happened to my *life*? Why *me*, Father? Why! Why! Why!" She went to the bathroom and blew her nose while Severin sat down again to surf the bands. Lavinia re-emerged, waddling toward him with a fat rusty tube in her hand. "I took this from the drawer," she said meekly. "Okay?" Some forgotten Coppertone cream. She seized the typed pages from his hand, brandishing them. He turned up the volume of the scanner. "What are you going to *do* with this? Your eyes are so bad you can't even *read*. What are you going to *do*?"

"What do you care? You get paid."

"People pay me to type for a *reason*, they have *scripts*, they have *jobs*, they're writing *books*. I don't understand your *reasons*—you're just eavesdropping on people's lives! People have a right to their privacy—"

"What are you, ACLU? You get paid to type. Period."

"I'd love to hear what *Chet Stoddard,* the Larry King of his *time,* has to say—maybe you could listen to *him.* But he probably can't *afford* a car phone. I hope he can't afford a *car* or if he can, he's living in it." Her face lit up like a battered jack-o'-lantern as she threw down the pages and backed toward the door, Baggied sandwich in hand. "If anyone ever finds out you're doing this—*illegally eavesdropping*—I want you to say you typed it your*self.* Not that anyone would believe it. Just tell them you found someone *else,* not *me,* okay? All right, Father? Because I do not want to be drawn in."

*

Free to listen to Voices again—shouting from canyons and on-ramps and driveways without letup, bungling into digital potholes on Olympic, dead spots on Sunset—shpritzing from palmy transformer-lined Barrington . . . Sepulveda . . . Overland . . . crying from electrical voids on nefarious far-flung PCH, dodging wormholes and power poles, festinating to beat devil's odds of tunnel and sub-terranean garage as one tries to beat a train across a track—prayers and incense to ROAM (where all roads lead)—trying to beat the ether. A blizzard of Voices fell from range, chagrined, avalanche-buried spouses in flip phone crevasse, electromagnetic wasteland of tonal debris. Neither Alpine nor AudioVox nor Mitsubishi-Motorola could defend against unnerving fast food airwave static: recrudescent, viral, sudden and traumatic—words dropped, then whole thoughts, pledges, pacts, pleas and whispers, jeremiads—maddening overlap, commingling barked-staccato promises to reconnect swiftly decapitated: Westside loved ones morfed to scary downtown Mex, collision of phantom couples in hissing carnival bumper cars, technology cursed, torturous redial buttons pressed like doorbells during witching hour—*hullo? hullo? can you hear me?*—symphony of hungry ghosts begging to be let in.

I'm losing you.

Rachel Krohn

She sat in the lobby of the storefront mortuary, nervously thumbing a Fairfax throwaway. An ad within offered membership:

ONLY $18.00 A YEAR
• Free Teharoh (washing of body)
• Free Electric Yartzeit Candle
• Recitation of Kaddish on day of Yartzeit

Rabbinical-types in white short-sleeved shirts came and went without acknowledging her; she wondered if they were apprentices. A smiling Birdie brought her back to the cluttered office.

"Your father was not murdered."

The old woman said it without preamble, like a teacher delivering a Fail.

"What are you saying?"

"Forgive me—but something in my heart told me it wasn't right to hide what I know. I thought it was God putting me next to you at the seder."

Rachel was dumbfounded. For a moment, she wondered if Birdie was someone in the grip of a religious psychosis. "What do you know? What happened to my father?"

"Your father took his own life."

Rachel let out a great sob. The old woman touched her, then withdrew. She handed her Kleenex and a cup of water, then calmly spoke of Sy Krohn's affair with a congregant—how the "lady friend" gave him a disease ("nothing by today's standards!"); how the cantor, realizing he'd passed the infection to Rachel's mother, chose to die.

"You said . . . your husband was there?" She spoke as if reading a script from a radio show. *Your father was not murdered*—Orthodox film noir. "You said at the seder—"

"*Here*—the body was flown back. But you know that."

"But your husband . . ."

"He performed the *taharah*."

"May I talk to him?"

"He will not speak to you. He was opposed to me telling what I knew."

"Was it *here* that he—" The old woman nodded, and Rachel thought she would faint; this is where the body had lain. She stood, as if to go. "You said those who do the . . . purification—are volunteers. Is that something I could do?"

"It's not for everyone."

Rachel shook, flinching back tears. "But it's for *me*!" The words came savagely, humbling the *shomer*. Rachel composed herself and said again, softly: "It's for me."

Birdie walked her to the sidewalk.

"You'll call?"

The old woman nodded. "I will."

"There's just one other thing I wanted to know. My father's buried at Hillside. How is it—I thought if a Jew killed himself, he couldn't—"

"There are ways around that. It was simply said your father was not in his right mind. Which he was not."

As she reached her car, Rachel imagined a string of women in the lobby, pending on Birdie—each with a revelation waiting, custom-made.

*

Sy Krohn was buried in the Mount of Olives on the outskirts of the park, across from a large apartment complex. On her way to the plot, Rachel tried remembering details—but that was thirty years ago. A worker on a tractor respectfully cut his engine as she stood over the stone. She was certain it was park policy; he even seemed to hang his head, BELOVED HUSBAND AND FATHER was all it said.

Rachel wasn't ready to confront her mother, so she drove to the mansion overlooking the necropolis. That's where the rich were interred—far away from the syphed-out cantor-suicides. Al Jolson's sarcophagus adorned the entrance. "The Sweet Singer of Israel" knelt Mammy-style while a mosaic Moses held tablets in the canopy above. Mark Goodson, game show producer, was across the way, the outline of a television screen around his name.

No one was inside but the dead. Scaffolding stood here and there in the hallways, as if the artists painting the ceilings were on lunch break. Small rooms off the main drags were filled with stacks of thin green vases. A few employees loitered outside, tastefully—they seemed aware of her browsing, and again, she wondered if by policy they'd left their workaday posts, awaiting completion of her tour. She entered an elevator as if it were a tomb and rode to the second floor. More couches and vases and yarmulkes and emptiness. She took the stairs down, past the David Janssen crypt. There were flowers and a big birthday card signed Liverpool, England. "We cry ourselves to sleep at night," it said. "We will never forget you." She passed vaults of "non-pros" with strangely comic epitaphs: HIS LIFE WAS A SUCCESS; SHE LIVED FOR OTHERS. Then came Jack and Mary Benny, and Michael Landon. "Little Joe" had a room to himself, with a small marble bench. The entrance had a glass door, but it wasn't locked. Anyone could go in.

*

"Who told you this?"

They stood in the hot, bright kitchen. The psychiatrist was between clients.

"What *difference* does it make? Why didn't you *tell* me?"

"I planned to," said Calliope. "At the time, there were so many other things . . . I was going to wait until you were a little older, but then—"

"Well, now I am!" A mocking kabuki mask, glazed with tears.

"Do you really think you would have wanted all the details, Rachel? Could you have *handled* them? Can you handle them now?"

"Don't insult me, Mother."

"Is it any better now that you know?"

"I'm glad I know the *truth*." A door opened outside. Mitch and a patient said goodbyes. "It's so . . . classically hypocritical!

The old cliché, isn't it? The psychiatrist who tells her patients that secrets kill—and here we are, all these years, living a lie? Can't you see how *insane* that is?"

Calliope whitened, trembling. "Your *father* was the hypocrite, not I! What I did, I did for *you*, Rachel, to *protect* you, you and Simon. If we had stayed here, *believe me* you would have been hurt. So don't talk to me about hypocrisy."

They heard footsteps. Mitch returned to his office. The women caught their breath, and Rachel resumed in subdued tones.

"Do you—do you know who the woman was? Is she still . . ."

"Serena Ribkin. She died last year. She happened to be the mother of a client, strangely enough." She sat in the banquette, limp. "There: now you even have a name."

"Was . . . was my father in love with her?"

"I imagine. Such as love is—though I doubt it would have lasted. But what the hell do I know? Maybe they were Tracy and Hep." She stood, energized again; her mother was always a quick recovery. "Rachel, I have to get back. Why don't we have a nice dinner over the weekend—we need that. We can go to that fabulous sushi place on Sawtelle."

"All right, Mama."

She fell into Calliope's arms and wept. Mitch was suddenly at the back door, but the psychiatrist sent him away with a shake of the head.

"That was a terrible, terrible time—you'll never know, darling, you don't *want* to. You and Simon were away, remember? I was glad of that. I used to literally thank God for Camp Hillel."

She stroked her daughter's head and kissed it. And then she cried and Rachel couldn't remember seeing that, ever. Her hair was thick and gray; at sixty-seven, she was still a beautiful woman. They strolled to the front door, arm in arm.

"Who was it that told you about your father?"

"A woman I met at a seder."

"You went to a seder?" She smiled, genuinely surprised.

"At my boss's." Rachel wasn't sure why she lied. "I had to, for business."

"And who was this woman?" Calliope asked, a paranoid glint in her eye. "Is she talking to people about Sy?"

"Not at all—Mother, it's nothing like that. It was an isolated event, a weird thing. She didn't even know who I was."

"She didn't know who you were yet ends up telling you your father killed himself. *Very* mysterious." Calliope smiled indulgently. There would be no more interrogations, at least not today. "Well," she said, kissing her daughter again, "you go home and soak—take a bubble bath. I'll call and we'll make a time."

Severin Welch

LesLeLes?

   what's hap ning with Obie

not so well

   . . . conscious?

no—. . . shou dn't say that, she—

   EL MUCH CHO DICE QUE DEBMOS ESTAR ALLI ANTES DE LAS CUATR

   shit

I didn't hear

   are y there? LESLIE? you there

   there you are. that was my friend Pancho

   ha, lovely

   hear me now?

she's unconscious—

just so hard to know

maybe it's time . . . her mother—what does her

mother

it's a bi mess right now, big mess

have you thought of i mean Les have you thought about you

know is there a

way

a legal way

oh i couldn't do that, of course, i've thought; yes. oh god, I couldn't

maybe someone else

it's all b come a major deal

are you going to the AIDS thingee

what?

award

for Gottlieb? 829—ESO QUEDA CERCA DE

SEPULVEDA SI SI

CERCA DE LA

ESCUELA Rochester is singing "Oh My Papa"—sounds like a buzz saw dying—Benny walks in from rehearsal. Benny keeps saying, "It's going to be a great show tonight! I think it's gonna be a great show!" In comes Don Wilson, asks if Hope's still mad that he makes a late entrance. Benny says Hope's a little hot under the collar but he'll get over it. Wilson leaves and Rochester gives Benny a shave. He's shaving and then he jumps back. "Uh oh, I think I cut you!" Benny says, "What do you mean, you *think,* can't you *tell?*" Rochester says, "It would help if you'd *bleed* a little!" Benny hears the orchestra play his theme, but he can't find his pants. Hope walks onstage—he's holding Benny's pants! Looks at the pants and says he's about to introduce a great entertainer: Gypsy Rose Benny. Says how strange it is working over at CBS—"that stands for Crosby & Benny's Strongbox"—feels out of place as Zsa Zsa at a PTA meeting. But CBS is right next to the Farmer's Market, so "you can lay 'em here and sell 'em there." Holds up the pants again. "Look at that material, ain't it wonderful? They call it 'unfin- ished payments.' " Unfinished payments—that was Severin's. The whole premise about swiping the pants so Jack couldn't go on was Severin's. And the "Road to Nairobi" sketch, with Benny and Hope in a cauldron surrounded by Zulus. There's a tiger hanging upside-down on a spit. When Hope swivels it around, there's leopard spots on the other side. Benny says, "The cat must have seen a vet—in Denmark." Hope says, "I wondered why it had its hand on its hip when I shot it." All Severin. Hope laughing so hard Severin didn't think he'd be able to finish. Martin and Lewis lit the cauldron bonfire at the end of the show. Must have been on ten seconds, tops, *i'm gonna fuck you up! take you to the*

cloisters, CUNT MOTHERFUCKER!
jerome, you didn't let me explain

explain! you cn explain.
xplain it to th mother fkng emergency room
how there's a bullet through your mothrfucked
up lyin head, you gonna be able to plain that,
freak? you cn explain everything else, answer
me, mother freak fucker!

jerome—
you ain w rth NUTHIN
jerome, i did not go AROUND with derrie i told you he was fuckd

    up that's why he's on the couch
  you what? you tol me what?
     i said i tol you he was fcked up, he was too Juckd up to drive—
and tha's why he was on the couch? Is that what you said, nigger?
  thats right

                  that what you said?

 thats right
             too fucked up to drive
   thats right
  do i luk like ed norton to you?
    crazy! Jerome
  i'm crazy
well you're acting that way, anyway, talkin about ed norton who is
ed norton
  i'm acting what way, nigger?

                  why d you keep

         repeating evrything I—

            i'm gonna burn your titties, drty
        cunt! motherFUCKER

     jerome, man, don't say that now, hney, you're scaring me!
  don't honey me, bitch, an im gonna do more than scare, nigger.
    what'd you thnk this is, hallowe'en? i'm gonna take the
tongs to your bumpy black ass
  your sick !

        shit down tha dick-sucking throat
      i am outta here
      go ahead, bitch, but i know you can't travel far with
        a dick in
      your ass
   jerome

cock like crack for you, gotta always be suking on that pipe, it like
    motherfuckin oxygen
    i'm going to to Chicago
    go, baby, go see mama an have fun.
cause you ain gonna live long, neither wunna you A clear, staggering sky; tonight, Severin could hear every word. He called Pink Dot for a pastrami sandwich, toilet paper, Lucky Strikes, Windex and chewing gum.

By the pool with the scanner, Santa Anas bent the stars, showering Voices down around like aurorae boreales. A boy called back to say they didn't have those kind of cigarettes, did he want some*around eight o'clock*
    oh darling hurry!do you love me?
                you know i do.
        then can't you come any soonr?
          sure'd like to. like
         to come a whole lot sooner
           don't be dirty!
        why not? it's fun to be drty
     people can listen on these phones
     let em get their jollies
you're bad!
sure bn thinkn abo t you
you have?
    uh huh all day
what?
    thinkin about you all day
        yr lying are lying?
            would i lie to you, honey? "now
            would i say something that
      wasn't true?"

> i like that song
> i'm asking you would i li—
> i like when you sing to me
> so you been thinking about me all day?
that's right, on and off
> i like the on part more than the off
> on and off that sur says it all
i thought you meant all day like "all day sucker"
w ellthat's what i am
> you are? or you wanna be?
> both
> i wish you were here right now
close your eyes and make a wish
> mmmmmmm. ok, i did
> what'd you wish?
> i can't tell you that!
> i thgt you told me everything
> just hry home
> is this spousal arousal?
i can't hear
> spousal
what?
> be home
hello?
> love

Pink Dot kid came with everything, a good kid, brought Camels, not the same as Luckies, but not too bad. Diantha used to smoke Kents.

Colder outside now. In half an hour came Tom Snyder, *there* was a survivor. Kissinger was going to be on, Kissinger and McNamara, could you believe it? What a time capsule.

He moved to the living room, scanner and all, this septuagenarian in his sprawly, musty bachelor pad with the giant vintage answering machine and Sinatra eight-tracks and *Playboy* towers sprung from the carpet: fiction by Styron, Mailer, Updike, Shaw. He submitted a story there once *you going to the Huston dinner?*

what's that?

the artist rights thing

fuck no, i'm going to the vneyard

you have your financing, Zev?

we just need one more piece

who's doing it?

Val Kilmr

i thought you had baldwin?

Baldwin's out

Kilmer is good

Demme loves Klmr

jsus i forgot you had Demme! are you gonna change the title?

what are you, from the studio?

Zev? Zev can you hear me?

i said what are you, from the studio?

hello?

there you are. i lost you.

i said, are you from the fuckin studio? they love to fuck with a good title

i love the title

then why the fuck would i change it

relax, Zev. jesus, jmp down my throat why don't you. i have a
wife who does that

i'll be your wife
yeah wll make me an offer
pay or play?
hahahahaha
i think you should have a proprietary cred t—like
"Caligula' what?"
jesus this phone is shit
Zev?
what
there you are can you hear me
yeah "Gore Vidal's Caligula"
that's what,
that's what you should do
call it
you should
call it ev Turl ub's DEA SOULS
what?
your breaking
ev
Turle taub's

DEH SOULS

Perry Needham Howe

Rachel found a dealer for the grande complication at the
Regency Beverly Wilshire. The fine watch emporium was
managed by a suave, self-effacing Frenchman. As things had

it, Henri Clotard was a huge fan of *Streets*. He was very sorry to say there were no Destrieros in the country at this time; he would have to make a few inquiries. Monsieur called the next morning to say he had arranged for a minute repeater to be sent by courier from the East Coast. Since Mr. Howe had never seen one, he thought it would be of interest. Perry went over as soon as the timepiece arrived.

*

He waited to be buzzed in.

Henri extended a hand, smiling graciously. "What a pleasure it is to meet you! Your kind assistant said you were a prompt man, and on this day I am most grateful, for I have been called away on a minor medical emergency."

"I'll come back another time."

"Nonsense, sir—I would not think of it. You are *here* and it would be bizarre to send you packing." He possessed the heightened, anachronistic politesse of a diplomat in a drawing-room farce. "I was fortunate enough to locate a complication here in the United States. Would you care to see it?"

The watch was similar to the Destriero, except its movement was concealed by a solid platinum case (the Destriero's was see-through). Perry strapped it on, feeling the full weight of its six hundred-some parts—perhaps one got used to the heaviness. The face was elegant, without bejeweled ostentation. To the untrained eye, there was nothing to indicate its worth; that was part of the allure.

"There are complications far plainer than this, sir. Two days ago, I had here an Audemars: one hundred forty thousand dollars. You would really not look twice. And yet, if you

buy yourself a ticket to New York next week for the auction at
Sotheby's (you don't have to fly first class!), you can put your
bid on a very simple-looking Patek Philippe, a minute repeater
from the year nineteen and thirty. But make sure," he added,
with a showman's grin, "to have half a millions in your wallet."

They walked through a catalogue. There were pecu-
liar-looking "jumping hour" models; Reverso Tourbillons;
Chronograph Rattrappantes; a Breguet (the premier genius of
watchmakers and Marie Antoinette's favorite) that measured
the length of each day as would be shown by a sundial; and
the wristwatches of Ulysse Nardin, portable astrolabes reflect-
ing the time and position of the stars all at once, in addition to
the month, lengths of day, night and twilight, moon phases,
astronomical coordinates and signs of the zodiac. The dials
were made of meteorite.

"The 'Astrolabium Galileo Galilei' is so correct," said the
Monseiur, "that there would merely be a deviation of *one day*
from the position of the stars after a period of approximately
one hundred and forty-four thousand years."

"Where does one buy something like this?"

"Oh, you can get them. Mostly, at auction—Genève. I was,
last month—*une grande farce.* Dealers should just stay away.
You see, the auctions are now open to the public, they are in
the hands of consumers who know *nothing.* I saw a watch that
retails for thirty-five thousand go at thirty-eight. It *retails* at
thirty-five, *new,* sir! There was an Italian on one side of me,
a German on the other and they just *did not stop.* They were
competing with one another—in a frenzy for the absolutely
insignificant. For things of no consequence. I said to the auc-
tioneer, 'Why are you doing this?' He said, *'Je ne fais rein.'* But
the auction houses . . . *alors.* Have you seen this?" He pushed at

him a photo of what looked to be an oversized pocket watch. "Patek Philippe: the 'Calibre 89.' I have a video I can show you. They sold one at auction to a group of Japanese investors for some three millions. Patek was *livid*—they thought it should have gone for seven. You see, the house set the reserve too low. They started at six hundred thousand when it should have been one and three-quarters millions. Only three 'Calibres' exist, sir!"

Perry undid the band, balancing the watch in his palm. "And how much is this one?"

Henri consulted another book. "One hundred and seventy-five thousand." He turned it over to reveal the engraving: "You see? One of fifty produced in nineteen ninety-five. It is also available—I would have to make a phone call, maybe two—with a platinum band. For that, seventy-five thousand is added. But if it is not in the country . . ." He winced a small, punishing smile; the dollar was weak. "You see, these kind of watches are made for a very elite group. And we are pushing ourselves into a corner, dealers and manufacturers alike. One day, I predict it will be very bad. They are making these in China now—in fact, I am going to Peking next month. They will make them at a fraction of the cost and sell low! They will say, 'This is authentic! Look, *we* are the oldest culture! We invented gunpowder! We! We! We!' "

The moment Perry had been waiting for was at hand: time to depress the repetition slide, the lever that triggered the chime. Henri set the hour at 11:57 and, without fanfare, keyed the mechanism with his thumb. The eleven meditative strokes of the hour were plangent and softly surprising, like a bell tower ringing in a distant town square. Perry thought of the shrunken city Superman kept under a glass in the Fortress of Solitude; he imagined the atom-sized inhabitants of a village—Schaffhausen?—going placidly about their business as the sealed world sang with the chronometric music of time. After the hours marked, there immediately followed the ringing of the quarters: three mellisonant double-chimes like delicate flares of wheat. To the sightless (and privileged), the clock had thus far "read" the hour as 11:45. Then, higher tones still, came an aborted minuet of minutes that remained. When this was done, Henri discreetly stepped away, allowing Perry the honors of initiating such a feast of minutiae and movable parts himself.

"I know a collector who has eleven minute repeaters," said the Monsieur as he returned. "Each a different maker. His joy is to set them off in unison. He lines them up in front of a microphone and broadcasts the cacophony over speakers—and these are not the normal speakers, I assure you, they are quite monolithic. I don't know what the neighbors think; it sounds like nothing you've ever heard before. It isn't necessarily pleasing to the ear—not to *mine*, but to his, yes. He is eccentric. You'll note I don't say crazy, I say *eccentric*. We all have a fever. My friend has his and you have yours, I can tell. I'm not sure what it *is*, but you have it."

Perry snapped to: "I've kept you far too long." The television producer longed to engage in the florid, mannerly volleys of noblesse oblige.

"It is perfectly okay," said Henri. "It has been my utmost pleasure, and of that, I am sincere."

"You've been exceedingly gracious" was the most the novice could muster. Then: "I hope whatever calls you away isn't serious."

"It is very kind of you to offer a comment and I thank you for that. My mother is ill, for some many years. She recently had the misfortune of taking a tumble and it seems she has taken another. Not to worry: fortunately—if one can say such a thing—this last unpleasantness occurred one hour ago while at hospital for the purpose of assessing hip transplant surgery. She is in good hands and I am assured all is status quo. I am headed there now."

Perry didn't buy the complication but felt he probably should have, if only for selfishly detaining his adviser. He bought a Tiffany watch instead, and told Henri it was for his wife. He would give it to Tovah as an emblem of their new project—knowing full well that was artifice. He would give it to her because it felt good and because he wanted to see her face when he put the box in her hand. It was as uncomplicated as that.

Ursula Sedgwick

Ursula kept calling ICM, leaving Donny messages that she needed to see him. When she told one of his assistants it was "urgent," the agent finally agreed, out of sheer paranoia. He was half an hour late for their lunch at Cicada.

"Phylliss Wolfe tells me you're big buddies."

"Phyll's great—and she's great with Tiffany. She really wants to have a kid."

"Yeah, well, she'd better hurry. Her hormones are almost in turn-around."

"She's very spiritual, too."

"So *Phylliss* is the one who got you involved with this shit! She tried to drag *me* to one of those fucking meetings."

"She didn't drag me anywhere, Donny."

"With the guy—Mahatma Hoot-muh—what do they call him?"

"His name is Sri Harold Klemp. He's called the *Mahanta*—"

"Right! Klemp! The guy from *Wisconsin*. Wisconsin, the dairy and guru state."

"You can sit and make fun all you want, but it's real. And so is reincarnation of Soul."

"You have to admit it's kind of hilarious, Ursula. I know I said 'Get a life,' but I didn't mean a *past* one." People stopped by to say hello. Donny didn't bother to introduce her. "Why don't we have the food to go and get a room somewhere? Someplace sleazy."

"I don't want to do that, Donny."

"Because of the boyfriend? I want to hear all about the boyfriend."

"He isn't a boyfriend."

"Then let's go."

"I don't need to do that anymore."

"Oh, I get it." He scowled. "*Past Life Therapy* . . . is that what this is?"

When she started to talk, he waved at a table. The luncheoners beckoned him over. Ursula used the wineglass to make imprints on the cloth, drawing faces in the circles with a fork. Donny sat back down and the same thing happened again, different players. He was gone ten minutes, returning as the salads were served.

"It was early in the fourth century—"

"Joan of Arc?" he asked cursorily, digging into the romaine.

"I was a wealthy girl—"

"Why is it that in past lives, poor people are always *rich*?"

She stared down at the scarified linen, collecting herself. "It was in Rome. I was born in Palermo, of a noble family. A powerful senator wanted to sleep with me, but I refused."

"Maybe that was Newt—Newt had to have a past life. Or Ross Perot! Al Gore?"

"As punishment for my stubbornness, I was forced into a house of prostitution . . ."

"*Now* we're getting somewhere. You know, I believe in past lives, I really do. I knew a guy who sold used cars. Always called them 'chariots.' Sweet guy, name of Benjamin—Benjamin *Hur.* But all his friends called him—"

"Donny, just listen!" The agent grew sullen and fidgety. "The only person who would help me was a boy who ran errands for the madam—"

"Right! The new boyfriend—your *hero.* I'm happy for you, Ursula. Maybe you can rule the trailer park together. But let me ask you something: does Mahatma Junior share the same little recovered memory? I mean, does he at least get the chance to *rebut?* You know: 'Hey, I don't remember that! That's not one of my past lives! I was King of the Zulus!' "

"Sometimes it takes a while to bring those memories from the Inner to the Outer. And Taj is very new—as am I."

"Taj?"

"He needs to come by it himself, and he *will.* If he lets the Mahanta guide him."

"What's his last name?"

"I don't know."

"Is it *Wiedlin?* What's he look like?"

"I don't see why that's important."

"You're right," he said, nodding at the waiter for the check. "Nothing's important. Including the fact you are out of your fucking mind."

*

Why did she even bother? She was grateful for all he'd done, especially for Tiffany. She wanted to release him, because Ursula knew her love had been overbearing. But to release him meant sharing the found vision of her passion play: smell of wet stones and burning wood, sting of incense, bordello voices (they seemed like Latin or maybe Italian, though she spoke neither).

She hadn't yet mentioned to Sara or Phylliss what girlhood memories and a trip to the downtown library had confirmed. When she was Tiffany's age, an aunt bought her a *Dictionary of Saints*. There was a painting of an ecstatic girl, implements of torture scattered at her feet. A man in a shirt with puffed sleeves held a sword to her neck. The story said she'd been forced into prostitution for refusing a rich politician; this hapless blonde, found on the Inner—who was Ursula, sad whorehouse girl exhumed from a dream—was none but St. Agatha herself. Now that her life made sense, she wanted to tell Donny everything, but how could he listen? Agatha had rejected the senator as Ursula had her father and his rough friends. Agatha consecrated her virginity to Jesus Christ; Ursula would make her vows to the Mahanta Sri Harold Klemp, the Living ECK Master. She must have known all this even as a tiny girl (it made her think of the Motorcycle Man at the potluck). Ursula was mildly embarrassed at the "bride of Mahanta" aspect, because she knew that wasn't at all something ECKists encouraged.

Maybe it was inappropriate. She'd talk to Phyll about it. Phyll would set her straight.

*

Tiffany was coloring her book with a child's fierce attention. Occasionally, she glanced up at *Fragile Rock.*

A woman came looking for Ursula. Taj saw her through the curtain; he knew Phylliss from ICM days and didn't feel like an encounter. He slunk to the bedroom.

For a few weeks, he'd been crashing there, unbothered, leaving in the early morning hours—but it seemed that the truth about Taj Wiedlin would soon out. Maybe it was time to call his sister for airfare home. He hadn't spoken to the family since Zev let him go. His mom was probably worried near to death.

When the coast was clear, he returned to the living room with a milkless bowl of Cheerios.

"Why did you hide?" asked Tiffany.

"I didn't hide."

"You're weird," she said, going back to her routine.

Taj couldn't believe he was offended by the little girl's dismissal. She shook her head, curling her lip in disgust as she drew. Taj began an "I'm weird" dance to break the tension, but her rejection congealed.

"When's Mama coming home?"

"I don't know, Crabby," Taj said, doing his goofy jig. "Come on and smile."

"I am *not* crabby and *stop* it."

"Crabby Tabby."

"You're *bothering* me," whined Tiffany. "You don't even *live* here."

"Ground control to Major Crab! Have a Cheerio and do the 'weird' dance. You'll feel better."

"I *hate* you." She didn't really, but now she'd said so.

"A little over the top, don't you think? And rude."

"*You're* rude." Less emphatic now.

"Why do you hate me?"

"Because you're *weird*."

"You mean I'm weird because I fuck your mother between the legs?"

Tiffany stood, agitated. *"Be quiet!"*

He started a "Be quiet!" dance, and she pushed him. Taj grabbed her head and held it fast so they were nose to nose, like player and ref. He made creepy, guttural sounds and Tiffany shook, squealing in terror. He screamed all over the surface of her head as if it were the earth, his cries satellite signals covering land, sea and polar cap. He dug nails into her chest and yelled at the top of his lungs in her ears, making funny kung fu faces as he butted Tiffany's head and yanked out a slim broomful of hair.

He dialed Zev's office, pounding her stomach while they had him on hold. "Hello? Are you casting yet for *Dead Souls*?"

He left her there, receiver propped to bloody mouth and ear.

Rachel Krohn

It was almost midnight when the old woman called.

Someone had died. Could Rachel make it to the *chevra* the next morning, say, eight-fifteen? The *taharah* would take an hour, maybe more. Birdie said it was a child and asked if that might be too upsetting. Rachel wasn't sure. She asked if it was an accident, and Birdie said the girl had been murdered. Was there blood? Birdie didn't know.

Rachel skimmed a handbook for grievers she'd picked up at the Jewish bookstore. It said mourners should cover mirrors and overturn beds. She turned out the lights and thought of the furnitureless mansion of her father's memorial park. She drifted to an ocean of bobbing canopy beds, each with wide-eyed child marooned. The beds bellied-up in the water until all that was left were their periscope-legs. She woke up drowning just after three and never got back to sleep.

Ursula Sedgwick

Donny argued with Phylliss and Sara, who were pushing for an ECK memorial, with readings from "The Golden Heart" and "Stranger by the River."

When his mother died, the rabbi explained how the human being was often compared to a Torah scroll, the parchment equivalent to the body; the divine names written thereon, the soul. The agent thought that beautiful. Serena's pilgrimage beneath the house had left her filthy, and Donny loved the idea of pious, level-headed strangers ceremonially scrubbing her down—wiping the pages clean—for the Journey. When he suggested the *taharah* would be a good thing, Ursula didn't speak. She smiled, grateful he was there at all—that anyone was who could help her Tiffany.

Donny called the rabbi and said Ursula was a Jew, and that is how her daughter was buried.

Rachel Krohn

Rachel was early. The girl's mother had been there all night with friends while the *shomer* sat with the body. The police arrested the boyfriend, Birdie said.

She sat on the couch and waited, wondering about the gore. What if the girl had been stabbed or mutilated? Rachel didn't think she could take that. She pulled a *taharah* primer from her sack. Some of the rules and regulations ranged from comical to macabre. All severed limbs were supposed to be tossed in the coffin. As blood was considered to be part of the body, it was kosher to be buried in the stained clothes of one's demise. And if a Jew wanted to be cremated, that was too bad—his wishes could be overruled by something called the Halachah, or Law. Birdie emerged from the back. It was time to begin.

The room was cold. There was a tiled floor with drain and slop sink. Buckets were filled with water and wooden two-by-fours lay stacked on a chair. The girl was on a metal gurney, wrapped in a bag. Another woman was there, around Birdie's age. She was the "watcher" who sat with the girl through the night, the one who recited prayers and reminded the body of its name "so it would not be confused before God." They washed their hands and put on gowns. Birdie offered surgical gloves, but Rachel declined; no one else wore them. The bag was removed. Rachel gasped—she was blond and looked like an angel. There was a bluish bump on her forehead and the chest was spotted with bruised whorls. *She will never have her period* went through her mind, like a mantra to keep her from sinking. A tube had been left in her mouth, and when Birdie tugged, it wouldn't budge. She took scissors and clipped so it didn't protrude, closing the lips and cutting the hospital bracelet. They covered the face and pubis with separate cloths, then the whole body with a sheet. Birdie tore pieces from the sheet to be used for the washing.

They tucked the sheet down and washed face and hair, drying afterward but not covering. The body was washed from right arm to shoulder, down torso to legs and then back. The process was repeated from the left side, Birdie washing while Rachel dried. Normally, rainwater or melted snow was required, but in this case they used water from the tap.

When the first washing was finished, they cleaned under finger and toenails with toothpicks. That was the most heartbreaking for Rachel, because the girl had painted her nails in different colors. They used polish remover that Birdie got from a metal drawer. Then the two-by-fours were placed under head, shoulders, buttocks and legs. The second washing—"the *taharah* proper"—began. Three buckets were used this time, and the girl was completely naked, even though Rachel thought the guidebook said that wasn't supposed to happen. They put a sheet over the body to dry it and the wood was removed. The other woman was ready with the shroud. ("After the *taharah* is completed," the book said, "the deceased is dressed in shrouds sewn by the hands of a woman past the age of menopause.") The sheet was lowered around the girl's head, and Birdie put a bonnet on her, as well as a piece that went around the face. Rachel helped with a collared, V-neck shirt—"you fuss with it. You have to learn," Birdie muttered—reaching in to take the little arm and pull. Both arms were brought to the head and manipulated through. The shirt had no buttons and was tied at the top. They slid the legs into the pajama bottoms, pulling them up to the waist. There, the string was twisted nine times, then made into three loops so it looked like the letter *shin*, which stands for God. Birdie tied strips of shroud just below the knee, and made a bow. The last piece they dressed her in was an overshirt, made the same way the shirt was, only longer. It was easier than before to get the arms through. They brought the wooden box next to her. Inside was a long strip from the shroud; when they lowered the girl in, it ended up around her waist. Birdie repeated the twisting procedure—it seemed like twelve or thirteen twists this time—then made the *shin* again.

The face covering was pulled down, and Birdie put broken pieces of pottery on the eyes and mouth. When the shroud was replaced, the other woman sprinkled dirt from Jerusalem over pubis, heart and face. The casket was lined with a very large piece of shroud that was then folded over the body, right side first, then left, then bottom and top. They put the lid on the casket and took off their gowns.

"To remove death," Birdie explained as they washed their hands from a hose in the parking lot. "When you come home from the funeral there's normally water outside the front door, for washing." Rachel stood there, numb and exhausted. "What a shame!" Birdie said. "Thank God it was not also a sexual assault."

*

That night, Rachel dreamt she stood pallbearer in a stream, guiding a raft into darkness. The chilly waters were deep and she carried a long pole. The little girl lay in her open casket, floating down this river that ran under Westwood. The bier became a barge filled with debris and Rachel climbed aboard, snaking her way past insolent men and passive women, searching for the vanished body. No one would help. Finally, she came to Tovah and a flying wedge of UTA militia.

"The cantor is ready for the second washing," said her smiling friend.

Severin Welch

Deh-souls! deh-souls! deh-souls!

ev

Turle taub's

DEH SOULS

"Well? What's he saying?" Severin bent over the recorder like a crone at a crystal ball.

The Dead Animal Guy hit PLAY, squinting hard. He'd been up to the house before—even to the daughter's. The Welches were clients from way back, when he worked for Three Strikes. Simon had kept in touch, and was simply delivering a carton of ciggies when he was suddenly drafted into a bit of the old *Our Man Flint*.

"Tell me! What is he *saying*? Is it 'Dead Souls'?"

Simon took in the scanner apparatus, gleaming at the gonzoid anarchy of it all. "Hey, this is off cellular!"

"Oh to hell with it," said Severin, exasperated. He shooed at Simon and retreated.

"Rad! You should let my friends post 'listen-ins' on the Net. Get the lotus-eaters where they live!"

As Simon rewound, the ancient auditor fast-forwarded to the William Morris façade. He saw the red brick edifice before him; they'd know in an instant if the Gogol property was being developed—by and for whom and how much. But who could Severin ask? Certainly not Dee Bruchner. He thought about Charlie Bennett, the expired Hitchcock collaborator. He'd call the Guild in the morning, see if he could drum up the erstwhile rep. Maybe it'd be someone amenable to—

"Hey, I think I know who that is!" cried Simon.

The old man stumbled over, fairly salivating.

"That's Zev Turtletaub, on Verde Oak! Around the corner—Ramon Novarro's old place. I was up there last week." They listened again. " 'Zev Turtletaub's Dead Souls'—hear it? *Big* producer. Did those canine flicks. And might I add, at the time of my housecall, the gentleman had a harem of, shall we say, 'lovers of the dog.' He is himself an extremely hairless Homo erectus."

Severin liked the dog pictures; he'd seen them on cable. His pulse quickened. "Are you *sure*?"

"It's him, I'm telling you, Zev *Turtletaub*. His Siamese got stuck in the wall: a very large and may I hasten to add messy problemo. A two-hundred-dollar job. *Mimsy! That's* the name of the mutt. Lotta people went to see those. I told him when I left that the next movie he makes should be more like *Casper*, only about the ghost of someone's pet who gets stuck in a wall— starring Jim Carrey as the Dead Pet Detective. But instead of *Casper*, you call it *Fluffy*! I do *not* think he was thrilled."

*

Severin called the L.A. *Times* research line and requested they send anything on Zev Turtletaub that mentioned *Dead Souls*. The Xeroxes came in the mail a few days later; Lavinia enlarged them for his bad eyes. The old man feasted on photos of this bald quarry. Friend or foe?

The "Calendar" profile numbered *Dead Souls* ("based on the Russian classic") among the Turtletaub Company's active slate. A number of projects were tied to Paramount and Severin found that of note. A few days after he received the clippings, Lavinia read an item over the phone from the *Times* "Hot Properties" section. It detailed Turtletaub's recent purchase of the former Novarro estate from actress Diane Keaton. The house was a Lloyd Wright jewel he'd bought "as a lark" while awaiting renovations on a home in Bel Air. Just last year, she read, the producer paid seven-point-two million for a Montecito villa adjacent to the Robert Zemeckises'.

The Dead Pet Detective slipped him the Verde Oak address and phone. Severin gave him a twenty for his trouble.

*

"Mr. Turtletaub?"

"Who is this?"

"My name is Severin Welch." He was nervous as hell and barely got the words out. "I'm a writer—"

"How did you get this number?"

"An old client of Dee Bruchner . . ."

"Dee Bruchner gave you this number?"

"Yes. Because I understand you're at the Morris agency now—"

"I'm surprised. I don't generally enjoy receiving calls at my home from people I don't know."

"It's about *Dead Souls.*"

"And you say Dee Bruchner gave you this number."

"I have been working on that script twenty years, sir!"

"What did you say your name was?"

"Severin Welch, Esquire. May I inquire of you, sir, are you using the script from the Paramount vaults?"

"What?—"

"All I am asking from you and Mrs. Lansing-Friedkin—"

Turtletaub laughed gutturally.

"All am asking is that my labors be acknowledged as seed work. As the inception. I do not have a lawyer, sir, nor do I intend to engage one; I'm not overly fond of the breed. You don't have a worry on that account. I merely ask that you consider the revisions I have painstakingly entered, with much attention to colloquial verisimilitude, over the last sixty-five-odd months. I am not seeking sole credit, sir, meaning that if another writer has already been contracted, there is no reason for him to be perturbed—writers are, easily so: I know, as I am one myself. If another has been engaged, more power to him! If we could just meet, sir, you might bring me up to date—"

"Who the fuck *is* this? Burnham? Burnham, is that—?"

"This is Severin Welch, sir, as I have said."

A long pause. Then, without levity: *"I said who the fuck is this!"*

"It's Homo erectus, you chrome-domed doggie-dick cocksucker!" shouted the tense old man in a fit of rheumy inspiration. "I already told you my name, sir, three times! I am the original writer of the adaptation of *Dead So*—"

Zev Turtletaub hung up.

*

Stepping jauntily from the house, Severin carried *Souls* script and trusty Uniden cordless, for comfort—its range a mere fifteen hundred yards, yet how could he leave it behind? He might have jumped in a cab, but his own locomotion felt revolutionary. Bracing: *Verde Oak, Verde Oak, baker's man, bake me a cake as fast you can*—pounding the pavement, hitting his stride, humming hap hap happy talk inanities. By the lights of Frères Thomas, *chez Turtletaub* was under two miles . . . *luck, if you've ever been a lady to begin with* left! left! left right left! Must concentrate on objective. Must take Turdetaub Hill— HUMP! two-three-four HUMP! two-three-four *trudge. trudge. trudge. trudge.* Company—ho! *trudge trudge trudge trudge.* Criminy . . . ho! What the hell, the houseman could drive him back. Have pity on an old man. Here we go, then: brisk, breezy downhill gait. Then he got lost. Asked directions from gardeners and sundry housewife types, proffering slip of paper with Via Verde venue—at which they stared grinning fixedly, illiterates. Cretins. *Homo Cretinus Erectus.* A toot! A toot! He blows eight to the bar (in boogie rhythm)—*knew* he was near because the Thomas Bros told him so. Murphy's Law for you. Yowza yowza yowza. The gig is up. The Gig Young is up. Not such a bad walk, a walk like this. Astonished to have been the fool on the hill for so long—fifteen years, excluding one emergency outing for gallstones, Diantha hauling him in the T-bird, drugged like a cat on its way to the vet. Jesus God he'd ruined that woman with his mad quarantine, mucked up her golden years but good—

huh? Severin heard digital chirp of phone, the a-pealing *ting* in his ear. He smiled with a start then looked around past curtains of exhaust-flecked ivy, storm drains and driveways, astigmat's eyes jump window to window to focus the locus—ring now clear as day. From whence it came? Ah! From him! Severin Welch! And he *knew* . . . shimmying off backpack, shoulder blades like crows' wings, disgorging Uniden and punching TALK—out of range! How cruel! Sobbing bitterly, like a child, a senile drama queen, how cruel to call me now, when you know I'm out of range!

ev'ry body's been KNOW ing
to a wedding they're GO ing
and for weeks they've been SEW ing
turned and marched up the hill in long, uneasy lope
ev'ry SUSIE and SAL!
stridulations louder until as if by yelping flames surrounded, he fell down on his march
the bells are ring! in! for me and my
bloodying his bony self, *Souls* script splayed on asphalt, hand clutching prop-like Uniden to chest
they're con gre gay! TING!
FOR ME AND MY GAL!
THE! PAR! SON'S! WAY! TING! FOR ME AND
pinned in the road like a bug by the knitting needle of a sky-high heart attack collections man.

Missing the Call.

Perry Needham Howe

It was a drizzly Saturday and he sent his wife to Aida Thibiant for some all-day exfoliatory pampering. As for Perry, he was on his way to San Diego with Tovah Bruchner.

The resolute agent had a new client. Arnold Eberhardt owned an animation house that churned out sarcastic, offbeat cable cartoons along with regular-fare programming for kids.

He was a railroad enthusiast who enjoyed renting a few private cars from Amtrak—a coastal no-brainer that got friends and families to Balboa Park around noon. A little low-key first-class fun. The all-aboard crowd was techie and un-Hollywood; Perry didn't know anyone, and that was always easier on the nerves. The couples played poker on the way down, using Sweet'n Low packets for chips.

Perry and Tovah sat in the dome car lookout with their screwdrivers. He was talking about one of the watches he'd boned up on—it could tell you exactly where the sun would rise or set on the horizon—when a man from another table spoke up.

"The Ulysse Nardin. Friend of mine has one."

Perry was pleasantly taken aback. "You're kidding. I never thought I'd hear anyone but a dealer pronounce that name."

"I'm a bit of a fanatic—or was. Be careful!" he admonished, with a laugh. "That stuff's crack for the wrist. Though I have to tell you most people consider those Nardins a bit tacky."

Jeremy Stein was the creator of *Palos Verdes*, a nighttime soap that was starting to smell like a hit. When he introduced himself, Tovah smiled the infernal, knowing way agents do, as if to say "Don't fight it—you're done for. Soon you'll be mine." The corner of his mouth subtly drooped, and Perry remembered some controversy surrounding the name. He'd have to wait for Tovah to enlighten.

"I just signed Arnold," said Tovah, suggestively. Again, the cocky devil-woman grin.

"Yes, I know. He's the best. We went to college together." He turned to Perry. "If you're interested, I can put you in touch with a guy who gets unbeatable prices—forty percent off at minimum, and I've seen him go high as sixty. Crichton's a customer; buys himself one whenever he finishes a project, as a little reward."

"I've been looking at grande complications," Perry said. "Did you ever have one?"

He shook his head matter-of-factly. "Never. I know Geena just got one for Renny. I should tell you, if you wear the things, they're gonna wind up in the shop. They're like Ferraris that way. Renny's had his in *four times*—he's a very active guy! It's important to know a watchmaker, that's why Berto's so great. He's the guy I was telling you about. I made the mistake of sending one of my Pateks to Geneva for a repair. *Here it comes,* eleven months later! Berto usually has a three-week turnaround."

Arnold's boy came down the aisle, engrossed in a hand-held digital game. Jeremy gathered him up.

"He's sweet," Tovah said. "Taking him to the zoo?"

"Absolutely. You know, San Diego has a taipan, if you're interested—probably the most aggressive snake in the world. Northern Australia. Last time I was there, a kid put his hand to the window and the taipan struck three times. They didn't realize until the end of the day that the damn thing had broken its nose!"

Tovah sought her client out below while the new friends bonded over the addictive nature of collectibles. Perry mentioned the eighteenth-century "Pendule Sympathique," a kind of carriage clock crowned with a half-moon berth to accommodate certain pocket watches; when the latter were placed within, they would automatically be reset and rewound by the "mothership."

"That's Breguet—did Napoleon have one of those? That kinda thing comes up for auction every now and then. They're millions upon millions, it just doesn't end. You can go to

Frank Muller—Muller makes one-of-a-kinds—for two hundred grand, they'll design whatever kind of watch you want."

"I'd love to get together," Perry said as they pulled into the San Diego station. "I've heard great things about your show."

"And I'm a *big* fan of yours. I'll bring Berto—know where we'll go? Ginza Sushiko, heard of it? On the Via Rodeo. Probably the most expensive sushi place in the country. You can get fugu there. Friend of mine in Japan took me for absolutely *exquisite* tempura—you know, one of these places where you eat out of eight-hundred-year-old bowls. Anyway, he said they had something *extremely* rare that I *had* to try. I said, 'Well now, what would that be?' And my friend Ryuichi says, 'Cow penis.' He began to laugh. 'I think you mean *bull*, Ryuichi—though cow penis *would* be rare!' "

*

They only had a few hours and decided to skip the zoo.

Tijuana was close but not close enough; Tovah said it wouldn't be such a good thing if they missed the return jog. They cabbed it to Hotel del Coronado for lunch. On the way, Perry had a grim laugh, imagining himself at the border like Steve McQueen en route to a miracle clinic. What ever happened to laetrile, anyway?

Tovah took a while in the restroom. When she entered the lobby, Perry raised a finger from the front desk, holding her off. She smiled and sat down, not really thinking he was up to anything. When he came over, she said, "I'm starved," but Perry said he felt like eating in privacy so he'd gotten a room and hoped that was all right.

*

"When do children learn to tell time?" She was trying to get him to open up about Montgomery.

He could see part of her through the door, naked, sitting on the bowl having her pee. He thought of Jersey, being scrubbed with seaweed. God knew how long it had been since he'd watched a woman in a bathroom, other than his wife.

"That depends," he said, listening to the tinkle. He wondered if she'd done this sort of thing before with other clients—the afternoon delight. Probably not with a dying one, anyway.

She came out in a white hotel robe. They should be getting back, she whispered, kissing him. "Why, yes'm," he said. He could smell her sex on his face and dreaded washing it off.

*

Floating past Capistrano, sitting on a depopulated divan, Perry remembered he had brought Tovah's gift. There was an impulsive purity behind its purchase, but now, after the act, such a gesture would seem old-fashioned and demeaning: reward for a job well done in the sack, a gold watch for fifty minutes of service. It wasn't expensive enough to give his wife and he wouldn't want Jersey finding it tucked away in a drawer, either. He'd bury the thing or bring it back to Henri, for credit.

Arnold's son passed, and then another reconnoitering boy, who stared at him a moment, causing a pang. He looked just like Montgomery—without the seizures, of course, or the medulloblastoma the size of Children's Hospital. Only six hundred cases a year and Montgomery one of them; he died at the beginning of March, making him number one-oh-eight, or thereabouts. The last few weeks he got chemo through a tube in his chest. When he curled into the fetal position, a doctor had the gall to say kids responded to trauma by "reverting to infancy." Perry wanted to scream "He *is* a fucking infant!" but something stopped him short—he was nothing if not civil. He stabbed at himself for months after, always holding his tongue, his whole life he'd been that way, even when it counted most, keeping a neat little room in the back of his skull to house the cheap inventory of unvoiced comebacks and polished, useless retorts, obsolete and carefully shelved. Jersey was the one who got rowdy, while Perry held the world together. He regretted never having had a big Shirley MacLaine *Terms of Endearment* moment. Instead, he'd capitulated straight down the line. Why had he let them torture his kid like that?

Tovah brought him a drink.

"Did you ever sleep with Jeremy Stein?"

"Oh please."

"Why not?"

"First of all, the guy is, like, totally into whores. From what I hear. And he had a *stroke*—it probably doesn't even work anymore."

"So those are the top two reasons you wouldn't."

"That's *not* what I meant! He's *not* my type. He's got a *kid.* Who he, like, *abandoned.*"

"But you want to sign him."

"He's got a hit show. The one thing in his favor."

He eyed her quizzically. "Why is it," he asked, "that agents always say, 'You got it'?"

"I know. I *hate* that."

"And now all the *assistants* say it. Every time you ask for something, they say, 'You got it.' No: 'You gahhhhht it.' You don't say that, do you?"

"I don't know who started that."

"Probably your dad."

"That's a horrible thought."

They watched bodysuited surfers catch a wave. The agent was pensive. Perry tried finding her smell on his upper lip, but the booze had killed it.

"You know," she said, "I'm not so sure that was such a good thing. What we did."

"Sure felt like one." He regretted asking if she'd slept with Jeremy Stein. Vulgar and flip.

"That's *not* what I meant." She smiled, blinking sultrily. "Are you okay with it?"

Perry was at a loss. He fell back on sheer age, which conferred a certain ready cool. He began to sing. " 'Strangers on a train, exchanging glances'—"

"Are we?" she asked, preparing to be hurt—now, or later. "Are we strangers?"

All women are mysterious, he thought. Without the twin antidotal axiom, there would be no game: *All women are insecure.* "Here's an idea for a film: Two strangers meet on a train and agree to kill each other's agents."

"How about lawyers?" Tovah asked, relieved to be steered from her mushy course. "I'd feel more comfortable with that."

"You gahhhhht it."

Ursula Sedgwick

Donny couldn't believe that Taj Wiedlin, his "shadow" at ICM for over two years, was the child's killer. He felt like Walter Pidgeon in *Forbidden Planet*—the scientist whose unleashed id runs murderously amok. After the funeral, the agent dropped from sight. Ursula reasoned her old lover finally understood what she'd tried to tell him that day at Cicada: life is a wheel that turns round and round, like a carousel.

She was going downhill living in the house where her daughter was bludgeoned. She slept a few nights at Phyll's, but the bungalow was small; the producer was pregnant and sick and it was hard on them both. Sara asked her to stay in a guest room of the Brentwood hacienda. The garden and clean, cool walls were welcome. Ursula liked that the streets had no sidewalks. During the day, she puttered around the old Venice house, straightening up, watching TV, sometimes napping on Tiffany's bed. Taj called from jail a few times and left messages on the machine—she refused to change the number because it still felt like a link to her daughter. Sara and Phyll couldn't argue with that.

She was wonderful with Samson. Sara's actress friends were always visiting, spinning bawdy, cynical Hollywood tales—so funny and compassionate and full of life—Marcia Strassman and Arleen Sorkin (she'd just had a little boy), Mary Crosby and Marilu Henner. And, of course, Holly and Beth Henley (Beth just had a baby too). Holly was so giving. She kept offering money and work. "Hey!" she shouted. "Be mah damn purrsonal 'sistant!" Ursula wasn't ready, but it was neat to get the offer. She knew Holly was sincere.

She found the infamous *Dictionary of Saints* at a used-book store on the Promenade and brought it to the children's section of the library to read. Ursula felt safe surrounded by all the big, colorful books and lilliputian tables and chairs. The women who worked there assumed she was a nanny—or young mother, which she was and would always be. She re-examined the barbarous painting, as if remembering a childhood fever. Saint Agatha was often pictorialized carrying loaves of bread on a tray. The text said those loaves were actually breasts, sliced off by tormentors—that's why she was simultaneously known as "the patron saint of breast disease and of bakers." It was silly enough that she laughed. In other illustrations, the breasts were shown to be bells; so too was Agatha "the patron saint of bell ringers and firemen." Something for everyone.

She didn't dream anymore about the Roman brothel but knew that wasn't a repudiation of her vision. She wasn't sure how she had been so wrong about Taj's role, but ascribed it to her lack of sophistication on the Inner. Ursula chose not to think about it for now. In her heart, she was certain Tiffany had been taken for a reason; in her heart, she knew the Mahanta was with her daughter at the exact moment she translated (the beautiful ECKist word for "passed on"). She had no doubts Tiffany was on the Soul Plane now. On one of his tapes, Sri Harold spoke about people translating because they had so much love for life that they needed more room to express it—that's why they went to a "higher channel." Ursula wondered if murder changed any of that; there was nothing in the Eckankar literature that pertained. Maybe Tiffany was ready to go but didn't want to leave her mother so she drew this person Taj to aid in her translation. Something like that may have been true for Saint Agatha as well.

She poured herself into ECK volunteer and study groups. Ursula would do good works for those who had shown her kindness. She would heal herself through dreams and seek the Inner Master's help in unwinding her karma.

Rachel Krohn

Aside from Tovah's encouragements, Rachel didn't know why she agreed. She couldn't even remember giving out her number. When Mordecai called, he said they met at the seder, and a casually crass remark brought it all back: the one with the braces who owned the messenger service. (He probably got her number from Alberta, the portly yenta. Rachel called her Alberta, Canada, but never to her face.) So there they were, Mordie and Rachel at the movies, an Indian art-house flick she had wanted to see for a while. Surprisingly, he was attentive and cordial—aside from the trademark verbal gaffes, Mordecai Pressman passed for gallant.

The film was about a man whose wife dies in childbirth. Unhinged by her death, he becomes a vagrant. After five years of wandering, he guiltily returns to meet his son. Raised by in-laws, the little boy is a terror-on-wheels; they want deadbeat Dad to reclaim him. The boy, grown used to stories of a debonair father who lives in Calcutta, rejects the visitor's paternal claims. In the end, the disconsolate widower refuses their pleas to take him by force, as would be his right. He departs alone. The child catches up on the outskirts of the village and asks if the man is going to Calcutta. "Yes," says the widower, "if you like. Come with me." The boy considers. "Will you take me to my father?" At this, Rachel cried—the true father before him and still the boy asks! The idea of a phantom father forever in Calcutta was so gorgeous and so sad to her, all at once. Mordecai handed her a handkerchief. "Don't mind the spots," he said, with a laugh. "It's only chutney."

They were supposed to go to dinner, but Rachel lied and said she had cramps. Mordecai dropped her off with a clumsy kiss.

She showered and slipped into bed. *Will you take me to my father?* The image of the cantor rose before her, crumbs of pottery on eyes and mouth, dirt on the heart. Then Tiffany Amber Sedgwick—for a week, she dreamed of washing her in a tub. As she soaped the tiny cello of her back, the little girl moaned like kids do when you try to rouse them for school, druggy and irascible. They just don't want to wake up.

*

Rosetta Beth Howe's bat mitzvah was celebrated at a temple in Bel Air, across the-freeway from the Getty. Tovah tagged along.

Around two hundred sat in pews—lots of parents Rachel's age, friends of the Howes' who'd come with their kids, Rosetta's classmates. Rachel was surprised all the hip-looking moms knew songs and Hebrew prayers by heart. Perry and Jersey flanked their daughter onstage. Eventually, Rosetta and the rabbi retrieved the Torah from its ornate tabernacle. The heavy scroll was placed in her arms and the girl, half hidden by its sacred blue-clothed bulk, held right as she marched among the congregation. Rachel forgot exactly why they made you do that, but it was an impressive bit of pageantry nonetheless. The girl's eyes deftly scanned the crowd as she dispensed sweetly modulated insider smiles to relatives and friends.

She was six months away from her own bat mitzvah when her father died. With the swift move to Menlo Park, the uprooting was complete—Rachel never saw her friends from Beth-El again. No more carpools and sabbaths, Succot and shofars, no more kissing of mezuzim on doorsills. Calliope donated her husband's "religious accessories," as she called them—his *tallit* and *siddur*—to the synagogue the way old clothes would be left at the Salvation Army. Each year, tradition faded while the Christmas tree grew gaudily redolent, its blinking, snow-sprayed branches heavy with goyische trinkets.

She made new friends in Menlo Park, and nursed a secret terror. Rachel had expected her period to come with the bat mitzvah; when that was broken off, she panicked. One by one her girlfriends fell to the red cabal, but for her the stainless months came and went like white clouds latticed across the sky. At night, flashlight under covers, she reread her under-lined Leviticus, desperate to be "unclean." They had studied the strange book in Hebrew School, with its ancient laws of sacrifice and defilement, delineations of forbidden sex and cat-amenial superstition: Rachel wanted the curse. She wanted to turn wine to vinegar with her touch or rust iron at the wan-ing of the moon. She wanted to make mares miscarry. It was said a woman on her period might cause the death of a man if she passed between him and another, and Rachel wanted to try that in the worst way—she wanted to feed her blood to the neighbor's cat and see if it would die. She yearned to be unclean, like the animals with "true hoofs but no clefts through the hoofs," like the creatures that lived in the water but had no fins or scales, like abominations of winged, swarm-ing things: eagles and vultures, falcons and ravens, ostriches, kites, hawks and gulls, owls and cormorants and pelicans, bustards, storks, herons and hoopoes and bats. She wanted the rhythmic drama of murderous potency, unclean. And when the bleeding stopped, she wanted to bring turtledoves and pigeons to the priest "so that he might offer the one as a sin offering and the other as a burnt offering; and the priest shall make expiation on her behalf, for her unclean discharge, before the LORD." So said the Torah, and this is what she read aloud. But the vaunted discharge would not come.

Until she was seventeen. The temple was awash in blood: she kept black beach towels in the dresser, rushing to menstrual intercourse. She wanted to be unclean and make others so. Through her twenties and thirties, Rachel studied laws of *Taharah HaMishpachah* regarding a *niddah*, or menstruant woman. This became her Jewishness and perversely circumscribed expertise—her Orthodox window of stained glass. Marathon running made her irregular; so the doctors said. With a sense of belonging, Rachel noted she was a *zavah*, "one who continues to bleed beyond the normal period of her menses or who has bleeding at a different time of the month." During that impure time, anything one slept, sat or rode upon (California King, LifeCycle, Land Cruiser) became unclean. The Torah distinguished between two types of vaginal discharges: a *mareh* was accompanied by specific physical sensation, while a *ketem* came with no warning—the stain simply discovered. The woman must always consult a rabbi to determine her status. Was she clean or unclean, *tehorah* or *niddah*? It depended on where the stain was found, its color and size. A *ketem* could only render a woman a *niddah* if it was the size of a circle around nineteen millimeters in diameter.

The woman must confirm by examination that the cyclical bleeding had ended. This was done with a three-inch-square cloth wrapped around the index finger, inserted deep into the vagina and rotated to detect any blood that might be hidden in the folds (a tampon wouldn't do). The inspection could be done a number of times during the day, between douching. If

questionable stains were still found on the cloth before sunset, it was to be put in an envelope and taken to a rabbi in
the morning. At the end of seven spotless days, the woman
would immerse herself in a bath called a mikvah; this was the
only way to make the transition from *tumah* to *taharah, tameh*
to *tahor.* It was necessary to submerge the entire body in the
water, and the immersion must take place at night, "after at
least three stars are visible."

As the service ended, Rachel's eye flitted to a passage in
the book of Torah that she held in hand. It was a preface to
Numbers and referred to the highest form of ritual defilement:
contact with a human corpse. The rabbis called the human
corpse "the father of fathers of impurity."

The Red Cow; Laws of Purification

The rules regarding the red heifer are often called the
most mysterious laws of the Torah. They prescribe a
process of purification for anyone who has been in
contact with a dead body . . . .

The congregants adjourned to the anteroom for blessings over
bread and wine. Rachel drank the little cup down, then quickly
had two more. The mood was festive as the guests filed in and
tore chunks from the challah. Rachel stood listening to the
klezmer band, entranced. The girl from the mortuary stared
through the glass—the sun white as the shroud shyly held to her
breast. The room whirled and the floor broke Rachel's black fall.

Ursula Sedgwick

She was in Century City running errands while Holly and
Sara were at yoga. Army Archerd said in *Variety* that Holly had

been set for *Sight Unseen,* a made-for-cable-movie "limning the
political and spiritual journey of an abused wife who gives
birth to a blind child" (timed to coincide with the publica-
tion of the book). Ursula thought that was brave—Holly could
do any kind of international role she wanted, but here she
was on Lifetime. That was the sign of a great actress: someone
interested in the work and the part, not the glamour and the
money.

Ursula got a hamburger at Johnny Rocket's and sat in the
sun, jostling Samson's carriage with her foot. People passed
and smiled and she remembered those times, rocking Tiffany
in a public place. Nursing her. Packs of oblivious girls rushed
by on their way to the cineplex—little foxes. They had long
blond legs, and she thought of Tiffany.

Ursula chewed her burger and unfolded the map. She
never knew odd-numbered routes went north-south and even
ones (Route 66), east-west. Well, that was a handy thing.
Minnesota was the "gopher state," fourteenth largest in the
Union—had only *been* a state a hundred and fourteen years.
Chanhassen, site of the Temple of ECK, was just southwest of
Minneapolis; she marked it in red ink. Sara said the Temple
was pyramid-shaped and suffused with the Maha Nada, the
great music of the ECK life current. Ursula couldn't wait. She
wasn't going to tell anyone about the road trip, though folks
would probably be relieved if they knew. If you fell in the
lake, you were supposed to grab on tight to the rope that was
thrown while they hauled you ashore—dry yourself off, shake
a few hands and move on. But Ursula was still thrashing and
no one liked to see that. People wanted results. That was only
human.

She decided to send the ladies postcards, keep an album of the whole trip. That would be fun. She'd been pasting together a very special photo montage: Ursula and Tiff and Sara and Phyll and Rodney the dachshund on boardwalk, pier and Promenade; Planet Hollywood and Dive!; lolling around United States Island's dry canals in their dungarees; carousing on the train to Sea World for an Eckankar family outing. She was going to have Kinko's laminate it to a beautiful piece of wood—Ursula did that with a "Calvin and Hobbes" cartoon, the one where Calvin stares out the window and says, "You know, Hobbes, some days even my lucky rocketship underpants don't help." She was going to give that to the Mahanta when they met in Minnesota.

Her first concern was fixing the Bonneville because, in its current shape, Ursula didn't think it would make it to Chanhassen. The alignment was bad. She should hurry, though—an ECKist friend had been to a gathering in upstate New York and the Mahanta appeared ill; as a vessel for so much energy, his physical body was often under siege. The friend didn't know where the Mahanta lived but was sure it couldn't be far from the Temple.

"Mama, look! Its eyes!" A boy stood over Samson, who was now awake. "What's wrong with its eyes?"

The mother grabbed him roughly by the wrist. She smiled at Ursula. "I'm sorry."

"It's all right."

"He's *darling*," said the mother, peering into the carriage. "But why are his eyes like that?"

"That is rude!" the mother exclaimed, mildly appalled. Ursula reassured the woman, then told the boy the baby was blind.

"But how did he get blind?"

"Well," said Ursula patiently, "it's just the way he was born."

"What's his name?" she asked.

"Samson."

"He is a *doll*. He'll have no trouble finding his Delilah."

"He already *has*," Ursula said with a twinkle. "Me."

The little boy asked his mother who Delilah was over and over until they were out of sight.

*

She was pushing Samson toward the Imaginarium when the two women collided. Ursula gasped, though wasn't sure why. "Do I know you?"

Rachel's eyes bugged, jaw trembling. "We—we met at—at the mortuary . . ."

Ursula fought for air. She sneezed three times, then burst into tears.

"Please, please don't!" groaned Rachel, weeping herself.

"My Tiffany! My baby!"—dumbly backing the carriage away.

"Please! I've been dreaming about her . . ."

"You!—" Then Ursula remembered this was the woman who had washed her girl; the last to see her translate from this earth. "Was she—was she beautiful?"

"Please!—"

"*Tell me!* Was she beautiful?"

"Oh yes! *So* beautiful! The most beautiful thing I have ever *seen*—"

"And you . . . took care of her?"

"Yes! We took *perfect* care of her." Ursula slowly deflated. "Are you . . . are you well? Can I—"

"Thank you!" shouted Ursula, abruptly heading for the long ramp beside Gelson's.

The part-time washer of the dead gave chase and shoved something into her hand. "Take it! It's yours!" Now it was Rachel's turn to flee.

She stormed off, stymied and haunted—like a witch whose potions had all failed.

Perry Needham Howe

Jeremy Stein made good on his promise to take Perry to lunch at Ginza Sushiko. He brought with him the free-lance dealer he'd mentioned on the train. Berto was a sound editor at one of the big post-production houses in the Valley. His family had been in the watch trade and from early on, he was attracted to the aesthetics of the old pieces they repaired.

They were the only ones there. Apparently, the restaurant was so expensive it didn't bother opening unless someone made a reservation; a hundred-dollar penalty was charged in event of cancellation. Perry said he wanted to try the fugu (you only live once, he thought) and was disappointed to hear its season came in November. It seemed fugu wasn't poisonous in itself but enjoyed eating something that was. At any rate, the chef said he served it "young," before too many toxins accumulated in the liver. The liver, of course, was the real delicacy—like most toxic things.

"You'd love it," Jeremy said. "It's rather like foie gras."

The chef scowled, his English not up to a riposte. "*Better* than foie gras."

"There's usually a residual toxin in fugu: first time I had it, my tongue started tingling *from the inside*. I almost shat myself! Finally got it together to inform the chef and he put me right."

Perry couldn't help but wonder if stage-four adenocarcinoma was a tasty treat out there in the star-speckled vomitus of the Big Bang. Somewhere, a galactic cook was serving it up "young" (before chemo).

The men were delivered soups that made the counter smell of forest. Then came bowls of hot water filled with leaves; they dipped shredded sashimi within and each grabful swelled like a white rose in time-lapse bloom. Perry felt as if he'd ingested a mild psychotropic.

Berto knew the creator of *Streets* was interested in a minute repeater. He admitted he'd never sold one but said they could be gotten, at a price. A Vacheron Constantin retailing around a hundred and sixty thousand might be had for about half.

"You know, there's a guy in Pennsylvania who will get the Swiss parts and make you a repeater, do anything you want. We're talking a *substantial* reduction. See, a lot of these super-complicated watches aren't *manufactured by* the companies that sell them. Look." He jimmied the back of his wristwatch, revealing the works. "(I know just where to press.) See: Patek bought the *ébauche*—the raw movement—from Le Coultre. The big names aren't necessarily the manufacturers. They *do* stuff to the watch, it's not like they do *nothing*. Take VCRs: there's ten thousand different kinds but only a handful of places that make the components. Okay?"

Jeremy picked his teeth with one of the hand-carved rarewood toothpicks that sat in tiny reliquaries before each man. Perry popped an urchin in his mouth that elicited a primitive sense-memory of ocean. He'd suffered a lot of epicurean bores in his day, with their gustatory boasts and simpleminded metaphors; now he was one of them.

"There's a European auction house called Habsburg you should know about, if you *really* want to go crazy."

"Oh, he's that already!" said Jeremy, eyes closed in ecstasy of octopus aftermath. "He's totally gone."

Berto pulled a Sotheby's catalogue from his valise and flipped to a dog-eared page at the back. Lana Turner stood next to a thuggish-looking man on her wedding day, nineteen forty-eight. "That's this guy Topping. There were two brothers, right? They inherited about a hundred and forty million." On the center of the next page was a plain-looking wristwatch with a black band. "One of the earliest perpetuals—Topping was the first real owner, bought it from Schulz—*and* it's a minute repeater *and* a one-button chronograph—that's in the crown—*and* it's got a moon phase. We're talking nineteen thirty!"

Perry took a closer look. "It says 'tonneau'—"

"Shape of the case. Like a barrel, see? It was made by this guy Schulz, who worked for Cartier."

"Schulz made the *ébauche*?" Perry asked.

Jeremy winked. "I told you he was gone."

"You're *learning* No," he said, pointing to the text. "See? It says the movement wasn't signed. Probably Piguet; they did a lot of the early complicated Pateks. This one sold for five hundred fifty thousand—and remember, we're talking nineteen *eighty-nine*. But that's an unusual piece."

Dessert was a drift of shaved green ice adorned by a Fuji-esque snowcap of crushed kiwi. The bill came to twelve hundred and thirty-seven dollars and fifty-six cents, without tip. The two men offered credit cards, but Jeremy refused.

"That's okay," said the benefactor. "My treat. Next time, buy me a watch. Hey, Berto," he joked. "Can you get a used Breguet for what we paid for lunch?"

"You could pay the *tax* on a Breguet—maybe."

Perry got the elbow as Jeremy nodded toward the dealer. "Would you buy a used Breguet from this man? Oh!" His face lit up. "Know what I heard? I heard there was a *black* American Express card."

"Yeah, Farrakhan has one," said Berto.

"I'm *serious.* Perry, have you heard of that? It's supposed to be for people like Bronfman and Gates. You can, like, buy *buildings* with the damn thing."

"Or minute repeaters," said Perry.

When they left, Jeremy gave the chef his card and made him promise to call at first fugu.

*

That night at the Century Plaza, Perry clutched his side and collapsed during the silent auction at a Luminaires fund-raiser for the Doheny Eye Institute. Jersey wanted to call an ambulance, but he stubbornly said the limo would do. The doctors were concerned the bowel had been perforated; they needed to go in and take a look.

"They might have at least let you keep on your tux," Jersey said as they wheeled her husband to surgery.

"Listen," Perry said groggily from the gurney. "I want my liver donated to the right restaurant—five-star."

"What?" She smiled, wiping tears away with the back of a hand. "What is it, darling?"

"I want—"

"Tell me what you want . . ."

"—none of this Mickey Mouse Mickey Mande *rejection* shit. And make sure it's in *season*—says so on my driver's license. Promise?"

"You're a crazy man, but I promise. And I love you."

She kissed him twice and he rolled away.

Severin Welch

Out of the ICU, thank God. Two days in that sonsabitchin place. They fished a catheter through his groin and cleared a blockage in a valve, that's how they did it now. Instead of a triple bypass they snaked in like plumbers through a pipe. Lavinia was there in all her weepy, slobby, hard-bitten splendor, like some kind of Kathy Bates. Frankenbates. She kept asking what was he doing in the middle of the street. Where was he going, what had *possessed* him? The old man thought it best not to answer. She'd have to move to Beachwood, she said—told anyone who'd listen—because her father couldn't be left alone. But she would need *help,* who could help? She'd call her ex, that fuck, he wouldn't lift a finger for anyone. Who, then? All his neighbors were so fucking old. Total care! Get *real*—that's what they were talking about—and who paid? Medicare? Medicaid? I'll tell you who: nobody! Nobody paid for total care, total care was for the rich! For English and Canadians, and the Swiss! But maybe the Motion Picture Hospital—Daddy, what were you *doing,* you could have been hit by a hundred cars! She railed against her rotten ex and Jabba the whore and the whole fucked up shitty planet.

"I'd like to have my radio, Lavinia." She knew what he meant. "I'd like you to get it from the house."

"They won't let you have that here," she said.

"Everyone has a radio."

"Not that kind. You'll be home soon anyway."

"I see. You're preparing my schedule? You're a doctor now?"

"That's right—so you better listen." She reached into a gold Godiva tin for a *marron glacé*. "This is *such* a beautiful hospital. The paintings! On every *floor*. It's like a museum."

"Why don't you move in, if you love it so much? You could give tours."

*

Three in the morning. The nurse gave him Dalmane, but he couldn't sleep. Lavinia refused to bring the scanner but he made her retrieve the script—its dirty pages gathered by paramedics from oil-stained macadam and, along with bruised Uniden, sealed in a Hefty bag—the very original draft of *Dead Souls,* put through anemic paces by Dee Bruchner so long ago. Pressed like a linty yellow flower within was the clipping from *The New York Times*:

> Charles G. Bluhdorn, who built a small Michigan auto-parts company into Gulf and Western Industries, the multibillion-dollar conglomerate, died yesterday while flying home to New York from a business trip

in the Dominican Republic. He was fifty-six years old and lived in Manhattan.

Jerry Sherman, an assistant vice-president and director of public relations for G.&W., said Mr. Bluhdorn, the company's founder, chairman and chief executive, was aboard a corporate plane when he died. Mr. Sherman said the cause of death was a heart attack.

Severin sat by the window, touching the cool security glass with a bunged-up finger. The nail still had a fissure, all the way from Brooklyn, 'thirty-one—looked like a miniature ice floe—when his best friend, Joey Dobrowicz, smashed it with a rock (by mistake, Joey said). Did he holler. He stared out the thick pane, trying to conjure faces, but the slate was gray, the drizzle dull. It was raining the night his Diantha died, in this very wing.

He went to the chair and sat down, winded by memory. There was something terrifying about chairs in hospital rooms, especially at night. An immense longing came upon him, and Severin revisited the time they first met . . . the Automat—*For Me and My Gal*—nineteen forty-two, the year Mr. Bluhdorn immigrated to America from Vienna. Severin was a Western Union messenger by day (extreme myopia would exempt him from the service), tyro novelist by night. Sometimes they threw him a few dollars to create a radio ad, but what he really wanted was to be an Author—do an *All Quiet on the Western Front,* or something in the Steinbeck vein—then hire out for the movies. When Diantha got pregnant, they took a bus to Hollywood.

He worked at Chasen's for a while—

began his career in a New York cotton brokerage house, earning fifteen dollars a week. In nineteen forty-nine, he formed an import-export concern that he operated until, at the age of thirty and already a millionaire, he bought into the Michigan parts company.

Among its hundreds of subsidiaries, the most widely known are Paramount Pictures, the Madison Square Garden Corporation and Simon & Schus

What could it have been like to live with him? Diantha saw less and less of those she cared for. Corraled by his sickness, she became a mirror, herself house-bound and bizarre. It had never been easy for her to make friends. She lived for Lavinia, grown unsavory and irascible before her eyes; turned to her granddaughter, but Molly was in trouble early on, evaporating around the time of Severin's own manic retreat—all that jail business broke Diantha's heart. His wife would have no rewards; when she passed, Molly had been gone almost five years. Severin kept hoping their grandchild would appear at Diantha's bedside and she did, yes she did, a day late, sores and scabs everywhere, tattoo covering her back, spidery rendering of a woman entered from behind by a skeleton with a scythe. For the last few years of her husband's madness—five, really—well, ten—what Diantha really had then was Lavinia. Overbearing, unkempt, gloomy, abusive Lavinia.

He saw his wife hanging in the air outside the window, a blown out, blighted angel dragged to hell by the gagman's caravan of black humors. Severin came to the Beachwood bedroom once and there she was, rocking, eyes slammed watery shut, hands over ears to evict the scannerbabble.

Mr. Bluhdorn's favorite expression, said an associate, was, "What is the bottom line?"

Didn't even bury her—too busy waiting, and waiting still! Why had he been so indulged? They should have *done* something, rancorous and violent, lacking decorum, caved in his head and smashed his machines, chased him down with wild children and devoured him on the beach.

It was pouring. A thousand gargoyles spat rain at the windows (Diantha gone now) with fatal, mischievous mouths. Severin slept.

Rachel Krohn

Oberon Mall was dead.

Mitch had a flu, and Calliope asked her to come to the service at Hillside Memorial Park. Rachel showered when they got off the phone. She was showering at least five times a day, skin chafed from overwashing. Mortuary parking lot lustrations hadn't been enough "to remove death," not by a long shot—in fact, the effort was risible. According to the Hebrew Bible, even a mikvah couldn't banish the intensity of the *tumah* of a corpse. This is where the red heifer came in.

The cow would be slaughtered, then burned with cedarwood (the mightiest of trees—HOPE), hyssop (because it grew in crevices—FAITH) and "crimson stuff" (from the scarlet worm—CHARITY) added to the fire. The ashes were to be mixed with living water, not stagnant, then sprinkled over the unclean—all *in addition* to immersion. That's what it took to emerge *tahor*. This particular law of Torah was one of four that remained unfathomable to even the most faithful of interpretants, the others being: marrying one's brother's widow; not mingling wool and linen in a garment; performing the rites of the scapegoat.

She put on the brown Armani her mother had bought for her birthday. To calm herself, Rachel recited the laws. When a wife entered the *niddah* state, she and her husband could not touch. They could not comb each other's hair, nor could they brush lint from each other's clothes. They couldn't even hand objects to one another, a small child being the rare exception. They were forbidden to sit together on a sofa unless another person—or, say, cushion—was set between them. They may not pour each other drinks, nor should a husband eat or drink from his wife's leftovers, though she could eat from his. If the husband didn't know the leftovers were hers, it was all right for him to eat. If someone ate from his wife's leftovers first or the leftovers were transferred to another plate, the husband could eat them too, as long as the wife had left the room. While she was unclean, he was not to sit on his wife's bed, smell her perfume or listen to the sound of her singing . . . .

*

They drove through a phalanx of paparazzi at the cemetery gate.

This, the green freeway-bound park where her father was laid.

It was Calliope's genius to stage a reunion via this bally-hooed alternative event. The psychiatrist was a public figure of sorts, a bitplayer perennial in the media drama—she would upstage the cantor (with a little help from Oberon), as he had upstaged her in that shattered time. She wanted him to feel her feathers as she swept past his table with the VIPs. Yes: it seemed to take forever but now all the bodies were in their proper place. Mother and daughter could have their mikvah.

Donny Ribkin and Zev Turtletaub said hello. They were joined by Katherine Grosseck. Calliope said she was glad to finally meet the real McCoy, and Katherine quickly filled Zev in on the impersonator *scandale*. Then the screenwriter said: How can I be sure you're the real Calliope? "By her hourly fee," said Donny, and everyone laughed. More jokes were made, belaboring the theme of the double. Before they broke off, Donny said he and Katherine were a couple again. Calliope offered congratulations. Zev said they were together only because Katherine's directing career needed jump-starting.

"Donny Ribkin was a patient of yours," said Rachel, reiterating what she'd already been told. She felt a bond with the agent, an illicit kinship.

"Not any longer. Not for months."

"Did he—does he know about Sy . . . and his mother?"

She nodded. "Just recently. He called to say he found her diaries."

"Well, didn't he think it a little *strange*? I mean, that you were the *wife* of the man that his mother was—"

"Of *course*, he thought it was strange. It *is* strange."

"I just can't see how—how you ever could have agreed to see him as a patient, Mother. Knowing that—"

"I made a choice, Rachel. Doctors make choices."

Rachel felt like making a choice of her own: to kick off her heels and sprint up the hill to the Mount of Olives, where the cantor awaited. She had cedarwood in her purse, and minty hyssop too—a small fire would be kindled at grave. She would perform the rites of the scapegoat while Aztec laborers shut off tractors, respectfully turning away.

Leslie Trott shook hands like it was a collagen convention. Calliope was always pushing her daughter to see him. A few years ago, Rachel gave in, but the emperor was overbooked. She wound up in a distant room, far from Big Star country—the Mount of Olives suite—where a dull colleague cheerily burned off a minuscule nostril wart.

"How long did you see Obie, as a shrink?"

"A year. A very troubled girl."

"Isn't it . . . *inappropriate* for you to be here?"

"I don't know where you get your ethical bulletins from, Rachel, but no. I'm a human being. I dance at weddings and I cry at funerals."

"You haven't cried *yet*. Did you visit her in the hospital?"

"Yes. She couldn't speak. At least, I couldn't understand her. She mostly blinked her eyes. The doctors said she knew what had happened to her—the mind apparently wasn't affected."

Rachel was startled to learn the Big Star was a Jew. She couldn't help wondering who prepared her for burial. In her mind, she saw the sexpot legs guided through Donna Karan pjs, silken string twisted nine times at the waist, then looped into the letter *shin*, which stood for God—though, at time of death, she was probably already clean as a whistle. When you're rich and paralyzed like that, private nurses were always sponging you down.

"You look too thin, Rachel."

"I feel fine."

"But *are* you? I worry—"

Rachel silenced her with a hug. Only a month ago, such a gesture would have been unthinkable for either one.

Calliope pointed out the mother of the deceased, a mountain of a woman who looked slightly deranged. Her enormous bosom heaved in laughter and tears at Leslie Trott's words. Eventually, he eulogized only to her and the grievers blushed to be privy to such intimacies.

*

They drove to the beach, north on PCH to points unknown. The sky looked like the bottom of an old porcelain bowl. When the rain began, it felt like the end of the world.

Calliope smiled dreamily. "We used to make this drive all the time, remember? San Simeon, Big Sur, Point Lobos . . . Do you remember what Sy used to sing?"

"We're off to see the Wizard!—"

"And Simon—what was that crazy song . . ."

" 'Hit the road, Jack' . . ."

Together: " 'And don't you come back no more, no more, no more, no more!' "

They laughed and sang some more.

"Well, how far should we go?"

"Till we run out of gas."

"Thelma and Louise."

"You know, she's a client—or was, for a while."

"Thelma or Louise?"

"Geena—whichever one she was."

The rain stopped. They got burgers and fries at a roadside place and crossed to the beach. Calliope had a blanket in the trunk. They spread it on a picnic table and faced the frothy gray-green tubes.

"This is nice," her mother said.

"Mama," said Rachel, plaintively. "I can't stop washing—since I found out—about Father . . . and then there was this—this *horrible thing*—a little girl—this *tumah*—we washed her—and this whole—and, and the red heifer!" She laughed, then sobbed with great embarrassing snorts. "I don't know, Mama! I think I'm going crazy!"

Calliope clasped her daughter's hands and looked deep in her eyes, like a hypnotist. "Rachel, you are *not*. It's just terribly sad and terribly confusing . . ."

"Well, I've been acting *pretty strangely* lately! Maybe I should—be—on an antidepressant or something."

"We can certainly investigate that. You wouldn't be the first."

"I don't know if anything will help."

"Just *talking* about it helps—a lot. *Believe* me."

"Oh yeah?" she said, sweetly chiding. "How would *you* know?"

"I have a little bit of experience in that area."

Rachel shook her head tearfully. "Everything is a *tumah*—"

"What is this *tumah*, darling?"

"Mama, I can't get clean! Haven't you ever felt like that?"

" 'Out, out, damn spot,' " she intoned, like a schoolteacher. "But there *is* no blood on your hands, Rachel! There just *isn't*. You know, sometimes there's a difference between the truth and what a child perceives to *be* that truth."

"Mama . . . did you know there's a moth that feeds off the tears of elephants? Human tears, too—I read about it in

National Geographic. It pokes the poor thing's eye just so it can drink the tears. What kind of world would have such a thing?"

"Darling, please—"

"And there's a bug—they call it a burying beetle. It digs the ground out from under dead things and buries them. I saw a picture of one, digging the grave for a mourning dove . . ." Rachel stood, unable to go on. She wanted to throw herself in the water, but her mother chased her down and held fast.

"No, baby! No!" she shouted as Rachel seized with tears, straining toward the maliciously indifferent surf. Calliope steered her back to the car, cloaking the frail, shivering shoulders in the blanket as if she were a princess—a mourning dove—who had launched her dead on a floating litter, toward unforgiving seas.

Ursula Sedgwick

When Taj Wiedlin hanged himself, Ursula took it as a sign for her to go. She went to Travel Shoppe and booked a deluxe sleeper—that's what Sara did when she visited her mom. Ursula wouldn't have felt safe on the road. She never got around to fixing the Bonneville, and besides, it was too big a target. They changed trains in Portland and began the journey east.

The cars were uncrowded. Ursula befriended a porter, a kind, fiftyish Captain Kangaroo-looking man. He was married, from Red Wing.

"Chanhassen," he echoed, a little unsure, then scratched his head. "That's a suburb—boy, I should know that place. Relatives there?"

"Sort of. What's the weather like now?"

"Well, it's going to be a pretty hot Fourth of July, I'll tell you. June, July and August are generally humid."

"My friend told me Bob Dylan was from Minnesota."

"Hibbing. Oh, we have many famous people. Loni Anderson, Roger Maris, the rock singer Prince—though my daughter tells me he doesn't call himself that anymore." Samson shifted in his sleep.

"Lots of writers, too," said the porter. "Sinclair Lewis—he wrote *Main Street*—and F. Scott Fitzgerald. *The Great Gatsby*."

"They made a movie out of that."

"Sure did. That was Mia Farrow. There's a woman who's had nine lives."

"And nine children, at least."

The porter thought that was funny. With a glance at the baby, he asked about her husband. Ursula said she was separated. "That's a shame," he said, tickling Samson's neck with a finger. "*You're* a pretty one, aren't you?"

"He's actually a boy."

"Oh, I'm sorry—never could tell them apart, even my own. You know, you really ought to go to one of the fairs while you're there. Best in the world. And come the Fourth . . ."

"County fairs?"

"Granddaddies of 'em all! Oh my, I'd guess St. Paul has the biggest fairgrounds in the whole country. There's Forest Lake, Pine City, the Cokato Corn Carnival. 'Princess Kay of the Milky Way'—that's a beauty pageant. Win, and they carve your face in butter."

"I'm not so sure I'd like that."

"When I was a boy, they had midways: sideshows and tattooed ladies, weird stuff in formaldehyde jars. Things are a bit different now—well, they're a *lot* different. Biggest entertainers in the world come by to sing. Garth Brooks, Tony Bennett. Anyone you can think of."

"Maybe I'll take my friend's mother. She lives in St. Cloud."

"Oh, she'll take *you*—we don't like to miss our fairs. She'll have you baking cakes and riding a greased pig."

"Well," Ursula said, standing with the sleepy boy in her arms, "I guess we'll be taking a nap."

"He's got a head start on you."

"It's contagious."

The bottle fell from the seat to the ground and the porter retrieved it. "That's a real pretty watch," he said, noticing it on the thin wrist as he handed the bottle back.

"It was a gift—an unexpected one."

"Best kind. Anyhow, you go ahead now. I hope I haven't talked your ear off."

"No, I liked it. Hope you'll talk some more."

"You just let me know if you need anything," he said, "with the baby and all. I'll bring you dinner in your berth, if you like."

*

Ursula weaved the clacking way back to their compartment. She locked the door behind her, closed the shades and lay down with Samson. They were still in Montana, with Malta, Glasgow and Wolf Point to go—then Williston, Stanley, Minot, Rugby, Devil's Lake, Grand Forks . . . St. Cloud. Sara's mom's was the third stop into Minnesota. Ursula thought maybe she would just drop the baby off. She'd been so full of hope at the start of the trip, sure that the Mahanta would meet her at the Temple because of her tragedy—then certain he'd lay healing hands on Samson's eyes and help him see. Now, the bottom had dropped out. What arrogance! Hadn't her friend said the Mahanta wasn't well? Who did she think she was with her false charity and selfish expectations, her profane misjudgment of the Light and Sound of God? Sri Harold Klemp was not put on this planet to lay hands on *anyone*, let alone at their convenience. She'd been so controlling; it was time to let go. There was nothing to do but fall asleep and hope the Living ECK Master would guide her.

She dreamed of her daughter. Tiffany waited at the Temple of Golden Wisdom and told her mother to follow. "Once you're here," she said, "we'll cry a river of tears. And when our tears dry up, we'll come back to Earth to live again." When Ursula awakened, it was night. She went and found the porter.

"Well, that must have been a good nap."

"Is it too late for supper?"

"I kept yours warm," he said, with a wink. "I'll bring it to your room."

She stood between sleeper cars, and the cold bit the tops of her cheeks. A man passed through and nodded. Ursula thought she saw a vast body of water out there in the dark. She wondered about it—too early for Devil's Lake. She looked at the watch the woman from the mortuary gave her that day in Century City. It was a Tiffany: that's how Ursula knew her daughter was reaching out. They belonged together, and now was the time. If they did return to Earth like she said in the dream (Ursula secretly hoped they would journey to a different plane), her only wish was to be far away from all the people and places that had hurt them. She stuck out her wind-clipped head and inhaled. How nice it would be to start fresh, to come back as anonymous passengers on a train—or summer cotton-candy eaters at a county fair.

Ursula smiled, raising her leg with its flowery tennis shoe atop the steel half-door. Princess Kay of the Milky Way, ha! hoisting herself up, Mama, come!—

Faces carved in butter.

Perry Needham Howe

It turned out to be old-fashioned appendicitis. When the doctor said there was something else, Perry got the gooseflesh: he didn't want to know. No, listen, said the doc, the nodules shrank, saw it on the preop X ray, plain as day. Little buggers were practically gone from the left lung altogether. But what did that *mean?* Naturally, the doc didn't know. Was it a good thing? he asked, animatedly cautious. Yes, said the doc, it was *definitely* a good thing. Then Perry pulled back emotionally because he didn't want to get sucker-punched—that's what cancer liked to do, ambush for a living. He asked what they were supposed to do now, and the doc said nothing, nothing *to* do but "follow it," eyes peeled, ears to ground. The producer giddily theorized he was making so much money even the cancer was intimidated and the two men shared a nicely cathartic moment of comic relief. Perry asked if he was still going to die, a bullshitty question but he wanted to know. It's a *good* question, said the doc. Then he gave him the trusty Zen of Common Sense standby, the old listen-whatever-you've-been-doing-don't-stop-because-you're-doing-something-right speech. When the doc left, Perry got on the phone to his wife.

*

Rachel brought mail and a videocassette to the hospital. She looked terrible. When Perry asked what was wrong, she broke down and confessed—she never returned the watch. She gave it away to a homeless person instead. Perry was further confounded when she handed him a personal check for fifteen hundred dollars, less than half the cost of the misappropriated item. She wanted to know if he would be kind enough to deduct the balance from her bi-monthly paychecks—unless, of course, he wished to prosecute. Rachel said she was prepared for that. When he pressed her to explain, she fled in tears.

Perry popped the "Calibre 89" into the VCR, perusing the cover.

Calibre 89

THE MOST COMPLICATED WATCH IN THE WORLD

Total development time: 9 years
(Research and development 5 years—manufacture 4 years).
Total diameter. 88.2 mm. *Total thickness*: 41 mm.
Total weight: 1100 grams *Case*: 18 ct. gold
Number of components: 1728, including 184 wheels—61 bridges—
332 screws—415 pins—68 springs
429 mechanical parts—126 jewels—2 main dials
24 hands—8 display dials.

The two-sided Patek denoted the time the sun rose and set; the date of Easter; the season, solstice, zodiac and equinox. There was an alarm too—when the carillon of its "grande sonnene" sounded, the melody was nothing short of an especially composed theme of some sixteen notes. A pinion drove an astral map with a night sky that, thanks to a "modern method of gold evaporation under vacuum," was able to show twenty-five hundred stars grouped in eighty-eight constellations. This supreme mechanism (forty-eight thousand man hours in the making) was even a thermometer. The tape showed its works in micro-, fetishized detail; one of the satellite wheels depicted within took four hundred years to make a single revolution.

"Where's Harold Lloyd?"

The sprightly old man from down the hall peeked through the door at the monitor. "Well, hey there. How you doin' today, Severin?" He freeze-framed while his visitor took a closer view of the enlarged cog.

"Where's Harold Lloyd?" he demanded. "Didn't you ever see *Safety Last*?"

"Now, which one is that?"

"Harold Lloyd! Hanging on for dear life from the hands of a big clock."

"I know the image well, but am embarrassed to say I've never seen the film."

"A beautiful movie. So when are you checking out? If you'll excuse my use of the term."

"Tomorrow morning. You know, I'm actually getting a lot of work done. I'm gonna miss the place."

" 'Please don't talk about me when I'm gone,' " sang the old man. "Heard the one about the guy who married an older woman?" Perry smiled, cocking an ear. "She comes out of the bathroom on their wedding night and Junior jumps her. 'Hey!' she says. 'Slow down! I've got acute angina.' And Junior says, 'I sure hope so because you've got ugly tits.' "

Perry began to snigger—guardedly, because he was already sore from the earlier jag. Then he couldn't help himself and laughed until he almost bust a gut.

Severin Welch

To be his age and so rich, with a cancer: sweet Jesus, but that was the hand you were dealt. The Kid said it was in remission, but that was always a crock—no self-respecting cancer knew from "remission." The Kid should be free and clear. *Turtletaub* should have it, right in the prostate or deep in the anus better yet, sitting poolside with his purloined scripts and Lady Schick'd legs. The old man prayed the cells were already splitting like sonsabitches, tarring up his stool but good.

Severin liked the Kid. The Kid was hung up on high-dollar watches. People were crazy any kind of way and so what. He could sure as hell afford it. The Kid was a swell connection to make; you never knew how you'd meet people (it helped if you left the house). He'd really opened up to the old man, gotten intimate about his disease and all . . . He could help him find an attorney, a Kid like that was bound to have them on retainer. Because I will have to deal with Mr. Turtletaub eventually, no way around it. He'd ask about it before he checked out in the morning—much as Severin loved the phone, some things were best done mano a mano. And pronto. No time like the present. Why wait. Kid seemed in pretty good shape. Good mood. Why not? Stroll over and watch some more of that crazy cassette, chat him up. Severin had already given him a little background. Not much, just a taste. The Kid was cordial—a real gentleman.

He turned and walked toward Perry's room, not caring anymore, not really. No expectations. Only wanting justice or a measure thereof—to be acknowledged and credited, partially recompensed. He'd solicit his new friend's help, his new friend who had to have as much money—more!—than any Turtletaub could ever dream. Plus he'd kicked cancer's ass, and how was *that* for clout?

Severin spied him at the end of the hall in a natty robe, sharing his super-complicated mania with the Vietnamese nurse. As the smiling old man got closer, he shrieked and toppled, eyes rolling back in his head. They were dragging him from a great pyramid; a stone had fallen and was lying on his chest. He surfaced on a bed. Perry held his hand and they had the old man's teeth out. He was crying. Doctors were everywhere and Zev shoved a needle in while Lavinia hooked him to a machine—the scanner!—wired into Voices of America like a switchboard Medusa. Why don't Molly ever come? What went so wrong with that girl? You wait and you wait and— *Can you hear me?* asked a smooth-faced Doogie. Someone kept lifting the stone and dropping it down, lifting and dropping, like him and Joey used to pin beetles with a rock on the thorax—*Can you hear me, Mr. Welch?* Tried to speak. *It's okay,* said Nurse Lavinia, the Kid nowhere in sight. *It's all right, you're going to be fine . . .* saw the Kid again, old man's vision suddenly lake-stream clear, bad Samaritan Perry just outside the door, helpless—he looked so pained and so lost, Severin wanted to talk to him, prop the Kid up and make nice, he felt bad, too much death in that extremely wealthy young man's life already, didn't want any part of that ghoulish diorama, he wished the Kid would just look away: hooked up now to his

Radio Shack gills, American Voices filling him up: house of the rising souls—*Can you hear me, Mr. Welch?*

There it was again, the idiot query. Dr. Bluhdorn leaning over, persistent, the mantric question again and again *Can you hear me?*

CAN YOU HEAR

can you—*me?*

hh

HEAR—

losing you

Mr. Welch!

The stab again, and stone settling down like a cold house. They worked like athletes, breaking ribs to rouse the heart: ringing, ringing, ringing—Mr. Welch would not pick up.

Rachel Krohn

After twenty-five years, Rachel stopped training for the unnamed, unannounced event. She left the track and stinging night air, cold turkey. Her mother once said she ran away from her life; Rachel thought that a lame analytical cliché. If anything, she'd been running toward it, trying to catch up.

*

"May I help you?"

"I work for Mr. Howe."

While the saleswoman retrieved the linen, she browsed the pillow puffs encased in delicate brocade. She found sheets she liked, Egyptian cotton at twenty-two hundred a set. Rachel smiled: there was no end to luxury. She thought of the torn shroud—so pure—and realized that for the rest of her life some part of each day she'd spend washing and dressing and tucking the little girl away. Such was the prayer now carried within, and Rachel finally understood. She would write to Birdie, thanking her for that mitzvah.

The saleswoman appeared with an elaborately gift-wrapped bag. Rachel hovered over the Egyptian bedsheets. "Aren't they extraordinary? Those are three-hundred-and-eighty-thread."

"Yes," she said, guiltily withdrawing her finger from the fabric folds. "A bit beyond my budget—I'd be too nervous to sleep."

"Oh, I think you'd sleep fine."

*

Rachel sat in the bath, scented candles burning. She'd told her boss the story behind giving away the watch—about the seder and the *chevra* and how she had bumped into the dead girl's mother in the mall. It moved him to share his own loss, something he had never done. He wished he'd known of the *taharah* "then," he said. He would have washed Montgomery himself. They talked a long while, but Rachel came away feeling something between them had been torn that couldn't be mended. She'd stay on a few months before giving notice. She was tired of living in the city, anyway. It was time to leave—time to surprise herself. "We moved swiftly." Wasn't that what the woman who killed the cougar said?

She felt flushed and, stepping out, turned on the light—the water was pink from her discharge. How wondrous, she thought, to be clean and unclean at once. That was her; that was Rachel Lynn Krohn, forever and ever. What were the laws regarding a woman who bled into purifying waters? Whatever they were, she would not abide.

She sank into bed, exhausted. She reached for the folded paper tucked under her alarm—the prayers said over the dead. She read aloud in slow, measured tones.

> His head is like the most fine gold, his heaps of curls are black as a raven . . . His eyes are like doves beside the water brooks, bathing in milk and fitly set . . . His cheeks are like a bed of spices, towers of sweet herbs . . . His lips are roses dripping flowing myrrh . . . His arms are golden cylinders set with beryl . . . His mouth is most sweet and he is altogether precious . . . This is my beloved and this is my friend—

It was her father she was reading to, and she hoped he wasn't suffering. Everyone had suffered enough, hadn't they? So, good night, Father! she said. I wish you hadn't left so soon, I've missed you! Good night now . . .

All is forgiven.

Perry Needham Howe

Perry navigated through the river of static. He knew Tovah was thanking him for the sheets, but she was hard to hear.

Can't wait, she said—something about—oh: can't wait to give them a trial run.

> *Perry, are you—*
> *whn . . . cming*
> *Perry?*
> *Perry can you hr*

She was breaking up and there wasn't a sunspot, canyon or high-tension pole in sight.

*

Tovah had a place near Beverly High, on Moreno. It was the first time he'd been over and that excited him. The two-bedroom was smallish, immaculate and bright. The decor was flowery, with a touch of judaica; he would have thought a middle-aged woman lived there. She showed him the Pratesi duvet and he kissed her, parting the robe to touch her bush. Tovah smiled, then modestly covered herself, retreating to the bathroom while Perry undressed.

"I have some meetings set," she said.

"I haven't even mentioned it to Jersey."

"Oh. Do you think she'll have a problem?"

"I don't know. She shouldn't. But I've been thinking . . . why don't we aim our sights a little higher?"

"Meaning—"

"Why don't we do it as a feature, with an A-list director—a Barry Levinson or a Jonathan Demme."

Tovah came back in and sat on the bed, hair spilling down around shoulders. "We can *absolutely* do that. You know who would really spark to this? Penny."

He nodded approvingly. "Or—I don't know. Maybe some-one like Jane Campion. Do you think she'd be interested?"

"I *love* Jane—we represent her. She's shooting, but we can get it to her in a second." She put her hand around his neck. "Perry, that's a *wonderful* idea."

"I just want to get the best people. Or at least see if the best people might want to be involved."

*

They pitched the story of Montgomery's life and death over the next few months. Nothing in Hollywood was a slam dunk, especially the story of a nine-year-old boy who, upon progno-sis of death, became a most peculiar savant.

He noticed his son's abilities one day when Jersey called out from the hall to ask the time. Montgomery responded to the second, from a feverish sleep. He had become a living chrono-graph, a perpetual calendar, a minute repeater—the boy with a caged tourbillon heart and titanium soul. The passage of hours suddenly had color and music and texture so that time was jazz and symphony, algorithm and blues, a drum and a psalm, a hootenanny that began in his forehead, washing over enamel of skin, his very joints the jeweled movement, head a cabochon crown, eyes the sapphire glass that read the jump-ing hours, organs the *ébauche:* the very expression of his being the grandest of complications. This child, who knew nothing of calendar arithmetic, gave the name of the week to dates ten thousand years in the past or thirty thousand in the future for each and every day of every year man had breathed or would give breath still: knew the sundial length and breadth of those days, and all the side-real noons and midnights—and more, had perceived the very moment of his death. Seven months and a handful of days before it arrived, Montgomery wrote it down in cool, untrammeled hand and laid it in a drawer.

Perry sat in the library. Jersey slept. Perhaps it was time to end his affair; he hated having used the cancer as an excuse to betray her. So graceless. He knew now that he was getting well.

A special two-hour block of *Streets* was on. He watched it in MUTE, sipping his gin. Tonight, the cops were in Venice chasing a creep who'd killed his girlfriend's kid. Christ, he looked like a kid himself. They brought him back to the house so she could ID him. The girlfriend peered through squad car glass, but the perp stared down till they forcibly raised his head. "That's Taj," said the woman, dead-eyed. Just then, the paramedics wheeled out the victim and loaded her into the ambulance, with the mom climbing in. Good show—you couldn't beat closure like that. Emmy time.

He slit the envelope and removed the card. There it was, in his son's sinistral scrawl: *March 7, 1989, 4:07:20 A.M.* He weighed the paper in his hand like a collector's curio—a watch that would remain unwound. It was heavier than anything Henri might have strapped to his wrist. The Monsieur said *chronograph* was Greek for "I write the time."

Perry stuck his finger in the gin and dripped a bead down. It bubbled over the ink. He rubbed until the numbers ran, smearing to illegibility. He smiled shakily, lower lip jigged by unseen leprechauns, holy creatures of time and space.

March 7, 1989, 4:07:20 A.M.—Montie's death, on the nose. How's that for closure?